Sean McGlynn

CONTROL FREAK

Vanguard Press

A CIP catalogue record for this title is
available from the British Library.

ISBN 978 1 784658 81 6

Vanguard Press is an imprint of
Pegasus Elliot MacKenzie Publishers Ltd.
www.pegasuspublishers.com

First Published in 2021

Vanguard Press
Sheraton House Castle Park
Cambridge England

Printed & Bound in Great Britain

Dedication

This book is dedicated to all those who have been abused, physically or mentally, by someone they loved, and trusted, without whose stories, it wouldn't have been written. I can only hope that, with the growing awareness, help and support, that is out there, they will become less and less. Remember, that if you are afraid to live your life, and to share your thoughts and feelings, for fear of retribution, it is not a loving relationship. It is time to get help, and to get out.

Acknowledgements

Special thanks to my wife and best friend, Catherine for all her support and encouragement, as well as her frank and honest feedback, and to my son, Charlie McGlynn, writer and artist, for the cover art.

INTRODUCTION BY THE AUTHOR

I began studying law in 1979. I had just married the person to whom I am still married over forty years later. One of the subjects I chose for my degree in 1982 was Family Law. It took my interest even at the young age of twenty-three. But the theory I learned in university, didn't fully prepare me for the reality. Soon after I opened my own practice, one of my clients was murdered by her husband, despite doing the right thing, going to court and applying for a barring order. It wasn't enough. He ignored it. The consequences of non-compliance with a court order do not cross the mind of someone who is obsessed with getting his own way, of owning someone. He didn't want anyone else to have her.

What goes on in private between a man and a woman, a man and a man, or a woman and a woman, is only known for certain by two people. And unless one of them speaks out about it, and that is unlikely to be the abuser, it will remain that way. But why don't more victims speak out, do something about it? Some do. According to the figures, domestic abuse is on the increase. But is it? Or is it that more people are finding the strength to report it, or do something about it?

It is not easy for someone to admit that they made a mistake, made the wrong choice, chose the wrong partner. Maybe he or she wasn't always that way. Maybe it was different at the beginning. Oftentimes it is, or was. So why can't it be the same again? Maybe because one person doesn't want it to be. Maybe it wasn't real. It only appeared that way. Domestic abuse is insidious. Abusers, and their ilk, don't have a particular look, don't fit into any particular category, have any particular occupation, or belong to any particular class. They are often handsome, charming, witty, romantic, complimentary, attentive. When they want to be. As in this story of John and Josephine. Although the characters could just as well be John and Jim or Jane and Josephine.

I am glad that we have moved away from the term 'domestic violence', because it's not always about the physical. Psychological and mental abuse can be just as bad, or even worse, can have longer lasting effects. Sometimes the survivors of domestic abuse have no physical scars. Have suffered no physical wounds. Or they have healed.

I have written this book in the form of a story, because, in reporting cases involving domestic abuse, in which obviously the parties remain anonymous, usually only the relevant facts and incidents are reported. These reports do not go into the fine detail, nor explore the thoughts and feelings of the parties. Abusive relationships can appear normal, or even perfect, to the outside world. But no one knows what goes on behind closed doors. Only the people who are behind them.

The characters I have created and the incidents I have depicted in this book, although fictitious, do have their basis in fact. However, neither John nor Josephine are based on any one person. Rather, they have been created from several persons or characters I have encountered, in both my professional and social life. I have, or hope I have, given them a life of their own. The reader may recognise someone they know in either, or both of them. And if you do, be assured that it is not them.

Some of the incidents I have depicted I know to have happened, some I believe to have happened and others I have just made up. In some instances, I have changed some details for dramatic effect.

Josephine's story, and it is mostly Josephine's story, is not all bad. Like any good story, it is happy at times, sad at times, funny at times, frightening at times, and tragic at times. There is no moral to this story, although it may be taken as a precautionary tale. That is not my reason for writing it. If it does make some people think twice, then that is a bonus. I did enjoy writing it, and my only wish is that you, the reader, enjoy reading it, that I have made it worth your while.

CHAPTER ONE
MORNING HAS BROKEN

Josephine realised, before she opened her eyes, that she was somewhere else, somewhere different, somewhere wonderful. She could sense the sunlight, feel the warmth enveloping her, even though she lay naked, uncovered. The bed was comfortable, more comfortable and softer than any she'd ever slept in. A long way from her own humble divan at home. The sound of someone breathing to her right, breathing slowly, softly. It was soothing, not frightening. Of course, she realised, she's in the Caribbean. On her honeymoon. "Heaven, I'm in heaven"; the words just came to her. Typical. She was always singing to herself, in her own head or sometimes so that others could hear. Then she would have to say, "Sorry, I was just singing again. I can't help myself."

But back to the present. Was she dreaming? She closed her eyes tightly, so tightly it almost hurt, before opening them wide. The ceiling was white, pure white, the room bathed in sunlight, the brightest sunlight she had ever experienced, or so she thought. It made it hard to focus. Maybe it was a dream. She pinched herself in the ass. It hurt. She had grown her fingernails for the wedding. No. She wasn't dreaming. She turned her head to her left. A blurred face came slowly into focus. Her husband. That thought filled her with delight. He looked so peaceful, child-like but handsome at the same time. She thought how lucky she was. She was so excited, it woke up every nerve in her body. He was facing her, his left hand gently clutching her left breast, his right hand under his head.

She wanted to get out of bed, but didn't want to disturb him. She took his hand gently by the wrist and carefully sitting up, so as not to disturb him, put it on her warm pillow. He stirred, but didn't open his eyes. She waited. He was still asleep. She crept out of the bed and went to the bathroom. She wanted to shower, freshen up. She closed the door quietly behind her. When she had finished, she wrapped a towel around her and went back to the bedroom.

He was awake, leaning on one elbow and looking straight at her. She felt his stare. A lustful look. She momentarily undid her towel while biting her lip. A quick flash of flesh.

His eyes widened.

"Get into bed," he said, pulling back the duvet.

Ooh! He was being so masterful, so demanding. She liked it. She dropped her towel and did as he asked. What happened next is private. It's also very rude.

When it was over and he was satisfied, and to tell the truth she was, too, she leapt out of bed and grabbed some clothes, intending to get dressed.

"What are you doing?"

That took her by surprise.

"I'm putting on some clothes. I can't go out naked, can I?" she said, laughing, as she approached the bed, resting both hands on it and looking into his eyes.

"Get back into bed." His voice was even but stern. There was no smile.

"You're such a stud. But we can do that again later. A bit of afternoon delight. Let's go out now. I so want to see this wonderful place you have taken me, breathe in the atmosphere."

"Get back into bed," he repeated in the same voice. Why was he not getting it, she wondered? Was he just playing with her? Okay, let's play.

"No!" she said jokingly. "You'll have to make me."

As he began to move, she jumped back playfully, as if to run away. He was quick, too quick. He had literally pounced out of the bed, grabbed hold of her by the arms, twirled her around and was staring straight into her face. His expression was unfamiliar.

Before she knew it, he had released her by throwing her backwards onto the bed so hard that it took her breath away, but not in the way Berlin sang about it. He was standing there, staring at her naked body. She felt him get on top of her. It hurt, but she hadn't enough breath to tell him to stop. She wasn't sure what he was going to do. Was this his idea of foreplay? He hadn't done anything like this before. He had always been gentle with her.

He was straddling her while holding her arms by the wrists above her head. She was looking up at him, looking into his eyes, looking for some inkling of what he was thinking, what he expected of her. Was he being dominant? Was he into S&M? Did he save it as a surprise? She decided to play him at his own game. She closed her eyes expectantly and gave him her sexiest pout. She felt his hot breath on her face. His forehead was touching hers. They were nose to nose, like Eskimos. Their lips didn't touch. His head was pressing hard against hers, so much so it began to give her a headache. She was about to say something, when he beat her to it.

"Josephine," he began. She could feel his voice more than hear it. "I want to sleep some more. I get grumpy when I don't have my sleep. You're my wife now. I expect you to do what I want to do, what I want you to do. Love, honour and obey. Do as I say, when I say. Understand? If you want this to be a happy marriage."

"What the fuck?" she thought, but didn't vocalise.

"I'm going to lie down now. You're going to lie still, and sleep, if you want to. Just as long as you don't disturb me."

Then he let go, rolled off her and lay down beside her. They were both still naked, uncovered.

The tears began to roll down both cheeks. She couldn't stop them. "What," she wondered, "had just happened?"

She didn't dare look at him. She kept her eyes on the ceiling. She felt herself begin to shiver. This was strange. Feeling chilly in such a hot climate. The room hadn't become colder, but something had, someone had. But why?

This is her honeymoon, their honeymoon. It's supposed to be the happiest time of their lives.

Why does he want to spoil it? She didn't know what to do. She replayed the history of their wonderful courtship in her head. The first night, the proposal, all the times they laughed together. All right, the wedding night itself wasn't the romantic deflowering she dreamt of as a girl, but then they had already known each other in the biblical sense. The wedding had been such a hoot: drink really did flow, and boy did it flow into John. Not that she was any sober sides herself. On the bright side, they did both make it to the bridal suite. Just about. Josephine slept on top of the bed, in her wedding dress. John didn't quite make it onto the bed. He was kneeling beside it with his head on her lap. She thought it kind of cute how they both still managed to be close to each other at the end of the night, despite their condition, especially John's.

But now this. She glanced to her right, without moving her head. His eyes were closed. She could tell by his breathing that he had fallen asleep. He looked normal, no sign of stress on his face. Perfectly relaxed.

"How could he just go back to sleep?" She felt like prodding him or shouting in his ear.

"Wake up." Not "wake up and make love with me", like the Ian Dury song. Rather "wake up and explain yourself."

"But then she thought of what he had said about doing what she was told if she wanted this to be a happy marriage. She did. She wanted this to be a happy honeymoon. If she challenged him now and didn't get the reaction or explanation she wanted, what would she do? Call the whole thing off, as Fred and Ginger had suggested? How could she? She couldn't pack up and leave, go home. She didn't have any money, any credit cards or debit cards. John had arranged it all, paid for it all. He had control of all the money. And anyway, where is home now?

John had rented a house for them, close to her work. She had given up her apartment. She had nothing. Well, she thought she had everything. A husband who was completely in love with her and she with him. A husband who had just threatened her. Or did he? He had told her in no uncertain terms to do what she was told if she wanted them to be happy. He didn't threaten to harm her in any way. He was like a stern parent.

"Do what you're told now, Josephine," she could hear her father say. But there was never any indication as to what would happen if she didn't.

According to John, they would be happy if she did. She wanted them to be happy. She wanted to be happy. She wanted him to be happy.

"Don't worry, be happy." Is that what she should do, needed to do? All this thinking was making her head throb. She closed her eyes and tried to stop. Yoga classes she had attended prior to the wedding had taught her how to put things out of her mind, how to breathe, naturally, evenly. Everything drifted out of her mind, up and away.

Time passed. She opened her eyes. Her instincts told her John was no longer beside her. She stretched out her hand. Nothing. No one. Then a sound, the sound of running water. He was showering. She had time to get out of bed and this time get dressed quickly. Before he would notice, could notice. She didn't want to seem upset, so she decided to cleanse her face and apply her make-up in extra quick time. As she sat in front of the dressing table mirror, she could see that her eyes were still red from crying herself to sleep; her mascara that she hadn't bothered to remove the night before was running in lines down her cheek, just like Lady Gaga on the cover of "The Fame Monster". But she hadn't any more time to think, the sound of running water had stopped. She had to work fast.

When John emerged from the bathroom, he was dressed in shorts and a t-shirt with the words "World's Best Husband". She had bought it for him as a surprise wedding gift.

"Good morning, darling! Why don't you get ready for breakfast while I go and stretch my legs?"

No mention of this morning's incident. All done, all forgotten. He approached her, and, bending over, leant his face into hers. She turned her cheek and closed her eyes. She felt her body tense up. He put one hand gently on the back of her head and, pulling her towards him, pressed his lips firmly against hers.

"Don't be long," he said, as he was leaving.

"Is that an order?" strayed into her head. She almost said it.

"What was that?" he said, looking back at her as he stood with his hand on the door handle.

"I love you," she said, thinking quickly.

"Love you, too," he replied, blowing her a kiss with his free hand, before exiting.

"Did I express my thought there without knowing it? Or can he hear my thoughts?" They did sometimes seem to know what each other was thinking.

She took a long, deep breath. John seemed to have got over whatever it was that had set him off. But he hadn't apologised. And she hadn't mentioned it. She didn't want to upset the apple cart. Partly because she was unsure of what would happen. Would he call it a day, call the whole thing off? How would it be if the dream was to end here? The shortest marriage in the world. Or maybe not. She had read, in some trashy magazines she had found at work, of husbands and wives cheating at the wedding reception. She had to admit that that would have been worse. John hadn't cheated. He wants to be married. He wants to be happily married. But here she was lingering a bit too long. He might think she was doing it on purpose. Would that make him angry again? She didn't want him to be angry. Although she had imagined their marriage would be the most wonderful marriage in the world, she knew in her heart that there would be little disagreements, arguments even. Not that she had expected anything like that so soon. When they talk about a honeymoon period, surely, it's supposed to be trouble-free. And so she resolved it would be. Forgive and forget. He had been under a lot of stress, working extra hours coming up to the wedding so that they could have the best honeymoon they could have. She should be understanding. They need to understand each other as well as love each other. Her inward smile began to return. And, according to the mirror, her outward one, too. She wasn't going to worry, she would be happy. Now and forever.

She moved to the window. She could feel the heat of the sun on her face. Closed her eyes. It felt soothing. Opening her eyes, she saw him. He was talking to one of the waitresses, smiling, laughing, probably joking. He was like that with women: charming, polite, endearing. Not like this morning. He was gently holding her hand. She felt somewhat jealous, although she didn't think for a moment that he would ever be unfaithful. After all, they were just married. But what about those men who cheated at the wedding reception? Stop it, Josephine. Her thoughts were wandering again.

John glanced up at the window. He saw her. She waved.

"Better hurry," she thought. Halfway out the door, she stopped, turned and grabbed her sunglasses from the dressing table, and put them on.

When she emerged from the lift, he was standing, waiting. He didn't seem impatient or annoyed. He smiled. He loved her. It was as if she was walking up the aisle towards him all over again. He took her hand. She felt elated. They walked hand in hand to the breakfast room. He guided her to a table, pulled out her chair for her and ensured she was seated comfortably, before going to get the food. It was a buffet breakfast, but no ordinary one. There was every kind of fresh fruit, freshly squeezed juices, choice of coffees, teas, cooked food. A banquet. John chose the food without asking. Brought it to her. It didn't bother her. It was what she would have chosen herself and more than she could possibly eat. Although she found that somewhat wasteful, it was time to forget about things like that, forget about everything except themselves, about each other. She enjoyed breakfast, basked in the sunshine and in the moment. For the rest of the day they explored their surroundings, got to know the staff and their fellow guests. John did most of the talking; he was good at that. She was happy to let him, happy to listen to the sound of his voice, regardless of what he was saying. How did she get so lucky? That night in bed, John was gentle and caring but passionate, just as he had been the night before. After, they slept in each other's arms. The next morning, John was up and at it early, before her. When she awoke, he leapt onto the bed beside her, kissed her passionately and told her how much he loved her, how lucky they were to have found each other, that she was his soul-mate.

The rest of the honeymoon was fantastic. They had gone on long walks. John was back to his best, laughing, joking, making her feel the centre of attention. One night during the hotel cabaret, he got up on stage and did karaoke. He couldn't sing, but that never mattered to John.

"Baby, I love you," he sang, or rather spoke, or did something between speaking and singing. But when he had finished, he took over.

"Folks," he not so much spoke as shouted, "I'd like to introduce you to my wonderful, beautiful, fantabulous wife, Josephine." She blushed and smiled as he pointed her out.

"Come up here, Josephine, come on." That was unexpected.

She felt embarrassed, but knew he wouldn't get off until she complied. She got up and joined him. He welcomed her on stage as if he was running the show. He was. At that moment he was. They let him. The funny thing. Everyone was enjoying it. It didn't matter that he couldn't sing. The organisers were loving it. It became interactive: others were getting involved, but not as involved as John was. But then there were not many Johns in the world. Maybe no other.

"A round of applause for the lovely Josephine, who is now going to join me in singing 'I Got You, Babe'." Everyone applauded.

"OMG!"

Before she could react, the music had begun. A microphone had been thrust into her hand. Even though she had, as a child, stood in front of the mirror, hairbrush in hand, singing along to her favourite songs, she knew she wasn't a singer. But then she couldn't be worse than John. She knew the words because her and John used to sing along to it when they had had a few drinks and were playing music randomly.

"Here goes nothing," she thought, before piping up.

"They say we're young…"

The people were clapping. Thank God. It sort of drowned out the singing.

When it was over, she actually felt good. John had pulled her into him all through the performance, and the song never seemed to end because they both kept singing "I got you, babe" over and over and over again. Until they became breathless. It was good while it lasted, but there was a little bit of relief at the end. A bit like sex.

"Did I just think that?" Josephine was surprised at herself. But not that much. She had come out of herself. Oops. Was that another *faux pas*? She was giggling to herself, when John noticed. He kissed her full on. She reciprocated. He was surprised. If ever there was a perfect moment in their marriage, this was it. The crowd were cheering, standing. It was the best night of the honeymoon and one of the best of their life together. She was waiting for them to shout "more". It wasn't that kind of crowd. But there was a disco of sorts afterwards. She and John danced and danced until they could dance no more. And so, to bed. And… Well, in the words of Shakespeare, "All's well that ends well." Breathless.

Apart from "the incident", the honeymoon was everything she anticipated and more. They had gone scuba diving. She had never done that before. John had. She was scared at first, but she thought of all those wildlife programmes she had watched on television, the ones filmed under the sea, and how magical and wonderful it all seemed. This was her opportunity to experience it for real, and she might never get another chance. She would do it. John held her hand the whole time. Once she was down there, it was so amazing she did actually forget her fears, but never let go of his hand. When they came up and got back on the boat, she was speechless. All she could think was "what a wonderful world".

They had swum, every day. They lay on the beach, the water washing over them just as in "From Here To Eternity". Was that where they were heading, she wondered. Eternity, together? They went into the water hand in hand and came out of the water hand in hand. She was so happy, she wished there was someone there to take their picture. There was. John had arranged it. John had insisted on hanging it opposite the bed. For their eyes only. She didn't know whether John liked it because he looked good in it or because she was looking at him as if she would never leave him. Or both.

CHAPTER TWO
SMALL-TOWN GIRL

Josephine was just a small town girl. In fact you couldn't really call where she lived a town. A village maybe. For a young girl, it really was a lonely world. But she was encouraged by the words of her favourite song. She never stopped believing.

Believing, that someday, she would get out of her small town and find the man of her dreams. Not that she had any idea of what he would look like, the man of her dreams. She wasn't one of those girls, or women, who insisted he had to be tall, dark and handsome or look like a movie star or one of their idols. Josephine was more pragmatic. She didn't rule anything, or rather anyone, out nor rule anyone in. She did, though, want him to be kind, intelligent and funny. Not funny in the sense that he was constantly making jokes. She wouldn't want the court jester. No. Funny in the sense of how he looked at life. How, like her, he wouldn't take everything seriously and could appreciate the lighter side of living. She would only know what he looked like when she had found him. As long as he had the look of love.

Josephine was one of six children, five girls and one boy, the apple of her father's eye. She was the youngest. Her father, Patrick, had been a farmer. But overindulgence in alcohol had ensured that he had a short life. He died when Josephine was fifteen. She had hardly known him. He worked all hours looking after the farm, and when he wasn't working, he was usually drinking. She would always remember being woken at night by the sound of him arriving home. Once, when she was very young, he crashed his jeep into the wall of the house. She looked out of the window and thought that he was dead. She was young. He was her father and she loved him. Naturally, she thought the worst. He was slumped over the steering wheel, motionless. Her brother had to go out and check.

He wasn't dead. He wasn't even injured. Miraculously, he had remembered to put on his seatbelt. Either that, or someone had reminded him to. Sometimes, when he had too much to drink, he would sleep for a while in his jeep in the car park of whichever establishment he had been drinking in at closing time. The owner or staff or sometimes a drinking buddy would help him to his jeep and put him in the driving seat. Although he drank a lot, he was never obnoxious or violent. Then, when he awoke refreshed, he would drive himself home. That was his way, and everyone knew it.

His luck ran out on the night of his fifty-fifth birthday, the seventeenth of March, St. Patrick's Day. His day started early as usual. He did what he had to do on the farm, before going into town to get his hair cut and treat himself to a new pair of shoes. A chance meeting with an old friend, James Brown, who had returned from living in America, resulted in them retiring to the pub for a traditional St. Patrick's Day drink, some catching up and some reminiscing. More local men joined the company when they realised a reunion was taking place, and more and more alcohol was bought and consumed.

Patrick loved and respected his family. So, despite being somewhat under the weather, he was aware that time was marching on and he needed to get home in time to wash and change for dinner. After finishing one more beer and one more whiskey, he said his goodbyes and left. He always considered himself a man who could hold his drink, but for some reason he was feeling a little bit unsteady. He had no difficulty, however, getting into his jeep and getting the keys into the ignition. There was no time to sleep it off this time. His family would be waiting. He started up the jeep and set off home. The town was busy, as every town or village in Ireland is on the seventeenth of March. And the usual parking laws were rarely enforced, even if the powers that be wanted to enforce them. It was impractical. Families were there to celebrate, watch or join in the parade and enjoy the day. There were cars and buses parked everywhere.

Patrick decided that his quickest way home was via a shortcut down a side street, avoiding the main road home, and any chance of being stopped or spotted by the Gardai, the Irish police, and checked for drunk driving. He managed to negotiate his way into and along the side street. He had almost made it to the other end of it, when he noticed a bus badly parked on his side of the road. He could barely see if the road ahead was clear, but not being clear-headed, decided to indicate and go around it at any rate. He was no more than fifty feet or so from the bus when a child leapt from the door onto the roadway. He had already started accelerating and was about to overtake. He couldn't swerve further to the right as there were people walking. His only option was to take his foot off the accelerator and brake hard. However, his reactions weren't as razor sharp as they would have been in sobriety. By the time his foot hit the brake, it was too late. At the same moment his jeep collided full force with the front of the bus. In his panic to get home, Patrick had neglected to put on his seatbelt. He ended up crashing through the windscreen of his jeep, his flight only cut short by his going head to head with a fifty-five-seater bus. He was killed instantly.

Instead of birthday celebrations, the family buried their beloved father three days later. Josephine noticed that her brother was wearing her father's new shoes. Her mother was nothing if not practical. "Waste not want not," was her motto. "Your father's not going to miss them," she told her son. "He'd want you to have them." Josephine had heard the expression 'dead man's shoes' but didn't know what it meant. To her it now had its own meaning. It was Josephine's first personal experience of death.

Despite the shock of her father's death, her mother, being a matter of fact kind of woman, carried on with her job of raising her youngest child and so Josephine was actively encouraged to carry on with her education and left school with more than respectable results. She was one of the smartest in her all girl school. Still there was little, or no chance, of her going on to university or third level education. Her sisters had already left home and P.J. was busy trying to keep the family farm going. So Josephine was put to work in a local convenience store as a checkout operator, so that she could help out with the household expenses. It wasn't what she had envisaged doing with her life. But, for now, she had very little option. Her father had left some debts behind, and being the stubborn man he was, had refused to take out life insurance, firmly believing that he had years ahead of him.

Although she had grown up in the digital age, Josephine had never used dating apps and the like. The main reason was that, given the rural location of her home, there wasn't any access to broadband. Nor would her father or mother would have signed up to it. And as for P.J., Let's just say he was less than technically minded and a little, or not so little, old fashioned. His only interests were farming, machinery, and cars. Not a child of the twenty-first century. So as far as romance went, Josephine had to content herself with television, movies and Mills and Boon. She was pleasantly surprised to learn that Mills and Boon had become rather more racy than the ones she had read as a young teenager, and even more surprised to find them in the local newsagents. They were described as sinful and seductive. But they were a poor substitute for the real thing. Not that she was going to find the real thing in her area. All the good ones, as they are termed, were either gay or married, and all the others were like P.J. Both in looks and attitude. It had to be said that she had her reservations when it came to P.J. getting himself a girlfriend, or wife. Not to be too cruel, but he was no Brad Pitt.

Working in a convenience store, although not all bad, was just not taxing enough for Josephine, so it was a pleasant surprise when she discovered that a woman she worked with was taking a night course at Letterkenny Institute of Technology. Letterkenny was the largest town in her county, County Donegal. She had often gone there shopping, or to go to the cinema. It was quite a big town but not a city by any means. It wasn't London or Dublin, but compared to her own little limited locality, it was New York. She would at least have some chance of finding a decent boyfriend there.

"Or a husband," she fantasised. Clearly she was reading too much. A boyfriend would suffice for now.

Her work colleague drove to and from Letterkenny every night, to attend her course, and if Josephine wanted, she could also enrol in a course and travel with her. So that's what she did. She enrolled in a computer skills course. The immediate reason was simply to get away from home for a few hours, but she hoped that in time it would enable her to get a better job. In a better place. Her father's debts would be paid in the not too distant future, and she would no longer be required to contribute. Her brother and her mother could manage between them.

The course was a joy, not just because she was escaping from her boring surroundings for a while, but there were more interesting people to talk to. And to look at. This course was not limited to the female of the species. And, oh boy, was that evident. There were some hot males, and we're not talking online services here. But nothing was going to happen as long as she remained living at home. Yes, she could talk and flirt and have coffee at break time, but there could be no follow up. Her mother would never countenance her staying in Letterkenny, even for a night. And besides, she didn't even know anyone living there she could stay with. She would have to wait. Not that it would be easy. But, as they say, all good things.

Luckily when she had finished her course, two years later, her mother had stopped depending on her meagre salary and it was time for her, at last, to fly the nest. She started applying for jobs. In Letterkenny. There had been one boy in her course she was particularly interested in. And he lived there. Was he into her? She thought so. She hoped so. So much so that she was desperate to land a job of some sort, of any sort. Luckily she had glowing references from her tutors on the course, and the head of her secondary school. As a result, she was interviewed for a secretarial job at Letterkenny University Hospital. She couldn't believe it when, just two weeks later, she was notified that the position was hers. Josephine was ecstatic. Even more so, when she discovered that her boss at the convenience store owned an apartment near the hospital, and that it had just become vacant. What a stroke of luck. Things were just getting better and better. The only thing was, it didn't come cheap. But, seeing as she wasn't a big spender, she reckoned she could afford it. Moving in day was the best day of her life, so far. To be away from home, from the watchful eye of her mother and siblings, to be an independent woman for the first time in her life. It was a wonderful feeling. And now she could pursue the object of her desire. Killian.

Time hadn't lessened her interest in him. In fact, the desire had grown stronger, week by week, particularly since the course had ended. It was almost at boiling point. Despite her living in a dead zone, as far as broadband goes, she was able to send him text messages. Casual messages. But now. Now it was time to ramp it up. Not that she was going to send him any intimate pictures, or copy him passages from those sinful and seductive Mills and Boon books. She wasn't that kind of girl. It would be more of a 'come up and see me some time' vibe.

Now that she was living in Letterkenny she could begin to use social media. Imagine her disappointment when she checked his Facebook page. He had a girlfriend, a serious girlfriend. They'd been together for a year. He had never said. But then why would he? They, he and Josephine, had never spoken in detail about their private lives, not that she had one. Nor had he ever crossed the line. He was friendly, very friendly, but not overly friendly. Not touchy feely. Maybe that's why she found him so attractive. He wasn't pushy, didn't overstep the mark. She just assumed he was a gentleman, but she could have sworn he had that look in his eyes when they were together. The one that says 'kiss me', or something more intimate. Obviously not. Unless, of course, he was a player. If so, she wasn't interested.

But she wouldn't rush to judgement. She would remain friends on Facebook, and who knows? There was no ring on it, on her, yet. She had noticed that. He might, in the future, need a shoulder to cry on, or just need to get under someone to get over her. "Is that right?" she thought. "Or should that the other way around? But then it's an equal opportunities world today, isn't it?"

And speaking of opportunities, wasn't she free and single, and ready to mingle?

There were bars and nightclubs out there, just waiting for her to grace them with her presence. And she did, for months on end, without success. It wasn't that she didn't have any suitors. She did have some intimate moments, but only at parties where there were others, especially other women, present. She knew, from watching too many crime programmes, not to put herself in a vulnerable position. She didn't want to be raped, or murdered, or both. She did want to be liberated but yet didn't want to go all the way. Why? Was she old fashioned? No, that wasn't it. She didn't embrace all that holier than thou religious teaching from the nuns in school, telling her that she would go to hell if she allowed a member of the opposite sex, or she supposed, a member of the same sex, see her naked or touch her intimately. Or even if she had bad thoughts, or masturbated, or both. She had. She wanted to have sexual contact, wanted to be desired, wanted to please and be pleased. Yet, when it came to penetration, to intercourse, there was something in her, some intrinsic feeling or need, call it what you want, that prevented her from giving herself entirely to another. Until she, and he, were fully committed to each other. Not that they had to be married, but they would both have to want to be together for life, forever.

Unlucky in love, for now, that's what she thought. But as against that, better luck in her career. There was an opening, within the existing staff, for a position as a private secretary to a gynaecologist, a busy gynaecologist, not only working for the hospital but also with his own private practice. It would mean more money. And more respect, she thought. She applied, and was surprised, when there were no other applicants. She would only discover why later.

The interview was less formal than she expected. Of course he, Dr. White, would already have her details on the hospital file, and everyone she worked with, including the doctors, were aware of how reliable she was, how efficient, how punctual, how personable.

"Do you drive, Josephine?" It took her by surprise. She didn't. Although she had considered it, the manner of her father's untimely death had made her somewhat nervous of trying. And there had never been any need.

"No, sorry, I don't."

He was perusing her C.V.

"But if it's necessary, I can learn" she added quickly.

"I see you live in town."

"Yes. Very close to the hospital. In fact I can walk to work in five minutes."

"Excellent. No need to learn to drive then. Unless, of course, you want to. It's just that sometimes this job entails extra hours, outside of the normal ones. I may need you to come in very early, or stay very late."

"That's not a problem, not a problem at all." Josephine replied with a relieved smile.

"Will it be all right with your husband, boyfriend, partner?"

He was being very PC. She supposed that was a sign of the times.

"I'm sure it would be. If I had one."

He looked at her over his glasses. There was a short pause. She didn't know if he was waiting for her to clarify or what.

"You will one day. A beautiful, intelligent, young woman like you, won't be alone for long."

She felt herself going red.

"You've got the job."

She was speechless. "How easy was that?" she thought. Still, never look a gift horse in the mouth.

"Congratulations. I need you to start first thing in the morning. I've sorted it with administration. Someone will cover your previous duties, and besides, you're still here if they need to know anything."

As she left his office she was beaming and singing to herself.

"The only way is up." For you Josephine, for you, but not for you and me. There was no you and me. Not just yet.

CHAPTER THREE
NEW LIFE

Working for a consultant was great. She was treated with respect. She was the first contact not only for patients but for other consultants, GPs, solicitors and their secretaries. At the same time, it didn't change her. She was still the same small-town girl, but no longer living in her small-town lonely world. People spoke to her now, important people, not least her boss. He was handsome, well spoken, respectful. He called her by her first name. They had conversations and not just about work. He was interested in her, her life, asked her how she liked living in Letterkenny, if she had found a boyfriend yet. He looked her straight in the eye when he spoke. Josephine had read (in some magazine article or other) that this meant he cared about her. He was at least ten years her senior, but she believed that "love knows no bounds". Downside. He was married, happily married from all reports. And "no", she hadn't found a boyfriend.

Josephine was taken by complete surprise when one Friday evening on her way out of the office, he called her back.

"Josephine?"

She turned to face him.

"Can you stay on for a while?"

While he had told her he might want her to work extra hours, she didn't expect that it would be on a Friday evening. Although she had no one to go home to, she still liked to go home and relax at the end of the week. How would she respond?

She noticed that his voice did not have its usual self-assured tone. Its usual authority.

She thought he looked sad. Something was wrong. She was hesitating.

"Unless there is some reason you can't," he added. He smiled a lingering smile. A please, pretty please smile.

Josephine was slightly unnerved by this.

"What's going on?" she thought.

"I just need someone to talk to. That's all," he added.

He was pleading with her. No one had ever pleaded with her, let alone such a seemingly important, self-confident professional. This was something new for her.

She slowly walked back towards her desk and put her bag on it.

"For a minute I thought you were going to tell me you didn't need me any more."

Despite having landed the job, she still thought it too good to be true.

"Sorry," he said apologetically. "I didn't mean to unnerve you. Let's go into my office. I'll lock the outer door. Don't want to start tongues wagging, do we?"

That comment made her hesitate; but then, given his position, she sort of understood where he was coming from. It didn't take much sometimes for an ugly rumour to be born. After all, it wouldn't be the first time a man cheated with his secretary. Wait! What was she thinking? This is nothing. There is nothing to hide.

"Josephine?" He was standing, holding the door open for her.

She went and sat in his office, in front of his desk, as if she were one of his patients, and waited for him to lock the outer door. She heard the click of the key. And then his breathing as he approached from behind. She was feeling more and more uncomfortable. She shivered, but not from the cold. Maybe she should have refused, made some excuse. She could remember that there was something urgent she had to do, a reason she had to go home. But that would sound lame. He knew she didn't have a significant other, and if it was urgent, she wouldn't have forgotten. As he passed her, he put his right hand on her left shoulder and squeezed gently. Hopefully, he didn't notice how that made her whole body tense up.

He went to the coffee machine, poured two coffees and put one in front of her. She took a long drink. She needed it. Thankfully, it wasn't too hot. He walked around the desk and sat, or rather slumped, into his leather chair. He sighed.

What, she wondered, did he want to talk to her about? She was only his secretary. Surely, he had friends, close friends, colleagues, family, buddies.

She still had her coffee in her hand. She had drunk most of it. Nerves. She put it down.

"Josephine, I'm sorry to burden you with my problems. I hope you don't mind me taking up your time."

She was now beginning to feel important. Why would this man, a man that everyone looked up to, want her time?

"No, not at all, Doctor White, no problem."

"Please, Josephine, I thought we were friends. Call me Lily."

He obviously noticed the shocked look on her face and gave a little laugh. "Only joking, Josephine. You know my first name. Please use it," he smirked.

She wasn't sure whether to reply. A Lou Reed song came into her head.

"Oh! Jim," she blurted out before she realised how that could sound.

It was his turn to look surprised.

"It wasn't supposed to sound like that," she said quickly.

"Oh, my God," she thought. "This is getting worse." She sat up straight in her chair, crossed her legs and clutched her knee with both hands.

"What did you want to talk about, Jim?" she added formally, before he could reply.

He put his elbows on the desk and leaned forward, as if he was about to give a patient some bad news.

"This is so embarrassing. I never thought I would be doing this, especially with my secretary."

She let go of her knee, retreated into her chair and raised her eyebrows. She was about to say something, but couldn't find any words.

He drew back and sat bolt upright. "Oh, my God, that sounds so bad!"

Josephine had to suppress her laugh.

"This is going from the sublime to the ridiculous," she thought.

Songs came into her head, as they often did when she was nervous.

"Go Now", "Run For Home."

She couldn't. The door was locked. That wasn't the real reason. She felt for him, even though he was older, wiser, or so it seemed. She began to understand the phrase "frozen to the spot". Sometimes, when you're in a situation you don't want to be in, it's just not possible to get out of it, to do anything about it.

"My wife is cheating on me."

Josephine was shocked. Not just because of the revelation. What was she supposed to say?

She said nothing.

"I know, Josephine, that you're too young and inexperienced for all of this, but I find that it's so therapeutic to tell someone. It has to be someone you trust, who won't divulge it to anyone else, not even their closest friends and family. I know, Josephine, from working with you, that you are that kind of person. I admire you for that."

She was so tempted to say, "You must have other people you can trust?", but then why was he talking to her?

She was like a rabbit in the headlights. She didn't know how much he trusted her, what he was going to divulge and in how much intimate detail. Some people might relish that thought, but Josephine didn't. She never thought of herself as prudish, but she was. She had to admit it to herself in this instant. It was all right reading about salacious stuff in cheap magazines or watching it on television, but it's different when there's someone there, expecting a reaction. Someone who is personally involved. And besides, she couldn't share it with anyone, not that she had anyone to share it with. Nor would she do it. She had too much respect for people's privacy. What if someone betrayed her trust, spilled the beans on her? Not that she had ever done anything worthy of spilling. But she might, some day. Then she wouldn't want it bandied about.

She wished her phone would ring. But who would call her? She didn't get that many calls. To tell the truth, she didn't get any calls, and didn't expect any, unless there was an emergency at home. And as yet there hadn't been. So all was well there, then.

What could she say? What would she say? It was her time to speak.

"Dr..." She checked herself. "Jim..." That was better. He was looking at her expectantly. "You know you can tell me anything. I won't judge you. We all have our problems."

"Shit," she thought, "I sound so grown-up. What the fuck am I letting myself in for?"

"I've only just found out. I think she thought that I was cheating.

31

She doesn't understand that I have to work long hours. She thinks that just because I'm a consultant, I can come and go as I please."

He paused and snorted. "She doesn't mind the money, of course."

"Have you talked to her about it?"

He got up, moved around the desk and put his left buttock on it, keeping his right foot on the floor. He was close, too close. She was looking up at him. She didn't have a peaceful, easy feeling — far from it. She shifted in her chair. He noticed. He leaned over and put his hands on her shoulders. Not forcefully, but she still felt trapped.

"Josephine, maybe you're just too young. When you fall in love and have a family of your own, you'll understand. It's devastating when someone betrays your trust when all you're doing is your very best to give them the best life they can have."

Josephine thought he was going to burst into tears.

He bent his head towards her, put his lips close to hers, and kissed her.

Although she hadn't known what to expect, she certainly didn't expect that. She hadn't resisted, drawn back. She couldn't. It was mostly due to the fact that he had a hold on her and that she was as far back in the chair as she could be. But the shock was also a contributor. She could have pushed him away. Her arms were free. She didn't. She couldn't explain it. Instead, she stood up. He hadn't let go of her. Instead, his hands had slid down from her shoulders and were now holding her upper arms, firmly but without hurting. He kissed her again. She couldn't believe that she was letting him. No. It was more than that. Her lips were accepting his. She realised she was returning his kisses. Was this some kind of unfulfilled fantasy? Had she fantasised about this very moment? She couldn't remember. She couldn't honestly swear that she didn't. And if his wife was cheating, well, it's all her fault. He wouldn't cross the line otherwise, even if he desired her.

Talk about being carried along on the crest of a wave. Everything happened so quickly. Next thing, she was on her back on his examination couch. Her legs were dangling over the end and he was standing between them, as was his penis. She couldn't even remember how he, or she, had removed her underwear. Something told her that this was wrong. Maybe her Catholic upbringing, maybe just her moral compass. Either way, she knew she should stop it now. Would he respond with "Don't stop me now"? After all, he was having a good time.

She had hesitated too long. She could feel that he was entering her, yet it didn't feel real.

How could this be happening? Well, he was a professional, and getting women to open their legs was his speciality. He was leaning on her with his upper body and forcing his tongue into her mouth. She was holding on to him, but not in a passionate embrace. She was afraid she was going to fall sideways onto the floor. Her mind kept on saying, "I shouldn't be doing this, I shouldn't be doing this." But then she wasn't doing anything. She was being completely passive.

Physically, she was feeling very little. In her head, everything was dream-like, as if she was an onlooker rather than a participant. Had he given her something, some kind of muscle relaxant? She knew from watching true crime programmes that there were drugs that rendered you helpless, yet awake. He, on the other hand, was far from helpless. In fact, he was becoming more and more vigorous, thrusting faster, breathing faster. He seemed to have got over his anxiety. And his wife's infidelity. And still she felt nothing. Neither pleasure nor pain. But that's not what mattered. A new thought told her he wasn't using a condom. She could become pregnant. She needed to do something.

Before she could get hold of him by the shoulders and push him away, it was over. He had stopped. He was finished, satisfied. It had obviously been infinitely more exciting for him than it had been for her. On a scale of one to ten, it was ten nil to him.

"Did he administer an anaesthetic before he started?" she wondered. "Was there something in the coffee?"

He had certainly numbed her senses. Taken her by surprise. This was not the kind of shock treatment she had read about in books or seen in the movies. But then, who knows what goes on behind closed doors? Now she did. She was part of the going-on. Except, it was over and she was wet. But it was his wet. He was out of there and pulling up his trousers, his back turned to her.

She was stunned. What just happened? Did it just happen? Would anyone believe this? Did she believe it? Maybe she had gone home and fallen asleep on the sofa. After all, she had had stranger, more unbelievable dreams than this.

He sat at his desk and lit up a cigarette. She could smell the smoke, the unmistakeable smell of a just-lit cigarette. Did that mean it wasn't a dream? She tried to erase all thoughts from her mind. If it was a dream, that might work. It didn't. He was still there, now sitting in his expensive, comfortable, pure-leather chair, leaning back and blowing smoke rings.

"At least someone is smoking," she thought, "and it's not me."

She sat up, taking care not to fall on the floor. That would just be so embarrassing.

"And what just happened isn't?" she reprimanded herself.

His phone rang. He put down his cigarette and answered it.

"Hello, darling; yes, I'm still at work. Had something urgent to attend to. I'll be home soon. Love you, too."

"Unbelievable. I've been had. In more ways than one."

She wanted to scream obscenities at him, run over and wipe that smug look off his face. Then she realised. She was sitting on an examination couch with a wet crotch, her knickers on the floor in front of her. How does that look? Hopefully, there are no security cameras in here. But then there couldn't be. It's a private consulting room. And anyway, did she think he wouldn't have ensured that what just happened was going to be totally private, between them? So that if it ever came up, he could deny it.

"What? She said what? And why would I risk my position, my career? It always amazes me the fantasies some young girls have about their bosses."

It never happened. How did it happen? How could she let it happen? Why did she let it happen? She looked at him. He had that self-same smirk on his face as when he had joked earlier about calling him Lily. Well, he wasn't lilywhite, was he? Far from it!

The coffee pot was within reach. She could grab it and throw it at him or smash it over his big fat arrogant head. What would he tell his wife then? That he tripped over his ego and fell into the coffee machine? He certainly couldn't have tripped over his penis. Feeling vengeful, Josephine? Yes. Of course. She stood up and looked at the pot.

Too late. Now he was gone as quick as he had come. Out the door.

And she was left to pick up the pieces. And her knickers. As she was still leaking sperm, she decided to go to the toilet and let it all out.

"Why would a doctor, a gynaecologist, risk his position, his job, his reputation for a fuck? And without a condom or any form of contraception? Did he think she was on the pill? She had told him that she didn't have a partner, she was free and easy, but that was in relation to working hours. It wasn't meant to be taken literally. Maybe he just assumes all single women in this day and age are promiscuous and are on the pill or using some form of contraception. Josephine wasn't.

She was sure she wasn't the first woman who had succumbed to his charms — no, not to his charms, to his lies. No doubt he had many notches on his bedpost. Or his examination couch. With that thought, she remembered looking at it, his couch, while contemplating her knickers on the floor. The frame did have an awful lot of scratch marks. Maybe this was his bedpost, and if so, she was very far from the first. Not that she was so deluded to think that she was. The first, the last, his everything.

Not in his repertoire. Maybe he fooled them all with his lying eyes, as he had her.

He had lied about his wife, his life, his intentions.

But what was she going to do about it? She could report him to his superiors. Not that he thought he had any — superiors, that is. She could go to the Gardai. How would that go?

"What's your complaint, ma'am?" Okay, that sounds so American, but she did watch too much television.

"I was raped. By my boss. He's a doctor, a consultant."

"And where did this happen?"

"In his rooms, his consulting rooms."

"So he dragged you in there and forced himself upon you?"

"Well, not exactly."

"So you went there voluntarily."

"Yes. Sort of."

"What do you mean, sort of?"

"He tricked me. He told me he wanted to talk to me."

"So did he? Talk to you?"

"Well, yes, I guess so."

"And then he attacked you, forced himself upon you?"

"Well, not exactly." There's that phrase again. A phrase you should never use in a formal interview, whether you're the victim or the suspect.

"I'm sorry, ma'am, but why don't you tell me exactly how it was."

"Well…" Not a good way to start a sentence. Sounds like you're about to make it up… "he sort of had sex with me without my consent."

"And you were subdued in some sort of way, tied up, rendered helpless?"

"Well, not exactly." At this stage, you just want to say, "Just forget it."

"Let yourself out." It was a real voice. Not the one in her head.

It took her by surprise. She was back in the room, and so was he. Back, but not for more, obviously. Not that he was ever going to get it. From her, at least.

"I'll see you Monday."

And he would. Unless she decided to take the day off. And if she did, what would he do? Fire her? It wouldn't surprise her. He would find some reason to be dissatisfied with her work, her performance. Well, here's the thing, Dr White — sorry, Jim — if it comes down to performance, maybe I should fire you. And speaking of fire, you're not as hot as you think you are. You're a cold-hearted bastard, as cold as ice.

CHAPTER FOUR
WOULD I LIE TO YOU?

Josephine was still working for Dr White, the bastard, despite his taking advantage of her. Well, to be honest, despite his raping her. But that fact would remain between them. Not because she didn't want to ruin his reputation or his career. When she had time to think about it, she realised that to do something about it would be a double-edged sword. It might ruin his reputation, his career, maybe even his marriage. But it would ruin her own reputation, as insignificant as it was, and her chances of making a life for herself. Even if she was believed and became the victim, she would always be the girl or woman that was taken advantage of by Dr White, or Mr White, as he liked to be known. Apparently, it gives him greater status. He liked to think of himself as a colossus among men. A god. After all, he was bringing new life into the world. Not literally, not like Arnold Schwarzenegger in "Junior". Rather, he was looking after the child-bearers of this world. And then it struck her. Why he felt he could have sex without a condom, without contraception. He didn't care if the women got pregnant. One of the crime programmes Josephine had watched on television involved a doctor who specialised in IVF and impregnated women he had drugged and had sex with. He had fathered multitudes of children. Maybe Dr White had the same aspirations. After all, if she had been in a relationship, she might just have assumed it was her boyfriend who got her pregnant, would want it to be her boyfriend who got her pregnant. But she had told him, Dr White, Jim, that she was unattached. But if she was promiscuous, slept around, it could be anyone's. Is that what he thought, had banked on? That if she became pregnant, she wouldn't be sure who the father was? And that brought her back to that horrible thought. Could she be pregnant? She hadn't even considered the morning-after pill, and now it was too late. One too many mornings had come and gone. In the coming weeks she continued to do her work as she always had, except that there was no longer any convivial conversation with you-know-who. Instructions now were delivered via dictation. Never in person. Although he still called her by her first name and used the word 'please'. Perhaps he was feeling guilty. Is he hell! He's just letting her know that he's the one in charge, her superior. He can do what he wants.

She just got on with her work, now that she had accepted that she wasn't going to do anything about it, except maybe try to warn any unsuspecting innocents abroad, new nurses or secretaries. In an informal, jokey manner, obviously.

"He's all right to work for, but he's got a roving eye, and other parts, if you know what I mean."

My god, is that what she was, she wondered. An innocent abroad. Maybe she should have stayed at home, as her mother suggested. That thought was only very fleeting. No. That would not have worked. She still liked her job, her place of work, her colleagues, living on her own. That hadn't changed. What's done is done. Onwards and upwards.

And then she missed two periods in a row. It couldn't be. Or could it? She needed to know for sure. But how? She didn't want it on record. Luckily, nowadays chemists carry pregnancy testing kits. Not only chemists, but shops, discount shops. There they were on the shelves beside the condoms. Made her think whether those condoms were less than effective. Else why would you need a pregnancy test? Or is it just so you could buy your condoms and pregnancy test at the same time. To be sure to be sure, as they say in Ireland. But it was too late for condoms. And anyway, he should have been the one thinking about them. No, not him. He's infallible. Nothing can go wrong. But then maybe nothing's wrong in his eyes. Nothing he can't fix. Well, now there might be something he needs to fix. But she wouldn't know until she had hold of that pregnancy test. She would go to one of the chemists she hadn't used before, where no one would know who she was, who she worked for. Why not those discount shops? Well, she thought, can I trust something I bought for one euro forty-nine cents, or one euro fifty cents since they decided to do away with those little insignificant coins? Not only that, but surely a chemist wouldn't stock something that doesn't work. Doesn't do what it says on the tin, or label? Aren't they licensed, regulated? On the other hand, discount stores answer to nobody, do they?

So the random chemist it was. As she was paying, she could have sworn she recognised the person queuing beside her, but he didn't speak and neither did she. Probably just her paranoia.

Going home was the most nervous, the most uneasy she had felt since that day in his office. When she got there, she didn't hesitate. She went straight to the toilet. It was positive. She was negative. This isn't happening. But it had. Happened. And she had let it. Why didn't she push him away, kick him in the groin? That would have put a halt to his gallop, dampened his ardour, brought him to his senses. Or rather to his knees. Instead, she allowed him to have his way with her, as they used to say back in the day, or in Barbara Cartland novels. She was joking with herself, but in reality the joke was on her. It was no joke. She wasn't laughing. He might, if he knew. But he would have to know. Or would he? She could go to England, have an abortion, as many had done before her. No one, not even him, would be the wiser. But why let him off the hook? She didn't think for one moment that he would ask her to give birth. He definitely wouldn't want that, or else he would deny that it was his. He might even claim to be sterile. The facts say otherwise. It was no miracle, the conception certainly hadn't been immaculate. Or memorable. It would have been a sleeping dog, but for the consequences.

Time was running out. She had read that in England abortion was legal up to twenty-four weeks. Although they were now legal in Ireland, time was short, maybe even expired, as if it didn't happen in the first twelve weeks it was complicated. Could be refused. And besides, she wouldn't want to risk people knowing, her family, her mother, her colleagues. Not for his sake, the bastard, but she didn't want to ruin her own life. And she was still looking for that man of her dreams, her dream lover, and when she found him, she didn't want him to think of her as easy or promiscuous. Especially as she was neither.

But could she afford it, the trip to England, the cost of the termination, as they like to call it nowadays, the time off? To be fair, that was probably the least of her worries. There's no way he wouldn't countenance a week's holiday in the circumstances.

"No going back," she thought, as she entered his office, without knocking. She was nervous. But why? For all her thinking and assuming, she really didn't know how he would react. Would he try to convince her to change her mind?

"Pull yourself together, Josephine," she told herself. "Do you seriously think he's going to ask you to have his baby?"

He was alone, as she knew he would be. She was his secretary. She knew his timetable, his appointments. He looked up, startled. His mobile phone was in his left hand. He covered it with his right.

"Josephine?" he blurted out.

Although she felt like giving him a smart answer, she didn't. Truth is, she couldn't think of one. Don't you just hate it when that happens? Never mind. She was focused on one thing.

Before she could speak, he lifted his mobile phone to his left ear and spoke into it.

"I'll have to call you back. Yes, as soon as I can. Me, too."

"Your mother?" Josephine said sarcastically. "Never mind," she added. "I'm not here to discuss your love life, or should I say your sexploits?"

He ignored that comment. "To what do I owe the pleasure?"

"Believe me, there's no pleasure in this for me. Nor for you, not like the last time." Her nervousness was being overtaken by her sudden bravado.

She could swear he cracked a smile.

"I think I'm pregnant. And don't ask whose it is."

It was his turn to be speechless. Except, he didn't seem that taken aback.

"Would I lie to you?"

He didn't respond, except to put his elbows on the desk and turn his eyes upwards, looking directly into hers, as she stood there in front of his desk. She hadn't sat down. Partly because of what happened last time and partly because she wanted to appear to be in charge of this conversation. To take control. Not like last time.

"Why would I lie about it?" she continued. "I promise you, I don't want you to leave your wife for me, leave your girlfriend, girlfriends, mistresses or whatever others you have hidden out there somewhere. I wouldn't dream of depriving them of your wonderfulness. I'll just have to look at it as a lost opportunity, I guess, the one that got away."

"There's no need for sarcasm."

"I know, but it sort of helps me cope."

"So, what do you want?"

"I want it to have never happened."

"How many…?" He stopped.

"He was going to say weeks," thought Josephine. How thoughtless, but no surprise.

"Are you asking me for an abortion?" he continued.

"Do you seriously want me to have your baby? What would your wife have to say? Hell, what would your girlfriend have to say. Why don't you call her back and ask her? In fact, call both of them."

"Point taken. What do you want me to do for you?"

"Seriously," thought Josephine, "does he really think I would let him touch me again? But then he did put…" she paused, "the baby there. Maybe he thinks he's the one who should remove him. Or her."

"I'll have to go to England. I don't want it on record here. Do you?" she replied, hoping that he would take the hint.

"There's another way." Now she really was afraid he was going to suggest the unsuggestable? But she had to hear him out.

"Go on, I'm listening."

"I have a friend in Dublin."

She looked at him quizzically. She felt like saying, "You have friends?"

"A gynaecologist."

"Are you not listening? I don't want it on record."

"Come on, Josephine, you're a clever girl. You've worked for me long enough to know that everything is confidential, that what is on record is what the doctor puts there."

"I don't follow."

"Maybe not. So I'll tell you how it works," he went on. "My friend does a D&C and it's done."

"And no one is the wiser."

"Exactly. Buried in the records. No questions asked. Nothing out of the ordinary. Just another woman having another procedure. Better than the alternative, don't you think?"

What she was thinking was she would love to have taken the chair she was holding on to, the very same chair where it all began, and smash it over his head. But what good would it do?

Back to the matter at hand.

"When?"

"Whenever you want."

"He's a very good friend, then."

"Yes, she is." That took her by surprise. But she wasn't here to discuss the modern-day ethics of the medical profession or which of the sexes was more ethical.

"Next week, Wednesday."

"Consider it done."

"I'll consider it done when it's done," she replied, as she let go of the chair and turned to leave.

"I'll email you the details," he called after her.

She paused as she reached for the door handle and glanced back at him. He was leaning back in his chair and putting his mobile phone up to his ear.

"You really are a bastard," she said, even though she hated stating the obvious.

He frowned, then smiled.

"Close the door after you, please, Ms Boyle."

She slammed it.

CHAPTER FIVE
SOMEBODY TO LOVE

Josephine had parted company with Dr White. By mutual agreement. And gone back to working in the general office. It wasn't as lucrative, but he had given her severance pay, so to speak. It was a generous payment. She took it. He could afford it, and no matter how many morals she considered she had, she wouldn't give him the satisfaction of refusing. She didn't think of it as compensation or hush money. More like "fuck-off-and-leave-me-alone money". Despite his having being aloof and not really speaking to her, she just couldn't help but wind him up or annoy him, at every opportunity.

"Oh! Dr White, can I have a word with you, in your office?"

"Certainly, Ms Boyle, but make it quick. I have a lot of appointments."

She knew that. That's why she was doing what she was doing.

"So, what is it you want to talk about?" he would ask when they were alone in his office.

"Nothing, really. I just felt like I needed to talk to someone. Someone I can trust. But then that's not you, is it? I should go."

And she would leave.

And now she was leaving for good. And anyway, the general office was much more fun. Sally was there. Her and Sally had bonded. Had the same love of music, the same sense of humour. The same hatred of Dr White. Maybe not for the same reason, but then Josephine had never asked Sally why she hated the self-assured, self-loving, arrogant, aloof twat. Maybe one day Sally would reveal what he had done to her, if anything. But she wouldn't wish that on Sally, on anyone, even though if it happened it happened, and nothing could change that. But Josephine was going to change, change her life for the better now that she had forgiven herself for what had happened. It wasn't her fault. She always knew that, but it took time to feel it. And now that the guilt had disappeared from her life, she needed something else. Wanted something else.

She wanted somebody to love, to love her back. There had to be a good man out there somewhere. She could try internet dating, but she had heard so many horror stories about psychos out there just looking for their next prey, paedophiles out there who befriend women to gain access to their children. She had seen the MTV programme "Catfish", that showed how people everywhere were making false profiles on Facebook, Instagram or some other social networking platform. It was impossible to tell who was genuine and who wasn't. There were lesbians pretending to be men, gay men pretending to be women. All sorts. She knew how to use the internet. Didn't everyone nowadays? But social networking didn't hold that much attraction for her. She still preferred to talk with people on the phone or in a personal social situation. She was surprised when she found that the local newspaper had a personal section where there were people looking for people, for various reasons: correspondence, companionship, relationships, fun. Fun? What kind of fun, she wondered, before the penny suddenly dropped.

"Oh! Fun. Maybe I'm too naive even for this."

She noticed that replies were requested in writing. To a box number, for obvious reasons. After all, you might not want someone looking for fun turning up on your doorstep when all you wanted was companionship. The whole concept made her giggle, as did some of the ads.

"Mature gentleman, GSOH, NS, RC, SD, VGL, looking for younger lively lady with a view to a lasting friendship and maybe more."

No mention of fun, then? But that could be what he means by "maybe more". Dirty old man.

It all seemed a bit archaic. Did people still write letters, put the paper in the envelope, lick the stamp and go to the post office to catch the post? Hadn't they heard of email, inbox instead of letterbox, send instead of post?

Still, she thought it might be fun to try it. Not that she was looking for fun. Well not necessarily, but if the right person came along. She wasn't that much of a prude. This is the twenty-first century, after all. Women are equal now. Why shouldn't she have fun? She couldn't

44

remember the last time. Her experiences with men since she moved to Letterkenny weren't what she would describe as fun, nor funny. Comic maybe, or tragic.

She scanned the adverts. "GSOH, NS, RC, SD, VGL." What the hell? What are they talking about? She was on the brink of giving up, when she noticed the key to unlocking these terms at the bottom of the page. Having read them, she cottoned on very quickly. She was a clever girl, just as Dr White had said. The people using the service obviously knew what each other were talking about, used the terms just as easily as the young people of today use text-speak. Bet they were very disappointed in finding out that their SD, NS, RC, GSOH was a raving alcoholic who smoked incessantly, never went to Mass and couldn't get the joke even if you explained it word for word. She found the VGL term particularly off-putting. What sort of prat describes himself as Very Good Looking? The sort that wouldn't be getting her reply, that's for sure. Move on, Josephine. Next.

"John. Boyish nature. Full of 'joie de vivre', loves good company, good food, good conversation, good music. Can talk, but willing to listen. Can read and write. Able to keep a secret. Technophobic. Facebook or Twitter. Neither. Just pen and paper. Looking for youngish female to share thoughts and time with, in real time, not virtual. Is somewhat old fashioned, so if you're interested send me your name and Box number. Write me or write me off."

What? No GSOH, no NS, no RC, no SD, and better still, no VGL.

She thought the "joie de vivre" reference a bit pretentious at first, but on second thoughts maybe he was just being playful. She was intrigued. It didn't tell her an awful lot about this person, but then none of the advertisements did. He sounded different. He wasn't just looking for fun. Or at least it wasn't apparent from his ad. Anyway, it would do no harm to reply. The good thing was that she didn't have to disclose any personal details. He wouldn't even know if she was using her real name. She would, of course. She didn't want to be seen to be deceitful. That wouldn't be conducive to any kind of relationship, even a friendship. She genuinely believed that if you want to get to know someone, you had to be honest from the start. And she would be. As she hoped he would be. If he writes back, she can continue the correspondence if he sounds interesting and interested, or simply end it there. She could send him a "Dear John" letter. She couldn't suppress the giggle. She was just about to send him one of those, a letter beginning "Dear John".

She wrote:

"Dear John, my name is Josephine. I saw your advertisement in the *Donegal Press*."

Good start, she thought. Genius. Show him you're intelligent by stating the bleeding obvious. But then sometimes you have to.

"You got my interest," she continued. "I am youngish and female, and it seems that we have similar interests. I can cook, but like to be wined and dined. I absolutely adore music, but I hope that my constant singing (although mostly to myself) isn't too annoying. You won't find me on Facebook or Twitter. So pick up your pen and paper and write me or write me off."

Is that it?

Yes. She was trying to get his attention, in the same way he got hers. Be mysterious, intriguing, give nothing away. Reel him in. Will he write back? If he does, well and good. If he doesn't, she can always scan the personal ads again for someone VGL. Only joking.

Josephine relaxed, put the letter in the envelope and addressed it to John, Box 22, *Donegal Press*. She would deliver it by hand to the newspaper office in the morning before she went to work.

It was a dreadful day, but she didn't mind. She felt excited. She was doing something to change her humdrum existence, cut through the monotony of work, home, eat, sleep, get up, work. You know the scenario.

She sang to herself under her breath as she walked: "Walking in the pouring rain..." Would she have a brand-new friend? A pen friend? That phrase sounded so outdated, so old. People were now Facebook friends, Twitter friends, friends reunited, all to do with the internet. But then it's all to do with communication, no matter how low-tech or high-tech it is. Skype really impressed her. Imagine seeing the person you're talking to, even though they could be thousands of miles away. It smacked of "Star Trek" or some other sci-fi programme. Now it was reality. Would her first glimpse of John be on Skype or in person? Would she ever get a glimpse of him? Only time would tell.

She didn't have to wait long for a response. She posted her letter on a Friday. She would give it a week. He could be busy at work, or just have a busy life. Come Wednesday, her curiosity got the better of her and she checked her box. There was a reply. This is the way it's done. Each person had a box number at the newspaper office. No doubt the owners were careful because of "data protection", or worse. Some creep could get your address and come calling, unexpectedly and uninvited. No one is safe nowadays, it seems. "Lock up your daughters", as they used to say. She had heard stories of stalkers and watched programmes on TV. The world is a scary place. And here she was, corresponding with a total stranger. Her father used to say, "There are no such things as strangers, only friends we haven't yet met." W.B. Yeats, according to him. "It makes sense," she thought. Her mother and father were strangers once; every husband and wife, every loving couple, were all strangers at one time.

She gently removed the white envelope from the box. Her name and address were handwritten. She hadn't seen her name appear in handwriting for as long as she could remember, not since school. She couldn't say if she had ever received an envelope addressed to her in handwriting. How strange to think that this was a novelty. In her youth, she remembered her grandmother getting letters home from her brothers who had emigrated to America years earlier. The envelopes and letters were handwritten. That's how it was. Neither her grandmother nor her siblings had ever used a typewriter, never mind a computer.

She hoped and expected that the letter inside was also handwritten. She had handwritten her letter to him. She did it from home. She didn't have a printer, didn't need one, and she didn't want anyone at work to know anything. She had good handwriting. She had no doubt that he would have been able to read her letter, easily. She had excelled in writing classes in school. They still had them in her school. She didn't know if they did in all schools or if it was confined to small local country schools like the one she attended. No matter, she was glad that she had acquired the skill. And it is a skill. Just like cooking or baking. Her mother had taught her those skills. In Josephine's opinion, the world was becoming too dependent on machines to do everything. Why should we need to spend money on a typewriter or computer and printer to write to someone, when all we need is a cheap pen and some paper? All she had needed to communicate with John.

She didn't open his letter just yet. She had to go to work. She would save it until she returned home later, maybe open a bottle of wine. Play her favourite music.

She wanted it to be personal, as if they were alone together. No one else could know, need know. She put it in her handbag, in the pocket, zipped it up. She went to work. Although she was always thought of as a happy person at work, people did notice she was happier, if that were possible. Remarked upon how happy she was. They wondered if something had happened, something good. Had she won money, the lottery? Her answer? Would she be at work if she did? No way! She denied that anything had changed. She was just being Josephine. "Can I not be happy?"

Of course she could, they said. But there's something different. She insisted that they were being ridiculous. One thing they did notice for sure was that she left work right on time, 5.30pm. Normally, she would linger, finish what she was doing. Not notice the time. Sometimes, someone would have to point out that it was time to go home. Not today. It was as if she was watching the clock. Not that anyone could complain. At 5.30pm, she was gone, on her way home quick smart. Curiosity had really got the better of her by then.

She had taken the envelope out of her bag once or twice during the day when there was no one else around, but resisted the urge to open it. It didn't seem as if there was more than a page or two. He could be a man of few words. As long as those words were meaningful, she didn't mind. Unless, of course, it was a "Dear Josephine letter". She laughed. She tried to imagine how he would begin. She supposed it would read, "Dear Josephine, thank you for your letter." Then that would be too predictable, but not unexpected. They were unacquainted. Formality is the best policy. She tried again.

"Dear Josephine, thank you for not writing me off." That sounded more like it. What next?

"I got your letter." That would be stating the obvious, but she had, and as she said sometimes, it's necessary. She was interrupted by the sound of someone coughing, purposely. She looked up to see Sally standing there.

"A penny for them."

"Oh, nothing, just daydreaming again."

"What's that?" Shit, she was still holding the letter.

"Oh, nothing, just a letter from home. My mother likes to write now and again," she lied.

Still, she couldn't stop thinking about it, the letter. She imagined that it was causing her blood pressure to rise. There was an apparatus nearby, not one of those up-to-date digital ones. The old one you have to pump yourself and read the dial. Probably long since unused. When she was sure there was no one around, she even put the sleeve on her arm, began pressing the bulb. Although it was old, it was probably still reliable. Just like her and John's pen and paper. It still worked. Before she could check the reading, someone came in. She quickly removed the apparatus and threw it away from her. She was sure that her colleague wondered what she was doing, but she said nothing. Neither did Josephine. She went back to what she should have been doing. Forget it, she thought, the letter. It's not long now. She looked at the clock. Three o'clock. Not long until home time. She tried to concentrate on work. It was the longest two and a half hours she ever experienced.

She walked home so quickly, more quickly than she had ever walked. She would have run, but didn't want to appear flustered in public. People might think she had been caught short.

And anyway, she wasn't dressed in the right attire, the right gear. Didn't you have to be dressed in brightly coloured Lycra these days in order to start running? But then she was never into that kind of thing. And besides, she had read that it was bad for your knees to be pounding the pavement or roadway, as the case may be. Isn't that why we have running tracks? Aren't they designed for running, for impact, so that people don't injure themselves or bugger their joints? No, no running for Josephine. But she was a fast walker, so much so that sometimes when she was walking along the corridor of the hospital with some colleague or other, she would find herself talking to no one. He or she would be five or six steps behind. Then she would have to slow down, lest the people she was passing thought she was talking to herself. But then those who knew her would expect her to be singing to herself at any rate.

She had decided to skip dinner. No time to cook tonight, not even time to stop for a take-away. Anyway, they say the most important meal of the day is breakfast. Then she remembered. She hadn't had breakfast. She had woken late and needed to get to her PO Box before work. Well, she had had lunch, of sorts. A yoghurt and a banana. That was all she could eat. Those butterflies were not far off, maybe still just caterpillars, but the possibility was there. She couldn't believe how excited she had become. Why? There was no why. Why do people always have to ask why, have a reason? Live in the moment. She was certainly living in this moment, but it wasn't a moment in the true sense of the word. This moment was lasting, maybe not forever, but for hours.

The letter remained in her handbag. She dropped the bag behind the sofa. Hidden. Hidden from whom? She knew how ludicrous that was, but it didn't matter. She went to the kitchen, took a bottle of wine from the cupboard, a Rioja, not expensive, but she liked it. She wasn't a wine snob, she wasn't a snob at all. As her father used to say, "A little of what you fancy does you good." It really did. As far as wine went, she simply tried them all, within budget, of course. She wasn't a big spender, or a big drinker. But she appreciated the effect a little wine had on her. She took the wine to the living room, put the bottle on the table, unscrewed the top. *Quelle horreur*: it was a screw-top. Well, screw you, wine snobs. It's good enough for me; and anyway, modern thinking is that it makes no difference. She poured herself a glass. A large glass. She put it on the table and sat on the sofa, reached behind it and retrieved her handbag. Before opening it, she took her glass and put it to her lips, intending to take a sip.

"Hell, I need more than a sip," she thought. She drank half and put it down. She took out the letter and looked at the envelope. What could she tell from the handwriting? How silly did that sound? But maybe not. Her thoughts returned to those true crime programmes. Murderers, blackmailers, criminals, all caught because of their handwriting. Some think that it can be as unique as a fingerprint.

"It's true, it's really true," she thought, remembering her teachers at school. They could look at an essay and know immediately who it belonged to, who wrote it. Based solely on the handwriting.

Writing is obviously revealing. Maybe not to the ordinary person.

But revealing, nonetheless. She had, as she promised herself, put on some music.

"Sweet Dreams," sang Annie Lennox.

"She's right," thought Josephine. Annie Lennox is right: we're all looking for something. And here she was, looking for love. She hoped it wouldn't be in the wrong place.

She opened the envelope, slitting it with a letter opener she had borrowed from work. Nobody was using it anyway. Probably there from the time of the Ark. She would return it some time, when someone noticed it was missing and an essential piece of equipment. She took out the letter and unfolded it. It was folded perfectly. None of the creases interfered with or obscured the writing. He was obviously meticulous. The paper was of good quality.

It read:

"Josephine (I bet you thought I was going to say 'Dear Josephine'), and yes, I did think that 'Dear John' as a start to an introductory letter was ironic. My second name is Joseph. I already feel a connection. Does that sound unreal to you? I don't want to freak you out or scare you off. I have been waiting for a response that makes me feel as if the person who wrote it might be worth corresponding with, might become a friend for life and maybe more."

She spat out the wine she had just put in her mouth.

"I hope he's not the mature VGL man looking for fun." She knew she was being silly now. Get a grip, Josephine. She composed herself; well, as much as she could with half a glass of wine down her top.

"I hope that you're the one," he continued. She had to re-read it. Oh! A friend for life, he means.

"It's obvious that you, like me, don't put your faith in social media."

He was right. But then she could just be desperate and trying anything. No. He knew. She had to tell herself that he knew.

"I believe that people should get to know each other before becoming intimate. I mean that both mentally and physically. My philosophy is this. Tell me about yourself, what you like, your tastes in food, music, books, movies, television. Don't tell me about your past, your family, your friends. I want to get to know you. Not them. Our tastes will not mirror each other's; that's just a myth, a fantasy, wishful thinking. They don't need to. We can grow and learn from each other. That's how it works. If we're both the same, what's the point in getting together? Better that we have something to offer each other. I hope that I have something to offer you and you have something to offer me. From your reply, I know that you, like me, think before you speak, before you write. Write me again…"

"Or write me off," she added automatically.

She poured another glass of wine. She read the letter again. How would she reply? Would she reply? She didn't have to think twice. Of course she would reply. It would take some time to compose it, but it would be all she would think about for the next few days. She had never felt such an instant connection with anyone. It frightened her. It excited her. She couldn't think straight. She didn't want to. All she could think about was John.

"Can't Get You Out Of My Head" played in the background as she eventually composed her next letter to him, her brand-new friend.

CHAPTER SIX
OH! WHAT A NIGHT

Even though their relationship, such as it was, had blossomed through correspondence, they had never met, didn't even know what each other looked like. They hadn't exchanged any pictures, as they had agreed their first sight of each other would be in person. Maybe he wanted to lose some weight or have some sort of makeover before that. Maybe he was afraid she would reject him. But it didn't sound that way from his letters. He seemed confident in himself, in what he liked. No, not in that way. They hadn't discussed sex or exchanged pictures of body parts. It wasn't Facebook or Instagram or whatever social media there might be for things other than faces. She shuddered to think what any such thing might be called. Maybe Bumchum, Bestbreast or Dickpic. Anyway, it didn't matter. She wouldn't be signing up.

Neither had they exchanged addresses. They still corresponded through Box numbers. She knew he lived and worked in Derry City and he that she lived and worked in Letterkenny. They were only about twenty miles apart. It had been months. They could have met at any time. Hell, she could have walked to Derry and back, or he to Letterkenny and back, several times. She had taken the bus to Derry once or twice. A fact she hadn't disclosed to John. She wanted to see where he lived. Although many people in Donegal worked in Derry and others went there to shop or socialise, she had never been. Her mother and father weren't the travelling kind. Shopping involved going to Donegal Town or Letterkenny and no further. Josephine realised just how little of the world she had actually seen. Not only had she taken the bus to Derry, but she had gone to the City Hotel, where John told her he worked, for coffee. Only once. She had hoped to catch a glimpse of him, but how could she? She didn't have a clue what he looked like. He hadn't told her what he did there and she didn't dare ask for him, as they had promised their first meeting would be special. She had just sat there and glanced at every male member of staff she could lay her eyes on. None of them gave her goose-bumps. Not the way John's letters did. But could she really have known him if she had spotted him? She convinced herself that she could. She concluded it must have been his day off. Either that or he was cooking or washing dishes in the kitchen. But then how many dishwashers know as much about food and can write as good as John can? Maybe he was the chef, the head chef. That would be cool. That would do her. She realised she had done the wrong thing. They had made an agreement as to how and when they would meet. He had led the conversation. He would make the arrangements. He was the man. She had gone along with it. Why not? She was taking a chance on him. Why stop now? And if she did, what would she do? She would be giving up. Far from the finish line. Not that it was a race to get there. They had taken it slowly. More like a marathon. Then she realised. It had been twenty-six weeks since that first letter. Before they would meet. She had been keeping count. And now it was here.

As promised, John had made the arrangements. He sent a taxi to her house to take her to Bridgend, a small village on the Donegal side of the border with Derry. He had told her that he would wait for her there. As soon as the taxi pulled up at the appointed place, there he was. He approached the taxi and, like a true gentleman, opened the door and took her hand.

"*Enchanté*," he said in his best French accent, before gently kissing the back of her hand.

He wasn't what she expected. In fact, she had no idea what to expect. He was taller than her. That wasn't unexpected. She was only five foot one. If he had been smaller, he would have been a midget or a dwarf. How would that have turned out? He could have been Dopey or Bashful. Instead, if not quite six foot, he was not far off, and Happy. He was of slim build, dressed in plain black trousers and a black polo-neck. She almost expected him to hand her a box of Milk Tray. He was clean-shaven, with shoulder-length hair parted on the left. It seemed as if his hair was its natural colour: dark but not black. She had the impression that he was older than she had imagined, and certainly older than her. He was one of those people who at first glance defied age. Neither a boy nor a man. But both at the same time. Young but aged. With wisdom, perhaps. But that remained to be seen.

"This way, mademoiselle," he gestured.

They walked side by side, he gently holding her right hand in his left. His grip felt secure but relaxed. They stopped at a beautiful Mercedes convertible, gold with a black roof. He turned and looked her in the eye, while at the same time opening the passenger door.

"Your carriage awaits," he continued, dropping the French accent.

"This is yours?" she asked incredulously.

"Ours. For tonight."

"Where are we going?"

"Ah! Ah! You agreed to leave it all to me. Just sit back and relax."

They drove for about five minutes along the main road, before taking a left at a place called Burt, adjacent to a distinctive round building with a conical roof. She knew it to be the iconically designed Catholic church or chapel. The road rose sharply. As they drove along, John put the roof down so that the wind was blowing through their hair. Was he letting her know for sure it wasn't a wig? What would she do if it blew off? How would she react? She stifled her laughter and hoped he wouldn't notice. She was thinking of the movie "Three Fugitives". Except, on this road it was more likely to end up in the trees or bushes. The birds could use it as a nest.

"Stop!" she chided herself. "You're on a date. This is supposed to be romantic." She had to admit it was. Alone in a fabulous vintage car with a handsome man on a mystery tour. What could be more romantic? Or scary? Even more so, as John didn't speak the whole time, and when she tried to initiate a conversation, he put his finger to her lips and turned up the music.

"The only way is up," sang Yazz & The Plastic Population.

She smiled. The road rose more steeply now, before they turned right along a narrow but level road. After driving a short distance, they turned left up a steep, narrow, winding road and stopped in an empty car park which seemed to be in the middle of nowhere. There was a full moon.

"Top Of The World" played as they parked.

"You're not going to turn into a werewolf?" she joked. "Like Michael Jackson in 'Thriller'?"

"No. I'm just a sheep in wolf's clothing. Come on, get out."

She looked around. Where were they going to go? There was nowhere. She looked out over the land. In the distance she could see the water, the sea mirroring the sky and in particular the full moon. To her right were the lights of Derry city. It was stunning. She was frozen in time for a moment. She suddenly realised that there was method to this madness.

"This way," called John, as he ran ahead. She turned and looked. In the distance she saw John heading towards a large round building silhouetted against the night sky.

"Am I mad or what?" she thought. "I could be raped and murdered, or just murdered, and no one would know where I am." She couldn't tell anybody where she was going, because she didn't know. She didn't even know John's second name or where exactly he lived. Or if he really worked at the City Hotel. She had her mobile phone. Should she send someone a text message? And say what? "I've been kidnapped in a Mercedes convertible, gold and black, driven to who knows where with a stunning view over Lough Swilly [she knew that much] and if I should go missing you might look somewhere of that description for my body." She really did watch too many true crime programmes.

As she made her way towards the building, she saw John standing at the wall. Because he was dressed entirely in black, his head looked like it was floating in thin air. It was spooky. As she got closer, she realised that he was shining a torch onto his face from below. The LED lighting was so white, it gave him a ghostly appearance.

As she reached him, he took her hand.

"Close your eyes," he said.

She had come this far; no going back now. She closed her eyes. If he was going to kill her, best she didn't see it coming. He was moving slowly, carefully, grasping her hand in his, guiding her all the way. The ground was uneven. She had luckily worn sensible shoes. Something had told her not to assume this would be a predictable dinner and dancing. Although her eyes were closed, she sensed it had got darker, if that was possible. The night air had become still and warm. They were in an enclosed space. She instinctively put her free hand behind her and moved it from side to side. There was a wall on either side of them. A passageway. The stone was cold to the touch. Suddenly, she could tell they were approaching a light. Either that or she was already dead. Going into the light, as people who had died and come back would commonly describe. They stopped. He pulled her around in front of him, gently. She could sense him standing behind her, close but not too close to make her feel uncomfortable. She could hear him breathing, but didn't feel his breath.

"Open your eyes," he whispered.

She was speechless. The rest of her senses were working perfectly.

In the middle of this fabulous historical ring fort there was a round table, with a white tablecloth and candles that reflected in the silver ice bucket that held a bottle of champagne. More impressive were the number of candles scattered about. On the ground, along the walls, on stands, everywhere. She was surprised that they hadn't lit up the sky from outside.

"Can I escort you to your table, mademoiselle?"

"*Certainement*," she replied.

He laughed. "I didn't expect that."

She had been good at French at school. Liked her French teacher. Also, she was a native Irish speaker. They say that if you know Irish, you can learn any language. She found languages easy to learn.

He pulled out her chair. She sat.

"Champagne?" he inquired in his best French accent.

"Oui," she replied.

"No, it's Dom Perignon," he chuckled.

She didn't get the joke, but laughed anyway. That's what polite people do. And those who don't want to appear stupid. Although, if you don't know something, you don't know it. Still, she didn't want to spoil the moment. So better to laugh. John would explain his joke to her later in the relationship. Assuming it lasted. At the moment, things were looking good.

He took the bottle from the ice bucket, wiped it with a snow-white napkin and opened the bottle without spilling a drop. The way it should be done. People who open champagne and spill half the bottle are plebs or morons, or so Josephine thought. Yes, they do it after football matches and Formula One races, but that's for effect. If you've paid for a good champagne, you want to drink it, all of it, not shower in it or mop it up

57

off the table or the floor.

She watched transfixed as he held two glasses, the stems between his fingers, and poured the champagne slowly and carefully into each, before putting the bottle back in the bucket, taking one and placing it down in front of her. He sat opposite and smiled.

"To us, to friends and lovers everywhere, to the future, whatever it may hold."

She blushed a little, but hoped he didn't notice.

He clinked his glass against hers and drank, draining his glass. She followed suit.

"Weren't you supposed to sip champagne?" she thought, but then she realised that tonight nothing is as it's supposed to be.

He caught hold of the champagne just as she put her glass down and poured them another glass each, this time without lifting the glasses. This time neither of them drank.

He was looking into her eyes. His, azure blue, sparkled in the candlelight. She didn't want to be first to speak, to break the silence, spoil the moment. It was like a game. Who would crack first? She did. She looked up. All she could see was the sky, peppered with stars, the full moon outshining them. The fact that she was sitting in the middle of a place with high walls surrounding her meant that all she could see was the sky. She wasn't going to complain. The night sky never looked so beautiful.

"*Excusé moi un moment*," he said, putting down his empty glass, before jaunting towards the doorway, the one they had come in through. Where was he going now? Although she liked surprises, she felt she had had enough for one night. Maybe he needed to relieve himself. Let's call a fig a fig. Maybe he needed a piss. She kept her gaze on him as he disappeared into the passageway. It wasn't long until he returned, emerging from the darkness with his LED light in one hand and a box in the other.

"Oh, no!" she thought. "He's going to eat my liver with some fava beans and a nice Chianti. And save the rest for later."

Her expression gave it away.

"What?" he said. "Not hungry?"

"Starving," she replied, as the smell of food wafted from the box.

"Not liver, is it?"

"No! Not liver!" He sounded bemused. "Did you want liver?"

"Do you have a nice Chianti?"

"Now I get it. But why would I settle for your liver when I can have all of you?"

"All of me," they sang in unison. They lifted their glasses, clinked and drank.

Now she was more relaxed, totally relaxed. It was only through her correspondence with John that she was learning to trust men again, or at least one man.

"Do I look like Hannibal Lecter? Am I scary?"

"Of course not. You remind me more of Patrick Bateman."

They both laughed and couldn't stop for a minute.

"So you would have preferred it if I had returned wearing a coverall and carrying an axe."

"Well, now that you mention it, I did think I heard you singing 'Hip To Be Square'."

"That's why you couldn't take your eyes off the entrance? And I thought it was love."

That made her laugh out loud. "So I should be singing 'I Will Survive', then?"

It was his turn to laugh. "This is getting ridiculous."

"So what is in the box, then, if it's not liver?"

The mood was so light they could have floated into the night sky, right there, right then.

John sat, put the box down and removed the lid. He placed a plate in front of each of them. She could smell a familiar aroma. From the box he dished out Chicken Chow Mein for each of them and handed her a fork, before taking his own fork in his right hand.

"*Bon appétit*," he said, and began to eat. Taking her cue from John, she took a mouthful.

"I couldn't manage a three-course meal without the proper facilities, and as you can see, there's no kitchen, running water or electricity. If I was Gordon Ramsay, perhaps I could have done a quick makeover with a little help from Channel 4."

"So you live here?" she inquired sarcastically.

"No, of course not. But it's…"

"Ours for the night," she interrupted.

"I knew from your letters you weren't so slow."

"I'll take that as a compliment, I guess."

They continued eating and drinking in silence, exchanging glances. Strangers in the night. Inwardly, she was bursting with pleasure and excitement, but was doing her best not to show it. Yet she couldn't help but beam from time to time. If he noticed, he didn't comment. Another sign of a true gentleman. He was so cool, so self-assured, that he made her feel comfortable, so comfortable. Eventually, she spoke.

"What is this place?"

"It's an ancient ring fort called Griannan Aileach. They say it was originally built around the time Jesus Christ was born. Appropriate, then, for the birth of our physical relationship, so to speak. The night we reveal our physical selves to each other. Don't get me wrong. I'm not speaking sexually, more metaphysically."

"What would Confucius say?" she interjected.

He looked lost, but only for a brief moment.

"I get it," he said. "Chinese, Confucius. You're pretty quick off the mark."

"Not just a dumb female?"

"Obviously. And anyway, who said all females were dumb?"

"Only blondes, then."

"That's blondist."

"I was only joking. And who knows, I might be blonde underneath it all."

"Dying your blonde hair dark? Well, I did know a girl once that did. She didn't want to be thought of as the proverbial dumb blonde."

"Was she?"

"Was she what?"

"Thought of as dumb?"

"I don't really know. I thought she was pretty cool. Don't get me wrong, she wasn't a girlfriend or anything. I didn't have a crush on her."

"Don't worry, I'm not the jealous type. Well, not yet anyway."

"Is that a threat?"

"No, just a warning."

They both laughed and toasted each other once more.

"Finish up. We don't want to stay here all night. The magical mystery tour's not finished yet."

"What about all the candles, the table, the chairs?"

"Don't worry, I have a friend who'll take care of all that. He's the caretaker here. I made it worth his while."

When they got outside, she was unsteady on her feet.

"It must be the night air," she told him.

"And not the champagne," he quipped, before putting her on his back, and giving her a piggy-back to the car. She hadn't had a piggy-back since school. She was slightly nervous, as he didn't take his time. It was a bumpy ride, and at times she felt as if they would both end up like Jack and Jill. They didn't. Their crowns were intact. She couldn't stop laughing as she dismounted. He was breathless. He appeared as if he wanted to say something, but couldn't. Instead, he simply opened the passenger door and she collapsed into the seat. He fell on his knees, holding the passenger door, and began laughing hysterically.

"Will he be able to drive?" she thought suddenly to herself. It was as if he had heard her thoughts and stopped laughing.

"I haven't had this much fun for years," he said. "And no, I'm not drunk; just happy. If you hadn't noticed, I only had two glasses. You had the rest."

"Oops," she thought, "it's not just the night air, then."

He lifted both her legs and placed them into the car, before fastening her seatbelt and vaulting into the back seat and from there into the driver's seat. He pulled on his seatbelt while starting up the car and off they went, back from whence they came. They were soon back on the main road and heading North, according to the signpost, to Buncrana. Josephine wasn't familiar with this part of Donegal. Her mother and father were from a farming background and lived in the west of Donegal, where there were many beaches that they took the children to in the Summer. They didn't travel far outside their own part of the world, or part of the county. Josephine knew the names of places from her geography class at school, but she realised how little of her own county she had actually seen. She was now seeing it by moonlight, and it was beautiful.

John kept changing the music. She knew it all, or most of it.

"The Night Has A Thousand Eyes."

"I Drove All Night."

"No Particular Place To Go."

"I Can Hear Your Heart Beat."

"Blue Moon."

John stopped at a late-night shop, before driving onto the beach. He found a secluded spot and parked the car. Again, being the gentleman he was, he came around to her side of the car and opened her door. He handed her a choc ice.

"Dessert, mademoiselle."

She smirked. "Cheapskate."

"What? But all women like chocolate and ice cream. Don't they?"

"Of course. Chocolate fondant and homemade ice cream."

"Next time. I promise."

He took a picnic rug, red and black checks, from the back seat and laid it on the bonnet.

"Allow me," he said, holding out his hand. She was unsure what was coming next. Before she could respond, he lifted her onto the bonnet. He climbed up beside her and handed her a take-away Cappuccino.

"Chocolate, ice cream and Cappuccino. Better?"

"You're forgiven, but only for now. I'm holding you to your promise."

"I'll make it myself. Gordon Ramsay, eat your heart out."

"Did you think it was his liver in the box earlier?" he added.

"Ewww. What would make you think I would want to eat any part of Gordon Ramsay?"

"Oops," she thought, "not sure that sounded the way I meant it to sound."

"I meant…"

He was laughing hysterically. He knew what she was trying to say. Best to shut up. He leant over and kissed her gently on the lips. She took it as if she expected it, but in truth she didn't.

"Time to relax."

He reached over the windscreen and pressed a button or two. The music drifted up from the speakers.

"Give me the moonlight, give me the girl." John was looking straight at her and miming the words.

"Oh no, I hate 'Lipsync Battle'."

He spat out his Cappuccino. "I guess romance is dead. I'll change it."

Some classical music she recognised, but couldn't name, floated out from the speakers.

It was soothing, relaxing. It seemed to synchronise with the sound of the sea lapping against the shore. The mood changed from playful to pensive.

Watching the moon, the stars, the reflections on the water and listening to that music was just hypnotic. She closed her eyes.

"'Moonlight Sonata'," he whispered. "And now I'll shut up."

He did shut up. She kept her eyes closed for the whole of the song; no, not the song, the piece. That's what they call it in posh circles, a piece. "It's still music," she thought.

The music could have lasted one minute or one hour. Time didn't matter. Josephine almost fell asleep; no, not asleep. It was more like a trance, a self-induced trance. The music flowed languidly to an end, leaving Josephine feeling more relaxed than she had ever felt in her entire life. She slowly opened her eyes to the sight of the full globe of the moon shining directly above, as if it was almost on top of her. It felt as if the car with John and her on the bonnet was floating slowly towards it. It would just be too much to believe John had hired a flying car. Then she had a horrible thought. She lifted her head quickly and glanced to her left.

"Phew!" she sighed a sigh of relief. The car was still on dry land. She imagined that the music had lasted for hours and that the tide had come in and carried them out to sea. That would be okay if John was James Bond and they had the Lotus Esprit from "The Spy Who Loved Me".

"Maybe he is a spy," she thought. He was certainly mysterious. "Do they have spies in Ireland, and why?"

"Let's walk."

The sound of John's voice interrupted her thoughts, her crazy thoughts. But then it was a crazy night. John was already off the bonnet and standing in front of the car. She threw her legs off to the left and leapt onto the sand. John was surprised.

"Get you!" he said. "Raring to go."

"I love walking," she said. "As you know." She had told him so in their correspondence.

He waited for her to come around the car and took her hand in his.

"Aren't you going to put the hood up and lock the car?" she asked.

"Naw, it's not mine, why bother?"

As they walked away from the car, she heard a sound behind her and glanced around to see the hood of the car close itself, click and the lights flash twice.

"It's automatic, it's systematic, it's…"

She gave him a withering look.

"Sorry," he mouthed. "I can't help myself," he sang.

"Stop it!" she scowled.

"Or what? Will you spank me?"

"You should be so lucky."

"I should be so lucky," he sang. Well, you couldn't really call it singing. Guess he'll have to stick to "Lipsync Battle".

"Aaargh!" she screamed.

"No more. I promise. Cross my heart," he said, making the sign over his heart.

True to his word, he led her along the beach, not uttering a word. He stopped, removed his hand from hers, sat down on the sand, took off his shoes and rolled up his trousers. He wasn't wearing socks.

"Time for a paddle," he grinned, before getting up.

Josephine bent up her left leg and removed her shoe. She repeated the action with her right leg and dropped both shoes on the sand. He took her hand again.

"One, two, three," he counted, before taking off like lightning, with her hand in his, in the direction of the sea. She just about managed not to fall face-first and, having steadied herself, not only kept up with him, but having extracted her hand from his, outran him and hit the water before him, splashing both sea and sand onto her dress, a plain little black number coming to just above the knee. She laughed, turned to see John arriving, bent down and threw two handfuls of water in his direction. He flinched and turned his head away as the water hit him on his chest. He charged at her, his legs white in the moonlight, appearing and disappearing in the water.

"At least he's not vain," she thought. "He doesn't do false tan."

She waited until he was almost upon her and quickly sidestepped him. She ran up the beach as fast as she could, assuming John would be chasing her. But when she stopped and glanced over her shoulder, he was nowhere to be seen. She turned and scanned the beach and the water several times. No sign. But then he was wearing dark clothes. Still, it was such a bright moonlit night that if he was there she would see him. There was nothing wrong with her eyesight. Maybe she was blinded by love. No. That's not it. Then she should only have eyes for him. A horrible thought crossed her mind.

"Could he have fallen over in the water? Could he swim?"

She couldn't remember if he had told her. He had been drinking, and she had heard of people drowning in as little as a pool of water. She called out his name. There was no reply. She called again. More anxiously.

"John, where are you? Are you all right?" She walked back slowly towards the sea as she continued calling.

"John, stop messing, it's not funny."

"I can't drive," she added, hoping he would pick up on her desperation. Not to mention the fact that he had the keys.

"I don't have my mobile phone."

She heard a suppressed laugh, as what she had thought was a rock unfurled, stood up and looked imposing. The zombie-like figure began moving in her direction with its arms outstretched. Although her eyes took a little time to adjust, the laugh was familiar.

"You bastard!" she screamed.

He laughed uncontrollably.

"Did I give you a fright?" he said, as she raised her arms and, using both hands, shoved him backwards onto the sand.

"How's that for a fright?" He was still laughing.

Regretting her impetuous response, she reached down her right hand to help him to his feet.

She let out a cry as he yanked her off her feet, landing her on top of him. They both rolled over so that they were lying side by side, face to

65

face.

"Hold me close," he sang.

She was sure he was going to kiss her again, more passionately. She closed her eyes.

Nothing.

When she opened her eyes, he was looking straight at her. He kissed her on the forehead, stood up, took her hands in hers and helped her to her feet. She realised he was playing with her. He put his arm around her waist as they walked up the beach, stopping only so that each could pick up their shoes.

"Did you think I had drowned?" he asked as they walked.

"I wish you had," she replied jokingly.

"Come on," he said, "you need to experience every possible emotion, every day."

She stopped suddenly and gave him a look.

"What?" he asked.

They walked on, hand in hand, to the car.

As she slipped into the passenger seat, she adjusted her clothing, checked her make-up and hair. She put on her shoes.

"Fasten your seatbelt," he said, as he donned his own and did a U-turn from the beach.

"Moonlight Feels Right" played as they drove onto the main road.

"I'm really glad you came," he said, turning down the music. "I've had one of the best nights of my life."

"Me, too," was all she could say. She couldn't believe she was choking up. She was holding back the tears. She wasn't sure what those tears were for. She felt elated and scared at the same time. She wondered if that was the effect he had set out to achieve. If so, he had succeeded.

As if he knew what she was feeling, he reached over and put his hand on hers momentarily and then turned up the music again.

"When Will I See You Again?" The song made her eyes well up even more. With happiness, that is.

Before she knew it, they were back where he had picked her up. The taxi was waiting. She thought maybe he would have driven her home.

"I've had a great night; it couldn't have been better. I could have driven you to your door, but I want our relationship to remain private for now, totally private, between you and me. No outsiders, no questions, no need for explanations. No nosy neighbours. I've paid the taxi, safe home. I'll be in touch, you can bank on it."

He went around the car and opened her door, took her hand and, kissing her on the cheek, escorted her to the taxi. As the taxi pulled away, he blew her a kiss.

Back at home, she lay in bed, unable to sleep. She had had a wonderful night, a night to remember.

"Oh, what a night," she sang to herself. And it wasn't even December.

When she eventually began to drift off, she had a vision of herself walking down the aisle in a beautiful white wedding dress. As she approached the altar, John was standing there smiling, dressed all in black. Holding a box of Milk Tray.

CHAPTER SEVEN
HAPPY BIRTHDAY

John had arranged for them to go to his favourite Chinese restaurant for her birthday. He loved Chinese food, in particular the food at "Chinatown". He had eaten there so often that he was personally acquainted with the owner. He had introduced Josephine to the take-away menu, but they had never eaten on the premises. This would be the first time.

John had thought about booking a more upmarket restaurant for the occasion, but he was never that impressed with such places. He referred to them as "Restaurant La-Di-Da". They usually served what became known as "fusion food". John called it "confusion food". The chefs referred to themselves as artists. They created masterpieces on a plate. After all, they say that you eat with your eyes. That's lucky, according to John, because what they give you would just about fill your eye sockets and nothing else.

Josephine didn't mind. She did like Chinese food, and the restaurant, although typically Chinese, was very comfortable. The atmosphere was just right and the staff couldn't be more welcoming and helpful. The owner came to their table and wished her a happy birthday. Obviously, John had told him. That was nice. It made her feel special. The owner was a handsome man, well-groomed and affable. He was well spoken and very complimentary. He complimented her on her appearance, her smile, and said how lucky John was to have met such a beautiful lady. The night was shaping up nicely.

When the owner had left them, a waitress arrived with a bottle of champagne. Josephine didn't know much about champagne, except that it was usually only for special occasions, at least in her world. She did, however, know, from John, that Dom Perignon was one hell of an expensive one, the same one John had brought on the night they met. She was surprised that a Chinese restaurant would have such a thing. John explained. "They let you bring your own wine. Or champagne. Do you like it?"

"How could I not like it?"

"It takes its name from a monk."

"Really! What was his name?"

"Can't remember, let's ask the waiter if he knows. I bet he doesn't."

"Don't, John" interjected Josephine quickly, grabbing the arm he was about to raise in the air to get attention.

"Don't embarrass anyone. It's not nice."

"I was only joking, my dear. Had you going, though."

"Stop it, it's my birthday."

"So it is. I'll treat you later."

"I'll hold you to that. But what was his name, the monk?"

"Obvious. Dom Perignon. He was French. Like Napoleon."

"And Josephine," she smiled.

"Of course, but not my Josephine."

That embarrassed her slightly. He noticed.

"To Dom Perignon," he chimed, clinking his glass against hers.

"To Chinatown," she replied.

"To us. Happy birthday, darling."

They each took a sip from their glasses and put them down.

He picked up his menu.

Want to order?"

"No. Not yet. Let's just enjoy the champagne. It's not every day I have champagne. Especially this one."

"Nothing's too good for you, baby. For us. I love you."

His words took her by surprise. In all the weeks, the months they had been together, he had never said "I love you". No one had ever said those words to her. Not her mother, not her father, not her siblings. No one. Maybe that's what was missing in her life. What age do you have to get to, how many people do you have to get to know before someone says "I love you"? For Josephine, it took until now. Why is it that people find it so hard to say? She did love her father, and if truth be told, her mother also. She never said it to them, nor them to her. For no particular reason. Was it taken for granted? But why? If your parents love you and you love them, why is it so hard for them to say it, to tell you, and for you to tell them? Why is home so comfortable to be in, but the people in it so hard to talk to, really talk to? That's the million-dollar question. I guess that things are what they are. People are people, and you don't get to choose the people you live with, as a child at least. Now in her twenty-second year, someone at last had told her they loved her. An involuntary smile came upon her.

John noticed.

"What's so funny?"

His tone was a mixture of upset and embarrassment. She had to act quickly.

"It's not funny, I'm not laughing; it's a nervous reaction. I didn't expect that. You took me by surprise."

He frowned.

"In a nice way," she added. She knew he was waiting expectantly. She had no option.

"I love you, too, John," she said in what she hoped was a low, loving, genuine tone. After all, she had no practice or experience.

John smiled and raised his glass.

"That's what I've been waiting to hear."

She raised her glass automatically. They clinked glasses. He leaned into her and pressed his lips carefully, lovingly against hers. She had closed her eyes. His lips lingered so long, she wondered if time had, in fact, stood still, which caused her to open her eyes and look straight into his. His look told her he meant it. He loved her. He really did.

Not like the last person who had kissed her. Not like Dr White. He loved himself, loved to get what he wanted. Didn't care what she wanted. Why should he? Why would he? He had his own life, his own wife. She was just a toy, a challenge. Well, not really a challenge. She hadn't even made him work for it. It was all too easy. Even when he found out she was pregnant. She had gone and had the "D&C" he had organised for her. A minor common procedure that thousands, maybe millions of women have every year. That's what the record reflects. Only they knew the truth, and maybe the friend who did the procedure.

"The procedure." She grimaced at the term. So cold, so utterly unfeeling, so final. But why was she dwelling on him now, at this moment, on what he had done, what he had put her through?

"A penny for them."

She had almost forgotten where she was.

"Oh! Nothing really. I was wondering if I'm dreaming. Will I wake up in a minute?"

"Do you want me to slap you?"

"Not here," she laughed.

"Naughty girl," he scolded.

"Do I deserve a spanking?"

"Don't push your luck."

"Aw!"

"All right then, later."

They both burst out laughing.

"Let's order before the champagne goes to our heads."

"I think it already has."

John nodded in the direction of the owner. He came immediately to the table and took their order. They spent the next five or ten minutes discussing how they met, how mad it is nowadays for people to meet that way. No Tinder, no Facebook, no Twitter, no Instagram, no PlentyMoreFish. That made her laugh. Sitting in a restaurant discussing PlentyMoreFish. Especially as she was waiting on her prawns.

"The duck spring rolls?"

She was back in the room. She heard John say, "Yes, please, that's mine."

"And the prawns?"

She had to suppress her laughter. "Yes, please," she almost shouted out, wishing the waiter would put them down quickly.

As he left the table, she looked across at John. He was laughing.

"There's plenty more fish where that came from," he said.

"That's what I like about you, John, always game for a laugh," she retorted, lowering her eyes towards his duck spring rolls. They both laughed and drank more champagne.

Josephine loved her prawns. She loved all seafood. She had grown up by the sea. She did like a good steak, though. Doesn't everyone? All restaurants offer steak in its various guises: minute, rib-eye, sirloin, fillet, T-bone and now flat iron. She didn't think that name too enticing. Does that mean that it's thin and tastes of metal, or, worse still, is as hard as iron? Anyway, it didn't matter tonight. There was no steak on this menu. Chinese usually had their own style of main course. She had chosen chicken curry. Dessert was banana split, a childhood favourite of hers. She still loved it, although it might seem childish, akin to jelly and ice cream. Funny, she loved that, too.

After dessert, they had coffee and the inevitable fortune cookies. John had insisted. The meal wasn't complete without the fortune cookie. She thought them a waste of time, but the night had been fun and she was sure John would make the opening of the fortune cookie interesting, put his own twist on it. He insisted on opening his first. He held up the paper.

"Tonight's the night."

As in every restaurant, music played in the background. Coincidentally, at that moment it was Rod Stewart singing "Tonight's The Night".

John sang along. "Tonight's the night."

The other diners could hear him. They were watching, listening.

She flushed with embarrassment, but was secretly chuffed.

"Open yours."

She reached for the fortune cookie and cracked it open. She expected something stupid like "Take me, I'm yours". She realised that John had arranged it all with the owner.

What fell from the fortune cookie made her hold her breath. She didn't know for how long.

John picked up the ring and held it out to her. She didn't know how to react. He took hold of her left hand and began to slip it onto her finger.

"Yes," she said almost inaudibly. John smiled. She guessed he knew she would say yes. He wouldn't have asked otherwise. She had come to know him that much. He was meticulous. He knew what he wanted, knew where he was going and who was going with him. She was.

The people in the restaurant were applauding and cheering, including the owner and the staff, but the noise only came to her ears gradually. It was as if she had gone deaf at the moment that ring hit the table. She couldn't even remember it making a sound. Neither had she heard John ask her to marry him. She couldn't be sure if he did or didn't. She was so focused on the ring and him putting it on her finger. She knew she had said "yes", although she hadn't heard herself. Amid it all, she was thinking, "I'm getting married," as "Love Is In the Air" played in the background.

CHAPTER EIGHT
FATHER AND SON

Josephine was so excited about the engagement, she almost forgot that she had never met John's parents. She needed to meet them. What would they think of her? Would they approve? It was strange, she thought, that John had never mentioned them. But then he had never asked to meet her mother either. She had told him her father was dead. The courtship (did she use that word? It sounds so old) was exhilarating, a whirlwind romance, or so she thought. No one else mattered; not friends, not family, not anyone, not anything. All that mattered now was them, their future together, their happiness. "Nothing Else Matters," she sang to herself as she thought about it. It was true. She was somewhere she never thought she would be. In love. Wouldn't it be great, she thought, if there was a place called "Love". They could move there, settle down. Then they would be in "Love" forever.

Joking aside, she would have to meet the parents, make a good impression. She would broach the subject the next time she was talking to John. He rang later that day. He rang every day now. They were inseparable, in mobile phone terms. It was good to talk, not that it wasn't good to write. Did this mean their relationship was moving into the twentieth century, not the twenty-first century, not Skype, not WhatsApp?

"Hi, John," she answered with obvious enthusiasm.

"How are you, gorgeous?"

"Better now I can hear your voice."

"When Will I See You Again?" he chimed.

"Come On Over To My Place," she replied quickly.

"You got me," he said with a reactionary laugh. "You're getting good at this."

They had developed a little game where if one referenced a song title in the conversation, the other had to reply with a song title. Josephine was proud of herself.

They had agreed to meet that night, as it was John's night off. They would go to the cinema.

It really was a traditional kind of courtship. They would go to a Chinese restaurant after the movie. "Chinatown", of course.

Josephine decided she would raise the issue of meeting John's parents after the meal.

"So when do I meet the parents?"

A look came over his face, a look she had never seen before. A long time seemed to pass before he spoke.

"They're dead. Both dead."

Now it was Josephine's turn to be silent. Saying she was sorry just didn't seem sufficient.

"I didn't know," she whispered, stating the obvious. "You never told me."

"I know. I guess I had to tell you some time. The opportunity just never presented itself. Our conversations were always happy, fun. I don't want that to change. I don't want anything to spoil that."

"But I told you about my dad."

"Yes, but I didn't want to make it seem like I was trumping you. Like your dad's dead, well, so is mine and what's more so is my mother, so there."

Josephine wasn't sure if she should laugh, but couldn't help it. She tried unsuccessfully not to.

"It's okay," said John, smiling. "You can laugh. It's a long time ago now. Shit happens."

"Did they die together? Was it an accident or something?"

"They both died accidentally, but not together. With my father it was a hit and run. He was drunk. It would be unusual if he wasn't. He was coming home from the pub, crossing the road outside the house. He almost made it. They never found the car. There was no one around. No witnesses. He lay in the gutter till daylight, when the milkman found him. People were so used to him lying somewhere, usually unconscious. He was a man of great renown."

"A man of the world," Josephine couldn't help interjecting.

"A well-respected man." His answer was immediate, automatic, sarcastic. He didn't smile this time.

"Well known he certainly was. Respected? That's a laugh. He wasn't even respected by his own flesh and blood. It was a godsend when he died, at least to my mother and me."

He stopped and took a drink of his wine.

"You know, in the beginning people would try to help him when he was prostrate on the roadway or footpath or lying through some hedge with his head in someone's flowerbed. I guess he wanted to wake up and smell the roses. He would be abusive to them, verbally, and sometimes physically, when he was able.

"'Get your fucking hands off me, fucking good Samaritan. Go and help someone who needs your fucking help.' No wonder people ignored him. Once, he broke a neighbour's nose with a head butt. Claimed afterwards it was self-defence. Poor man was helping him up by holding onto his coat lapels, when he suddenly shot his head forward into his face. The man let go, causing him to hit his head on the footpath. He was the victim of an attempted assault and robbery. Didn't the man have him by the lapels. It was the only way to get him off the ground; he was no lightweight."

"What happened?"

"Nothing. My father was well known to the police as well. Did a bit of work for them. He was a locksmith. They tried to prosecute the unfortunate man whose nose was broken. Made him out to be the aggressor. My father would have been less than reliable as a witness for the prosecution. They knew that. So did the other man's legal team. They were both right. On the day of the hearing, he turned up late, drunk, drunker than usual for that time of day.

"Drunk and incoherent. Wasn't even sure why he was there. It was strange that he did actually turn up, knew there was some reason he should be there. When the police officer told him what he was there for, he was surprised. Why would he make a complaint against someone who was trying to help him? There must be some mistake. He even went to the man and apologised for the 'misunderstanding'.

"'Between you and me, I think the police got it wrong. But say nothing. We don't want to upset them. Do you want to go for a drink? It's on me.'

"Needless to say, the poor man made his excuses as far as the drink was concerned. He was smart enough to realise that he should get as far away as possible from him. And the sooner the better. He knew for sure not to drink in the same establishment, never mind in the same company.

"After hearing the circumstances and the fact my father was contrite, the judge threw it out. Apologised to the other poor man for the inconvenience. It was all much ado about nothing. It did, however, make the local newspaper. 'GOOD SAMARITAN GETS JUSTICE HE DESERVES.'

"From then on, everyone knew not to go within ten feet of my father. They would cross the road to avoid going near him. He could go to and from the pub with the whole footpath to himself. Kind of fitting that the same footpath killed him. The car broke his leg, but the footpath cracked his skull. Might have lived if he had been treated within a reasonable time. His own bloody fault that nobody bothered. Funny there was very little blood. He was a hard-headed bastard, took a few knocks in his time, would start a fight in an empty pub. Fitting end for someone from the school of hard knocks, that a hard knock finally killed him. He would be proud of that in his own demented mind. My mother was nonchalant when she heard the news. The milkman and the police arrived at the door at the same time. She took the milk, thanked them all and closed the door. Didn't even bother to go out and see him. She refused to go and officially identify him. Wouldn't let me do it, either. I wasn't yet eighteen. Let his family do it. The funeral was a quiet affair. Some people attended out of decency, but no one was sorry to see him go. There were no tears."

"I take it you weren't close."

John gave a derisive snort.

"How could anyone be close to the cruellest, most vicious, uncaring bullish man that ever walked this earth?"

"But he was your father?"

"That was my misfortune. In the words of Harper Lee, 'you can choose your friends'.

"I vowed I wouldn't let him ruin my entire life. So it's time to stop talking about him. I would not have let him attend my wedding, our wedding. I would have killed him first."

From the look in his eyes, it was apparent he might well have.

"My mother was the victim of alcohol abuse from the day she met him. Even after all she suffered at his hands because of drink, she became an alcoholic herself after his death. Fell in with another drinker, but this time she drank with him, became abusive herself in drink. Changed from my protector to my tormentor.

"'John, don't ever leave me. John, come and have a drink with me. John, where are you going?' John, John, John was all that I ever heard. This from a woman who let her husband abuse me all his goddamn life. Now she was doing the same. I was seventeen. Old enough to leave home. So I did. I went and got a job in a hotel kitchen in Belfast, washing dishes. It wasn't much, but to me it was the great escape."

"If you like Pina Coladas," Josephine began to sing under her breath. Or so she thought. She had been staring at her drink while John talked. He had stopped. She looked up. He was grinning.

"You win again," he chimed. They both laughed.

He leaned across and gently kissed her.

"I'm glad I escaped. I might never have met you."

She blushed.

"I have one question, though. Do you like Pina Coladas?" They laughed again.

Although she didn't want to spoil the moment, Josephine wanted to hear what happened to John's mother. Also, she didn't want him to think she was dismissing his story.

"What happened to her, your mother?"

"Eventually, she suffered the same fate," he carried on as if he had never stopped. "Fell down the stairs in a drunken stupor, died from a swollen brain. I'm just glad I wasn't there to witness it. I know maybe if I had been at home that night, she might not have died. But I've learned not to have regrets. Better to accept what has happened, look at it as the inevitable. In her case, I think it was. Better for her. She wasn't happy. Don't think she ever would have been."

"Do you miss her?"

"Not the person she became. I miss the person she was, the person I loved. She was never going to be that person again. I stopped loving her long before she died. I had accepted that you can't turn back the clock, make it like it was."

He finished his wine.

"Anyway, enough nostalgia. Can I take you home, little girl?"

"Ready to go," she replied with a smile. He reached over and took her by the hand.

She stood. It was totally automatic. They were partners now. And just like dance partners, someone has to lead. In their case, it was John. Although he was smiling at her, there was sadness in his eyes.

She felt sorry for him. Even though her own father was fond of the drink, as they say in Donegal, he was never abusive to her mother or the children. He was what you might term "a happy drunk". But then her mother was a patient woman. As long as he brought home the bacon, figuratively speaking, she was happy. She was a woman of simple tastes: a roof over her head, a fire in the hearth and food on the table. That's how she was brought up. She was never going to take the world by storm. She was happy to let him do what he wanted. Not that he did too much wrong. Drinking was his vice. He would have called it his pleasure. That and sexual intercourse, Josephine supposed, seeing as he had fathered six children and the fact that her mother confided in her that the way to a happy marriage is to give him what he wants. Josephine decided she wasn't going to be like her mother. She didn't want to be "the wife", "the little woman", "the housekeeper". She wouldn't be. John wouldn't want her to be. Their marriage would be different. She would go as far as to say unique. They would be best friends, lovers, everything to each other.

"You are everything." That's what they would sing to each other.

CHAPTER NINE
HAPPY TOGETHER

Josephine couldn't believe she was engaged. At times she would gaze at the ring on her finger and wonder if it was really there, or was she just imagining it? She would take it off, feel it, hold it up to the light. Then slip it back on her finger. It was really happening. She hadn't been much of a jewellery wearer before this. In fact, she wore little or no jewellery. There was, of course, the crucifix around her neck that she had worn since her first Holy Communion. Her father bought it for her. It sparked a topic of conversation one night during dinner with John. She had cooked for him.

"Is that Jesus around your neck?" he asked.

"Yes. Why?"

"No reason. Do you still go to mass? Apart from funerals and weddings, I mean."

"Not any more. Not since I lived at home."

"I don't blame you. Can't remember the last time I was there. Probably my mother's funeral."

Josephine wasn't sure where this was all going.

"So, are you still a Catholic, Josephine?"

"I'm not sure."

"Well, for example, do you believe in abortion? Do you think that it's murder?"

That one came out of left field and stopped her in her tracks. He was waiting for an answer.

"It depends, I suppose."

"Non-committal then, just like most so-called Catholics."

This wasn't John, his usual carefree self. Something just didn't feel right.

"Let me put it another way. Would you ever consider having an abortion?"

That really threw her. She almost choked on her Bolognese, had to take a drink of water. She had stopped imbibing fizzy fattening drinks. After all, she would be getting married soon, and that meant looking her best. Maybe she should cut out the pasta as well.

When she had put down her water, John was staring at her. It was one of those moments when she wondered if he knew everything about her, even the things she hadn't told him.

But how could he? She did feel sometimes as if they were the one person, "2 become 1". Isn't that what marriage is all about?

All this thinking took time, too much time. He was staring at her. He knew something. Or at least he knew there was something going on in her head. Even though they had promised to be completely honest with each other, she could never bring herself to divulge her biggest secret, and hoped she would never have to. But at the same time, she had never lied to him in the sense of always giving an honest and truthful answer when he asked her about her past, things she had done or about her thoughts and feelings.

"I have," she said eventually, averting her eyes, "had one. An abortion. I had to."

She couldn't look at him now, but simply waited for his response. He kept on eating, chewing. She could hear him, but didn't dare look up. She didn't want him to see that she was breaking down.

Josephine felt as if she should explain, but wanted him to ask, to take an interest. She didn't like the awkward silence. She had never experienced that with John. He always made her feel at ease, relaxed, that nothing else mattered. Now it seemed to her that the past was coming back to haunt her, haunt them. She didn't want it to. She wished she had bitten her tongue, changed the subject. But that wouldn't have worked. When John asked a question, she always had to answer, not because she felt threatened, but rather she needed to please him.

"You don't have to explain."

She was shocked. She was already beginning to speak, although John hadn't noticed. The worst thing. Now she wanted to explain more than ever. She looked up.

"But I want to."

He was looking at her, but with no hint of feeling. He had never been unfeeling. They had never been unfeeling with each other. Everything had always been so intense.

"He tricked me. I was stupid," she said, lowering her eyes again. It was easier to talk that way, to explain, to try and explain.

Now she felt more than stupid. That was such a cliché. But she had to carry on.

"He was a doctor. My boss. I was in awe of him. Made me think he was having marital problems. His wife didn't understand him. Fuck. I didn't understand him. He played me. It only happened once. In his private rooms. It was quick. I don't even remember what it was like."

There was no longer the sound of someone eating, only the music that was playing in the background.

"The Secrets That You Keep."

She had paused and coincidentally the song came to an end. You could have heard a pin drop. Except the floor was carpeted, so you probably wouldn't have.

"I think he might have drugged me," she continued, to fill the silence.

It now felt as if she was talking to herself, ruminating, remembering.

"I couldn't believe it when I found out I was pregnant. Neither could he. Can you believe it? A doctor who believes he can have unprotected sex with someone and they won't get pregnant. Who does he think he is? God? Turns out he doesn't have to be. He has friends, friends who will, in his words, deal with it. He had a friend who did. I had a D&C."

He wouldn't know what she was talking about. Why would he? He would have had no reason to be familiar with the procedure. There it is again, that word, procedure.

"D&C. That's dilation and curettage. Women who have had a miscarriage have it done, but it's also done for other reasons. Not usually for the reason I had, as far as I know. They remove stuff from your uterus. They removed everything from mine. I don't have to worry. I can go on my merry way. I can't lie. I was relieved. How could I explain it? I wasn't immaculate, it wouldn't have been a virgin birth. I certainly wouldn't have been welcome, in my condition, at the Hospital Christmas Party. Funny…" She was about to say "it", but checked herself. "He or she, I never knew which, would have been due on 25th December. According to my calculations."

"But then I'm not a doctor," she added, before joking, "so what would have happened if Joseph had said 'he's definitely not mine, get rid of him'?"

She realised she was rambling, as she was prone to do when she was nervous. And boy, was she nervous! She had gone from not wanting to tell to telling everything, including her wandering thoughts. What would John think? Would he run away? Was he still there? She hadn't looked up since she started talking. Would he not want her any more? He knew she had sexual encounters of sorts with boys, but nothing serious. Would it make a difference that she had had sex with her boss, that she had had an abortion? He wasn't religious. He wasn't pro-life, as far as she knew. And he did say that all that mattered was the person she was now, that her past wasn't important. But she knew that talk is cheap. People don't always react to something or know how they would react to something the way they say or imagine they would.

All the while she was recounting this sordid tale, she had her eyes firmly on her partly finished meal. She was waiting for John to say something, but the only sound was the background music, and it wasn't "Tonight's The Night" this time.

"Don't dream it's over" sang Neil Finn of Crowded House. This was it, the shortest engagement in the history of the world. She looked up. Through the tears in her eyes she could see that John was looking at her. She couldn't read him. She never had to before. He was always talking, filling all the awkward silences.

"Do you want your ring back?" was all she could say.

That drew an immediate reaction.

"Why would I want my ring back?" he asked, with a quizzical look on his face.

"If we're not getting married, I don't think that I should keep it," she said almost inaudibly.

"We're not getting married?" He now sounded confused and disappointed.

The tears began to come faster. She was trying to brush them away with her napkin. She really didn't know what she was doing, what she was saying. She wanted him to take charge of the conversation as he normally did. At least then she would know where she stood. It was as if he was reading her mind again. He took her hand and squeezed gently.

"Dear Josephine, love of my life, my future wife, please stop talking and listen. None of us are saints or angels. I'm certainly not. I've done things I'm not proud of, things I wish I'd never done. But as they say, what's done is done. I'm not going to judge you on what has gone before. I'm in love with the Josephine who first answered my ad and the one I have got to know since. Of course our past matters; it helps to make us what we are today. Sometimes we have to go through things we wish we didn't. We learn from them. Bad decisions don't make us bad people. They just prove how human we are. To err is human."

"To forgive divine," Josephine added automatically, interrupting him.

"Not true. We're all capable of forgiveness and being forgiven. But the only person who can give us forgiveness is the person we have wronged or, more importantly, ourselves. So you don't need it from me. And the answer to your earlier question is no, I don't want my ring back. I'm hoping to add another one to it as soon as possible. Unless you don't want me to."

Before she could answer, she was distracted by the sound of Gladys Knight singing "You're The Best Thing That Ever Happened To Me".

"I was just about to say that," she thought to herself. Now it would just sound as if she was taking her cue from the music. She began to laugh, but tried to hide it by putting her face in her hands. He got up from his seat, came around the table and hugged her. He obviously thought she was sobbing. She was shaking, with laughter. She didn't know how to tell him. Instead, she reached for her napkin and pretended she was drying her eyes. He sat down again.

"You okay now?" he said caringly.

"Yes," she replied, as soon as she could suppress the laughter and sound upset, as convincingly as she could in the circumstances.

"For a moment I thought I had messed everything up, that I had opened my mouth and put my big foot in it, both of them. I know that I should have told you before, but I was scared, afraid of what you would think of me, that you would hate me, just like I hate myself. For being so stupid more than anything else. I don't know if what I did afterwards was right or wrong or if I'll burn in hell for it. But then I don't believe in hell."

John raised his glass.

"I'll drink to that. To hell with religion and the devil."

They clinked glasses and drank.

"Anyway, Josephine, if we're wrong, the worst that can happen is that we'll end up there together, together forever. Isn't that what everyone says they want. We may end up getting it."

"You have a way with words, you old devil you."

"Less of the old."

This was more like it. Now she was enjoying the night.

"Okay then, you cheeky young thing."

"You're heading for a spanking, if you're not careful."

"Oh! Yes, please."

"Hurry up and finish eating, then."

They couldn't stop laughing. Josephine was laughing so much, she thought her bladder would burst.

"I need to go to the toilet before I pee myself."

"Don't leave me this way," John sang.

Now she really did feel she was going to pee herself. She made it just in time. Sitting on the toilet, she felt relief in more ways than one. Things had come good, despite the unexpected beginning to the night. Although she was one of those people who laughed a lot when they got nervous, she wasn't nervous any more. John had accepted her despite her shortcomings, despite her keeping secrets from him; well, one secret at least. She now wished she hadn't, that she had told him a long time ago. She had plenty of opportunity, during their correspondence, during their courtship. Oops, did she just use the word "courtship" again? She was still an old-fashioned girl. Maybe that was it. She still had that old-fashioned attitude. No need to tell. What he doesn't know can't hurt him. How then is it that the subject raised its ugly head? Why did he have to mention the word "abortion", ask her if she would have one? She was convinced someone had told him. But who? She never told anyone. She found it very hard to believe that Dr White was going to spread it around. Strike that. Of course he was spreading it around, the bastard, but not the fact of her pregnancy and termination. So how did John know, or did he?

85

Probably not. Was it just his intuition? Can people really read your mind? Can he read hers? But she wasn't even thinking about it. Not tonight, anyway. Not that she was aware of. But then there's the subconscious.

She wanted him to know, wanted to tell him, but didn't know how or when. Well, maybe "Tonight's The Night" should have been playing. Just as he chose the time and place for their engagement, her subconscious had chosen this time and place to come clean. Better late than never. Better now than later. She wasn't the Virgin Mary. John knew that.

He accepted that. But this news tonight was a different ball game. It could have changed everything. She was glad it didn't. She vowed no more secrets. That would be what would keep them together, forever. In heaven, not in hell. After all, according to Belinda Carlisle, "Heaven is a place on earth", and Josephine had found it.

"I thought that would surprise you, dear," he said glibly.

"When did y-o-u decide this?" she enquired.

"Oh! A long time ago."

"What then with the Dublin or Las Vegas option?"

"You know what they say, 'a man can hope, dream even, and times his dreams come true'."

Really? And who are they, these purveyors of wisdom?"

E.L. James, actually."

You're quoting 'Fifty Shades Of Grey'? Don't tell me you've read

e shot her a look of incredulity. "I'm more of a Shakespeare man . 'Romeo and Juliet' and all that."

But that didn't end well, did it?"

No, there was no Romeo and Juliet the sequel. Let's just settle on Well That Ends Well', then."

et's hope it does. You do realise we'll have to invite all my

here is that. But hey, it's only for one day."

he day at a time, sweet Jesus."

as one of these nights, nights where things were perfect between hey played off each other, kidded each other, spoke as if they ious, but each knew the other was laughing inside. It was like a ompetition. Who would crack first? Who would laugh or let the own? Best thing. They usually did it in unison. They would each heesy grin, snigger or simply burst out laughing. There was so od feeling in those moments. Magic moments.

it was decided, or rather that John had decided, they would ake plans. What would she wear? She wasn't like one of these ho say they have dreamed of their wedding day all their lives, were a child, spent their life looking for the perfect dress. Did hink about getting married? Probably. Doesn't everyone? That ean that she ever sat down and planned it, dreamed about it. he did dream of John waiting for her at the altar when she was eep at the end of that first wonderful night. But although she f dressed in white, she hadn't seen any detail. She couldn't, if isualise any aspect of the dress. Now she was going to have

CHAPTER TEN
ESCAPE

John had said, "Let's elope. The way young lo

She recognised the Van Morrison refere
joking. But he wasn't.

"It'd be so romantic," he continued. "No
were or what we were up to until it was all o
the biggest party, pretending that it's an enga

"We'd make our big entry to 'Crazy Ii
playing loudly as we entered the building."

And then in his best MC voice, "And
give it up for Mr and Mrs John and Josephi

"I can just imagine their faces. I'd hav
take a picture of them at that moment. I'd ha
Be the best wedding photograph ever."

Josephine had gone along with the
suggested various locations they might es
to as far as Las Vegas. Las Vegas would
They would have been married by Elvis
Now Or Never" and followed by "The
visualise it. God, no! The Celebrant in
Vegas Elvis suit and John in his black le
Forget Las Vegas. Dublin now sounde
earth. Neither of them were rich. Well,
wasn't. Else why would he be wor
Manager. My God! Maybe he's an un

"So," she said to John one night,

He sat up from his slouching pos
taking a sip of Jack Daniels, replie
wedding."

"Well, knock me down with a fe

some

it."

H
mysel
"F
"N
'All's
"L
family.
"T
"O
It v
them. T
were se
staring
façade d
wear a c
much go
Now
have to n
women w
since they
she ever t
doesn't m
But wait.
falling asl
saw hersel
she tried,

8

to. She wasn't that close to anyone that she could ask to go wedding dress shopping with her. No one whose opinion she would value. She wasn't inspired by any of her sisters' wedding dresses. But then they didn't share her taste. They didn't think outside the box, didn't travel outside their own environment. But Donegal wasn't New York or Milan. And so didn't offer the same choice. She wasn't insulting the people of Donegal or her sisters, but she wasn't one to run with the pack. She wanted something different. She wanted the best. After all, she had found the best man.

She had grown quite close with Sally from work, but not in a best friend sort of way. More like best work colleague. When at work, Sally was the one she would talk to most. They didn't socialise outside of work, for no particular reason other than they each had their own lives. And although the subject of their relationships with their other halves sometimes came up for discussion, it was only in a superficial or general way. There was no in-depth conversation, nor did it seem that either wanted one. It was a bit like talking about men in general, what they do and don't do.

"He never puts the toilet seat down." How often has a woman said that? As long as he lifts it up before he uses the toilet, Josephine thought. She remembered her mother having to clean after her father on the morning after a long night at the pub. He hadn't just missed the mark as far as getting it in the hole in the seat. He didn't even notice that the lid was down. It was a case of "splashing it all over", except it wasn't Brut aftershave.

It wasn't that she wouldn't respect Sally's or anyone's opinion, but she just wouldn't know if their choice would be the right choice, or good enough to impress John. That sounds terrible, but even though she never considered herself choosy or fussy, she naturally wanted him to see her and think she was the most beautiful woman in the world. She would have to trust her own judgement. Her family still weren't on board with it all. When she told them she was engaged and getting married, both her mother and sister said, "We'll see." They really knew how to put a damper on things.

She could, of course, ask John to help her choose, but even though she was practical and pragmatic, she was still a little superstitious as far as some things go, and her husband seeing the dress before the wedding was one of them. That and the fact she wanted the big reveal. She wanted him to see her and cry. With awe and happiness, that is. Not because he was making a mistake, she laughed.

John had a few days off from work and decided they would spend them together. He convinced her to skive. Call in sick. She felt like a schoolgirl again. They would go out of town for a few nights, book a hotel or something, have breakfast in bed and do nothing. It sounded good to Josephine, too good to refuse. She called work.

"I don't think I'll be in for a few days," she told them in the office, speaking in a low voice, trying to sound ill. She realised how stupid that was, how false it would sound, but it would sound even more stupid if she now began to speak normally.

"I feel terrible. I must be coming down with something." She thought about coughing, but decided against it.

"Do you want me to send you a doctor?" said the voice on the other end of the line.

Josephine fell silent, before realising it was Sally. Josephine burst out laughing, as Sally continued, "I guess not. After all, three's a crowd. Go and enjoy yourself. I'll cover for you."

"Thanks, Sally, I'll return the favour."

"You certainly will, Josephine. Now get off the line, I have work to do."

She was relieved. It couldn't have gone any better. Now she could relax in the knowledge that no one would suspect. Who was she kidding? No one really cared.

Work sorted, all she had to do was go and pack her suitcase. All? She would have to choose what to wear, and seeing as they would be spending two nights together, what about bedwear? She had always slept naked. She felt uncomfortable in pyjamas. Maybe it would be best to be comfortable in her own skin. John had already told her how gorgeous and sexy her body was. Why cover it up? But neither did she want him to think she wasn't making the effort. She realised that she didn't have any sexy underwear. No time to order from Lovehoney or Ann Summers. There was a lingerie shop in the town. She had seen it advertised in the local paper. One problem, though. She didn't want anyone from the hospital to see her. And John had told her to wait in her apartment for him to collect her, but not at what time. She would have to go with the see-through option.

Her thoughts were interrupted by the sound of a car. John. She looked out. The gold convertible Mercedes. What else? She was chuffed. But then what if someone from the hospital sees it outside her apartment? No one from the hospital lived there, but it wouldn't be so out of the way that someone might not drive or walk past. Now she was just being paranoid again. She began to sing the Black Sabbath song.

"Stop, Josephine," she chided herself. Then realised she hadn't packed. Too much thinking and not enough doing. John was at the door. She let him in and kissed him. No. He kissed her. Passionately.

"Ready To Go?" He was laying down a challenge. Song titles. Here we go again.

"Take Me, I'm Yours," she replied.

"You Really Got Me." He was quick.

They both laughed.

She wished she could have sung "another suitcase in another hall", but it was still in the bedroom and still empty.

"I'll just go and get my suitcase," she said, before heading upstairs. She would have to grab some clothes quickly and practically throw them in. Luckily, she was that kind of person. She would ponder for ages what to wear, but then when it came to the crunch would make a snap decision. Thing is, it would usually work out for her. And so she hoped it would be the same today. She didn't want to keep John waiting.

"Just doing my make-up," she shouted, just in case he wondered what she was doing.

She hoped he hadn't noticed that she had already done it. But being a gentleman, he probably wouldn't mention it if he had. He might just think she needed the toilet.

"Oh, no! I hope he doesn't think it's a number two." She had never let him know when she went to the toilet for that reason. She would always make the excuse of having a shower and leave the water running as a cover.

"It's great that you brought the Mercedes," she shouted, hoping he would realise it's nearly impossible to speak and push at the same time.

She didn't get a reply, nor did she expect one.

When she appeared with her suitcase, he was already in the car. She suspected he was arranging the music, just as he did on that first night. He was.

As she climbed into the car, the Pina Colada song was playing. She expected nothing less. She liked it. The song, that is. She had never had a Pina Colada.

He looked at her and grinned.

"Is my timing immaculate or what?"

It was. His timing was. He had it all worked out. So much so, she knew that these few days would be wonderful. She was "So Excited."

"I wish I could drive."

He looked bemused.

"Then I could sing 'Move Over Darling'."

"And I could sing 'Baby You Can Drive My Car'."

"But I can't, so I guess you'd better start us up."

"And 'I'll Never Stop'," he replied.

"Well, at least until 'This Is The Place'."

"Maybe we should get going before 'The Going Gets Tough'!" they said in unison, laughing.

And they did. Get going. She wasn't sure where. As usual, he didn't tell her. She didn't ask. Why spoil the surprise. It really didn't matter where they were going, as long as they were going together. It could have been anywhere, nowhere. Now she was singing to herself again.

"In The Middle Of Nowhere."

They ended up by the sea. She loved the sea. And not just because of that first night. She always loved it. The fresh sea air, the waves, the colours, the horizon. That's the thing. The horizon never looks so beautiful anywhere else. It's like going back to the days when sailors thought you could fall off the end of the earth. Looking out over the sea to the horizon, it was believable. Don't they say you can sail off into the sunset? Well, only when it's getting dark, presumably. But it is hypnotic. The horizon. The sunset. It makes you want to forget yourself, your life, where you are. It's magical. A little bit of magic in your life. Sitting on the sand, looking at the sea, waiting for the sunset.

As she was lost in her thoughts, he leaned across and gently put his head on her shoulder.

"Put your head on my shoulder…" she began to sing in her head, just as he whispered in her ear.

"Are you thinking what I'm thinking?"

That is a question you just can't answer. If you say yes, then he might ask you to tell him what you're thinking. And it might be way off the mark. If you say no, then it's always going to be the wrong answer. So the only thing to do is to do what, as a child, you were always told not to do. Answer a question with a question.

"What are you thinking?"

"I'm thinking I want to make love to you, right here, right now."

They were parked by the sea and it was getting dark. There was no one around. So that answer didn't surprise her. But he was right. She was thinking the same thing. Except making love for them fell short of sexual intercourse, as they were sticking to their agreement to save that most intimate act until their wedding night, to make it special, two people in love, totally in love, giving themselves to each other totally. To some people that might sound hypocritical; sex is sex. But they weren't pretending to be puritanical or taking the moral high ground. It just made sense. At any rate, it was their decision and it doesn't matter what anyone else thinks. The way it should be. It's called intimacy because it remains between the participants, two people. Not three or more people, not for discussion by the busybodies on Facebook, Twitter or Instagram. Just the two of us, you and I.

"My God," thought Josephine, "this could be the longest foreplay in the history of the world. Except, is it foreplay if you have an orgasm?"

"Who the fuck cares?" she thought, just before she lost herself in the moment.

CHAPTER ELEVEN
DRESS YOU UP

After their romp on the beach, they drove a very short distance to a beachside chalet.

"This is it. Our very own love shack," thought Josephine. Not that it was a shack, far from it.

The lights were on in the living area. Obviously, John had told the owners they would be arriving in the dark, or maybe the lights were on sensors. Either way, she liked the look of it. Wood framed with a veranda looking directly out to sea. And it was on its own. No neighbours. They could do what they want, when they want. Everything a getaway should be. What's the point in getting away if there are people next door? It so surprised Josephine that people bought a holiday home by the sea beside several other holiday homes by the sea. How is that getting away from it all? Out of the frying pan. And into... Well, into a crowd of people you don't know.

They settled in quickly. They hadn't eaten, but John produced chicken curry and rice from what seemed like out of nowhere. Well, actually out of a cold box.

"Here's one I made earlier," he said, before plating it up and putting it in the microwave. But it wasn't your usual microwave meal. He had actually made it himself. He served it with champagne. Maybe not everyone's cup of tea, but it just seemed like John was a champagne-with-everything kind of guy.

Afterwards, he made them both a Pina Colada. Josephine's first taste. Did she like it? Yes, she did. It had rained before they finished on the beach, but then she didn't mind getting caught in the rain in that situation. Only thing, she was into Yoga. But never mind.

She was feeling really, really relaxed, laid back, partly because of the sex and partly because of the alcohol. Yet sleep wasn't on her horizon. She was waiting for what was coming next. She was sure John was not going to let this night end so soon. Maybe more sex. Maybe something else. It was. Something else.

John had left the room and gone outside. She heard him open the car, the unmistakeable sound of the alarm being triggered. The flashing of the indicator lights reflected on the window pane. What more could there be?

"Oh, no!" she thought. "He hasn't really read 'Fifty Shades of Grey' and is expecting me to embrace the bondage thing or want me to sign a slave contract."

"Oh! Bondage up yours," she thought.

As he came back in, there was no clanking of chains, no bag of tricks. However, he was carrying what looked like some magazines or brochures, a bunch of them.

Were they going to plan the honeymoon, tonight? She didn't want to. She didn't want to do anything. To escape to her meant getting away from everything, forgetting about everything.

He came and sat beside her. Put the magazines down on the coffee table. She looked at them.

"Irish Brides."

"We need to get you a dress."

"Not tonight," she thought to herself. But how could she say it to him?

Before she could say anything, he had opened the first magazine. He had marked the page.

"This one would look good on you."

Josephine wasn't interested. She really didn't want to feign it. All that was in her head was "the only thing that looks good on me is you". She felt like saying it to him, singing it to him, in her lowest, sexiest singing voice, like Marilyn Monroe when she sang "I Wanna Be Loved By You".

She realised he was waiting for an answer.

"That would look good on anyone. It's gorgeous. Not cheap, I bet."

"Only the best for you, Josephine. Don't worry about the price. But never take the first option. There's more."

He pulled a loose page out of the magazine. She was speechless. She was looking at a dress with a high lace neck, long lace sleeves and a skirt that reminded her of the knitted dolls her grandmother used to cover the toilet rolls with when she was a young girl. What was she going to say? She wasn't a Southern Belle or a Wild West bride. Would she be honest? Would that hurt his feelings?

"What do you think?"

"It's… it's not me." She could see he was holding it in, the laughter.

"It's hideous!" she screamed.

He burst out laughing.

"You're taking the piss."

"Just testing."

"So if I turned up in that, would you still marry me?"

Now it was his turn to squirm.

"I'd marry you if you turned up naked."

"Not sure that's going to work for the priest or the congregation."

"No. But we could consummate the marriage there and then."

"There might be murder in the cathedral."

They laughed.

"I think I need another Pina Colada."

She never dreamed she would like Pina Colada. She had imagined that they would taste like Mikado biscuits soaked in alcohol or a liqueur version of a Bounty Bar. Neither of which sounded appealing. And, to boot, she had tried Malibu and Coke at the insistence of a friend in her teenage years. It made her ill, literally. So she was surprised to be enjoying the taste.

John put two more drinks in front of them and discarded the top magazine. There were at least four more. Maybe she could pretend to be asleep. He would wait until she awoke. That was John. He might even spend his time flicking through the magazines. There was no TV, purposely. It was a getaway. A real getaway. Except for Josephine. She wasn't getting away from what John had planned for her tonight.

He kept showing more and more dresses. Asked her if she could see herself in them. She couldn't. Solely because she wasn't interested in so doing, not in the slightest. Maybe if he had cut out a picture of her head and superimposed it on them. Even then she couldn't have chosen, said yes to a dress. She could have asked him if he could see her in them. What his favourite was. She didn't want to. She didn't want John to know what she would be wearing. She was afraid that if she told him that, she might hurt his feelings.

"I'm tired," she told him.

"Of me?"

"No. Of course not. Just tired."

He took her in his arms. She felt so close. And then she almost fell asleep. She could hear herself beginning to snore and opened her eyes. He was gazing at her lovingly. She could feel her lips morphing into a smile, a genuine smile.

"Should we go to bed?"

"Yes, please." They did. But not for sex. For sleep. And it didn't take long. Literally as soon as her head hit the pillow.

The next morning, she noticed the magazines were in the bin. Just where they belonged.

John was cooking breakfast. Eggs, sausages, bacon, black pudding, hash browns, beans.

How was she going to get into any dress if she continued to eat like this? But this wasn't an everyday breakfast. It was an occasional treat. And everyone has to have one, don't they?

They both knew what good food was, what healthy food was. And food was John's business. She would do what she needed to do, eat what she needed to eat in order to look good on their wedding day, to look good for John. Even if it meant eating like a rabbit. She laughed. Hopefully, when the day was over they would be doing something else like rabbits. Sometimes, Josephine was ashamed; no, not ashamed, maybe aghast at the thoughts that came into her head. But they weren't bad thoughts. Just naughty thoughts. And she had always had them. She figured that they were doing no harm, so no point in denying them. Besides, they made her laugh, and laughter is the best medicine. She may be a bit crazy like her thoughts, but that made her Josephine. And that's why John loved her.

"Breakfast's up."

She laughed, thinking of John Cleese in "Fawlty Towers". "The game's up, up there, a bit of game pie got stuck."

"Is it game?" she said jokingly.

"Not game, Josephine, but if you enjoy it, will you be game for something else afterwards?"

"You know me, John, I'm game for anything."

"If I had known that, I'd have made duck surprise."

She laughed. He had trumped her again. One of these days, or one of these nights, she would get the better of him.

He hadn't been joking. After breakfast, they ran down to the sea naked. There was no one around. Well, it was just before dawn. And as there was no one around, why not do what pleases you, what pleases both of them? And they did.

These were some of the best few days of their lives together. Josephine didn't want them to end. They wouldn't, though, would they? After all, they were getting married. But she had seen what marriage had done to people. Her sister for one. Was she making a mistake, the biggest mistake of her life? But how could she say to John, "I don't want to get married."

Maybe she could explain. Why spoil a good thing? Would he understand? He had made such a big deal of getting engaged. Taking her here to discuss wedding dresses. All for her, everything for her. How could she tell him she didn't want it? She couldn't. She might lose him. So she would do it. Get married. Choose a dress. Her dress. Now she knew the dress she wanted.

"John," she said, on the second morning as they lay cuddled up in bed, her head in the crook of his arm. He looked down just as she looked up. "I want to choose my own dress. I want to surprise you. Just as you surprised me on the night we met. I don't think you'll be disappointed."

"You could never disappoint me, Josephine."

"Even if I turned up naked?" She couldn't resist it.

"Especially if you turned up naked."

They looked at each other and kissed.

"You can choose," he said, when their lips parted. "After all, you chose me."

"We chose each other," she responded immediately.

"That's true. True love."

"You and I have a guardian angel," they sang in unison.

She knew it was all good. Although her arms were already around him, now they were tighter, as were his. They both closed their eyes and relaxed.

CHAPTER TWELVE
LITTLE LIES

In the early days of their romance, John and Josephine didn't indulge in serious sexual activity. They held hands, they kissed, they cuddled and caressed, but never touched each other sexually. That lasted for all of three weeks. They were both hot-blooded people, and so they got to know each other intimately. Yet they had agreed they wouldn't have sexual intercourse until their wedding night. They considered their relationship special, very special, and wanted to have something special left to share on their wedding night. She thought of it akin to some people who like to save the tastiest part of the dinner to the end. It was more special to Josephine as it was John who had suggested it. She would have given herself to him entirely the night he proposed, or even before, if the truth be told.

"Slut!" she laughed to herself. But then she would do anything for love; well, almost anything.

They knew they were going to be together, forever she hoped, and so they would surrender to each other fully on their wedding night, just as people did in those Mills and Boon books she used to read as a teenager, the milder romantic ones. They were blessed to have found each other. If blessed was the word for it. John was an atheist, or so he said, and although brought up Catholic, Josephine just wasn't convinced God really existed. She certainly didn't go to church or read the bible. At the same time, she did so want to get married in a church. Apart from anything, she wasn't sure if her family and in particular her mother would even attend the wedding if it wasn't the traditional church ceremony. That wouldn't have stopped her doing it, but it was important to her that her family recognise that she and John were, in fact, married. And she had to confess that, although she knew that non-religious ceremonies were nevertheless valid in the eyes of the law, she would feel more married, if that's possible, emerging from a church.

She had heard that some parish priests were less than accommodating. If you weren't a regular attender, they simply wouldn't even consider letting you get married in their church.

She hoped that wasn't the case in Letterkenny. It was a cathedral town and there were a number of priests in residence, so to speak. Hopefully, they wouldn't know or ask whether she was a regular in the congregation on a Sunday, or Saturday night. That's the way it was nowadays: your Sunday obligation could be fulfilled on a Saturday night. How is that keeping holy the Sabbath day? But then other religions have their Sabbath on a Saturday. Typical of the Catholic Church, hijacking someone else's idea. Perhaps they want people to defect and still be able to celebrate the Sabbath on a Saturday, or is it just that they can collect money from people before they spend it all on Saturday night?

"What if the priest asks me if I'm a virgin?" she suddenly thought.

"I could lie. I might have to lie." He wasn't going to be able to verify her answer. And with all the sins she had already committed at this stage in her life, one little lie wasn't going to make any difference.

She caught herself, as she often had to.

"What the hell am I talking about? If I don't believe in God, don't practise my religion, why should I be worried about lying to the priest?" But she was. It was some weird sense of morality, rather than a fear of breaking one of the Ten Commandments or the fear of eternal damnation. Her upbringing, despite not inspiring her to join the ranks and become Sister Josephine one day, thank God, did leave her with an inbuilt sense of right and wrong. And she still believed it was wrong to lie, especially to a man of the cloth. What does that even mean? Sounds more like a tailor. But then she had heard her father use the term cloth of heaven, referring again to W.B. Yeats, as he often did. Maybe they're cut from that.

But surely he wouldn't ask, the priest. What if he insisted she go to confession? She would have to go. She would have to confess something. But not that. Certainly not that. Then that would be a lie by omission. This was getting worse. Maybe they should just get married in the hotel or something?

But then John had already decided they were having a church wedding. Although he didn't say it, it was probably because he knew that's what she wanted. That's what would satisfy her mother, her family, even though they still weren't on-board with the whole marriage thing. They hadn't known each other long enough, they didn't have a traditional courtship, they should wait a while longer. That was her mother and sister's opinion. Not that they didn't like John. They didn't know John. He didn't know them. He didn't really want to get to know them. She had made the mistake of telling him that she wasn't that close to her mother or her family. That she didn't go home too often. That things just weren't the same since her father died. That she needed to get away from them for fear she would be the one stuck at home looking after her mother, forever. Hence, he wasn't interested in seeing them.

"I'm not marrying them, Josephine," he would say, "I'm marrying you. I don't need to get to know them. I don't need to see them."

"You and me, babe, you and me," he would say, "together forever, and nothing will tear us apart."

No, she couldn't tell John she had changed her mind about the church. He had already "set the train in motion". The love train was on its way to its final destination. Next stop matrimony.

She just had to hope that the priest wouldn't ask too many awkward questions or that she could practise looking young and innocent. And if it comes to the crunch, she would lie for love. She just had to focus. If the awkward question arises, tell him what he wants to hear and then change the conversation quickly.

"So, Josephine, are you a virgin?"

"Of course, Father. And tell me, Father, what's the policy on our having popular music at the ceremony?"

"Popular music?" That was just being diplomatic. Surely, he would understand what she meant. What other way could she put it? Would he know who the Ramones were, the song "Baby I Love You"? After all, the original version was recorded by the Ronettes in 1964. But then he could be young, the priest. Anyway, it didn't matter. She could explain it to him. After all, the question was only to deflect attention from herself. Thank God their song wasn't "Like A Virgin", she laughed. She was sure that "Wake Up And Make Love" wouldn't fly.

"Okay," she decided, "I'm going to roll with it. Let's do it, the big church wedding, the whole nine yards. Or whatever length the aisle is."

She was beating herself up about her sex life, which was virtually non-existent until she met John. No, she wasn't a virgin, not now, not after Dr White had taken advantage. Before that there might have been some doubt. But that was down to some stupid one-night stand in Letterkenny when she had too many drinks, although she wasn't one hundred per cent sure she had been penetrated. It was all over in a flash: a sight of a penis, a slight feeling of pressure between her legs and Bob's your uncle. It was over. She felt wet. On the outside. She was convinced she remained a virgin. But then her ideal scenario for this wedding was spoiled by Dr White, or Mr White as he would correct people. Well, what's done is done, and isn't there a place for everyone in the house of God, even a sinner, especially a sinner? As long as they are repentant, sorry for their sin. And boy, was she sorry that the whole Dr White incident happened, that she had let it happen. But as John told her, it was time to forgive herself. And so there was a place for her in the house of God. Sorted.

"It's all set," John said the next day, when they were out for breakfast.

"What? What's all set?"

"The wedding. The church. It's all systems go. We have blast off."

"You've booked the church?"

"Why do you sound so surprised?"

"You're an atheist. How did you manage that?"

He laughed at her. He couldn't stop himself.

"What are you talking about? I simply asked the priest to marry us, that you wanted a church wedding... sorry, that we wanted a church wedding."

"Did he not ask if you were a Catholic. If I was a Catholic?"

"No. He probably assumed that we were. He told me we needed our baptism certificates. I have mine. I assume you have yours. Or can get it."

"So he didn't ask you if you went to mass. If you were a virgin?"

"Whaaaaat?"

"Don't we have to confess our sins?" she continued unabated.

He stopped eating and put his face in his hands. She could swear he was praying. He wasn't. Well, not really.

"Holy God!" he said eventually.

"What's wrong?" She was bemused.

"The Spanish Inquisition ended in 1834. We're getting married. We're not trying to book our ticket to heaven. You don't need a ticket to heaven. I can take you there any time."

He was nothing if not cheesy. That was part of the reason she loved him. He wasn't cheesy in a cheesy sort of way, more in a lovable sort of way.

He had, in his own way, taken her to heaven. For Josephine now, heaven was a place on earth. Right here, right now. Being with John was like discovering herself, her sexuality. That sounds so crass, but for Josephine it was true. She had a sexual awakening. She was able to let herself go. Never before had she been able to admit to someone that she liked sex, had fantasies. Fantasies she had hitherto kept to herself. Not involving John at that stage, obviously, not involving anyone in particular really. Yes, there were rock stars and movie stars she wouldn't have kicked out of her bed. Not that she would ever have to worry about that. Her fantasies were more abstract, more about her, what she would like someone to do to her. And although what John had done to her wasn't exactly in line with those fantasies, it was enough. For now.

"Do that to me one more time," she sang in her head, although she knew that would never be enough with a man like John.

CHAPTER THIRTEEN
WHITE WEDDING

All her family and friends told her it was fashionable to be late. Ten minutes, maybe fifteen. Not for her. Not for John. She would not be late. She wouldn't keep him waiting. If they were going to vow never-ending love to each other, then they would respect the formalities. They had chosen as the song for their first dance "Never Ending Song Of Love" by the New Seekers. John thought it would be fun to dance to, rather than something boring like "I Will Always Love You" or something stupid like "You're Still The One".

"You're Still The One?" On your wedding day.

"I should bloody think so, otherwise there's no hope for the future," John had said one night, as they browsed through their options.

John was right. This wasn't a case of holding on. They were solid, solid as a rock, just like Ashford and Simpson. And now they were being cemented together, forever. Their love would be never-ending, just like the song says. They had practised their dancing, but only when John had had a good few drinks. It was a sort of jive-cum-twist-cum-tango, if you get the gist. They were obviously no Torville and Dean, although sometimes it felt as if they were dancing on ice. They had fallen over on more than one occasion, usually her landing on top of John. In her mind, he ensured it happened that way so that she wouldn't hurt herself, or maybe he just liked her on top. They would both burst out laughing. It was obvious that John was not worried about a sterling performance. Neither was she.

"Who wants to be normal?" he asked her. "Our parents have been there, done that. Lived a normal life, died a normal death. Not us, Josephine; we're going to make an impression that people will remember.

She couldn't sleep on the night before the wedding, nor did she want to. Her mother and sisters insisted she went to bed. She stayed in her room, listening to music through her headphones so they wouldn't hear. She listened to all the songs she had loved since her father had bought her the first portable radio. She had kept it playing under her pillow every night. She loved the retro stations. Sixties pop, Seventies glam rock, disco, power ballads. She had no favourite band. The song mattered more than the singer.

She remembered a song her mother used to sing when she was a child. "I'm getting married in the morning. Ding dong! The bells are going to chime. Kick up a rumpus, but don't lose the compass. And get me to the church on time."

That was it. She would get to the church on time, come hell or high water. The wedding car had been booked. A vintage Rolls-Royce. Gold. John had arranged it. It was for him, really. When he was young, five years of age, he had holidayed with his parents in a seaside resort. On the last day of the holiday, the day they were due to go home, he was playing on the beach. His father had bought him some Corgi toys, a cement lorry and a gold Rolls-Royce. He loved them both, but especially the Rolls-Royce. He buried them in the sand, fully expecting to dig them up again. Being a child, he didn't mark the spot. When the light started to fade and the car was packed, he had already dug more holes than his young mind could count or care to count. He would gladly have dug a million holes to find his beloved Rolls-Royce. His mother had come to take him back to the car. He had a tantrum, screamed, kicked, threw away his plastic spade — to no effect. He was going home. They, his parents, were bigger and stronger; resistance was futile. He couldn't win. Not long after he was put in the car, he was fast asleep. Next thing he remembered was being tucked up in bed by his mother. She kissed him and pulled up the cover. He was so exhausted from digging holes, he slept through the night. I bet he never dreamed he would be riding in a real Rolls-Royce one day.

At 6am, she showered and put on her underwear. It was ivory. John knew she wasn't a virgin, didn't care that she wasn't a virgin, so she didn't want to be virginal, even though she did consider that she would be doing it properly for the first time that night, doing it with John. They had stuck to the plan of not fully engaging until after they were married.

On their wedding night they would finally connect in a way they never did before. And although it would have been nice to be able to tell John that he was her first, her last, her everything, she had that night in the restaurant, voluntarily or maybe not so voluntarily, divulged how Dr White ensured, whatever doubt she had in her mind, that she was no virgin. She never dreamed of asking John if he was a virgin. She just assumed he wouldn't be. Don't men take pride in how many sexual partners they have had, how many conquests? It didn't matter anyway. Would she call it off if he had slept with more than three women, more than four, more than ten, more than a hundred? No. This is it. Other women didn't matter, no matter how many. Obviously, he never loved them. She was his true love, now and forever.

Her dress was white. John agreed. His opinion was the only one that mattered. And besides, no one else knew, except Dr White. And he wasn't invited. Even though people might expect that he was. They would just assume he was too busy, being such an important asshole and all that. It was her day. His and hers. They would do what they wanted. "Nothing's Gonna Stop Us Now," he told her, and although it was just another song title, and she was used to him using them in everyday conversation, he really meant it, he really, really did.

She sat there in her underwear and dressing gown, listening for someone to stir. She thought that her mother would be awake. Maybe hoping she would come to her and tell her that it was all off, that she had changed her mind. Not that she, her mother, had tried to persuade her to. She wasn't like that. Silence was her weapon of choice. It said it all. She wasn't pleased. It wouldn't work this time. Not that it had worked in the past, not with Josephine. As much as her mother was silent, Josephine was defiant. Yet neither changed. Nor would.

She looked into her mother's room. She wasn't there. She knew she'd be in the kitchen. She'd be drinking tea. Her drink of choice. Although she did like a sherry or white wine on special occasions. As she opened the kitchen door, her mother was sitting in her usual place at the table, facing the door. She could usually anticipate her mother's mood, but on this occasion she was unsure. No matter how much she had tried to convince her mother she was doing the right thing, that she was truly in love with John and he with her, it wasn't working. Her mother had expected to meet him more than once, get the measure of him, decide if he was right for her daughter. It just wasn't right that she was marrying someone that her mother had only met once in a formal setting. John had agreed to a dinner date with her mother and sister, to appease Josephine, so that they could see that he was real, that Josephine wasn't making it all up. She thought that it had gone well. John had been his usual charming self. But that wasn't good enough for her mother.

"Why did he not have the decency to come to my home to meet me? What kind of man is he? He's got you wrapped around his little finger anyway. Not a good start to a marriage."

Her mother was not the eternal optimist. Her motto should be, "If something can go wrong, it will go wrong."

"What's up, Mum?"

"What makes you think something's up?" she replied, taking a drink from her teacup.

"I know you. There's something. You don't want me to marry him."

"I don't know if I do or if I don't. How could I? I've only met him once."

"I've told you about him, how good he is to me, how good he is for me."

"Josephine, it's your life. He's your choice. You're the one who has to live with it, with him."

"I will. But can't you be happy for me?"

"I'll be happy for you when you're happy for yourself."

"You don't think I'm happy now?"

"I don't think you know. You know how things can go, you've seen your father and I. From what you've told me, he drinks a lot. You're drinking a lot."

"I didn't say he drinks a lot. He enjoys a drink; all young couples enjoy a drink from time to time."

"Maybe, but you don't know where it can lead. Sometimes there's no going back. Once a drunk, always a drunk. Your father was always giving it up, always tomorrow. The drink didn't control him, he controlled it. So he believed. It more than controlled him. It killed him."

Josephine could feel her eyes beginning to leak. Her mother noticed.

"Dear Josephine, I'm not going to ruin your day. I'll be a model guest. I'll even congratulate the happy couple. I'll dance, I'll speak to everyone. I'll keep my opinions to myself. No one else will know or suspect anything I won't make any trouble." And she wouldn't. Josephine knew she wouldn't. She was a woman of her word.

"I'd better start getting ready," she added, getting up and washing her cup in the sink, drying it and hanging it up. She was like that. A place for everything and everything in its place.

"Excuse me," she said, as Josephine stood aside to let her through the door.

That was typical of her mother. "I'm not going to ruin your day." Not half. She had just made a very good effort. Josephine decided she had to win this battle. She didn't win many battles with her mother. That just made her more determined. She would enjoy the day, in spite of her mother, to spite her mother. She would have as little contact with her as possible, and keep John away from her. Tomorrow it would be over and they would be alone together.

Forget about her mother, forget about the rest of the world. That night they would stay in the hotel, but tomorrow they would be heading for the airport and the Caribbean.

"Last-minute nerves?"

Her eldest sister stood in the doorway in a pink dressing gown, rubbing her eyes. "Is there tea in the pot?"

"Yes, I mean no. There's tea in the pot, but no last-minute nerves. I'm ready to do this. It's the happiest day of my life."

"I believe you," Mary said, pouring herself a cup of tea.

"What is it with this family? I've already had this crap from Mum. I don't need any more."

"Well, if you got it from Mum, I guess you've had enough."

"Have you tried your bridesmaid dress this morning?"

"No. Do you think I've put on weight since last week?"

"I don't know, have you?"

"If I have, it's too late to do anything now. Tell you what, if it doesn't fit, I won't be a bridesmaid. You have your other three sisters."

"You're right, I have had enough. I'm going to get ready."

"See you later, alligator."

"In a while, crocodile," she replied automatically with a little smile.

She felt more tears coming, but exited before Mary could notice.

Those were the words she exchanged with her father every time he left the house, the same exchange that took place the day he died.

She realised that Mary was worried about her: she was her baby sister. Mary's own marriage hadn't gone so well. Her husband cheated on her, left her for another woman. The children had grown before he left, leaving her entirely on her own. Josephine thought that was cruel, selfish, thoughtless. He left it late enough that she would find it difficult to fall in love again. It becomes harder as you become older, not necessarily because of age, but let's face it, it's difficult to love again, trust again; you're set in your ways, you've grown accustomed to one person. When she married Jake, she thought she had got it right. He was handsome, had a good job, didn't abuse drink, didn't smoke, was passive, never raised his voice, didn't turn a word in her mouth. All through the marriage he had been perfect, as far as she knew. Did everything for the children, for her, got on with her mother. She should have known. If a man gets on with your mother, there's something wrong with him. He has no balls. That's how it turned out. Moved all his stuff out when she was away for the weekend with her girlfriends. Left her a note:

"Dear Mary,

Don't blame yourself, but I don't love you any more. I've found someone new. Now the children are grown you have time to yourself and you'll find someone, too. I hope we can still be friends.

Love Jake.

P.S. I'll be in touch."

She didn't blame Mary for being sceptical. But she didn't have to rain on her parade. We don't all make the same mistakes. Mary played it safe. John was anything but safe. He was energetic, unpredictable, exciting. She was looking forward to the honeymoon, their homecoming, their future. Together, always together. That's how it would be. People would say, "Aren't they a lovely couple? You never see one without the other; imagine they're married for twenty-five years." Josephine always had a vivid imagination. She pinched herself on the arm in case she was dreaming. It hurt. I'm getting married, she screamed from within.

She took herself back to her room, where she gathered up her dressing gown, shower gel and towel. She went to the bathroom to take a shower, as it would soon be time to go to the hairdresser. Her sisters would accompany her, and no doubt when they returned to the house it would be pandemonium. It was, but she got through it; they all did. When the Rolls-Royce arrived, she felt the butterflies in her stomach for the first time. As she got into the back of the Rolls, she noticed there was an MP3 player, with a sign: "Play me". She knew it came from John. He couldn't let the opportunity pass. She put the miniature headphones in her ears. At least he realised that she couldn't wear full-sized headphones. She pressed play.

She recognised the tune immediately:

"Come Softly To Me."

"Let's go," she said to the driver.

"Let's go all the way," she thought to herself.

CHAPTER FOURTEEN
MISS YOU NIGHTS

Josephine was excited at her new role as Mrs Clark. What excited her more was having someone to share her bed with. Although they had sex from time to time in her bed, and other places, they had rarely spent the night together. It wasn't that they didn't want to, but usually John had to leave in order to be back at work the next day. That, and Josephine was still afraid or rather paranoid that someone would see him leave in the morning and it would somehow get back to her family and in particular her mother, who still believed she was being a good Catholic and practising what she had been taught about boys and sex. Obviously, she wasn't. But she didn't want to upset her mother, especially as her marriage was imminent and she would no longer have anything to hide in that department. Not that she was going to do it in front of her mother. Rather that her mother would assume, and rightly so, that she was doing it, that her and John were doing it.

The occasional, or rather not so occasional night of passion didn't make her feel like they were a real couple, man and wife. Now it would be different. They would go to sleep together and wake up together. She was singing in her head again, "I wanna wake up with you."

She wanted to celebrate, so she decided she would make a special night for them, cook a special dinner. It was John's day off the next day. He was still working at the City Hotel in Derry, but had been promoted to Restaurant Manager. He finished his shift tonight at eight. It would take him about twenty-five minutes to get home. They used to go to the Chinese on nights like this, or John would bring home a take-away. They rarely had a home-cooked meal. She would ensure that her meal would exceed anything they ate out.

John loved meat. Didn't all men? Her father did. Beef, lamb, chicken, pork. According to him, a meal wasn't a meal without it. And her mother never made one without it. Breakfast was bacon, sausages, black pudding and the rest. Lunch would be cottage pie or beef stew. Dinner was steak, lamb, chicken or pork chops.

"A hard-working man needs meat," her mother would always say.

Well, she was going to ensure that her new husband would get his. She giggled to herself. She had planned that, too.

For starters, she was making Chicken Satay. She had Googled the right way to do it. She had practised it again and again when John was at work. She had practised it so much, she worried she had put on weight. She actually took time out to go to the bedroom, take off her clothes and look at herself from every angle. She still wasn't sure, but then she hoped that John would be so impressed with her cooking and so enamoured by her efforts in the looks department that when he got to the bedroom, he would be singled-minded, blinded by love.

"Shit!" she thought. "Here I am standing looking at myself, when I should be cooking."

Back in the kitchen, the Satay was ready. Now for the main course. She laughed. She hoped she was the main course, but she was only the last course. Scratch that. She was the best course, the big finale.

For the main course she had chosen fillet steak, only the best for her husband. John liked his burned on the outside and practically raw on the inside. "Black and Blue," he called it. She had also practised that. And she ate it. It was delicious. Not what she was brought up with. Her father liked his steak "well done". In Ireland that meant cremated, tough as old boots. She remembered her mother beginning to cook her father's dinner about an hour before he was due home. Vegetables cooked to a pulp, frying pan on, steak cooked through. It took him half an hour to eat it. He chewed and chewed. He practically inhaled the vegetables. The one thing that was right was the mashed potato. That was so tasty, so smooth and full of butter. Same as she was doing tonight. John would appreciate it, she was sure. And she was making a pepper sauce, á la Delia Smith.

She had what she thought was inspired for dessert. Strawberries and champagne. Served in bed. The same bed they would share from now on every night of their married life. She had even bought heart-shaped lights that she had pinned all along the headboard.

She needed a drink to curb her enthusiasm. But she didn't want to be drunk or tipsy when John came home. Even so, she gave in to temptation.

Temptation, the only thing that Oscar Wilde couldn't resist. Like many others, she assumed.

Like her tonight. Hopefully, like John later. She had a little nip of gin. With tonic. Well, to tell the truth, she had two or three.

Now she was ready. She decided to go and get dressed. No, she wasn't the naked chef. She wouldn't be naked until later, and she certainly wouldn't be cooking at that stage. Well, not in the conventional sense at any rate. She had to get it right, her attire. Not that she had that many choices. Fancy clothes weren't her thing. The only time she got properly dressed in her youth was on a Sunday for mass. As a child, she would be dressed in the same things, day after day; but come Sunday, she had to impress, as did all her siblings. They all had to look good for God. But then didn't God see all, every day? It seems that on Sunday he sees more. Sees everyone. He might just miss you on any other day. Or maybe he just doesn't care what you do six days a week, as long as you make the effort on Sunday. That's how it seemed to Josephine, even as a teenager. The vilest people acted like saints on a Sunday, or at least until they left the confines of the church.

"You'll see him on a Sunday eating the altar cloth," she used to hear her grandmother say. She was right. She didn't take any prisoners, her grandmother. She was more tuned in than her parents. They say that wisdom comes with age. With her grandmother, that was so true. She was the wisest woman she had ever known. She loved spending time with her. Josephine was closer to her than anyone in her life. Until now. Now she had found the love of her life, her soul-mate. She wasn't sure what that meant. Soul-mate. We're all supposed to have one, a soul. But is it the case that we all have a soul-mate, just one other soul that we're supposed to spend our lives with? And how do we find him, or her? She had enough of her wandering thoughts. She had found hers, and that was all that mattered. And she wanted to look nice for him. She wanted to look beautiful, desirable. She wanted to look so good that he couldn't keep his hands off her. After he had eaten his dinner, of course.

Tonight, what she would be wearing wouldn't be what would be suitable for Sunday mass. Far from it. God might even blush.

She waited. Eight thirty came and went. She had resisted the urge to drink more gin.

Nine o'clock came around. She felt like calling him. He told her not to do that. In a nice way.

"Josephine, I know this might sound a little odd. But please don't call me when I'm at work. Unless it's an emergency. They don't like me getting calls. It's unprofessional. Frowned upon."

She thought about it and decided she would wait. After all, she didn't want to jeopardise John's plans to move quickly up the ladder, to improve his life, their lives. Still, it was hard to resist. She wished he would appear.

She began singing in her head, again.

"Baby please come home."

A John Martyn song was one of those that played the first night they had sex: "May You Never." What beautiful words. She loved that song. It was so suited to this night. From now on she would never have to lay down her head without a hand to hold, John's hand. She got up and sought it out. She found it. She was definitely going to play that one just before she enticed him to bed. She never thought of herself as a temptress before. She never had the confidence, the desirability, or so she thought. Now it was different. He wanted her. Always. He would want her more tonight. She would make sure of that. She had shopped from Ann Summers. See-through bra, see-through panties. She worried: would he prefer a thong? Not on himself, she giggled. On her. Well, she thought, he's going to be so distracted, it won't even cross his mind. The blood flow is going to be somewhere other than in his head. She realised the gin was going to hers. Sober, she wouldn't be thinking such picturesque thoughts. But she liked it. But she wanted to be, if not sober, no more than tipsy. Welcome her man into their new home, make a perfect meal, take him to bed, and satisfy him. And herself, now that she had become a liberated woman.

She looked at the clock. Nine thirty. She was a patient person. Or used to be. She would wait forever for a pizza to be delivered, and even then, give the delivery boy a generous tip. But tonight, her patience was running out. She realised that it wasn't just the fear that the meal would be ruined. Her Ann Summers underwear was making her sexually excited.

"Oh, my God," she thought, "I'm horny." She never had that thought before. She never imagined that marriage could do that. Shouldn't it be the other way around? Whatever! Her patience was now thinner than the underwear. Suddenly, she heard the key in the door. She jumped up. She wanted to be there, standing right in front of him, looking sexy, seductive, alluring. Too late. He had made it to the living room. Worse than that, he was carrying a Chinese takeaway and a bottle of wine. He smelled — no, stank — of alcohol. Her disappointment was palpable, at least it should have been. Not to John, it seemed. He simply thrust the food into her hand.

"Take that while I open the wine."

"Take that?" She caught herself before she said it.

"Just have a little patience," she heard Take That singing in her head. She had had quite a lot of patience tonight. What's a little more? She took it, the food.

He practically ran into the kitchen and grabbed a corkscrew. Returning to the living room, he began to plunge it into the top of the bottle, before realising it was a screw-top. Now she was sure that he had one over the eight, or maybe eight over the eight. Firstly, John would never bring home a screw-top. That just wasn't how wine was meant to be bottled. And secondly, who needs a waiter's friend when you have a screw-top?

John flopped down on his favourite chair, bottle in hand, and unscrewed the top.

"Get two glasses, Josephine, tonight we're celebrating."

So much for the cooking, so much for the underwear, so much for the effort. The excitement was turning quickly to exasperation. She tried not to show it.

"What are you waiting for?"

That jolted her into action, but not the kind she was hoping for. She went to the dining room and grabbed two wine glasses from the table she had so lovingly set earlier. As she held them out in front of John, he poured the wine until they were half full. Leaving enough space to take in the aroma, as John always did before tasting. Except tonight it wasn't about the wine. He put down the bottle, took a glass, clinked Josephine's glass loudly and said:

115

"To new beginnings." He drank it all.

Josephine stood speechless, glass in hand.

"I got the job."

She was utterly confused. What job? What is he talking about? Am I that forgetful?

"I'm going to be Assistant Manager."

"But you were already promoted to Restaurant Manager."

"No, silly, forget about that. I'm talking Assistant Hotel Manager."

She wanted to participate in his enthusiasm. Say she was happy for him, that he was great, brilliant. But she still didn't know what he was talking about.

"Well done," she said, for the sake of saying something.

"Only thing," he began, "it means I'll be away from home, away from you a few nights a week."

"What? Why?"

"Well, I can't drive to and from Belfast every day, can I?"

"Belfast?"

"Yes, Belfast; that's where the Europa Hotel is."

"The Europa Hotel?"

"Where the job is."

Her head was reeling. She didn't want the wine. She wanted something stronger, another gin, a large one. She handed her wine glass to John. He took it. He had already refilled his own and drank every drop again. Another sure sign he was under the influence in a big way.

She went to the kitchen and poured herself a gin, an extra-large one with a little tonic.

She felt like asking him how this all came about, but reckoned tonight wasn't the night to do it. He was so excited, it would be a waste of time. Not her favourite waste of time. John decided he would celebrate with some music. He picked out a CD and put it on.

"Simply The Best" blasted out from the speakers. He began dancing around to it, looking at himself in the mirror that hung above the fireplace, the mirror he had insisted on buying and hanging there just because he had loved a Hammer Horror story involving an antique mirror that granted it's owner whatever they desired. With dire consequences. This mirror wasn't it, it wasn't even antique. A replica, a bad replica. But

John wanted it, and that's all that mattered.

Josephine needed a pee. While in the loo, she decided it best to remove the Ann Summers stuff. Tonight, was not going to be the night. And as for her food. Maybe tomorrow. The Chinese takeaway was still sitting there on the worktop. Would she try to get John to sit down and eat it? No. She felt betrayed, crushed. This was going to be such a good night. Now she just wanted to go to bed and sleep. No chance.

"Josephine!" He was looking for her. "Where are you, darling?"

"I'm here."

"Come and dance with me."

She would. She would dance with him. He was her husband, after all. And he wanted to dance. Funny thing is, she enjoyed dancing with him, even when he was in this state. They enjoyed dancing, together. And they did, to the tune of "Freebird". John loved that song. Played it often. Tonight, it has relevance, she thought. He would be leaving here tomorrow or whatever day he had decided he would take up his new position in Belfast. And although he wasn't leaving for good, she wouldn't know how many nights she would be without him, without a hand to hold. She thought they were equal partners in this marriage, all for one and one for all. Now it seems that she was just second in command. John had the last say. He would decide how this marriage would work. He would decide their future. He had decided their future. The future was here. He would be in Belfast when required and she would stay at home. She would be there when he decided to come home to her, waiting. There would be miss-you nights. And they would be the longest.

CHAPTER FIFTEEN
COME BACK AND STAY

"I was thinking I could get a job in Belfast."

John stopped eating his breakfast and looked at her, mouth open. She could see a chewed-up sausage on his tongue. It wasn't a pretty sight.

"What?" he said eventually.

She knew he had heard her. He just had a habit of saying "what?" when he was taken by surprise and didn't like what he was hearing. But Josephine was determined to have this conversation.

"So that we can be together every day, like a proper husband and wife."

He put down his knife and fork, smiled, reached across the table and took both her hands in his.

"Josephine. Dear Josephine. We are more than a husband and wife. We are soul-mates. We are the one for each other. We don't need to be conventional. I don't want us to be conventional."

The last part was spoken evenly but firmly. It made her think of that first morning of the honeymoon for the first time in as long as she could remember. She felt like he was telling her "no" in a way one would speak to a child asking for something in a hopeful way, rather than an expectant way. But this was going to be her only chance. So she responded.

"But I'm lonely here, and my job doesn't mean anything to me. You've always said what a crummy hospital it is and how the hospitals in Northern Ireland are so much better, so much more efficient. A new job would be a new challenge for me. And I would be paid in pounds, just like you. We would be better off."

He let go of her hands and sat back in his chair. He lifted his knife and fork. He still had some food on his breakfast plate.

"Just let me eat this."

For the next few minutes, she watched him eat. He never looked at her. She knew this wasn't going well. She now wished she hadn't even mentioned it. She was going to tell him something else, but now she daren't. She had applied for a job in the Belfast City Hospital and had been given a date for an interview. She was going to surprise him. She would ensure the interview was on a day John was at work so that they could have lunch together. And hopefully she would be successful. They could both live in Belfast. Surely there are apartments to rent. There was nothing tying them here. The house was rented and they could leave on giving one month's notice.

Her thoughts were interrupted by the sound of John putting his cutlery down on his plate. Correctly, naturally, at the 6.30 position, with the prongs of the fork pointing up. He was picking his teeth with the fingernail of his little finger and making fizzing noises as he tried to remove the bits of bacon from between them.

"Forget it," she felt like saying, "I was just being silly." She hesitated.

He got up and came around the table. He knelt down beside her, put his right hand on her shoulder, took her right hand in his left and looked into her eyes. She shuddered. She could feel her eyes welling up. She wanted to close them, but didn't, as he was gazing into them.

"Josephine," he spoke softly, "I know you're lonely. It won't always be like this. I won't always be in Belfast. Do you think I want to be an assistant manager for the rest of my life?

"No, Josephine. One day I'm going to have my own restaurant, we're going to have our own restaurant, and no one will tell us what to do."

She recalled how John had told her about this dream before, but she thought it was just that, a dream. Pie in the sky. Wow, she thought. Maybe he'll call his restaurant that. John was good at dreaming. But then she had dreamed of getting married as early as that first wonderful night. And it came true. So maybe John's restaurant isn't pie in the sky. Except, maybe, for the name. All the while she was thinking, trying to organise her thoughts, he was still kneeling there in front of her. He wasn't going to propose. He had already done that.

He kissed her on the forehead and began speaking without taking his mouth away.

"I really, really want to be here with you. Every minute of every day.

But for now, it's not possible. You going to Belfast wouldn't work. Even though I choose to work there, it's just another step on the ladder. It's not a place I would choose to live, that I would choose for us to live. For you to live. It's a city, and like any city it can be dangerous. There are lots of people. All sorts of people. No one knows anyone else. You would be alone, totally alone, while I'm at work."

That statement registered with her quickly. "But I am alone, totally alone, here," was all she could think. "What would be so different?"

"You wouldn't be safe there. I would be frightened that you might come to some harm. You're safe here. I know you're safe here, and that makes me happy. I would not be happy with you living in a city. In Belfast. I love coming home here, to you. Where we can relax, be alone together. Far away from Belfast, far away from my work. It's two different worlds. And this is the world I love, our world. No one would expect me to drive nearly a hundred miles to Belfast at the drop of a hat. If I lived there, if we lived there, they would feel free to call me into work any time, any day, any hour. Is that what you want? For our time together to be interrupted at every turn? Not to have our special times to ourselves?"

He stopped talking and laid his head on her breast. Not in a sexual way. Her natural reaction was to hold his head with her free hand. Without realising it, she was petting him.

Now she could no longer hold back the tears. But it wasn't bitter tears. He had melted her heart. Not for the first time. He lifted his head and brought his face close to hers. His eyes seemed glassy, but before she could see any tears, he put his head on her shoulder and hugged and held her. She could see her reflection in the glass of the oven door. Tears were streaming down her face.

She couldn't help but sing the words of "The Tracks Of My Tears" in her head.

Even though her tears had turned to tears of happiness — no, not happiness, tears of relief — she still couldn't smile. She had broached the subject with an expectation, a happy expectation, and her hopes and expectations had been dashed. In a diplomatic and loving way. John's way. What could she say? What could she do? Nothing.

"Let's go back to bed."

He still had hold of her hand as they made their way to the bedroom. The love-making swept it all away. She was feeling good again. She wouldn't go to that interview. She wouldn't think about moving to Belfast, ever again. She would remain here in their love nest. She was lying in the crook of his arm, head on his chest, listening to his heart. She felt comfortable, safe, loved. She didn't want to leave this place. Didn't want him to leave her. But he would. Tomorrow. But like Arnold Schwarzenegger, he would be back. And she would be waiting. They had vowed to be together forever, but that doesn't have to mean every day. After all, absence makes the heart grow fonder. Josephine would console herself with that thought until it was time for him to be back for good. She began humming to herself. The song?

"Come Back And Stay." For good.

CHAPTER SIXTEEN
HIT THE ROAD, JACK

Josephine didn't like the fact that John had to stay away from home, from her, several nights a week. But she did look forward to his days off. And he did arrange that he would have a free weekend at least once a month. Then he was ready to party. To go drinking and dancing. The house they had rented was in the town, just off the main road and next to a local hotel. It was a nice older house and within walking distance of Josephine's work. And across the main road and down the next street there was a nightclub. A party girl's dream location. Except Josephine had never been a party girl, until now. But only with John. Never alone. And when they partied, they partied hard. A few drinks, dinner, a bottle of wine between them, an after-dinner drink or two, and then off to the nightclub. And another few, or not so few drinks. But then home was just around the corner, or two.

Walking home from the nightclub became second nature, eyes closed most of the time, holding onto John. Not that he was sober. Far from it. But she trusted him and he always got her home in one piece. More than she could say for himself. One Christmas there was snow and frost. Their house was halfway up a steep street, quite a steep street. That's why she took her grandmother's advice and wore thick woollen socks on her feet until she got to the bottom of the hill and changed into her high heels, putting her wet socks in her handbag, in a re-sealable plastic bag. So that she would have them for going back up the hill. On that fateful night, John was incapable of guiding her home. So she had to take the lead. Isn't that what marriage is all about, give and take? Tonight, she was taking, taking charge. She hadn't much option, unless she wanted to leave him wandering the town until he sobered up. Never mind lost in France, he would be lost in Letterkenny. She put on her socks and they weaved their way home, she leading him, hand in hand, her shoes in the other. She was struggling somewhat as John was no lightweight, both in terms of his body mass and his drinking. Even after having too much in the restaurant, he had continued to drink himself silly. Josephine, whether she saw it coming or something in her psyche told her to sober up, decided not to have any drink at the nightclub. Despite her sobriety, she was losing the struggle to retain a hold on him, no matter how much she tried. When he began to go down, there was no stopping him. She felt his hand slip out of hers. And then a terrible thud. He was lying face down on the roadway. She wasn't too concerned, as he did fall down on occasion. Funnily enough, he would usually let go of her hand before he did, so as not to drag her down with him. That's true love. He protected her at all costs. Even to his own detriment. Tonight, it might not have been voluntary. She could usually hear him as he fell.

"Oops, I've done it again!" he would blurt out, before he started giggling to himself. It used to be "Fuck it", but she had asked him to please stop swearing. She never expected him to listen. It was a pleasant surprise, and quite funny the first time. This time was even more surprising. The sound of silence. He lay face down, motionless. Could he have fallen asleep that quickly? As she bent down to hear if he was breathing, she saw the blood begin to flow from his head. A pool of red quickly became visible in the pure white snow. She jumped back, landing heavily on her ass. It hurt.

"Fuck!" she thought. "My bum is wet, and cold and sore." It was. And she had sworn. But that wasn't the problem now.

"Shit, John's dead."

He wasn't. She heard a moan and then a giggle. And then, "Fuck, I fell."

She was still on her ass. As he raised his head, he was looking straight at her. He was staring. The blood was streaming down his face from the cut on his forehead. It was like one of those zombie movies. "Night Of The Living Dead." She felt frightened, but only momentarily. She very quickly noticed that his eyes were focused on one thing. Her legs were open and the hem of her short dress had fallen down around her thighs. She felt good. He still desired her.

He had the look. He rolled over and sat up. She took his hand, intending to help him up. Instead, he pulled her onto his lap and kissed her. Hard. She could feel he was excited. They couldn't do anything here, or could they? She pressed against him for a second. The sound of a police siren changed her mind.

They were only a hundred feet away from the main street. There was every chance someone would come along sooner rather than later. If that happened to be law enforcement, as they say in America, they would be nicked.

She stood up and took John by the hand. When he was this way, in the expectant state, he would follow her lead. He walked past her, turned and stopped. They stood face to face. He kissed her passionately. She moved past him and took him by the hand. He did it again. The passionate kiss. It wasn't far to the front door, but if they kept this up it would be daylight before they got there. When they did get there, he was alert enough to get the key in the door. He slammed it behind them. By the time they were halfway up the stairs, they were naked. Not naked and afraid, naked and excited. He didn't take his hands off her all the way to bed.

They woke up some time later, entwined. The sun was creeping through the open window. They were on top of the bed. She was on her back, he on his front. He had one hand between her legs, the other above his head. She felt happy. As she focused, she saw that his white pillow cover was almost completely red. The events of the night before came flooding back.

"John, John, John?" She was shouting louder and louder.

"When do you think I started wearing earplugs to bed?" he mumbled from where he lay.

That made her laugh. He sat up and looked at her.

"Well, this is a nice surprise. Breakfast in bed." There was a glint in his eye. The same glint that was there when he was raised from the dead the night before.

"Perhaps he should bang his head more often."

No sooner had the thought entered her mind, than he was on her again. He was still in the mood for love, regardless of what she supposed must be a thumping headache. Should that not put him off?

"Sorry, dear, I've got the worst headache; not tonight, or rather not this morning."

But it seemed to be having the opposite effect. And guess what? She didn't mind. She wanted it as much as he did. When it was all over, she reminded him that he had hit his head. He went and cleaned it up. It began to bleed all over again. He had to have stitches. He didn't care. He referred to it as "another battle wound in the war of life".

"I'm not sure you should be battling with the road too often," was her reply. He agreed.

"I don't think that's what Ray Charles meant when he sang 'Hit The Road, Jack'," she added.

They both laughed.

CHAPTER SEVENTEEN
BREAKING THE LAW

They didn't always go straight home from the nightclub. Sometimes they stopped in the hotel. They had gotten to know Joe, the night porter. For anyone who doesn't know what or who a night porter is, he's — and it's nearly always he — the one who has the unenviable position of re-admitting the drunk and incoherent late-night partying residents and serving them more alcohol, if they want it. Well, at least that's the way it was in that particular hotel. Even though they weren't supposed to be there, Joe had become a good friend, and good friends break the rules for each other, especially when John made it worth his while. On this night, there were quite a few in the late-night bar area. Around one table some men and women were playing cards. John decided that he wanted to join in. So they did. Josephine knew how to play poker, but not seriously. After a few games it became apparent that it was all just a bit of fun, but the drink had gone to John's head. He was becoming his own drunk antagonistic self, as some men seem to do. Well, let's not be sexist, some women, too.

"Let's make it interesting," he quipped, throwing down a twenty-euro note on the table.

They had been playing with coins before that.

"You're joking, mate," said one of the men. "Where do you think you are, Las Vegas?"

With that, a rather large girl in an orange top, who had been sitting at the table but not playing, began laughing.

John stood up, grabbed his twenty and putting it back in his pocket, flashed her the dirtiest look.

"I don't know what you're laughing at, you big fat ugly tangerine dream."

John went and sat at the bar. Although Josephine felt like apologising for his behaviour, she could feel that he was watching and listening. She wouldn't risk offending him in the mood he was in. Although he could be the most funny and compassionate person when sober, in drink he could be harsh and cruel, really cruel. Not in a physical way, but some of the things he would say, even to her, the love of his life, were unrepeatable. She simply got up and followed him. She did notice that the poor girl had begun to cry. As she sat down next to John, a tall, blond, chubby man returned from the toilet and sat at the table. He began to console the crying female. John was drinking another double brandy.

"Hey, Josephine, forget about those losers, and have a drink. Joseph, a double for Josephine, please."

He was nothing if not formal, even when drunk. To some people.

Before Josephine could warn John that the blond man was approaching, purposefully, a closed fist struck him on the side of his head, knocking him sideways into Josephine's lap. She was just able to steady him enough so that he didn't actually fall to the floor. The assailant simply turned around and went back to his table. For a moment she could see that John was lost for words. A silence descended on the bar. She wasn't sure whether that was because everyone was watching what happened or just that John had shut up. And that didn't happen often, not when he was out on the town.

"There's a first time for everything," they say.

This was it for John, at least as far as Josephine knew. He hadn't realised what had happened. Joe did. He saw it all, even though he was pouring Josephine's drink. It was still in his hand. He set it down in front of John, who was in the process of standing up.

"Don't," he said, grabbing John's wrist. "It's my job on the line."

Surprisingly, that seemed to stop John in his tracks. He actually did care about someone other than himself. When it suited him. Or maybe the punch on the head had knocked some sense into it. He sat down again and threw back Josephine's double brandy, in one go. She didn't know whether to laugh or cry. She wanted that drink. No, needed that drink. As if he was reading her mind, Joe put another double brandy down in front of her. She looked at him and smiled. He winked.

"That's the sign of a good barman," she thought. She took her drink, held it up so that Joe could see what she was doing, mouthed "thanks"

127

and drank, almost half of it. Joe feigned a shocked look.

Leaning over the bar, he whispered in her ear, "You should get him home."

"I was just thinking that," she whispered back.

John, who had since rested his head on the bar, sat up and, looking around, slurred, "Let's go home, and have a drink."

"This place is full of assholes tonight," he added, so that some people he wanted to could hear it.

"He probably isn't including himself in that statement," thought Josephine.

Josephine was relieved. She was worried that if she had made the suggestion he might have resisted, ordered another drink, put Joe in a position. Still, there was something she had to do.

"I just have to go to the toilet," she said, as she got up from her stool.

That was an excuse. She wanted to talk to Joe. Or rather, quiz Joe. To know who he was that had assaulted her husband. Even though he probably deserved it, she was affronted. No one does that to my husband, no matter how much of an ass he makes of himself. He's my asshole and if he needs chastising, I'll do it. Maybe the drink had gone to her head a little, or maybe, like they had agreed, they would stick together no matter what.

"So who is he, the fat bastard who hit John?"

Joe was shocked.

"Sorry for swearing. I'm sure it's not the first time you've heard a woman swear."

"It's the first time I've heard you swear."

"Sorry. I won't do it again. Has it changed your opinion of me?"

"No. Not at all. Let him cast the first stone and all that. We all do it. Why should I expect you not to do it?"

"So who is he?" she persisted.

"Nobody. He stays here from time to time. He's a travelling salesman."

"What does he drive?"

"Why?"

"No reason."

He knew she was lying. "You know I can't tell you that."

128

"Okay. What's his name?"

"I can't tell you that, either."

"Tell me something about him."

They were standing in the reception area. Joe went over to the guest book and opened it.

"I have to go check on the bar," he said. And he did. And there in the guest book was his name and the details of his vehicle. A white van.

Josephine went back to the bar, where Joe was clearing up and John was waiting.

"Let's go home and have that drink," she said.

And that's just what they did. They had a drink, and then another, and another. Until…

"John?"

"Yes?" He was polite now. He had forgotten it all. He had become a happy drunk.

"You know that man who punched you in the face tonight?"

There was no reply. She didn't expect one. She just wanted to get his attention.

"Well, I can see his van from here."

He looked at her blankly.

"I think we should teach him a lesson."

Josephine had recently watched "Beverly Hills Cop". Learned the banana up the exhaust pipe trick. She went to the kitchen. Luckily, there were some bananas. More than enough.

She ran across the road and stuck one up the exhaust. It disappeared.

"Surely that can't be right."

She ran back to the house for another. She decided to take them all, just in case.

She added another. It disappeared.

"Fuck it."

She put all five in the exhaust. They all disappeared. She made a mental note to buy bigger bananas, just in case she needed to do this again. But what now?

She ran back to the house.

"Sugar."

She had heard somewhere, sometime, of someone putting sugar in someone's fuel tank. The bag was almost empty. Nonetheless, she would try it. As she got to the door, John snatched it out of her hand.

"I don't think so."

She was surprised. He was the sociopath.

"Fun is fun, this is serious."

It didn't faze Josephine, not that night. She went back to the kitchen and grabbed the Fairy (washing-up liquid, that is). She ran out the door and squirted it all over the van, on the doors, on the locks, on the roof.

And then. She noticed that someone had cut the grass around the car park. It was just lying there, doing nothing, serving no purpose. It would now. She lifted bunches of it and threw it on top of the van. She kept on doing it.

"Well," she thought, "it's no longer just a boring white van."

They both stood back and looked. They laughed. They went home. Went to bed and fell asleep.

The next morning, Josephine woke early. She sat bolt upright with a start. She shook John vigorously.

"What the fuck?" he growled.

Josephine jumped out of bed and went to the window. She stood to the side of the window and gingerly pulled back the edge of the curtain. It had rained. And we all know what happens to Fairy liquid when you add water.

There in the car park was Mr Blond with the hotel manager. They were standing there motionless, just staring quizzically at an unexpected spectacle. There was no permanent damage to the van, no thanks to Josephine. But who would do such a thing?

"What are you looking at?" she heard John grunt from the bed.

"Come and see for yourself," Josephine said, as she gestured him over to the window.

John pulled back the curtain and looked out. They didn't see him, obviously, as he was stark naked. He laughed heartily.

"Fuck you, you ignorant twat," he shouted, as he stuck up his fingers in front of the window. Just as he did that, Josephine noticed Kathleen, their elderly neighbour, a retired nurse and widow, walking past their house. She must have heard John, because she looked up.

She pulled him away quickly. He staggered and fell back onto the bed. She just hoped that Kathleen hadn't seen him, or at least it was one of those moments when you say to yourself, "Did I just see what I thought I saw?" and decide you couldn't have. Hopefully, she hadn't heard him, lest she think he was referring to her.

"What did you do that for?" he growled, but not in a nasty way, more in a "I'm still drunk and stupid" way. He was. Both.

"Kathleen's out there. She just looked up."

"Well, it might have given her a thrill. I'm sure she hasn't had one in ages."

She ignored that comment.

"What if they call the Gardai?"

"Why, Josephine, are your fingerprints on the bananas? Surely you didn't leave teeth marks? You might be on 'CSI Letterkenny' next week."

She couldn't help but laugh.

"Do you think Joe's going to finger us? Besides, he's probably gone home at this stage."

"Hopefully he saw your handiwork. It'll give him another story to tell his customers."

Typical of John. So blasé. No one will ever catch him out in anything. He has an answer for everything.

"Why would I do that to someone's vehicle? That's more like something some young scoundrels would get up to."

They would believe him. He has that sort of self-confidence about him. No one would doubt him. He could put on the innocent little boy act when he wanted to.

They stayed at home that morning. It was Saturday. Josephine kept expecting a knock on the door. It didn't come. She never saw the van leave. She did, however, see two members of staff wash it down with buckets of water. She wondered what happened to the bananas. Were they still there, frying with every mile, or were they ejected in front of some unsuspecting motorists who were wondering whether a fruit and vegetable van had sprung a leak?

She would never know. One thing's for sure, there would be no banana split for dessert that day.

CHAPTER EIGHTEEN
MR SOFT

Josephine had been invited to a wedding. A colleague at work. John hated weddings. She decided she would put the invitation in the fire without even telling him. She had taken it out of her handbag in the bedroom and forgot about it.

"What's this?" John asked the next morning, while she was still half asleep.

She lifted her head and looked at him.

"Oh! It's a wedding invitation. A girl from work. I meant to put it in the fire."

He stopped reading it and stood looking at her.

"You don't like weddings. I knew you wouldn't want to go."

"I might," was his immediate reply.

She was taken aback. She pinched herself in the ass. No. She wasn't dreaming.

"In fact, we will go."

It wasn't a suggestion. He didn't ask if she wanted to go. It was typical of John. He had decided. There and then. Just as he had decided he was taking the job in Belfast, the job he had applied for and didn't tell her. That didn't mean he wouldn't change his mind. He often did. He had stolen a woman's prerogative in that regard. This time he didn't. He even suggested she get something new to wear. She wondered if he, John, had been whisked off to Stepford and replaced with the perfect husband.

One thing bothered her, though. John's drinking had become a problem. Something, she now realised, that went with the job. It was fun when they drank together, even if they over-indulged. But that was occasional. It's not fun when one person does it and does it almost every night. That person being John. And a wedding meant alcohol. Beer, whiskey, brandy, champagne. If John was in the mood, he would get through it all.

When the day came, it all went well, far better than she expected. John was the perfect gentleman. He dressed all in black. He always refused to wear a suit outside of work. He looked as he did on the first night they met. She had dressed in black and white. She had to admit that they cut a dash as a couple. John was charming to everyone. He danced with her. In fact, he barely let her relax. They had a ball.

After the meal, they had sat with some of her colleagues from work in the smoking area, even though neither of them smoked. But since smoking was banned in licensed premises, the smoking area had become a place for people to congregate, smokers and non-smokers.

"I wanna go where the people go," thought Josephine. It's so true. Why else would non-smokers be here in the smoking area?

A conversation got up among the men about Viagra.

"I get mine on a three-monthly prescription and sell them for €50 a time" said one guy.

"I use mine, all four of them," said another.

"You only get four a month?" Josephine asked.

"Yes, that's all you're allowed on your prescription," was the answer.

"I'd need more than that," laughed John. "If I needed them, that is."

He did. Need them. Things in the bedroom had been a bit flat recently. Or should that be flaccid.

"It doesn't work like that. You don't have to take it every time. You only have to take it once a week."

"Even if you're not having sex?" asked Josephine.

"Yes, of course."

"But can you go out after you've taken it, you know, with the effect and all."

Everyone laughed. Except John. He was just as clueless as she was.

Josephine felt so stupid. She could feel her face turning red. She felt the hand of a colleague on her shoulder.

"It doesn't work instantly. It's like putting yeast in your bread: you have to add some heat, some stimulation, let it do its work," he whispered privately in her ear.

"Yeast, heat, stimulation?" What was he talking about? The penny dropped.

"Oh! To make it rise."

"You got it," he replied, before walking away.

She felt as if everyone was looking at her, except John. When she looked at him, she could see that he was taking it all in. She looked for signs of anger or jealousy in his face. There were none, and she would know. It was more a look of enlightenment. With everyone else the conversation had moved on.

Both her and John had finished their drinks, so they decided to return to the function room. John went to the bar and refreshed their drinks. He continued drinking Guinness. No spirits, no cocktails. They had another dance and returned to their table. They were on their own now. Everyone else who had been at the table had drifted away, talking to other people, in the smoking area or in the bar. John suggested they go home. Josephine acquiesced, as she always did. Except this time she was happy to. It had been a long day and even though it had been an enjoyable one, she did feel tired. John called a taxi and said he had to go to the toilet. He told her to go outside and keep a lookout. Other people were leaving, and even though the taxi was booked, it was not uncommon for taxi drivers to take the first person who jumped into their car.

As the taxi pulled up, John appeared at her side and, taking her hand, opened the back door for her. He was being a true gentleman, as he had been on that first night. He even tipped the driver. When they got home, Josephine needed a drink. Water. Lots of it. She wasn't used to drinking that much and that long. John, to her surprise, went straight to the bedroom.

"What?" she thought.

She expected him to go to the living room, after pouring himself a large Jack Daniels, and put on some music. Turn it up loud. Look at himself in his bad replica antique mirror.

Not only would John look in his mirror, he would talk to it, or maybe it was himself he was talking to. It was hard to tell. Josephine only ever watched him through the glass in the living room door, so she wasn't privy to the conversation. She tried to imagine it.

"Mirror, mirror on the wall, who is the handsomest, cleverest, funniest of them all?"

And the answer is. Well, he didn't really expect the mirror to answer, did he?

But tonight the mirror would be lonely. He stayed in the bedroom. But why? He hadn't seemed tired. In fact, he was still buzzing. She felt somewhat uneasy. All this was too good to be true. But what was she supposed to do? She tiptoed into the bedroom. He was already tucked up in bed, covered from head to toe, or rather neck to toe. All she could see was his head. As she looked at him, his face seemed to be glowing. The only thing lighting the room was the mood light he had purchased the week before. It sat on the bedside table. It changed colours according to your preference. John had chosen red.

"Red light spells danger." Isn't that what Billy Ocean told us?

Well, tonight there was double danger. John's face was as red as, if not redder, than the mood light.

The covers on her side of the bed were pulled back.

"Take off your clothes," he said in a commanding voice. She was used to taking commands, but tonight she welcomed it.

"Leave the stockings on."

She did. Although sometimes it scared her, his masterful tone on this occasion was making her tingle. He patted the bed with his hand. She moved to the bed and sidled in beside him.

They kissed. He was hot, hotter than he had ever been. In a purely physical sense, that is.

Especially his face. It almost burned her skin. He took her hand and guided it to his groin. He wasn't yet ready, although not completely soft. She tried to encourage it. It wasn't happening. She took his hand and placed it on her breast. He was stroking her stockinged leg with his other hand. He was moving up through the gears now, but not quite at maximum overdrive. She rolled over on her back and allowed him to get on top of her. She opened her legs. He began to press himself against her. She could feel him, his penis, pressing against her. She looked at him. He was getting redder. She was afraid he was going to have a heart attack or a stroke. How would that pan out?

"911, what's your emergency?"

"Well, um, my husband's on top of me. I think he's dead."

"How did he die?"

Naturally, I think."

135

"Is he breathing?"

"Well, he was a while ago, quite heavily."

"What about now?"

"He's just heavy, really heavy."

"Can you check his pulse?"

"No. He's on top of me."

"There's an ambulance on its way."

"Is it all right if I push him off? Only he might fall on the floor. I don't want anyone to see me like this."

"Well, madam, we do recommend that you wait for the emergency services."

"Does that mean people are going to see me naked?"

"I'm sorry, madam, I can't answer that."

"So they're going to see me naked?"

"I think you should concentrate on your husband, madam."

"It's hard not to, but if he stays where he is much longer, I might have to toss him off."

"Excuse me, madam, are you saying you haven't tossed him off yet?"

Her thoughts were interrupted by John's swearing.

"Fuck it, it didn't work." He hadn't managed to get fully erect, to penetrate her.

He rolled over on to his own side of the bed. She lay there, afraid to ask what went wrong. He was upset, really upset. Not only had he not penetrated her, he hadn't orgasmed. For John, this was a massive failure. He prided himself on being a stud. Even though it was all in his own mind. If he was satisfied with his performance, then she obviously had to have had a good time also. Tonight he was far from satisfied. As was she. His ego was shrinking along with his penis. He got out of bed and put on his casuals, which he always kept nearby. This was it, time to get out the Jack Daniels bottle and play some music. She decided to leave him to it. It was his way of winding down. Not that he had to wind down far tonight. Naughty, naughty Josephine. He would pour himself a generous Jack Daniels, put on some music from his sizeable CD collection, relax in his recliner for a while until his glass was empty, before pouring himself another. Then he would get up, change the CD, drink a little, dance a little and stand before his mirror, glass in hand, bottle placed strategically on the mantelpiece for him to return to again and again, looking at himself in the mirror every time. Or maybe he really believed this was the mirror and he was making wishes. God knows what he was wishing for? Whatever it was, it wouldn't work. She had tried it, the mirror. She wished John would give up the job in Belfast and move home, that they would be together every day and every night. It didn't work.

She turned over and went to sleep. Would he be back before morning? Unlikely.

In the morning, she got out of bed and put on her pyjamas. It was Sunday. Before going to the kitchen for her morning coffee, she looked in on him. He was asleep on his recliner.

She decided to make him breakfast. As she cooked the tomatoes, it reminded her of the colour of his face the night before. It was a strange night. Before she went to sleep, she had heard the music from the living room. "Too Hard To Handle" by the Black Crowes. Ironic. She wouldn't tell him.

When the breakfast was ready and plated, she went and shook him gently. He awoke. He looked up at her and smiled. Obviously, it was all forgotten.

"Breakfast?" she said in a friendly tone.

"Thanks," he replied. "I'm starving."

They sat together at the kitchen table. He ate like a savage. His body needed something to soak up all the alcohol. He finished his breakfast — sausage, bacon, eggs, black pudding, fried bread, tomatoes, mushrooms and toast — in extra quick time.

"What happened last night?"

This question took her by surprise. He normally didn't ask. Pretended he remembered everything.

"Don't you remember?"

"Would I be asking if I remembered?" he replied sarcastically.

Now she had to decide what to tell him and what not to tell him.

"We came home and had sex."

"Was it good?"

It wasn't. For either of them, apparently. But it was one of those times when a little white lie was the lesser of two evils.

"As always." That sounded weak. "You were insatiable," she added quickly.

"Wow. I can't even remember. It really works."

She caught his eye as he looked up at her with a glint.

"The Viagra. I dropped one," he said, as if talking about ecstasy or some such thing.

That threw her. It was on the tip of her tongue to say, "What Viagra?" She took a deep breath and bit her tongue.

"I didn't realise it would be that good. I'm going to get some more. Watch out, babe."

She couldn't bear to tell him. But what if he's sober next time? It might be different. Hopefully. Brewer's droop might have played a part. She'd have to wait and see. Red face or no red face? "Too Hard To Handle" or "Mr Soft"?

"Life is full of ups and downs." That thought did make her chuckle.

CHAPTER NINETEEN
THE THRILL IS GONE

Although Josephine had heard people talk of how their marriage had gone stale, that the excitement had disappeared, she never thought it would happen to her, and certainly not after less than six months. But then John had disappeared very quickly, disappeared off to Belfast. And when he was home he was more interested in eating and drinking than sex. So much so that he had put on weight, a substantial amount of weight. He wasn't the same slim figure that had greeted her that first night. If she had seen him as he is now, she might well have sent him another Dear John letter very quickly. And it wouldn't be asking for a second date. She could imagine them sitting side by side on the Channel 4 programme "First Dates" and being asked if they wanted to see each other again. She would be diplomatic, of course, but would have to be honest.

"You were great company and I had a good time, but I don't feel any connection."

But would she really have blown him off if he looked as he does now on that first night? Blown off the blown-up John? After all, at that stage they already had a connection, had formed a bond. She didn't like to think that she was shallow, that looks were all that mattered. They weren't. Not to her. But her current thinking was tainted by how the relationship had panned out. She still couldn't get over how or why John had to take that job in Belfast. And no matter how much she tried, she couldn't convince him to move home. He was sticking to the plan. His plan.

Each of those mornings she awoke alone in her bed, when John remained in Belfast, her mother's words echoed in her head.

"I've made my bed." That was her mother's answer to why her life was as it was. As if that one decision in life determined everything thereafter and there was nothing that could change that. But Josephine didn't believe in her mother's defeatist attitude. Things can change, things can always change. It just takes the will and determination. And she had both.

She didn't want to go on feeling hopeless. She wanted to get it back. The excitement, the thrill. They needed to reconnect. And the best way to reconnect for a man and his wife is through sex. Isn't it? She would have another try at seducing him. She hoped it wouldn't work out like the night he disclosed his new job. That was a disaster.

A little better planning was needed. She would ensure that John knew there was a treat waiting for him, a special treat. And that it was nothing to do with confectionery, or with food. She didn't believe that it truly was the way to a man's heart. The way to a man's heart attack, maybe. She would find a better way, a more healthy way. Sexercise. For two. It didn't have to be today or tomorrow, but soon. She had disposed of the Ann Summers underwear. Burned it when John wasn't there. Why? She wasn't sure why. Embarrassment, disappointment, uncertainty? Would John have liked it, or would he have thought she looked slutty? She had never asked him what he preferred her to wear in bed. For special occasions, that is. And he had never told her. One thing she did know. John liked stockings, the feel of them. She actually found him taking some out of her drawer one night. He was sitting naked on the edge of the bed, running them through his hands. She could swear he was about to put them on if she hadn't accidentally interrupted him. He jumped up and pretended he was taking them out for her to put on. There and then. He was excited. They had sex. He never mentioned it again, nor did she. She wished she had. She wouldn't have minded if he wanted to wear them if they turned him on. If she was sure that was his intention, she would even encourage him. Maybe she should buy a few pairs. They could both wear them. That is, if it was only a sexual thing. John wasn't a transvestite. Well, as far as she knew. She had an awful thought.

"What if he's parading around Belfast dressed as a woman?"

No. She couldn't imagine it. He didn't shave his legs. And boy, were they hairy. That thought sort of changed her mind about the stockings. How would they look? But then did that matter? It was just the two of them. And she certainly didn't want him to shave his legs. Even though she didn't mind him having a feminine side, she didn't want it to extend to John looking feminine. She liked a man to be a man. And to act like a man, especially in the bedroom. She remembered once when she was single, a guy had asked her to dance and began talking about how nice it must be for her to be able to wear a dress.

"It must be nice wearing a dress, feeling the cool air rising up and circulating around your body underneath it."

She wasn't sure whether he wanted to change clothes or what. Needless to say, she didn't save the last dance for him.

Back to the plan. See-through underwear incinerated, she chose a basque and stockings. Black, of course. Back to black. She loved Amy Winehouse. Who doesn't?

Father's Day was coming up. That would be appropriate. Maybe their new-found passion would lead them to starting a family. Josephine still hoped for a child. But John still wasn't ready. It didn't fit with his master plan. Children cost money, and all their money had to be reserved for John's restaurant, a proper restaurant with proper food. No nouvelle cuisine, no two peas on a plate — proper food, proper portions.

One of the nurses at the hospital confessed to her that she had put a hole in her husband's condom in order to conceive her second child, but Josephine just couldn't do that. It was dishonest. And risky. John just might not believe that he was the father. Then the shit would hit the fan. Not only would John not embrace his role as a parent, he would disown his child and his wife. Of that she was sure. He always told her that truth and honesty were the cornerstones of a good marriage, a lasting marriage.

John would be home that night at eight. He would be staying in Belfast for the previous four nights. Let's hope that absence does make the heart grow fonder and the fire of passion glow brighter. She impressed herself with her poetic thoughts. He would be off the following day, Saturday, and the following day, Sunday. Father's Day. They could stay in bed, and who knows what might happen.

She seized her opportunity on the Monday morning. She had lain awake for an hour or more. John was still asleep. As she lay looking at him, she realised how much she was still in love with him, despite her unhappiness at her situation. Her mind was wandering back to all the good times, the happy times. The alarm hadn't broken the spell yet. She didn't want it to. It would spoil her moment. He would wake with a start, realise he had to get ready for work and jump out of bed. Instead, she turned the alarm off and shook him gently ten minutes early.

"Let's do something special this weekend. We haven't done anything for ages. I miss you. I really miss you."

He hugged her.

"I'm sorry, Josephine. I know I've neglected you. I'm just so focused on the future, our future. But I do love you. You're my everything."

"You are everything," he sang softly in her ear. That gave her little thrills. His breath as he sang tickled her earlobe. But in a good way. It didn't matter that he wasn't in tune. They were back in tune, and that's what mattered.

"Will you be home on time on Friday night? Please."

"I promise."

She leaned her head into his chest. She wanted to stay there, stay this way, as long as she could. But she could see the clock. It was 6.30. He had to get on the road. Leave her again.

She felt like singing to him. "Stay With Me."

But he wouldn't. He wouldn't let them down, his employers. He was the consummate professional. And besides, he needed the job, the money. It takes capital to start a restaurant; you can't do it on a shoestring. And according to John, the more he worked, the more he could save.

He kissed her gently on the forehead and moved away, out of the bed and into the shower.

She got up and went to the kitchen to make his breakfast. She wanted to look after him, to care for him. She made a bacon sandwich, even though she thought he should be cutting down, eating more healthy food. But today wasn't the day to broach the subject. Everything between them had to remain positive. For their marriage to be positively charged. And for the weekend to be sexually charged, as planned. This wasn't just a case, as her mother told her, of giving him what he wants. She was going to give him far more than that, show him that she was good in the bedroom, good enough to not only make him feel excited, but make him feel loved, make him feel wanted, all at the same time. Show him what he was missing by being away from home so much. That the thrill is here.

It was time to get ready for work. John had long gone, having devoured his bacon sandwich and downed his morning coffee. A happy camper. Not as happy as he would be this Friday night. And if everything went as planned, not as happy as she would be.

She sang "Happy" to herself as she showered and got ready for work. All her misgivings, all her fear and disillusion had evaporated. She was back on cloud nine.

It was Monday, but she had Friday on her mind as she walked; no, not walked, sprang, to work. In work she had a sense of déjà vu. The day she had received John's letter. The day she couldn't wait to get home. If this is how she is on Monday, what will she be like on Friday? God, she might even have to resort to wearing Tena Ladies, but not for the usual reasons, if you get the gist. Her bladder was still working efficiently. But her imagination and expectation were working overtime.

She wondered if John was feeling the same. But wait, it's different for men.

"If he's as excited as I am, it's going to show. That's not going to go down well with customers."

She burst out laughing.

"I hope that it doesn't need to go down."

She had to curtail her thoughts again. She had reached the hospital. Better concentrate on work. And she tried.

But working in a hospital, there was always gossip. Who's sleeping with whom? That's putting it politely. And sometimes the gossip gets graphic. Not what Josephine wanted to hear this week. She had to excuse herself on occasion. It wasn't the thought of other people doing it. It was that the very mention of sex made her think of the weekend. And it seemed that there was more talk of it this week than at any other time she could remember. Did all her colleagues know what she was planning? How could they? Had she let it slip? Certainly not. She would never divulge such intimate details, no matter what other people divulged to her.

On Friday, she didn't leave work right on time. She left an hour early. She had arranged it with Sally. If anyone asked where she was, she had an appointment. She did. A very special appointment with her husband. And he with her. She was on her way home to make it a night to remember.

CHAPTER TWENTY
WHERE DID OUR LOVE GO?

Not only had Josephine left work early that Friday, but she rushed home, even faster than that day she had received his first letter. So fast that she almost fell flat on her face when she opened the front door. That would have put a spanner in the works. Unless John found black eyes and a swollen nose a turn on.

"Black eyes." She didn't need them, not tonight.

Luckily, she was still holding the key which was still in the lock, so that she simply swung on the door, swivelled and hit her ass on the wall. Although it hurt, she would suffer the pain and concentrate on the ecstasy.

There was going to be no dinner, no food, no distractions. They could send for a take-away afterwards if John was hungry. He certainly wouldn't be hungry for love, not if things go to plan. So now all she had to get ready was herself. And the bedroom, of course. She wanted him to know she had gone to a lot of trouble, that she still wanted to please him, that this part of their relationship, their marriage, was still important to her. She still had the red light-up hearts which she pinned across the headboard. She had placed the mood lamp on the bedside cabinet. It would give the room a nice glow. The bed sheets and duvet cover had been laundered not once, but twice. They would feel and smell fresh and inviting, but not as inviting as Josephine. She had showered after work and longer than usual, washed and blow-dried her hair and sprayed herself and the pillows with perfume. Angel by Thierry Mugler. She loved it. Smelled like chocolate and vanilla. Appropriate, she thought, as John's passion was food. But not tonight; tonight, he would be saving all his passion for her. She would be his sole object of desire. And she didn't want to disappoint.

While showering, she noticed the beginning of a bruise on her buttock, so she applied some concealer. She really didn't want to start explaining it to John; no distractions, nothing to spoil or detract from the mood. Looking in the mirror, she was unsure as to whether she had put on weight or if her ass was beginning to swell. Probably a little swelling, she concluded. Now it was time to don the sexy stuff. Looking in the mirror, she no longer felt any insecurities. She was looking hot. She couldn't wait for John to see her. Then she would be feeling hot and hopefully so would he. She slipped on a small black dress that he could remove for her. The same little black dress she had worn that first wonderful night.

"Tonight's the night," she sang over and over to herself, remembering when the ring on her finger had fallen from that fortune cookie.

It was all coming together nicely. She put on some appropriate music.

"I'm so excited," sang the Pointer Sisters.

"The Pointer Sisters? It'll be something that'll be pointing tonight when John gets a load of this," she laughed, pointing at herself with both index fingers.

Time was marching on. Time for the final flourish.

She had bought some red tissue paper and using skills learned from school art class, fashioned loads and loads of rose-petal shapes from it. She laid a trail of these from behind the front door all the way up the stairs and into the bedroom. She would wait for him on the bed with the champagne, two glasses and some strawberries, just in case he was peckish. Nothing to do with kinky sex or anything. Well, who knows? They say variety is the spice of life. And she had sprinkled some black pepper on the strawberries. She had read it made them more tasty. But not too much, she hoped, that they would take his breath away. She wanted to do that.

The door would be closed and as he opened it she would be lying seductively on the bed. She practised, watching herself in the mirror. Should she pout? The mirror told her no. Better just to lie with her head resting on her hand, flashing her baby blues as he opened the door. That worked, she thought. It was approaching the time, and her heart was beating faster as she sat on the edge of the bed. The house was silent, so she would hear his key in the door. As she sat waiting, anticipating, she remembered something. She hadn't switched off her mobile phone. Not that anyone was going to call her. No one ever did, except John and some random people doing surveys for who knows what, at random times. Just her luck that she would get one tonight at the wrong time.

Someone wanting to know if she has bladder problems, if she uses Tena Ladies. Or maybe wanting to know how often her and her husband have sex. She would have to tell them that she was having it right now and that her husband wasn't particularly pleased that they had called.

"My husband says fuck off and stick your Tena Ladies."

Not how she wanted it to go. So best to turn it off. It was on the dressing table in her handbag. She leapt up and just as she got to the bag, it rang. The ring tone "I'm your man".

It was John. Her heart sank. Was he going to be late, even though he promised not to be. He was going to ruin everything. Why else would he be calling? He never called on his way home. Maybe he had broken down. Hopefully nothing bad had happened to him.

She answered.

"Josephine, it's me," he said, stating the obvious. "I'm sorry, I'm not going to make it tonight."

"No, no, no, no!" she almost said out loud.

She felt weak at the knees, and not for the right reason. She fell back on her ass on the bedroom floor and let out an "ouch".

"Josephine, are you okay?"

She wondered how to answer that. She was and she wasn't.

"Josephine," John shouted. There was a hint of panic in his voice. Should she stay quiet and let him rush home to her aid? Would he be so glad to find that she was all right, take her in his arms and make mad passionate love to her? Wishful thinking, Josephine. He would just be furious that he had to come all the way from Belfast to find that he had been fooled. He would drive all the way back there and then, just to spite her.

"I'm fine, John. Just a little let down." That pun wasn't intentional. She wasn't laughing.

She didn't feel like laughing. She felt like crying.

"I just can't get away; there's important guests staying, real important guests, and I have to be here in case they want food tonight and I have to be here first thing for breakfast. It can't be helped. I'll make it up to you, I promise."

She felt like telling him to stick his promises. You mean to tell me he didn't know this on Monday morning. Either that or he's making an excuse. A bad excuse. Maybe, just maybe, he's saving all his love for someone else.

"Josephine," he said softly, "I love you." But not enough, John, not enough.

"I love you, too," she replied weakly.

"I'll be home tomorrow night. We'll go for a Chinese," as if that makes it all right. No, John, tonight would have made it all right.

"See you then, gotta go," and he did. Go wherever he was going, wherever he had planned to go long before Josephine had hatched her plan for tonight. He forgets that I've got to know him well, very well, too well. Sometimes it's better not to know too much.

"Well, there's one consolation, the one thing she was trying to get him away from: food and drink. Strawberries and champagne.

If she were of the mind, she could go on the internet, talk to people, post some selfies.

"Hot Or Not," or some such site. Maybe there's a man nearby who might appreciate the effort she went to. She could send him a message.

"Come on over."

Instead, she would probably just lay in bed, eat her strawberries, drink her champagne and sing,

"All by myself."

CHAPTER TWENTY-ONE
PICTURE THIS

Once in a while, John did come home between shifts instead of staying in Belfast for the night, those nights when he was finished at eight and wasn't due to work until eight the next night. Then he just wanted to eat, drink and watch television. Problem was, he never knew what he wanted to eat, or rather, had forgotten what he had said he wanted to eat before he took himself off to work that morning.

"What's for dinner, then?" he would ask, as soon as he was in the door.

Josephine used to remind him what he had said he wanted that morning, but he rarely wanted it when he came home.

"I've changed my mind. Is there nothing else in the house? I'll just have to order a take-away. You can eat that."

So she decided to adapt. She would buy the ingredients for what he had said he wanted, and if there were two moons in the sky and he wanted the same thing when he came home, she would go into the kitchen and cook it while he busied himself getting shitfaced. He was now drinking excessively, drinking himself into a stupor at every opportunity. His way of coping with the fact that his plan wasn't coming together quickly enough. The end, or rather the beginning, wasn't in sight. That and, as he often said, "All work and no play, makes John a dull boy." He was wrong: he wasn't a dull boy, he was an angry man, a very angry man.

This night she had decided to take a chance. He always loved her spaghetti bolognese, told her it was the best he ever tasted. Complimented her every time on her cooking skills. She should have been born Italian.

"Just like Mama used to make," he would say in his best, not so good, Italian accent. But then he learned it from Super Mario Bros.

"What's your fancy?" she said, trying to seem as accommodating as possible.

"Surprise me." He was throwing down the gauntlet. The only way she could genuinely surprise him would be to stick something up his self-entitled ass. Maybe that wouldn't surprise him either. She long suspected he was cheating on her, but sometimes wondered if it was with a woman or with a man. Stranger things have happened. As John was staying in Belfast at least three nights a week, she took to reading to pass the time. Not intellectual reading. Not Shakespeare. She had enough tragedy in her life. Trash. Those weekly magazines with true-life stories where mothers slept with their daughters' boyfriends or husbands left their wife for another man. She actually knew of a local woman who left her husband and seven children for another woman.

Then she remembered how he had changed. What self-respecting gay man would put up with such an asshole? Oops. That's something she shouldn't express about her husband, even to herself. But he was an asshole, even though he could be a nice asshole when he wanted to. Not that she had ever looked closely at that part of him. Now she was being ridiculous. Then that was just how she was. Random thoughts just came to her, more so when she was nervous or angry. And she was both.

"I'll be in the living room," he said, taking his glass and bottle of Jack Daniels with him.

As soon as he left the kitchen, Josephine poured herself a glass of wine and drank it, before pouring herself another. It was now the only way she could cope. She would have to open another bottle and take it to the living room before serving the food. John would be there, changing channels constantly, watching no more than a few seconds of each one. How he knew what the hell he was watching was beyond her. Fleeting images. He rarely reacted, except when Gordon Ramsay appeared.

"Gordon fucking Ramsay. Who the fuck does he think he is? Fucking asshole."

And so, to the next channel, and the next one, until it came around again to Gordon Ramsay.

"Gordon fucking Ramsay. Who the fuck does he think he is? Fucking asshole."

"It's Groundhog Day, or rather Groundhog Night," thought Josephine. Not just for him, but for her. She put her head around the living room door.

"Will it be tonight?"

He was nothing if not sarcastic. She decided to play him at his own game.

"Have another drink, why don't you. I'll be back with the food."

She closed the door behind her quickly before he could respond.

That would annoy him. He liked to have the last word. She would have to return with the food quickly. Otherwise he would appear in the kitchen with a reply to her last comment. He would be getting fed up slating Gordon Ramsay. She quickly plated up and brought a freshly opened bottle of wine and two glasses to the living room. He had now decided to actually watch something. "Fawlty Towers. Gourmet Night."

"Hope he isn't expecting duck," Josephine sniggered to herself. He won't be getting it. Neither did the guests at Fawlty Towers. He was laughing to himself. But then he loved Fawlty Towers. It was one of the programmes they could watch together and enjoy. They both got it. Maybe this night wouldn't be so bad after all. She put the wine and glasses on the coffee table. He looked at her, then at the bottle and smiled.

"Pinot Noir. Good choice, Jo." He called her Jo sometimes. Usually when he was in a good mood. He reached out. She went over and took his hand. They kissed, not passionately, just a soft touch of the lips. He gently let go of her hand. She was chuffed. She wasn't expecting this. She retreated to the kitchen to get the food. She was smiling inwardly. She had relaxed. She thought John had, too. She remembered the open bottle of wine, put the cork back in it and hid it under the sink. John was bound to come into the kitchen at some point. She didn't want anything to spoil the mood. He wouldn't approve of her helping herself to a glass of wine without sharing, never mind two or three glasses.

She plated the food and took them to the living room. John was still laughing at Basil Fawlty. He was explaining that "Duck Surprise" was the duck without oranges or cherries."

"Good," she thought, "he's still in a good mood." Except she noticed the bottle of Jack Daniels was well on its way to being depleted. Not a good sign. She hoped he was hungry, hungry enough that he would appreciate what she had made him. Yes, it had been one of his favourites and he had told her that hers was the best, but all that had changed. Nothing was as it had been when they were in love. No, not when they were in love. When she thought he was in love with her. When she was in love with him. Was that a "*faux pas*"? Was her love for him in the past? She didn't know. To be honest with herself, she cared less. Like tonight, it was just a case of "let's get through this". She knew that wasn't right, wasn't enough. But like a lot of people, she didn't know what to do, how to change it.

As she put down the plates, she felt his stare. Not at her, at the food. He had stopped laughing. She felt a change in his attitude, his demeanour. She was so tuned in to him that she could detect the least hint of displeasure. She really wanted to go back to the kitchen, retrieve that bottle of wine and finish it. She noticed that John had already poured the Pinot Noir. So she lifted hers and took a mouthful, a good mouthful. That was a mistake.

"Not waiting for me, then?"

"Sorry."

"Worried about something?"

"No."

"You should be. This doesn't look at all appetising. But seeing as Gordon Ramsay is able to taste everything no matter how shit it looks, I'll do the same."

She felt like running out of the room, running out of the house, running away from the situation, from John, from everything, and keep on running.

But she knew she wouldn't, couldn't. Instead, she would just stand and wait for her master's voice, his critique. It wasn't going to be good. That was obvious. She felt like taking another drink of wine, what was left in her glass. She wouldn't dare.

He took up his plate. Looked at it with disdain. Sniffed it longer than was necessary. Put it down in front of him, took his fork, wound some spaghetti around it and put it in his mouth. He pulled a horrible face, a more horrible one, if that were possible, but still swallowed it. He took his fork and smashed it down on the plate, causing the sauce to splash all over himself.

"Fuck!" he swore, as he lifted the plate and, turning to Josephine, fired it in her direction. She closed her eyes, but didn't move. She had become used to him throwing stuff. Nothing had ever struck her. It was the same tonight. The plate flew past her head and smashed against the wall above the fireplace, narrowly missing the mirror that John loved so much. That might not have been unintentional. John was still blatantly aware of what he was doing, even when out of his head on alcohol. She had never known anyone who could be so precise after a bottle of Jack Daniels. He could throw things, usually his glass — empty, of course — and not break or damage anything, except the glass. But they were dispensable. As long as they hit something harder, usually the wall, all was good in John's world. The true sign of a sociopath. He only breaks what he wants to break. Hence, he missed the mirror.

"No seven years bad luck for John, then."

"Did that mean they would stay together or that they would separate?" John had said he wished he had never married her. So if his luck was going to hold out, they would separate. So her luck would improve accordingly.

Her thoughts were interrupted by his maniacal laughing. He was pointing at the wall above the fireplace, where strings of spaghetti and red sauce were running down. He found it funny.

Hilariously funny, it seemed. Josephine turned around and looked. She couldn't stifle her own laugh. In some perverted way, John's actions had cut through the uncomfortable atmosphere.

"We should frame it," he said between giggles.

She knew what he meant. It was beginning to resemble something. She wasn't sure what. It was just like those pieces of modern art where people ask you what you see: do you not see the tiger, the lion, the woman, the face of Jesus, or whatever?

"Oh. My. God. It is," she thought. "The face of Jesus in the spaghetti, complete with crown of thorns and the blood running down his face."

"Not so much a Botticelli as a Vermicelli," she said.

That set them both off. They couldn't stop laughing. John stood up and came to her. They embraced, both shuddering with laughter. This was what she wanted, what she craved. Closeness, togetherness.

"Let's stay together," she felt like saying to him.

"Let's go to bed," John whispered in her ear.

She didn't answer. She didn't have to. He took her by the hand. They went to bed. They didn't sleep, for a while at least.

Josephine awoke with a start at 5am and sat up in bed.

"My mother and sister are coming to visit today."

She didn't realise she had said it out loud.

From under the covers, John replied, "Don't worry, I'll sort it."

Even though the Vermicelli was still in her mind, she knew he would.

"Thanks," she replied. She had to go to work. Her visitors were due at six. John had said he would sort it. He would. He didn't often break his promises to her. He had just promised her a miracle. He would deliver. He would make Jesus disappear. She went to work confident in his ability. Was she right? She was. John went out, bought a can of paint to match the colour of the living room wall. Came home, cleaned it all down and repainted. No spaghetti on the wall. No sign of madness. No sign of anything out of the ordinary. It was as if it had never happened. John had done a good job. So good, neither her mother nor her sister noticed. Their only comment, "It's a nice room, but where did you get that hideous mirror?"

She didn't like to say she felt the same, so she just said, "John chose it, he likes it." That didn't surprise them. They didn't realise that it could have met an untimely end last night. It didn't. Worse luck. Or was it? If he had smashed it, he would not have been so happy. And she may not have been so lucky. As it was, there had been a happy ending, for both of them.

CHAPTER TWENTY-TWO
WAITING FOR MY MAN

Things had changed. John had changed. He kept changing, every day, every week, every month. She didn't know who or what he was going to be at any given moment. Her sister had told her before the wedding, "Once that ring is on your finger, the honeymoon is over." Josephine thought that statement quite odd and meaningless. Little did her sister know, she was right. The honeymoon was over, not quite as soon as the ring was on her finger, but too soon for Josephine's liking. She glanced in the mirror as if she expected to see herself as she was on that first morning, red, teary, uncertain eyes, black mascara-stained cheeks. She did, in her mind. She thought of all the abuse that had been inflicted on her since. More mental than physical. And even the physical was not physical in the sense of her suffering bodily injury. John had verbally abused her on many occasions and had no hesitation in throwing things around when he was in a bad mood, just as he had thrown the spaghetti, plate and all, against the wall. She hadn't been struck yet by anything, except a little glass that landed in her hair or on her clothes. On one occasion when she couldn't take it any more, she took a snap decision to fight back. She had found a tea set her mother had given her for a wedding present. Six settings: cups, saucers and side plates. She washed it and left it to dry. John spotted it when he came home. He had already said how much he disliked it. Told her to get rid of it.

"What the fuck is that doing here?"

"Nice to see you, too, darling," she replied sarcastically.

That didn't go down too well. He grabbed some of it and headed for the back door. To the bin, presumably.

"John," she shouted. He stopped and turned to face her.

"Give them back. They're mine."

He laughed.

"They're ours, your mother gave them to us."

"But you don't want them, you don't like them. You said you hated the whole thing."

"I do. But it's half mine, and I'll do what I want with it."

She charged towards him and tried to grab them out of his hands. A cup and saucer fell on the tiled kitchen floor, smashing in the process.

She stood back. She could feel the tears coming. Her mother hadn't given her much in her life.

"You bastard!" she shouted, picking up one of the remaining cups from beside the sink and hurling it at him. It missed. Only just, and smashed against the back door.

"So that's how you want to play it."

He returned fire with a cup, followed immediately by a saucer and then a plate. All three whizzed past her head and smashed against the wall behind her. That did it. This was war.

Josephine was never a violent person, but something came over her. She started grabbing cups, saucers, plates, whatever she could, and threw them at John, one by one. She could hear smashing, but wasn't looking to see whether any had hit home. She did feel one or two items brush her arm or shoulder, but she had the most ammunition. She went to reload, but realised there were no more bullets. She stopped in her tracks. She expected a counter-attack by way of hand-to-hand combat. It didn't come. He had never hit her. Yes, he had grabbed her on occasion and held her while ranting, but he had always let her go without any lasting pain, save for a slight nip or bruise on her arm.

Her bravery had subsided. She looked up slowly. He was just standing there in the middle of the debris, grinning, waiting to catch her eye.

"Well, that was fun. I need a drink."

"I suppose you'd better put this lot in the bin," he added sarcastically.

And that's how it always went. Resistance was futile. He had won again. And here she stood, the loser.

She had played into his hands. As usual. He would never apologise. Why? Because he was never sorry. He just did what he did and would laugh it off. Next day, or sometimes next minute, everything would be forgotten. It didn't happen. Josephine used to try to reason with him. Tell him he was frightening her, that he was out of control. He would just give her a big hug and explain that it was all part of their relationship, part of any relationship.

"Ups and downs, Josephine, ups and downs. Every good relationship has them. We wouldn't appreciate the good days without the bad days."

Funnily, it sort of made sense, or did it? She didn't want to emulate her mother and father's marriage, wouldn't put up with that mundane existence that her mother had. Same old thing every day of every week, every week of every month, every month of every year.

"I've made my bed, I have to lie in it," her mother would say in answer to everything.

But it's funny how you can never control your own destiny. Here she was, just like her mother. Trapped in a loveless marriage. So confused, she couldn't get out. Except, she wasn't confused, not any longer. She knew she was trapped. John had taken over her mind.

That didn't mean she couldn't take it back. Be herself tonight, tomorrow, every day.

"It's my life," she thought, "and I'll do what I want." But would she? Not while she was under his wing, his supervision, his control.

She hadn't yet worked out how to extricate herself from him. From this life. What had she gotten herself into? She didn't know, not really. She thought it was love. But it wasn't, or was it? Past tense. What is it now? Does he still love her? Sometimes it seemed he did. Other times he seemed to hate her. But she didn't know what hate was. She had never hated anyone, not even Dr White. But then that was a one-off. Fool me once. How many times had John fooled her? And how many times did she not realise? Too many. Was she still his fool?

"Fool if you think it's over."

She was still thinking in song titles. But she liked music, always had. This was the one thing that was still fun between them. They could still have those moments of laughter when they would try to outdo each other in getting song titles into the conversation. If only everything else between them could be half as much fun. But fun wasn't a word you could associate with what was happening outside of those times.

Josephine was feeling so depressed, she dreaded home time when she knew John would be there. He was being an absolute bastard. He thought, for some reason, she was cheating on him. After all, she was home alone a lot of the time, a lot of nights.

"That's rich," she thought. "He was the one who chose to go to Belfast and leave me here."

But that didn't matter to John. She had the opportunity, and so it might be true. And he wasn't going to stop until he knew for sure.

He came home early one night when he was supposed to be working late, or at least that's what he had told Josephine. She was in bed, as he knew she would be. He was drunk.

"Too drunk to fuck," she thought.

All the better. It took him ages to undress; one shoe was cast aside, then a pause, then the other. Taking off his shirt was the most interesting. He stood up to do it. It was just like John Travolta doing "Staying Alive". Right arm up, left arm down. She wasn't really sure how that was going to work. Then both arms up. No. That wasn't going to work either. Next, he tried crossing his arms, grabbing it by the seams and, bending over at the waist, beginning to pull. Naturally, he fell forward as the shirt wasn't budging. Luckily, he was facing the bed. She had anticipated this inevitability early enough to pull her feet and knees up so as not to disturb his soft landing. Maybe he should have opened the buttons. Now he realised that. He got up, sat on the bed and started fumbling with them. He might as well have tried the camel through the eye of the needle. She was going to need a needle to sew them back on, as he decided the only solution was to rip it off. Now, if he had been sober and she had been in the mood, he might have seemed so macho. Now he just looked ridiculous. Even more so when he decided to rip it up. How dare that damn shirt not come off when he wanted it to. He would probably appreciate a shirt that removed itself, or more likely someone who would remove it for him. Josephine remembered the times when she had, and had to admit she felt a slight something. But not enough that she was going to engage in anything akin to sex tonight. She couldn't. If taking the shirt off was a comedy, trying to get him to engage in anything resembling a sex act would be a tragedy.

And speaking of the poor shirt, at least it was one less for her to iron. John didn't know what an iron was. He thought shirts came out of the washing machine pristine and ready to wear. And if they didn't, he just bought another one. He would need to visit the shop tomorrow. This one was beyond resuscitation. It was for the bin. She wished that she could bin him, too. No such luck. He would still be here tomorrow.

Shirt off, it struck him. Why he had come early, or so Josephine supposed. To catch her in the act, or at least find some evidence of her infidelity. The wardrobe, a natural hiding place for a lover. He got down on all fours, put his head between the open doors, looked right and then left. Nothing. He looked up. No one hanging there.

"How could he see anything anyway?" thought Josephine. "He was blind drunk. No, not drunk, paralytic." Paralytic was a good Irish term for unable to walk, talk, hear, see or think.

Even though there was nobody in the wardrobe — well, nobody apart from John — he remained there for a while. She suspected he had fallen asleep. It wasn't long before the snoring confirmed her suspicions. That was all very well, except she knew he would wake up sooner rather than later. No point in trying to get some sleep herself. And anyway, she was enjoying the show, in a perverted sort of way. And it wasn't long before the interval was over. He began to move, in reverse, stopped and turned himself around, still on all-fours.

"Where else could a lover hide? Under the bed, of course. Brilliant deduction, John."

She was way ahead of him. He began crawling under the bed. There was no one there. Josephine knew that. Now John did, too.

She waited. Turned her head so that she could see the other side of the bed. He would emerge, sooner or later. Oops. Here he comes. Nose to the grindstone. Well, not the grindstone, just the carpet. He had trouble extricating himself from under the bed. Good job he wasn't the bogeyman.

"Shit!" thought Josephine. He is, he actually is the bogeyman. Except, he's real and more frightening.

But not tonight. Frighteningly pathetic, perhaps.

She was watching him intently. It was fascinating. She had never seen him act so randomly. He always had a plan. If he had formulated one in this instance, he had long forgotten it. He stood up, loosened his belt, pulled down his trousers and shorts. They were around his ankles. He obviously wanted to remove them. He bent over and promptly fell forward. Jesus — sorry, John — falls for the second time. He narrowly avoided splitting his head on the door jamb. How would that have panned out? Well, first of all there would be blood all over the cream carpet. That wouldn't please him. Not to mention the blinding headache. But he might not notice that in his present condition.

Then he would have to go to the hospital and be embarrassed. Of course, it wouldn't surprise her if she got the blame.

"My wife is always leaving her shoes and things all over the bedroom floor." It wouldn't even cross his mind that it would be patently obvious that he was fluttered. But in John's mind that wouldn't be the cause. There still must have been something on the floor.

Worst-case scenario, he would be dead, or is it? The worst-case scenario?

"Stop, Josephine," she corrected herself. For all her wishing that she was out of this situation, not once had she wished him dead. She still didn't. That was just a little naughty moment, just like when you see someone bending over and are tempted to put your foot on their ass and give them a gentle push. She was actually relieved that he didn't split his head, but maybe just a little hit would have knocked some sense into it.

He remained motionless. And then. Snoring. The loudest and most unnerving snoring that was ever heard. His nose was stuck to the floor, so that it sounded like someone trying to start a clapped-out motorcycle. His naked ass was visible from the bed. It wasn't a pretty sight. It was pretty hairy. Josephine hadn't noticed that before. No crack back and sack there, then. But then maybe he was planning a hair transplant. Aren't they all the rage for men nowadays?

"Is it possible to transplant hair from your ass to your head?" Josephine wondered.

She tried to picture how it would look on John. All she could think of was Kilroy, as in "Kilroy was here". She decided to have some fun. For some odd reason, John had a black marker in the drawer of his bedside cabinet. Even though she never felt the urge to look in there, she had decided to do some extra cleaning one day. And there it was, a black marker, among the other crap he kept there: spare batteries (for her vibrator, among other things), phone chargers (even those for phones he had long since discarded), a screwdriver (she couldn't explain that one) and some plasters, as if he was going to cut himself in bed. Wait, maybe they were for her when she cut herself on him, seeing as he was so sharp.

"Well, tonight," she thought, "I've found a use for one thing, at least."

She took the marker and, moving carefully and quietly, not that anything could be heard above the revving of the motorcycle, knelt behind him. She laughed to herself. It was usually the other way around. He liked to do it doggy-style and she didn't mind. Providing it was vaginal. There was no way she was going to go anal. John was anal enough for both of them. Josephine was convinced that he was the one that was cheating, was seeing someone else, maybe more than one. He was charming, after all, when he wanted to be, before he made you his sex slave, cook, launderer. Wife, in other words.

She took the marker and, moving it gently, made a large "A" on his left buttock.

She took a deep breath, mainly to stop herself laughing out loud. She held it. There it was again, engine revving, but no movement.

She adjusted herself. An absolutely unthinkable thought crossed her mind. Her vibrator was in her bedside cabinet. Okay, the batteries were somewhat run-down, but then John had more than an adequate supply in his drawer. Would he notice if she subjected him to a little surprise? It would be no noisier than his incessant snoring. It might jolt him out of his stupor. No, not might, it most certainly would. But then he might like it. If he was cheating with a man, it might not even be a new experience. Remember those articles in those magazines.

"John leaves wife for Fred."

Well, maybe not quite that, but that's the gist of it.

And it's not for the company or because they both like football. She wondered, just for a split second, what he would do if he awoke with a vibrating object up his ass. She could just leap back into bed and pretend she knew nothing, be fast asleep. This was a golden opportunity. He was so out of it. Funny, the vibrator was gold. John had bought it for her.

"Only the best for you, my dear," he had said, "for when I'm away," he joked.

She had felt like saying, "You know what you can do with your gold vibrator."

Now she had the opportunity to follow through. Before she could decide, he let out the loudest fart she had ever heard in her life. Luckily, she had stood up. Now she really did want to put a plug in it. She brought herself back to earth. No point in gilding the lily. She wanted a good night's sleep. So she continued with her original plan. She knelt back down, but only after she deemed it safe. Took the marker and made a large "H" on his right buttock.

She hoped that the first person to see it would be his girlfriend. Or boyfriend. But she was giving him the benefit of the doubt. Would she tell him? Would she ask him?

"Why have you got 'AH' written on your buttocks? And what does it mean?"

John would know. He might wonder how the hell Gordon Ramsay managed to get access to his ass. Gordon's revenge.

She wondered why John didn't shave his ass, seeing as he was so meticulous about his appearance; but then maybe she, whoever she may be, likes a hairy ass. There's no accounting for taste. In all their time together, although Josephine had seen John's ass, she really couldn't recall it being that hairy, or as big as it was now, for that matter. Nor did she caress it or grab it in the throes of ecstasy. Now here she was, face to face with it. It moved, but only slightly, to the left. She was still feeling naughty, so she prodded the right buttock. It worked. It realigned. "A place for everything and everything in its place," John used to say. For him it was all about his precious CDs. If she played one, she had to put it back in its cover; but not only that, she had to put it back in its place. And its place was determined alphabetically, but then alongside its compatriots. All CDs of the one artist or one band belong together, and all artists and bands belong in alphabetical order.

"And, dear Josephine, if they're not in order, you are out of order."

That should have raised some red flags. Except at that time she was too naive or too controlled. Tonight, she felt free. She had learned to keep her mouth shut but her options open. She was making her mark, literally. There were baby wipes in the en suite. She could relent, clean it off, pretend it never happened. He would never know. She took it back: she didn't really want to wipe his ass. And if she could help it, she wouldn't be around to do it when he needed it. No. What is done is done. She

161

would live with it. Would he figure it out? He wasn't Sherlock Holmes, certainly not. If he was, he would have figured long ago that she wasn't happy. Tonight brought her a little bit of happiness, a little bit of control. She looked at her handiwork and laughed inwardly to herself. But then let herself go. Laughed out loud. He wouldn't hear it, not above the sharp intake of breath that had now become like a jack-hammer. How can one man make so much noise? She remembered that outburst from a minute ago and stood up. Just in case. More than ever she wanted a gin. He was in front of the door. Even though she had had her fun with him, she was unsure that she could get out of the bedroom without him waking up. He seemed to have a sixth or even seventh sense. If she moved out of his presence, even when he was in this state, he seemed to know. It was an animal instinct, his only remaining animal instinct. He certainly wasn't an animal in bed any more. More like a teddy bear. She had to hold on to him lest he fall off. That wouldn't be a problem tonight. Seriously, she was so enthralled with his charm in the beginning. He actually told her in the early days that he wanted her to be his good luck charm. And he had been the epitome of a charming man. Always pleasant, always attentive, always complimentary. Everything a woman wants. Or wanted. And he knew it. She fell for it, fell for him and his charm. She should have known better. She does now. But what is she going to do about it? She was too tired to think about it just now.

She went back to bed. In the morning, she woke up to the sound of John showering. John didn't shower for four or five minutes. It took at least twenty. He used one of those loofahs on a stick. He was obsessed with removing all the dead skin. She wondered if he had seen his ass. Probably not. He only ever regarded himself from the front. That was apparent from all his nights in front of the living room mirror. If he was cheating, she wouldn't see her handiwork, she wouldn't see that he was an asshole. But it's all right, she would know soon enough.

CHAPTER TWENTY-THREE
TOTAL CONTROL

Although they were both working, they weren't left with that much disposable income when the bills were paid. So some nights were just spent in front of the television. There was always enough money for John to have a full bottle of Jack Daniels, and even a few back-up bottles of beer. His concession to Josephine? A bottle of red wine. Granted it was usually a decent one. Pinot Noir, Fleurie, Cabernet, Chateauneuf. Always French.

"French wines are the best wines. Altissimo," he laughed.

Josephine knew from school that "altissimo" was not a French word. Italian, she surmised. But this was John's little joke. He used to tell her how he hated the pretentious people who frequented the hotel restaurant. Didn't know their Amarone from their Albarino. You had to let them taste it. Show them the label, get the nod of approval, open it and pour a little in their glass. Then came the floor show, or rather the table show.

He, or sometimes she, would swirl it around their glass. Longer than necessary.

"Don't they ever think there's other people waiting to be served? Not at all. They were here with people they wanted to impress and they were going to do it. At all costs. After the swirling, they raised the glass and buried their nose in it." Sometimes, John admitted, he wanted to nudge their head at that point — accidentally, of course, just like Basil Fawlty in "Fawlty Towers". But although he played it out in his head, he never did. For all his bravado, he valued his job.

Eventually, he or she would put the glass to their lips and taste, while the others at the table tried to look interested. Once, a man at the table had the cheek to take a slurp of his whiskey during the performance. She, the woman who was tasting, stopped and glowered at him. John had to turn away and pretend to cough. He really wanted to laugh out loud.

The man responded by putting his glass down and looking suitably chastised. She continued, ironically, by making that annoying sucking sound, pretending to take in some air so as to get the full flavour. John waited impatiently for her to swallow it and give him the nod, as people are wont to do, rather than speak, for whatever reason. Supposedly, it's more professional. Or maybe it's just like people who click their fingers when they want attention instead of saying "excuse me".

She spat it back into the glass.

"What the fuck?" John could only just refrain from saying it out loud.

She looked up at him.

"Are you serious?"

How do you answer that? "About what? Yes, I am, are you?"

"This is piss."

John was shocked. Everyone at the table was shocked. It showed in their faces. The man who had slurped his whiskey lifted an empty glass to his lips and realised there was nothing in it. Yet he held it there.

"Would you like me to change it?" John was being diplomatic. It wasn't the done thing, to challenge a customer and tell her she was a charlatan. Even if she was. And she was, on this occasion. The wine was fine. John should know. He drank it later.

"Of course. You don't expect me to drink that." "That" was said with some disdain.

John lifted the bottle, her glass and left the table. What to do now? He forgot to ask if she wanted the same wine or another. Something told him to bring another bottle of the same. So he did. She loved it.

"That's more like it," she said in her most authoritative tone. At the same time, John had arranged for a member of staff to bring another whiskey, a double, for the poor man she had reprimanded with a withering look, while she was busying herself trying to emasculate him. Something told him he might be her downtrodden other half. He thanked the waitress and, looking over at John, gave him a wink before focusing on the dragon and rolling his eyes, just as she said, "I hope I won't be charged for this, or the last one."

Now comes the truth. You know nothing about wine, or maybe you do, but you know everything about scamming.

John could have challenged her there and then, told her there was no

164

difference in the two bottles, that he was somewhat of a wine connoisseur himself, told her what he thought of her, told them all to leave — but that's not what the hotel would want. Bad publicity. Even if he was right. Right to kick out pretentious pricks who think that they are so important they deserve to get freebies.

"Of course not, madam." He felt like adding, "Would you like me to clean your boots? With my tongue or a nice Chianti?"

John didn't let her make it a shit night. He had one ally at the table and he fed him whiskey all night long. Just to cause some annoyance. And it worked. Turned out it was her husband. He grew some balls over the course of the night and told her to "shut the fuck up". That's when the party broke up and they went home.

"So who will I charge the whiskey up to?" asked the waitress.

"To experience." She looked confused.

In the end, John put it on his account. It was worth it.

Back to tonight. They were watching TV. Josephine loved "Real Housewives". She didn't know why. Not what she had grown up with. Then, TV was all about fantasy, drama or comedy. Oh, wait, nothing's changed there, then.

When John came home, he would take charge of the remote control, just as he had this night. He flicked through the channels and decided there was nothing he wanted to watch. He took himself off to the kitchen.

Josephine grabbed her chance, took the remote control and put on "Real Housewives of Beverly Hills".

She was enjoying it when he reappeared. With a new bottle of Jack Daniels.

He sat down again in his recliner. He focused on the television while pouring himself a large one.

"Oh. My. God! Plastic fantastic."

She knew what was coming next.

"Some day when we can afford it, you, too, dear Josephine, can look like that."

At that point, Josephine knew it was time to change channels. She did. Now it was murder. Literally.

Larissa Schuster. She murdered her husband and submerged his body in hydrochloric acid. "Looking for a way to get rid of me, my dear?"

Josephine knew when he kept using the word "dear" in his usual sarcastic tone, he was spoiling for a fight.

So she changed the channel quickly. But he wouldn't forget. At least not tonight.

Next channel.

"Wives With Knives."

She pressed again.

"Friends" — it was just beginning.

"I'll be there for you…"

"'Friends'," he shouted. "I love that programme."

She couldn't believe it. Now she could relax. But not for long.

"Change it."

The programme wasn't over. It was just the break. But she did as she was told.

"Ramsay's Hotel Hell."

She managed to press the button quicker than a contestant on a TV game show, just as John began to say, "Gordon fucking Ramsay…" and before the usual "fucking asshole" was drowned out by the sound of "Whole Lotta Love". A vintage episode of "Top Of The Pops" was starting.

"Leave that!" he almost shouted, as he shot forward in his chair, almost spilling what remained of his Jack Daniels. Almost, but not. She swore he could have somersaulted with the glass in hand and still not spill a drop. He once fell, or rather slid, down three steps at a barbeque party and landed on his arse. His hand with a two-thirds-full glass of Jack Daniels was held high, perfectly horizontal. You could have measured it with a spirit level. He took better care of his Jack Daniels than he did of her. She thought of all the glass-throwing incidents. It was always empty. Just goes to show how much in control he was. Even in anger. Or was it anger? He never really spoke in anger. But, as the saying goes, many a true word is said in jest, just like when he told her she was getting fat and he wondered what he had seen in her in the first place, and laughed.

But now he was singing along to Ian Dury and The Blockheads.

"Hit me with your Rhythm Stick…"

She wished she could hit him with something and shut him up. For the rest of the night. Even though she did like the song and had danced

166

to it with John on many occasions, it didn't last long, his joyfulness. They had the cheek to play "Staying Alive", and even though he had inadvertently tried his own interpretation late one night in the bedroom while undressing, he hated the song.

"Turn that shit off!"

Josephine obliged. She could just have given him the remote and relaxed with her wine. But there was a reason she didn't. You see, John had a habit of playing "Smash the TV". Not like the old Nintendo game "Smash TV". This was literally smash the TV. The idea was to make the TV go off using the remote control, but not in the conventional way. For normal people it was simple. Press the on/off button. Simple. Not for John. He had his own unique method.

"I've left the Jack Daniels in the kitchen. Get it for me will you, Josephine? And leave me the zap."

"Shit," she thought, as she handed him the remote, "I'd better hurry." But then she knew once he had it she wasn't going to get it back, unless, of course, he fell asleep. She almost ran to the kitchen. She couldn't see it. Where did he leave it? Normally, he just puts things down on the nearest surface. There's no way he would put it in a cupboard. But sometimes when we're desperate to find something, we just can't see that it's hiding in plain sight. She closed her eyes and focused her thoughts. She opened them and focused her eyes, scanned the kitchen. No. It's definitely not there. Did he forget where he put it, or was he purposely telling porkies just so he could get hold of the remote? She was just about to turn around and go back to the living room, when she heard a familiar sound. The unmistakeable sound of another TV biting the dust. The only saving grace is that flat-screen televisions don't explode all over the place. It's just a case of a loud crack, a sizeable dent in the screen and a multitude of little white lines radiating outwards on the dead-black surface. She froze. And then the sound of music. No, not the movie. Remember, the TV doesn't work any more. The strains of "Another One Bites The Dust". It was time for John to play his music. He was nothing if not sarcastic.

Believe it or not, he had gone through three televisions in the last three months. He even had the cheek to bring the broken ones back to the shop for recycling when buying a replacement. He didn't care what they thought.

"I must get someone to secure it properly to the wall this time," he joked with the shop assistant. Not that they would buy it. They didn't care, as long as he continued buying televisions. More commission for them. So what make and model would he appear with tomorrow? Bigger and better, probably. Not that that was the reason he destroyed them. It was just something that he did. A habit. Another of his bad habits. Not that he saw it like that.

"It's only a television. And anyway, it was crap. We needed a new one."

"Every few weeks?" she felt like asking.

He would still be wanting his Jack Daniels. But where is it? She would have to ask him.

As she entered the living room, there he was, glass in hand, replenished, drinking, dancing and singing to himself.

Ironically, he was playing "The Sun Always Shines On TV". Not tonight, John. He was never a fan of A-ha, but he had dug out one of his 80s compilation CDs and, knowing John, he was playing it for her benefit. He smiled, or rather smirked, as he spotted her.

"Found it," he said, pointing to the bottle on the mantelpiece.

"Of course you did, John, of course you did," she thought.

"Okay," she smiled. "I've got to work in the morning. I think I'll go to bed."

He stopped dancing and approached her. Kissed her on the cheek.

"Goodnight, Josephine darling. Sweet dreams. I'll be up when I'm done."

When the bottle was done was what he meant. And even then, he might not be up immediately or at all. He could pull an all-nighter in his chair or creep into bed at sunrise. He wasn't working the next day. Obviously. He had never missed work because of alcohol or got rat-arsed when he had to work. He was always in control, total control.

CHAPTER TWENTY-FOUR
AFTER THE LOVE HAS GONE

Although there seemed to be very little love left, they were still sharing the same bed. And even though Josephine felt this marriage was fading fast, there was a slight glimmer of hope remaining. If only they had had a child. If only they could have a child. Is that grasping at straws? Maybe that's what's missing. Although John wouldn't agree. Yet he still wanted to have sex with her, although his performances had not been Oscar-winning. No matter how hard he tried. Hard? Oops, Freudian slip. Joking aside, it was the truth. He needed help.

She wasn't sure if he was still using Viagra, but if he was it wasn't the answer. He didn't say as much, but it was blatantly obvious. He did manage on occasion to penetrate her and orgasm, although he could be faking it. Sometimes there wasn't much semen to write home about. Not that she would. Write home about it, that is. Her mother wouldn't want to hear it. She might even say, "I told you so." Not specifically about the sexual side of things. Having said that her mother wouldn't revel in her misery. It would just be a case of "you should have listened". Her mother would have wanted her to get married, of that she had no doubt, just not to John, or his like, as her mother would say. But her mother played it safe. She wanted security, children, routine. She got it. She settled for it.

But not Josephine. Yes, she had married, just as her mother had, but she had married for love. But where did the love go? She consoled herself with the thought that they were still together. That John still wanted her, desired her. Yes, he was having his problems and maybe, just maybe, that was the problem. She tried to talk to him, but no matter how much she coaxed him, he would not go to the doctor, admit that he was impotent. So macho. But hey, if Pele can admit to it, why can't John? Josephine was by no means a football fan, but who hasn't heard of Pele? John, for one. She said to him one night, "Don't worry, Pele was impotent and he's the world's most famous footballer."

"Who?"

He was serious.

"Brazil, Mexico 1970, one of the best football teams ever, if not the best."

"Football? You're talking about football? Why? I know nothing about football."

It was true. He didn't. Never watched it on television. He did watch current affairs. Was so glad when Theresa May stepped down.

"Not before time," was his comment. "Who the fuck put a woman in charge of the country anyway, stupid bitch?"

To John, at times, every woman was a bitch. Including his own dear wife. Not something she had known when they got together. Then every woman was precious. And she was the most precious woman on earth. He treated her accordingly. Now? Well, now she wasn't sure what she was, what her value was. Maybe nothing. Nada. She had been learning Spanish. At home on the internet. Babbel. It's so easy nowadays. Just think, when she becomes fluent, she could get a job in Spain. Imagine John's face.

"John, I've something to tell you. I got a new job. Only problem is, I may have to be away from home, away from you, for a few nights, quite a few nights, quite a few weeks, quite a few months, quite a few years."

Her thoughts were interrupted by her phone ringing.

"I'm Your Man" — her ring tone. John put it there. She hadn't dared to change it. Sometimes when they were both at home, she would hear it, "I'm Your Man."

"Shit, I called you by mistake. I just can't get you out of my head." He would laugh.

He could laugh it off; he could laugh anything off. He was a true sociopath. He didn't care what she thought. He didn't care what anyone thought. He was living in a box, his own little box, and he always would be.

"I'm your man..." It was still going. She answered.

"Josephine?"

Who did he think was going to answer?

"Yes, darling," she said obligingly.

"Are you all right?"

"Yes. Why?"

"It took you a while to answer."

"I had to wipe my ass," she lied. She was becoming tired of his suspicious ways.

"Are you being facetious?"

"What? I can't go to the toilet now?"

She could almost feel the heat of the smoke coming out of his ears, but knew he wouldn't want to stay on the phone long. He had other fish to fry, no doubt. She didn't know exactly what he was up to recently, but she just knew there was something happening. Wives know these things instinctively.

"I won't be home till late. Things are hectic here. Don't wait up. I love you."

Same old shit, same old excuse. She knew he was waiting for her to say something. The same thing she said the last time, the same thing she would say the next time.

"I love you, too. Don't work too hard." There's that word again. Hard? She almost laughed. She had to put her hand over her mouth.

"I'll see you when I see you."

"You will," she thought.

She had no way of knowing she would see John sooner than she expected.

She had sat up for a while watching television. The true crime channel. Why, she wondered, did she watch programmes about rapists and serial killers when she was here alone in the house? What if one were to visit her in the night? She had no way of defending herself.

Except to tell him her husband would be home soon and he's probably a bigger psychopath than you. She laughed to herself. He wouldn't believe her. Fool. When she had enough of hearing what these bastards did to women, she turned off the television and retired to bed.

She was no sooner asleep, after reading her Kindle for a while, than she felt a presence in the bedroom. She didn't believe in ghosts, although she had seen the movie "The Entity", where Barbara Hershey was repeatedly raped by someone or something invisible. Was this going to happen to her?

"Chance would be a fine thing," she laughed. Quietly, so as not to

171

let on she was awake.

But if it was John, why didn't he wake her? And besides, he said he would be late. Maybe he got off early. It wouldn't be the first time he lied or just didn't bother to tell her his plans had changed. The lines of communication had grown cold, as had their love for each other. Perhaps he was hoping to catch her in the act this time. It would have to be an act, as nothing was happening for real. But it wasn't that long since he rang. Unless she had been asleep longer than she imagined.

But it has to be him. How would anyone else get in? Had she left a door or window open? No. Her OCD made her check every door and every window every night, without fail. And being a light sleeper, she would certainly have heard the sound of breaking glass.

She was somewhat relieved now that she had convinced herself it was John, but still listened intently. He was trying not to wake her. She knew by the way he was breathing. Slow, measured, controlled. She could hear what sounded like the removal of clothing.

"Well, at least it's not an entity," she thought. "Surely, they don't wear clothes, even invisible ones? And she knew from those programmes that a rapist's first priority was to subdue his victim, not neatly fold his shirt and trousers.

She felt the duvet move. And then someone moving into the bed beside her. She smelled a familiar smell. Alcohol. It was John. And to her surprise, he was hard. Very hard. Harder than she could remember. As hard as, if not harder, than those early days of hot, passionate sex. "Those were the days," she thought.

Although she felt somewhat excited, she was mad with him. Why did he lie to her? Why did he just not tell her he was coming home? Why did he not just tell her he had his mojo working again?

She turned to face him.

"Honey, I'm home," he said.

"You scared the shit out of me."

"Why, darling? Is it because my cock is hard?"

"No. It's because you didn't tell me you were coming."

"Well, that's because I'm not coming, not just yet."

"That's not funny, John. Why the hell did you tell me you would be late?"

"I thought the element of surprise might make you more excited."

"Excited? Any more excited, and you'd have had to do CPR."

"I've got a little something for you," he sang.

Typical of John. He's not taking this seriously. He's focusing on himself again. And tonight, his self is stiff.

"I just wanna make love to you," he sang.

She didn't know whether to laugh or scream. With anger, that is, not fright. She had got over that.

He's got something and he wants to use it. He wants to stick it to me. If he had gone the right way about it, she would have been a willing participant. Let herself go. Enjoy it. It had been a long time since she had. Enjoyed it. But he had not only made her feel frightened, but annoyed, extremely annoyed. And when Josephine became annoyed in that way, she just couldn't shake the feeling. It would just be a case of John doing what he wanted to her and her becoming more and more annoyed. She really was not in the mood, unless that mood is called furious. Before she could gather her thoughts and say anything, he was on her. She didn't want it. She really didn't. John failed to sense her displeasure. He was only thinking of his own. He tried to stick it in her. Not successfully. He missed. He wasn't even close. He was panting. Too much for her liking. He was persistent. She had decided that he wasn't going to get it.

"Get off me."

"No way, babe."

She hated that word "Babe". Does anyone think that "Babe" is a term of endearment, that it makes anyone feel sexy or desirable? Did Marvin Gaye sing "Let's Get It On, Babe?" Maybe John's a Styx fan. But it wasn't her giving him the strength or courage tonight.

Something else had given him that. Maybe Jack Daniels. Although that normally had the opposite effect. What happened next shocked her.

He grabbed her from behind, turned her over on her front and got on top of her. He was still hard and getting harder, if that were possible. Why, she wondered? That didn't matter. She didn't want him. He didn't listen. He was prodding her with his member. She laughed inwardly. Had she just used the word "member"?

He was still trying to put it in her, unsuccessfully. She was resisting. She was afraid it would slip into the wrong slot. It felt as if he didn't care where it went. She decided to try another tack.

"I think I'm pregnant," she blurted out. He stopped for a moment and laughed, or rather, snorted derisively.

"I don't think so."

Not the reaction she expected. What did he mean by that? She wanted to ask him to explain himself. She felt herself getting even more angry. Before she could say, "What the fuck are you talking about?", he was prodding her again. Without success. Not even close. But then she wasn't helping. He was becoming more aggressive, frustrated. He grabbed her by the hair and pushed her head into the pillow. She couldn't breathe, let alone speak. He was pushing into her from behind, while at the same time leaning on her with his body. She tried pushing herself up with her hands, but he was too heavy. A result of his ever-increasing appetite for food and alcohol. She felt like she was going to suffocate, and he wasn't even aware of it. Now she was afraid for real. Maybe it was because she couldn't see his face. She couldn't gauge what he was thinking. Or if he was thinking at all. With his brain, that is. If she couldn't breathe, she couldn't remonstrate, and he was just too strong for her to do anything about it physically. It was one of those times when resistance really was futile.

She decided that the only way she was going to get out of this situation was to let him get what he wanted, just like her mother had told her. But she had to make sure he wasn't going to pop her other cherry, if you know what I mean. She reached back, took hold of it and pushed it into her. Where she wanted. He released his grip on her hair, grabbed hold of her hips and began pushing, eventually getting into his rhythm, huffing and puffing as he did so. He wasn't exactly the fittest guy in the world. No gym bunny, although tonight he was humping like a rabbit. She just wanted it to be over, but had to admit she was feeling a little turned on despite herself. Maybe she should just let herself go and enjoy it. But she didn't want to. Not tonight. Not now that he had made it all about control. It was over before she had finished gathering her thoughts.

He slumped over her and remained still for what seemed like an age. He didn't seem to be losing the erection as she would have expected. She wondered why, but didn't really care. She wanted him to pull out and get off her so that she could quiz him about his snide comment. He was still, silent. Until the snoring began. He had fallen asleep.

"Shit," she thought, "how the fuck am I going to get him out of me now." He was heavy, heavier now that he was asleep. She thought about it for a while.

He was limp — his body, that is. What a quandary! A hard dick inside you and a limp dick on top of you. What to do? She put her hands on the bed and pushed herself into the cat pose. Thank God for Yoga. Now all she needed was a quick pelvic thrust. Thank God for the Time Warp. Even though it was hard, it wasn't long. She laughed. And she was free. Or at least her bottom half was. He was still a monkey on her back. But not for long. She slid out from under him. He just fell face first onto the pillow that she had just vacated. A horrible thought crossed her mind. She could smother him now, lie on his back and push his head into the pillow until he stopped breathing. But then they would figure it out, the detectives. They always do. And she really didn't want to spend the rest of her life in a women's prison. She so did love sex, done in the right way, but she had no lesbian tendencies.

Better to leave him. Let sleeping dogs lie. Down, Fido. But she could see that he still wasn't down. Down and out, maybe. It was like he was wearing a strap-on. Not his own. But closer examination disclosed it was. His own. But invigorated. Enough to get what he wanted tonight. It hadn't mattered what she wanted.

"Why," she wondered, "after the love is gone, do men still want to make love, or pretend to, just so that they can have sex when they feel like it. That women, and probably men, too, have to suffer the humiliation of being no more than a warm body, somewhere to put it?" "If you can't give me love," she thought, "go look for somebody else."

She knew that once he fell asleep, especially after having too much to drink, he would not wake up for hours. Her feelings were alternating between disgust and pity. She couldn't hate him. She couldn't hate anyone. That was just how she was. But she could love. She had loved him for so long. She remembered the good times. Making love. Not like this.

She left the room. She went to the kitchen. Boiled the kettle. She took a cup from the cupboard and put a spoon of coffee in it. Paused. Added another spoon, before taking the boiling kettle and pouring the

175

water. She went to the fridge for the milk. As she put it back, her big toe caught on something on the floor. It was half hidden under the fridge. She felt a stabbing pain. She bent down and picked it up. An empty syringe with a small, fine needle attached. Neither she nor John used any injections — well, not that he had disclosed. Then she noticed that the lid of the kitchen bin wasn't fully closed. Something was keeping it open. She lifted it out. A box with the words "Caverject 20mg".

Something had got into John, literally. She got out her laptop and logged onto Google. Good old Mr Google. You can ask him anything without being embarrassed or ashamed. He doesn't judge you. Although she was sure someone out there in cyberspace knew everything you were looking at. That's why we get all those ridiculous advertisements we didn't ask for. God knows what she's going to get after this. She typed in "Caverject" and didn't know how to react to what she read. It was what might be called a remedy or solution for male impotency. Only available on prescription. To be injected directly into the penis.

"A little prick for a little prick," she laughed. Joking aside, it seems to work. But where did he get it? She found it hard to believe that John had eventually decided to consult a doctor, admit that he couldn't get it up, that he was anything other than all man. John had always told her he had connections, he could get anything he wanted. Maybe he was getting it from a friend, or rather an acquaintance. She didn't know if he had any friends. She had never met any.

If only he would have confided in her, let them both enjoy his new-found libido. Not John. He found it and he was going to enjoy it. He was so self-centred, an egomaniac. She took the box with its contents, including the syringe from the floor, and would ensure that it was disposed of properly at the hospital. She would say nothing to John. Why bother? The last glimmer of hope had vanished from her mind. It was over. There would be no child. John had as much as told her so. It was just the two of them. But not for long. She just had to find the strength to get out. The love was well and truly gone. And what used to be right is wrong.

CHAPTER TWENTY-FIVE
DON'T GET ME WRONG

"Josephine?"

She looked up.

Are you okay?"

"Sorry," she replied, "I was miles away."

Paul, the newest A&E doctor, was standing in front of her desk, with a concerned look on his face. Josephine began to pull her hair down over her left cheek, surreptitiously, or so she thought. He noticed and gently took her hand in his. He lifted up her hair with his other hand. She thought about pulling her head away, but knew it was too late.

"What happened?"

She was embarrassed. John was drunk again the night before. He had thrown his Jack Daniels glass in her direction after an argument. She didn't believe he intended to hit her. He never did before, and he had thrown many a glass. No matter how drunk he was, how many drinks he had, he could make sure it sailed just past her right or left ear and smashed against the wall behind her. He was like a knife-thrower, except with glasses. All she had to do was sit still. The first time it happened, she didn't even have to think about it. She wasn't looking. They had argued over something or other. She couldn't remember. She had decided to ignore him and continue eating her dinner. She felt the whoosh and heard the crash. Smithereens of glass landed in her dinner. And some in her hair. She wasn't hurt. Not physically. She was shocked. It took some time before she could look up. When she did, he was just standing there with a grin on his face.

"That got your attention."

It hadn't been a serious argument. That much she could remember. Probably about something ridiculous, such as how you should make your curry sauce. It was curry they were eating. She remembered thinking to herself that the curry wasn't as hot as John's temper.

But rather than ranting or shouting, he was standing there as cool as a cucumber.

"So what is it that you wanted my attention for?"

"I need another drink," he replied laughingly.

She put down her fork, walked past him to the living room, brought back the bottle of Jack Daniels, got him a fresh glass and put both down in front of him.

"Thanks, darling."

He was so blasé about it, about everything. He unscrewed the top, poured himself a large one, a very large one, and took a drink.

"Don't think you should eat any more of that curry. Have mine. I've had enough. Leave the glass. I'll clean it up in the morning." And he would.

Then he took himself off to the living room to play his music.

The bruise on her cheek, the black eye, was just the result of a reckless act. He was drunker than usual. He misjudged it. It could have struck her face dead centre. Instead, it caught her cheek. Thank goodness he wasn't really a knife-thrower. She thought the concealer she applied that morning had done its job. Obviously not a good enough job.

She felt like saying, "It's nothing, really; the hairdryer fell while I was trying to get it from the top of the wardrobe. I should have used a step ladder."

She thought better. Paul wouldn't buy it. After all, he was used to treating victims of abuse. He had told her that he had spent some time working with battered women's shelters. Should she come clean, tell him the truth. It was getting to that point where she needed to talk to someone, but was still reluctant. She and John had agreed that, as long as they lived, their relationship would be totally private. No one else would be admitted, no one would be allowed into their little bubble, lest it would burst. It was only big enough for two. Their bond was sacred. Once broken, it could never be repaired. But the bubble was about to explode. She could sense it. Was she ready to talk about it? Not yet. But she had to get rid of Paul somehow.

"I can't tell you right now. It's not private here, someone could overhear. Another time."

"Okay," said Paul. "When and where?" She didn't expect that. He waited.

Josephine thought for a minute. She didn't want him to tell anyone else. Maybe if she confided in him, he would agree to keep it to himself. After all, he knew all about confidentiality.

"John won't be home tonight, he's staying in Belfast."

He gave her a searching look.

"That's the nature of his work," she added embarrassingly. "He's got a lot of responsibility. He wants to earn enough to open his own restaurant."

He was silent, waiting for her to go on.

"Why don't you come to the house at eight?"

"If that suits you," she added, to fill the silence.

"Okay, I'll see you then," he said finally.

She had already told him where she lived. He was looking for somewhere to live and she told him it was a nice neighbourhood and not far from the hospital. She had noticed a few "house for rent" signs recently and told him so.

She wasn't too worried about the neighbours. She didn't know them and they didn't know her. She only spoke to them to say hello in passing. John had never even acknowledged them. Not his kind of people. She wasn't sure what his kind of people were. He had never introduced her to anyone he knew. Their social life involved dinner for two or some function involving her work or acquaintances. She had no close friends. No confidante. All as a result of their preserving their own little bubble.

John called her at work that afternoon. He rarely made contact with her at work. He never needed to. He usually told her in advance what he was going to be doing that day; whether it was accurate or not, she never knew. But more importantly, he told her what she was going to be doing. Sometimes, she would write notes to remind herself what he had said as soon as she got to work, lest she forget. She didn't want to hear John say, "You never listen to a word I say, do you?" one more time. She had heard it often enough, generally followed by some more choice language and John taking himself off to the living room with Jack Daniels. The drink, that is; he didn't have a friend called Jack Daniels — well, not as far as she knew. The bottle was the friend he spent most of his time with now. Of course, when John was in that mood, it didn't matter that she had, in fact, listened, had written it down. John made the rules, and whatever he said in the morning wasn't necessarily what he remembered he had said when he got home.

"I don't feel like chicken tonight. What made you think I wanted chicken tonight? I told you we were having Chinese. I'm sick of chicken. Put it in the bin."

She knew not to argue, even though she hated wasting good food. She would do as she was told, as usual. However, when John left for work, she would retrieve the chicken and exchange it the next day for something else, or cook it up in a curry or stew and freeze it. That is, until one night when she went to the bin, she found that the chicken had been removed from the packet and buried among the kitchen waste. How is it that she could never hide anything from him? She often thought that he had hidden cameras watching her. Even if he had, what would she do?

"Hah! I found your hidden cameras, John."

"What hidden cameras?"

"The one in the living room clock and the one in the bedroom ceiling."

"You mean the security cameras, the ones I put in so that I could check on you when I'm not here, especially at night? What if someone broke in and was attacking you, how would I know? I'll tell you how. Because I can check those cameras on my phone whenever I need to — they're connected to the internet. And I do check them regularly, just so that I know you are safe. Isn't that what people do? Protect their valuables, and there is nothing more valuable to me than you, my love."

And she would have to apologise and tell him that he thinks of everything, that he is so wonderful. Why would she object to them, unless she was doing something she shouldn't be doing? What else could she say?

"Bullshit. You just don't trust me. You're a stalker. What man stalks his own wife?"

Well, she could imagine how that would go down.

She was afraid that John knew she was planning to talk to Paul. How could he? Impossible. She was just being paranoid. There were no hidden cameras. She would know. John may even take pleasure in telling her that they were there. Just to make her paranoid; or, rather, more paranoid.

She considered changing the location of her and Paul's meeting, but he would have already left the hospital as his shift was over, and she couldn't ask anyone at the hospital for his contact number. There had already been some rumours about why she parted company with Dr White. Just another small part of the rumour mill that runs continuously through hospitals and such places. None of them, the rumours, were accurate.

"Josephine," John had said, "I just called to say I love you."

She couldn't think of a song title to reply with. She was still thinking, "Why is he calling?"

Realising there was going to be no response, he continued.

"As you know, I won't be home tonight, but I'll see you after work tomorrow. I'll do dinner. Love you, Pumpkin."

"Love you, too, John. Thanks for calling," was all she could say.

"Anything wrong?" asked John.

"Oh, no, sorry, I was distracted. Someone here was trying to talk to me."

"Who?"

"Just one of the doctors, nothing important."

"All right then, gotta go, see you tomorrow." He was gone off the line.

She had decided to get a couple of bottles of wine on the way home. If she was going to tell someone about her problems, she would need some Dutch courage. But there was no Dutch wine, or at least none that she knew of. So she stuck with French. John had told her French was best. And she did so love Fleurie. So light and still full of flavour. So she went with that. Two bottles. She didn't want to seem stingy. But three would be too many. They weren't going to make a night of it. She figured that if they drank one bottle each, although she didn't intend that they would, that would be the height of it. She would never drink more than one bottle herself, unless, of course, John was in a wild mood. Then he would pour her more and more drink until she could take no more. But tonight, the wine would just serve to lighten the mood. She wanted the atmosphere to be casual. More importantly, she wanted to feel relaxed, take the edge off. She didn't want to seem nervous, make it seem as if the marriage was in trouble, real trouble, that she was in some sort of danger. She would disclose just enough, but not so much that Paul would feel that he had to intervene. It would just be two friends or colleagues getting together for a little chat.

But John could never know. He wouldn't approve. No man could set foot in his house, unless he invited him in. And he never had. In all the time since they were married, no man had set foot in this house, not even Josephine's own brother. Not that she ever thought of inviting him. Like the rest of her family, he had no time for John and not much time for her either, now that she had chosen him. She had never before thought it strange or unusual that they had never had a male visitor. Until now. Paul would be the first. But not by design. By chance. That made her feel uneasy. It's wrong. Why? Because this house is ours, mine and John's. Too late. It was one minute to eight.

Paul was dead on time. She had told him not to ring the doorbell. Even though she didn't know the neighbours, she suspected that there would be at least one nosy one. There always is.

"Did you see that fellow going into number 16 last night? It wasn't her husband, you know. I've never seen any man other than her husband go into that house. What do you think is going on there, then?"

She was being ultra-careful, even though there was little or no chance of it getting back to John... or was there? Next thing you know, John would be making friends with the widow Sue at number twenty-two. Dropping in for coffee. Nothing else, hopefully. She appeared to be in her sixties. But then stranger things have happened. She was distracting herself again. And Paul was at the door.

"Text me when you're outside," she had told him. She had been sitting on the sofa for ages, her mobile phone in hand, staring at the screen. She wanted to have a glass of wine before he arrived, but she was brought up to have good manners. She had, however, opened the bottle to let it breathe. "That's what you do with red wine, Josephine," she could hear John say.

"Red, red wine," she sang in her head as she opened it.

Her and John's love of music and song titles had remained with her despite the sorry state of their relationship. It was one of the things that had made them so close.

"It's funny," she thought, "with all the bad things that are going on in our lives, the little things still mean a lot." She couldn't help it. It was part of her life, her marriage.

A marriage that had been a happy one in the beginning, that had made her feel happier than any other time in her life. She was still clinging to those good times, those happy times, those happy feelings. And they hadn't gone away completely. Yet they were too few and too far between.

"Where there's life, there's hope, isn't there?"

"Fuck, Paul's on the doorstep." She had better open the door. As she did, the smell of aftershave invaded her nostrils. Jean Paul Gaultier, "Fleur Du Mâle". She liked it. She once suggested to John he should buy it. Came in a bottle shaped like a male torso, white and glazed like porcelain. He dismissed her immediately.

"You suggesting I'm gay?" he laughed. "You might as well suggest I wear perfume. What kind of impression would that give people?" He was no metro-sexual. Totally hetero. He'd probably prefer something more macho like "Bad Boy" or "Brut". After all, that's what he'd become. Or what he was all the time underneath that smooth exterior. On that first night, when he said he was only a sheep in wolf's clothing, he was lying. He made it sound so true. That's what men can do. And women, too. When it comes to pulling the wool over the eyes of another, we're all capable: man, woman, transsexual, transgender, bisexual or asexual. And whatever other term anyone cares to describe themselves as nowadays. It's not about what orientation you are or think you are, it's about how much of a human being you are. As someone said in the Bible, maybe Jesus, "Do unto others as you would have them do unto you." If only more people were aware of that quote and lived by it. She did. Or tried to.

"Shit!" She was hesitating again. She unlocked the door and flung it open.

Paul was huddled in the doorway as if that made him invisible. He smiled at her. Neither of them said anything. She just stepped aside and let him in. She gestured him into the living room. He went on in as she closed and locked the front door. He stood until she invited him to sit. She ushered him away from John's recliner and into the armchair. It was enough he was here in their house, but for him to sit in John's recliner would be a step too far. Josephine would certainly not be able to relax. For one minute. When Paul was safely ensconced in the armchair, she sat on the sofa, the glass occasional table between them. She poured two glasses of wine without asking. He didn't object. He lifted his and took a sip.

"So tell me," he said. She wasn't surprised at his directness. After all, this was why he was here. She bowed her head and began speaking. She wanted to hide her embarrassment, didn't want him to see the sadness in her eyes.

"I feel as if you already know what I'm going to tell you. You've had experience. John's changed since we got married. He's under pressure, he's putting himself under pressure. He's working too much, wants to get enough money to open his own restaurant. He's been drinking, quite a lot, actually. It makes him angry. I have to walk on eggshells."

She paused to take a drink of the wine she had been swirling around her glass the whole time. There was no response. She heard him take another drink of wine. She looked up. He caught her eye and held her gaze.

"Don't get me wrong," she continued, "the bruise you saw. It wasn't intentional. He just vents his anger and frustration by throwing things, glasses usually. Empty ones."

She turned her eyes to stare at her feet, which were on the sofa, almost under her backside.

"He keeps bringing more home from his work. Perks of the job, he calls them. I sometimes think he could fill the recycling bin with them in a week." She turned her eyes towards him.

"But he's never hurt me intentionally. It's just the alcohol. He's self-medicating, looking for comfort in the bottom of a glass. He doesn't realise that I feel his frustration, that he can talk to me, that I'm here for him, always."

She stopped. Partly because she felt like bursting into tears, but also because she had said too much.

She took a long drink without looking at Paul, composed herself and looked at him. He began speaking right on cue.

"I suppose I did know, or thought I did. I have noticed how fragile you seem. How you rarely mention your private life, your husband or your relationship. How you get nervous sometimes at home time, how you react when you get a text message. I always assume it's from him."

"Him?" That sounded strange to Josephine, especially the tone with which Paul said it.

"I didn't want to say anything," he continued. "Put you in a position. You know I have experience of this sort of thing. Truth is, I've tried to help women before, and what happened? They went back to their husbands. I was the bad guy, tried to break them up. What did I know? I wasn't in their relationship. 'He loves me, he really does, in his own way.' they would say, or 'He needs me, he has no one else.'"

He was ranting. This was not what Josephine had expected. He was supposed to listen, be a sympathetic ear. Give her some friendly advice, advice to help her heal her marriage. He kept going.

"I don't understand the hold these men have over women. My mother used to say, 'There's nought stranger than folk.' She's right."

Josephine had put on some music before she let Paul in. She was distracted by it for a moment. "People are strange," sang Jim Morrison. It struck her that she hadn't even changed the CD John had been playing the night before. She didn't know if Paul had picked up on the irony.

There she goes again. Distracted by the music, the song lyrics, rather than listening to the person talking to her. The lyrics were there, even when she wasn't listening to music. She would sing them to herself, under her breath. Sometimes people would ask her what she had just said.

"Oh! Nothing," she would say; "just talking to myself."

They probably thought she was nuts. Always talking to herself. She didn't care. She had learned not to worry what others thought of her. From John.

"Josephine?"

She was back in the room. The song had finished. She looked at Paul, stared for a second. He looked worried.

"How bad is it?" he asked.

She honestly didn't know how to reply. She wished now that she hadn't asked him to come. She felt she was cheating, being disloyal to John. He was still her husband. The only man she had ever loved, been truly intimate with.

"Excuse me a minute," she said, as she got up and put her empty glass on the coffee table.

She went into the kitchen and out the back door into the garden. She prayed he wouldn't follow. He didn't. Probably assumed she needed the toilet. She needed a break, time to think. And to take some deep breaths. Inhaling the night air seemed to disentangle her thoughts. She knew what she needed to do.When she returned to the living room, he had poured himself another glass of wine. Had changed the CD.

"I Want To Make It With You", David Gates and Bread. It was kind of creepy in the circumstances.

"Shit," she thought. She was about to ask him to leave. It was all a mistake, a big mistake.

"Don't get me wrong," she began, "I really appreciate your concern. What you think you know, well…" she paused, "it's not the way you think it is. I love him, I really love him. It's just a phase. It'll pass. I can't imagine being without him."

He took a long drink. The glass was almost empty. There was an uneasy silence. She had been staring at the floor as she spoke, avoiding eye contact. She looked up. He was staring at her.

"I thought you were different. I thought I could save you. From him." There was that same tone, same inflection again. He finished his wine.

"From yourself. And who knows? We could have been good together."

What was he saying? What was she doing? She had totally misjudged this man. What's new? She needed her own space.

"You should go."

Surprisingly, he stood up immediately, empty wine glass still in hand. She flinched. Hold on. This wasn't John. He would have flung it across the room in her direction, as he did last night. Paul didn't. He walked across the room towards her, handed her the empty glass, which she took automatically, kissed her on the cheek, and spoke in her ear.

"Not tonight, Josephine."

She shuddered, but managed to walk him to the door, unlocked it and let him out. He didn't look back. What was she thinking? This night could have turned out so much worse. She raised her eyes to the sky, blessed herself. She recited "Angel of God".

Why, she wondered, did she still pray when she had lost her religion a long time ago? Not so much lost her religion as lost the religion her mother had brought her up with. She still prayed, even though she didn't really know who or what she was praying to? Maybe the universe, even though all the prayers contained the word "god". There's comfort in praying, she found, whether it means anything or not. It doesn't have to.

She held her breath, checked the door was locked, checked her phone was on and went back to the living room. She needed another drink. Wine wasn't strong enough. She opened the drinks cabinet (so christened by John). It was a cupboard. There was no gin. There was an unfinished bottle of Jack Daniels. She had tasted it before: John insisted she tasted everything.

"If you don't try it, how are you going to know you don't like it?" he used to say. Not just about alcohol.

Tonight, it wasn't about like or dislike. She needed the strong hit. She drank from the bottle. It took her breath away, but that's what she needed now. It didn't taste too bad. She couldn't remember if she had liked it before. It didn't matter. She stood in front of the mirror over the fireplace and saw herself holding the bottle in her right hand, lift it to her mouth and drink.

She had ejected Bread. Reinserted The Doors.

It was an act of defiance. I'm drinking your whiskey, John. I'm doing what you do in your sanctuary, playing your music, drinking your favourite alcohol, looking at myself in your mirror.

"What does he see?" she wondered. "Why does he look at himself so much? He looks at himself more than he looks at me. Does he even see me any more? Does he see how sad and broken I am? Does he still see me as he did on that first night, in those first heady days of love and romance? Or have I changed?"

"My Eyes Have Seen You," sang Jim Morrison.

To Josephine, that sounded like something a stalker would say. Had John stalked her? In his own way. He had captured her, captured her heart.

She sat in his chair and swivelled from right to left, left to right, pausing to take another drink. She had drained her wine glass just so that she could use it to drink Jack Daniels. It was another act of defiance. John would be horrified. Not only was it not the correct glass, but it wasn't clean and fresh. But tonight's the night, John, the night that you can't tell me what to do. I'm in charge, in charge of this house, this space. I can do what I want tonight.

I might even watch some "mind-numbing" reality television: "Real Housewives of Beverly Hills", "First Dates" or "Come Dine With Me". But they would only remind me of my own sorry situation. Here I am, a real housewife, but without the money, whose first date brought me to this point, wishing that my husband would come dine with me more often."

In the end she had drunk so much Jack Daniels while contemplating her next move that she didn't feel like or couldn't get out of the chair to retrieve the remote control. She was jaded. There was nothing left in the Jack Daniels bottle and the music had finished. She wasn't just drunk. She was pickled, soused. She laughed, thinking of the episode of "Fawlty Towers" when the Spanish chef, she couldn't recall his name, fell in love with Manuel and drank all the wine when he was rejected.

She looked at the empty bottle and began to sing "The Devil Went Down to Georgia".

Whoops, that was Charlie Daniels, not Jack Daniels. She was ready for bed. "Better the Devil You Know," she thought, as she climbed the stairs.

CHAPTER TWENTY-SIX
SUSPICIOUS MINDS

Josephine opened her eyes. Her head hurt. Not so much hurt as was filled with cotton wool. The crisp sound of the birds that sang outside her window every morning was being drowned out by the thumping bass in her head. Black wisps, like fleeting shadows, floated across the snow-white ceiling that she had painted herself only a few weeks ago. She closed and opened her eyes several times before they disappeared. She knew it was nothing serious. What time was it? There was a clock to her left. Seven minutes past seven. It was okay to get up. Her OCD. The numbers matched. She was born on the second of February. The second day of the second month. Hence, she loved doubles. She often wondered if she had been a twin and that the other twin died at birth or was naturally aborted before being born. Ever since having taken the job at the hospital, she had read many things in the course of her work and had taken more interest in the workings of the human body. That, and the fact that she still wanted to give birth. To be personally involved in the miracle of life. Not just because she had aborted Dr White's baby. No. Not Dr White's baby. Her baby. It was never his baby. It was never a baby at all. The beginnings of a baby. But like her twin, it might not have survived. She would console herself with that thought. And she would never know if she had had a twin, not for sure. But then nothing is sure in life. She had been sure that Paul was a genuine caring person. And look how that turned out.

She thought about the night before. Paul leaving, walking away from her door. She would have to face him, today, tomorrow, again and again. Why did she even consider confiding in him? She had misread the situation, his motives. Was she really that naive? She married John, after all. They do say that we repeat our mistakes. Is that what she is destined to do? Choose the worst type of man? She could always become a lesbian. No. Not really. She wasn't physically attracted to women. Men were her thing. She liked their thing. She began to giggle, but stopped herself, as the movement was beginning to make her feel nauseous.

She just remembered that she hadn't eaten the night before. Maybe that was a good thing, as she really didn't want to be physically ill. She could never be a bulimic. She had only thrown up a few times in her life, and she absolutely hated it. And anyway, they say the stomach acid rots your teeth, and she didn't want to lose hers. Dentures really scared her. They just didn't look natural. As a young girl, she had seen her grandmother remove hers at bedtime and put them in a glass with some sort of tablet. Steradent. That was the name on the tube. The same tablets she, her grandmother, would put down the toilet.

"Why are you putting those tablets down the toilet?" she asked her one day.

"They remove the limescale, darling, keep the toilet clean."

To a girl of tender years, that was so confusing. Are dentures made of the same stuff as toilets? Well, they're both white, gleaming white after grandma uses those tablets. Maybe they are. Are grandma's dentures as hard as the toilet? She tapped on it, the toilet, with her small, fragile knuckles once. It was hard, really hard. She thought of the Red Riding Hood story her mother used to read to her.

"What big teeth you have, grandma?" "And hard," she now thought. But then grandma wasn't grandma in the story. She was the wolf. And he had already eaten grandma.

"He wouldn't have eaten my grandma," she thought. "She might have eaten him with her hard, white teeth."

Her grandma was no shrinking violet, never showed any fear, always knew what to do. Always told her to stand up for herself, to be brave, and that the only thing to fear is fear itself. She was wrong. She never knew John, wasn't married to him. Although maybe she was right. Maybe it was time to stop fearing him. After all, he's only human, flesh and blood.

Back to today. She needed a shower, to wake her up. Jack Daniels! She remembered. What was she thinking? She wasn't. Still. It felt good. Being in John's shoes. Maybe not his shoes: his world, his music, his alcohol, his mirror, his mind. Did she really get into his mind, his brain? He had gotten into hers. Sometimes she felt as if they were one. "One and One is One." At other times there was a chasm between them.

"Who are you, John?", "What do you want?", "What do I want?"

"I can no longer answer that," she thought.

She had washed and put away the wine glasses, tidied up, sprayed the room with air freshener, lest John get a hint of "Le Mal". But then he would think she was entertaining some gay guy. But even that wouldn't go down well. He might be bisexual.

In her panic to get to work, she had almost forgotten about the empty wine bottle, the empty Jack Daniels bottle. How would that have turned out? Inspector Clousseau, aka John, would have a field day.

"Let me see, ma chérie; an empty bottle of wine and an empty bottle of Jack Daniels. There is only one conclusion. Two people." And what's worse, the other person was drinking his alcohol. She would have to own up. She was feeling lonely, afraid. He was never home. She bought herself a bottle of wine and drank it. It didn't settle her nerves, so she had to have some Jack Daniels. After all, he had introduced her to it. He wouldn't believe her. Not with his ever-increasing suspicious mind.

"Suspicious Minds." She liked that song. She wondered why. It's not a love song. How could it be? Someone who sings they're caught in a trap isn't in love. It's not a trap. It shouldn't be a trap. It should be where you want to be. Not only that, but the person you're with should want to be there with you. So why was he gone most days, most nights?

Luckily, her OCD told her to check everything again before she left the house. And one of those things was her behaviour the night before. And the evidence of her behaviour the night before. The text message. She had forgotten to delete it. Not so much forgotten as had been so distracted it went completely out of her mind. She did it now. But what if she had left it?

Would John have checked her phone? To be fair, he never had. As far as she knew. But then if he had, would he have told her? Not unless it suited him. Not unless he had caught her out. So she surmised that her decision to delete it was right. Better safe than sorry.

And then there were the empty bottles. She took them in her handbag and disposed of them in a public litter bin on her way to work. She chose one. Not the nearest to the house and not the nearest to the hospital. That's where he would look first, if he bothered to look. Now she realised how utterly ridiculous her paranoia had become. Watching too many crime programmes. Don't leave a trail. He already thinks he has enough on you. That's a laugh. There's nothing to have on me. But that doesn't matter to a jealous husband. To John.

Even how she disposed of the evidence made her feel guilty. What would John say if he knew? "You did what? Put empty bottles in a public bin? But you know we recycle all our bottles."

He might even kill her for that. After all, they had watched the movie "Serial Mom" together. And she was death on people who didn't recycle.

In reality, that wasn't going to be a problem. A more immediate problem was how she was going to handle seeing Paul today. She always felt comfortable at work. In recent times more comfortable than she was feeling at home. Now that would change. What would she say to Paul? Would she say anything? Be convivial, friendly, nonchalant? Or avoid and ignore him altogether? She really didn't feel like pretending nothing happened. Didn't want him to think that his behaviour was acceptable. She wanted him to know that she was disappointed in him, angry with him, that she realised that she had made a mistake. She wanted him to know what an absolute bastard he was to try to take advantage of her in a moment of weakness. He thought he could take advantage of her because of her vulnerability. What's wrong with me, doctor? I'll tell you what. Nothing. I'm a married woman, happily married. I don't need no doctor. Been there, done that. Heartless bastards, both of them. But what about John? We he heartless also? Did he have a heart? Could he be loved? Could she continue to love him?

"I don't know how to love him" popped into her head. It dawned on her that this was the truth. She had come to realise that John loved himself more than anyone, more than her. He had a hatred for everyone else to one degree or another. He never had anything good to say about anyone. Behind their back, that is. To their face, he was ever the charmer. It was difficult to reconcile his many faces.

She couldn't believe that Paul was not at work that day. Someone told her it was his day off. She felt cheated. Had he planned it? He hadn't told her he was free the next day. He didn't have to hurry off to bed. But then maybe he expected to be in her bed. Men lie. She should know that by now. Sometimes not by what they say, but by what they don't say. But then it wasn't Paul who had chosen the time and place. She did. But he agreed. Maybe it was a case of opportunity knocking for him. She still felt a sense of relief. It would have been difficult to see or speak to him. Enough that she would have to face John later and act naturally. OCD wasn't her only overwhelming condition. Guilt was another. For some reason, whether it was her religious upbringing or just a part of her character, when she had done something wrong or something, in retrospect, she shouldn't have done, she found it hard not to confess. She really did believe that it was good for the soul. Not that she was going to confess to John. That would surely be a case of "whatever you say will be taken down and used against you. Again and again, for the rest of your life."

And anyway, even though it was an error of judgement, she wasn't to know what Paul was really like. But she did put herself in a position. What position? She was in her own home and although Paul was pushing his luck, she didn't really think he would try anything. After all, what would an allegation of sexual assault do for his prospects? No, this is an episode that John didn't need to know anything about.

"Least said, soonest mended."

Josephine had hoped to get to the off-licence at lunch time to get a bottle of Jack Daniels and leave it at home before returning to work. She had forgotten that Sally had planned a lunch with some of the staff for a colleague who was leaving. She would just have to get that Jack Daniels on the way home and get it in the drinks cabinet before John would notice. Maybe he would be late home, maybe she would get there before him. Fingers crossed. She left work fifteen minutes early so as not to be late home. Her handbag was big enough to conceal the Jack Daniels.

She was actually looking forward to dinner. John could cook. He had attended a course as part of his training. He had a very good repertoire. He could cook everything — meat, fish, vegetarian — and make it tasty, very tasty. She was sure her expectations would be met, if not exceeded.

As soon as she opened the door, he was there in front of her, greeting her with a tender kiss on the lips. Not passionate, just welcoming. It made her feel at ease.

"Hello, baby," he had said. "Go and change. Wear something nice, something that makes you feel good, sexy, desirable."

"What was the occasion?" she thought. She couldn't think. She looked at the date on her phone. Nothing came to mind. Regardless, she did as John suggested. It took her a while to decide what to wear. Eventually, she played safe and wore a little black dress, the one that John loved so much. She didn't wear any panties; she had become confident in herself since meeting John, and didn't want to spoil her figure, her silhouette. She wore them to work lest John suspected something, but when possible, she went commando. She glanced at herself in the mirror. She looked hot. John would be pleased. She still wanted to please him, despite all the troubles in their marriage. Hope springs eternal. She was elated. She didn't know what had prompted him to make this night special, but she had no complaints. She took one last look at herself and walked from the bedroom to the living room, where John was waiting with drinks. He handed her a G&T. He had poured himself a Jack Daniels with ice.

"Wait," she thought. She had finished the bottle the night before. The one she had bought on the way home was still in the bedroom in her handbag. He had intercepted her before she could sneak it into the living room, into the drinks' cabinet. So where did his drink come from? Was she just being paranoid? Had he bought another just to have enough? He could have. He never had enough. He didn't give her time to think any more.

"Cheers. To us." Their glasses clinked.

John downed his drink in one.

"Another?" he asked.

"I haven't even touched mine yet," she replied.

"Don't worry, let me change it. Jack Daniels okay?"

She didn't know how to reply. She was getting nervous, very nervous. She said nothing.

"Cat got your tongue, dear?"

Dear? That's a word he'd rarely, if ever, use to address her. His use of the word dear didn't sound endearing.

He took her G&T from her hand. She didn't resist. Truth be told, she was in a state of fear. He could have done anything he wanted, walked up the walls and danced on the ceiling, and she would not have moved. He opened the patio doors and emptied the glass. He took some ice from the bucket, poured over Jack Daniels, a lot of it, what looked like a double or treble. It was hard to tell, with the amount of ice in the glass.

He poured himself another one.

"Down the hatch," he said, putting the glass to his lips. He paused. His eyes were fixed on hers. She drank. One mouthful. It made her feel sick. She tried not to show it.

"I thought we did everything together. On the count of three. One… Two…"

His gaze was unwavering. She felt compelled. She had to drink.

"…Three…"

She drank. Finished it all. So did he, but only after he knew she had. He was smiling. Not so much smiling as grinning. Amazingly, she didn't feel sick this time. She could go again. She realised now how resilient she was. She was feeling defiant. She was looking good. A bit of her wished that John would stop this now. That he would look at her the way he used to, that he would have that glint in his eye, the self-same one he had that night he had fallen on the ice and snow and hit his head. That he would make her feel desired. Not frightened. That feeling was beginning to overwhelm her. How was she going to escape this situation? There was no escape. She lived here, with John. She had dreamt of living on her own, without her husband, without the hassle, the abuse, the control. She realised that John was singing or mouthing something.

It was only now she realised that there was music.

"Your Cheatin' Heart" by Hank Williams. It was playing now in the living room, the room where she had entertained another man. No, that's not the right words. She had neither entertained another man nor any untoward thoughts. That was him. She was innocent, wasn't she? But something was wrong, very wrong. She realised that she knew it from the moment John greeted her at the door. She should have turned on her heels. It was too late. She had to play the game, his game.

"That felt so good," she said with conviction. Or so she hoped.

He was taken aback. He was used to being in control. Now he had to outdo her. He poured another two drinks. Jack Daniels without the ice. He took his and rather than drink it this time, he sat into his recliner, slumped into it. He stared at her as she lifted her drink, expecting another challenge.

"You look so good tonight, Josephine, good enough to eat."

Was this night going to end well after all?

John killed the moment, absolutely obliterated it.

"Is that what you wore for him?" he spat out. "Or did you wear anything at all?"

He didn't expect an answer. He didn't get one. Now she was the one with a fixed gaze. She was fixated on his eyes. His pupils were growing ever larger, almost filling his eye sockets, like a demon in a horror movie. Except this wasn't a movie. She knew she was in trouble, again.

"Handsome doctor, I presume. I didn't think you would settle for anything less. You have aspirations. Moving on to better things, pastures green, dear Josephine?"

"John…" she began in an apologetic tone, but suddenly changed her mind.

"Fuck you!" she said, and downed her Jack Daniels in one. She almost choked, but was damned if she would give in this time. She steeled herself, walked over and reached for the bottle and poured herself another. John laughed.

"The bastard," she thought. He couldn't even allow her this one moment in control. He had to be the one in charge. He had taken everything from her, her confidence, her happiness, her self-worth. He would take her life away from her if he could.

She put the drink down.

"I'm going to bed."

She marched out of the room and went directly upstairs to the bedroom. She sat on the bed for a time, listening. She knew he was down there, thinking to himself, talking to himself in front of the mirror. Just as he did every time they had an argument or falling out. One minute he would be dancing to the music, the next he would be lying back in his recliner, singing along. Suddenly, he would leap up, take his drink in hand and stand in front of the mirror, mouthing to himself. She couldn't hear him over the music. Sometimes he appeared so angry, other times he seemed to be in heaven, then he would be laughing uncontrollably.

There were so many emotions contained in those ten or fifteen minutes.

Once she saw his reflection break into tears. He didn't know that she was watching. The mirror didn't pick her up as she hunkered down outside the glass doors. She could hear the music. "Knocking On Heaven's Door" by Mark Knopfler and Ted Christopher. Released following the Dunblane massacre in Scotland. For all his faults, John had a soft side, a vulnerable side. Not one he showed to others, not even to her any more. He rarely showed it at all. But he did that night.

John loved children, wanted to protect them, was emotionally wounded at hearing of any physical or mental abuse of them. Probably because of his own childhood, the cruelty that had been inflicted on him by his father. What his mother had become after his father died. He seemed to have empathy with children. But for some reason he didn't want a child. She didn't believe it was just the money, that he wanted it all for his restaurant. He was frightened, frightened that he wouldn't be a good father. That he would do to his own child what his father had done to him. He was confident in many ways, but when it came down to it, he had insecurities like the rest of us. She couldn't help but think that things might have been different if they had had children. She was sure John would have loved them. It was adults he hated. But why did he hate her? How could he hate her? She had given him everything, trusted him implicitly, would do anything to protect him, give up her life for him.

Her thought process was interrupted as she realised the music was getting louder. Either he had turned it up or he was on his way. The bedroom door was closed but not locked. John had insisted there would be no locked doors in his house and had hidden the keys to all the doors. They were open with each other and so their house would be open.

She could hide under the bed or just get under the covers. Either way, he would know she was there. It was an instinct, they could find each other. That used to be a good thing, a positive thing. She remembered a dreadful party they were at and became separated. She escaped outside and dared not go back in to find John lest she be cornered again by some guy boring the ass off her with his talk of healthy eating and exercise. It was supposed to be a party, for God's sake. A time to indulge. Why would you want to be reminded how unhealthy it is to eat fried food, salty snacks and drink alcohol?

"Guess who?" someone whispered in her ear, as he put his hands over her eyes. It was John.

"What are you doing out here?"

"I needed to clear my head."

"I know what you mean," he replied. "Come on, let's go home." She was never so glad.

But not tonight. She heard the footsteps on the stairs. She knew the number of stairs, and when John was in this mood, he wasn't the lightest of foot. She was counting. He was getting closer now. Her options were no longer open. She ducked under the covers, still wearing her little black number, and pretended she was asleep.

The door opened — no, not so much opened, as it was almost flung off its hinges. She couldn't help but peek from under the covers, eyelids half shut. He stood in the doorway, silhouetted against the landing light. It reminded her of a Dracula movie, except that Dracula didn't make enough noise to wake the dead. She thought about holding her breath, but then realised that if she was feigning sleep she would have to breathe normally, deeply. She could do that.

She did it before, so many times.

"I know you're not asleep," he barked. "Did you do it here, in our bed?"

She was tempted to answer, to tell him he was acting like an idiot, that he was wrong, that she truly loved him despite everything, that she couldn't cheat, couldn't break his heart. She was almost there. Perhaps this truth would melt his anger. Too late.

"Get up!" he roared. With that, he bent down, grasped the side of the bed with both hands and upended it so that she found herself trapped between the bed and the wall. She was neither lying nor sitting, but somewhere in between. The duvet was lying around her bottom half. She was staring at the mattress, which stood in front of her like the wall of a padded cell. For her own protection, she thought. Surprisingly, she wasn't hurting, at least not physically. But what now?

He was standing on the other side of the upturned bed, his face gazing down on her.

She didn't bow her head or hide. Instead, she decided to look him in the eye. She wouldn't back down, let him win.

His malevolent eyes now turned to amused, uncaring eyes. She was disappointed. She wanted a reaction to her defiance, she wanted him to be challenging, violent even, though it was frightening. There's nothing worse in this situation than an apathetic opponent.

He turned and walked away. She heard him leave the room, chuckling to himself.

Would she follow him, goad him, make him show some emotion? No. She knew she wouldn't. Even though she craved his attention, she was still afraid of him. Of what he might do next. Even though he was a control freak, he was losing it, losing his own self-control. Better to leave him alone. She would rearrange the bed, get into it and go to sleep. In the morning, he would be there beside her. He wouldn't talk about the night before. Neither would she. All gone, all forgotten. Back to this wonderful life, another day in paradise.

CHAPTER TWENTY-SEVEN
MIRROR IN THE BATHROOM

Josephine was right. In the morning, it had all been forgotten: no mention of the night before nor any sign of the madness that had taken place. John, although not overly loving, did the usual routine.

"Morning, baby," he said casually, as she awoke, and he gave her a peck on the lips before he got out of bed.

"I'm making dinner this evening, so don't worry about shopping on your way home." It was his day off.

"Thanks, baby," was all she could say, was all she wanted to say, before he took himself off to the kitchen for his morning coffee. No point in asking what last night's charade was all about or trying to discuss it with him. And besides, she still didn't know what he knew or thought he knew about Paul's visit. Dragging that subject up again wasn't in her interest.

When she was dressed and ready for work, he was sitting in the living room, drinking coffee and watching the television, or rather, changing channels as usual. Except Gordon Ramsay wouldn't be on at this time of morning, so he would have nothing to swear about. There was a time when he would have breakfast ready for her on his day off. They would eat it together and on occasion he would convince her to call in sick so that they could go back to bed. That was then. Today there was no breakfast, no going back to bed. She would have to grab some tea and toast and eat it on her own in the kitchen. She really didn't want to engage with him, as she still felt that there was something bubbling under the surface of this another-ordinary-day façade.

And she didn't want it to erupt. Perhaps given time to himself, time to relax, whatever it was, it would subside. He would have time to reflect, to realise that there was still something between them, that there were still some embers that could be reignited. Maybe that's what he had in mind for this evening. She could only hope.

Josephine glanced up from her computer. The clock said 5.50pm. It was past home time, considerably past home time. She hadn't noticed. Today of all days, he would expect her to be home on time. Today of all days, she wanted to be home on time. The dinner would be ready. The wine opened. If she doesn't hurry, John will have polished off the first bottle, might even be on the second. As she had confided to Paul, his drinking was now totally out of control. She had challenged him about it, but that just set him off. Like a petulant child, he would rebel, drink even more. Finish the bottle of Jack Daniels, then go scrabbling in the cupboard or the kitchen for wine, beer, whatever there was. And if there wasn't any, he would go out and get more. Once, he took the car and was gone for almost an hour. She heard the scraping of the bumper on the ground as he drove it back into the driveway. He had lost control and driven headlong into the gatepost of a house. It was solid stone. Luckily, the house was unoccupied at the time and no one had notified the police. He was laughing as he came into the house and, opening the bottle, poured himself another drink. Glass in one hand, bottle in the other, he recounted the story.

"Had a bit of a mishap." He was laughing.

"Thank fuck I always wear my seatbelt. What a good law-abiding citizen I am. Not like your old man." That hurt.

"I only hit a gatepost. I think some of it fell on the bonnet. Bumper's had it."

Josephine was disgusted, but had to stand and listen so as not to antagonise him. She felt like telling him he was an idiot. He was. She had come to realise that. But he was a dangerous idiot.

"I'm okay. Thanks for asking." Now comes the sarcasm.

"I didn't get the chance. I was worried about you."

"Were you, Josephine, my darling? Really? Or did you wish that I wouldn't come back?"

"Now you're being stupid, John."

"Oh! I forgot. You work with people who are so much more educated, much more refined."

She realised he was spoiling for an argument, a reason to rant and rave, to vent his hatred, and it was her turn. Again.

"I'm just glad you're not hurt." She went over and kissed him on the cheek.

That took him by surprise. He looked at her.

"I'll make you something to eat," she said, trying not to show her disapproval.

"Why don't you sit down and relax. You could be in shock." He was now. It showed on his face.

She got herself quickly to the kitchen before he could respond. She stood by the cooker, listened. Music. Music, drink, dance, mirror, drink, drink and more drink. Until he gets to that place known as oblivion.

She pondered whether to make him something to eat, as promised. She finally decided he wouldn't remember. In that state, he would forget about her, about everything but himself.

He was in the throes of self-loving ecstasy. She would make him breakfast. She went to bed happy in the knowledge she would have an undisturbed night's sleep. He would spend the night entertaining himself until he fell asleep in his recliner, the one he had to have. It was good for his back; after all, he was on his feet all day. She could picture him, lying there, mouth open, arm dangling over the side, empty glass in hand. He was so intrinsically mean, he always drained the glass before he passed out.

Nothing came of the car incident. He told the insurance company he had crashed on the way home from work avoiding a stray dog on the road and hit an old drystone wall. The wall wasn't damaged, he told them, except for a few loose stones that landed on his bonnet. There was no need to call the police. The dog was long gone and the owner of the land could simply put the stones back where they came from. As for the owner of the gatepost, they will probably never know who's to blame.

Now, in real time, as she got to the door, she could hear music. "I'm Still Waiting" by Diana Ross. John had obviously been on the lookout, saw her approach. The choice of song didn't do anything to calm her nerves. She expected him to greet her with some degree of sarcasm dripping from his wine-stained lips. The door opened just as she was about to put her key in the lock.

"Here she is, the birthday girl." She had forgotten. Had things got that bad? He took her handbag and dropped it on the hall floor. He hugged her so tightly she could hardly breathe; then, releasing her, he kissed her in a way he hadn't done for as long as she could remember. She almost went weak at the knees. She felt breathless. It was as if he had sucked all the oxygen out of her lungs. He seemed to be sober. That in itself lifted her mood. Maybe this was a turning point. Maybe she was right in what she thought this morning.

As he released her, he kept hold of her hand, guiding her into the dining room. The blinds were pulled, candles glowed everywhere. It was reminiscent of the night they met. What was happening? She followed his lead, just as she had that night. This time there was no passageway, she could see and knew where she was going. He pulled out the chair, ushered her into it. As she looked at him, he put his finger to his lips. "Don't speak." She couldn't help but play the song in her head. She hoped they were going to play the game they always used to play when they first met. That they were going to have a conversation, a stupid but usually loving conversation, using only song titles.

She never realised how fabulous the room could look. John took an open bottle of champagne from the ice bucket on the side and poured two glasses and handed her one, which she took without hesitation. He sat opposite and looked into her eyes. His bright blue eyes, the eyes that she fell in love with, sparkled in the candlelit room.

"To us, together forever."

"To us," she replied automatically.

He drained his glass, as he had done on that first night. She did likewise.

She expected him to refill the glasses. Instead, he laughed.

"Miss clever clogs can't even remember her own birthday."

She was flabbergasted. How could she fall for such a ruse? Of course it wasn't her birthday. But in the moment…

She felt like telling him he was such an asshole.

"Wait," she thought. His blue eyes had lost all of their sparkle. His pupils were becoming so dilated they seemed to fill his sockets. It wasn't "Don't It Make My Brown Eyes Blue". Rather, "Don't it make my blue eyes black". Black and menacing. He wasn't going to make this a night to remember in the way he had done on the night they met.

"I'm out of here," she thought.

The door was right there, right behind her. It was open. The table was between her and John.

She stood up, and, using her ass, her ever-expanding ass, as John now lovingly referred to it, shoved the chair across the floor behind her as hard as she could, before turning and bolting for the stairs. She knew she could make it to the bathroom before he had time to catch up.

She had made it her panic room, and boy, was it time to panic. Little did he know that, despite his rule that there would be no locked doors in his house, in their house, she had found the key to the bathroom. Not by chance: she had sought it out. Why? Because she feared that someday she would have to hide — no, not hide, to protect herself. And how would she do that save behind a closed door? Now the time had come. The key that John had hidden months ago, the key that she had found, she had hidden under the bathroom sink. As long as she could get there, she could lock the door. And she did. But it wasn't right that she had to lock herself away from her husband, to be afraid of her husband. Yet she had no option. She had prepared for this night, and now it had come.

John had told her more than once that he would rather see her dead than with another man.

She was now beginning to wonder if, in fact, he knew more than he was letting on. His past remarks about "a good-looking doctor" stemmed from her confession about Dr White, but she had told him that she was the victim. That she hated the bastard. But suspicion is not logical, nor requires evidence. The clue is in the word.

Was he watching the house on the night Paul came? Came to the house, that is. Her OCD was playing up again. Not that he came that night, nor was there any chance of it. But if he was watching, he wouldn't have been able to let anything happen, not that it had. After all, she was the innocent party. Or was she? Not in John's eyes. There was something in that suspicious mind.

As she reached for the bathroom door handle, she took time to glance over her shoulder. She saw nothing, heard nothing. He couldn't have made it there before her. Or could he? No.

This wasn't a horror movie. "No," she thought, "this is worse, this is real life." She was tempted to tiptoe to the top of the stairs and look down, but thought better of it. He could be lying in wait. She decided it was best just to go with the preconceived plan. Stay in the bathroom until morning. The bath mat was more than comfortable and it was, for her, a safe place.

She retrieved the key from under the sink and closed and locked the door. It surprised her that the key was still there. That John hadn't discovered it in his exhaustive search for evidence of her infidelity."

But then he wasn't home that much any more. He seemed to be doing a lot of overtime. Or was he?

She waited for him to come to the door and start his crazy talk.

"Why were you late home? Was Dr White feeling lonely again? Did he need some comforting? Or something more? Maybe you thought you could have his baby this time. After all, you're always saying you want one."

Instead, tonight there was silence.

Listening intently, she couldn't hear him coming. But then he could be stealthy when he wanted. He was sober, or appeared to be. He could be on the other side of the door, listening, waiting for her to make a mistake, to open the door.

"Not a hope in hell, John."

Maybe he was simply prepared to let her linger, give her time to reflect?

"He treats me like shit," she thought, "so maybe he thinks I belong here."

She sat on the toilet and did a pee. She might as well, she thought, as she was here anyway.

Just as she was finishing, she froze.

The door handle. It was moving, down. The door. It's locked. I'm safe. It opened. His face appeared around the door. Grinning.

"Hello, baby," he said in the style of the intro to "Chantilly Lace".

Talk about a compromising position. She almost shat herself. Well, no better place. No one could say she had lost her sense of humour. She had heard it said that some soldiers laughed going into battle. Now she understood the phrase "you have to laugh".

Rather than try to pull up her knickers, she quickly pushed them off, taking her shoes with them, and stood up. He was there in front of the door, having closed it behind him. He held up a small metal spring.

"It's wonderful how such a small thing can make such a big

difference."

He paused, giving her time to think. He did know about the key — he did something to the lock.

"When is a door not a door, Josephine? Obvious. When it's ajar."

"You're not laughing. The joke isn't funny any more, is it?"

"What have you been up to, my dear?"

She felt like saying, "What does anyone get up to in the toilet?"

"Cat got your tongue? Shall I answer for you?"

"You see, rather than hurrying home to your beloved, to whom you pledged your never-ending love and devotion, you choose to dally elsewhere. I haven't yet worked out exactly what you think you're doing, but things will become clear eventually, clear as water."

She followed his gaze as it moved from her to the bath. Only now did she realise it was full of water.

"Oh, crap!" she thought, just as she was lifted off her feet and unceremoniously immersed, causing her mouth and nose to fill with water. He was stronger than his appearance belied.

She instinctively grabbed both sides of the bath and pulled herself up. He was standing there with a satisfied grin. She knew this was only the beginning.

She shook her head and drew breath. Ready for the next onslaught.

He bent over her, grabbed her by the shoulders and pushed her back down. She was able to hold her breath, for a while at least. She kept her eyes open so that she could look at him.

She never seriously thought he would kill her, but if he did, she was going to look him in the eye, show him she wasn't afraid. She was. He didn't avert his gaze. It was a staring contest. Who would crack first, and how? Funnily, she didn't feel any hatred from his stare. It was almost devoid of feeling. It was a simple battle of wills. If he was looking for fear in her eyes, there was none. He didn't seem disappointed. It was just you and me. Again.

"What is this all about?" she wondered. Is she being punished by dunking, as were scolding women in medieval times? Is he trying to get her to confess? Even if she had something to confess, she wouldn't dare, as he would ensure that she would be punished. Again and again.

He had released the pressure on her shoulders, but she hadn't noticed, as she was concentrating on staying in control, in control of her breath, in control of her bladder and bowel. She wouldn't be humiliated by him in that way. That was just a step too far.

She could have moved, risen and taken a breath. She wouldn't satisfy him. She never did, according to his abusive tirades. She was useless, only cared about herself, her appearance, her job, her friends. What friends? She wasn't allowed any.

"What do you think you look like, Marilyn Monroe?" She didn't. She never wanted to.

Why, she wondered, did he make that comparison? She could never understand why Marilyn Monroe was the benchmark for all women. She wasn't the only attractive female that ever walked this earth.

It was getting too difficult to hold her breath any longer. She didn't have to. He grabbed her by her upper arms and lifted her upper body over the side and left her hanging there. Her bedraggled hair hung down from her head onto the cold tiled floor. She imagined she could feel it. Or maybe it was the cold shiver of what was to come. Time stood still. For her at least. She was expecting something to happen more quickly, immediately. It did now. She felt him take her by the hair. Half of her body was still in the bath. If she resisted, she feared he would pull it, her hair, out of her scalp. Putting her hands on the floor, she dragged the rest of her body out of the bath and onto the floor. It hurt. It caused John to lose his grip. But only momentarily. He bent down and grabbed her by the hair again, vice-like this time. Rather than be pulled along, she managed to turn herself around and get her feet flat on the floor so that she could at least have some control over her movement. He had his back turned to her.

"That's a bonus," she thought. "I don't have to look at his ugly face."

Just as she had control of her footsteps, he stopped suddenly, causing her to buckle in the middle and her ass hit the floor. No sooner had she come to terms with this, than she was yanked into an upright position and made to face the bathroom mirror. He was there, behind her. She could swear she felt his cock prodding her behind. He was enjoying this. She wondered if he had had his Caverject. He put his head on her shoulder. But not like the night they had escaped, parked on the beach. This time was different. He wasn't going to ask her if she was thinking what he was thinking.

She couldn't help but smile. Involuntarily. But he wasn't to know that. He hesitated.

He was expecting fear in her face. He pressed himself into her. Her smile disappeared.

"No," she thought. She didn't want him to do that to her one more time. A horrible thought crossed her mind. In their most intimate moments, she had said the only thing she would never do with anyone, even him, is anal sex. John had a good memory, the best memory of anyone she had ever known. Had he remembered her greatest fear?

He grabbed her hair again, pulled her head back so that his face was there next to hers, but more in front of hers. He was the star of this show.

"Look at you," he snarled. "Not so smart now, not so self-assured. What would your boyfriend think?" That one is hard to answer, seeing as she doesn't have one.

"You might need to change that mascara for a waterproof one."

That made her notice the streaks on her face. She hoped he didn't think it was from her tears. There were none. She wouldn't cry. She had been like that as a child. No matter what her mother did to her, she wouldn't cry. Funny, it wasn't the physical abuse that made her feel like crying. Her mother could have beaten her, slapped her face or punched her. She never did. Sometimes she wished she had. But one time her mother told her she never loved her, that she was too much like her father. As a child that was hard to take, hard to understand. Why did her mother not love her father? Why did they get married? It wasn't until that night before her own wedding that she understood. She didn't want me to make the same mistake.

"You're pathetic," he whispered. "Not worth my time. Did you think I was going to satisfy you?

"I felt you clenching your buttocks. That's when I knew you were scared. No danger of shitting yourself now, then. Maybe when I'm gone."

He raised his right arm. She flinched. Nothing. She opened her eyes in time to see him take a picture of her on his iPhone. What would he do with it?

"A keepsake," he giggled. "Don't you think that my prospective replacement should see you at your worst before he commits to anything?"

As he released his grip, her body sagged. She grabbed the sink and almost threw up. Only water came out, the water she had swallowed earlier.

She heard the door open and waited for it to close. It didn't. It made her look up. He was standing there, waiting. He was waving goodbye, as if he was just going out for a while. He had a massive grin on his face. He stopped waving and raised his left hand as if to throw something. She closed her eyes and held her breath. She heard the splash as his little metal spring landed in the bath. As he turned and left, she could hear him humming to himself. She recognised the song.

"Nowhere To Run."

"Nowhere to hide," she added instinctively.

CHAPTER TWENTY-EIGHT
I WANT TO BREAK FREE

Sally said she should end it. Josephine just had to confide in someone, and at least Sally wasn't going to try to take advantage. Sally was right. She needed to get away from John, move on. She had been fooling herself for too long, even though they had only been married for months rather than years. She was still young. Many women remain in what the professionals would call a dysfunctional relationship for years, thinking things can only get better or for the sake of the children. She and John didn't have any. She came to realise that was by design. John's design. That night of the rape, and she now realised it was rape, he had told her as much. He laughed when she said she thought she might be pregnant. There was no hint of doubt in his mind. Even though they had used a condom on many occasions, there were times when John didn't seem to care, when they did it "au naturel". That included that very night.

But from John's reaction, it wasn't going to happen that night, or any night. Why, then, did she miss her period? She had done a home pregnancy test, which was negative. But she had to be sure. Although it was against her better judgement, she went to Dr White and asked him to do a proper test. As soon as she had broached the subject, she wished she hadn't. He had laughed, before jokingly saying, "Don't look at me." She realised just how stupid she was being. Just how desperate. Of course, there were other reasons women missed their periods, not least stress. And boy, was she stressed. She was married to John. But her marriage to John was done. And so she had accepted Sally's recommendation for a solicitor to commence the beginning of the end.

She would have to juggle her working day in order to keep her appointment with him, the solicitor, Mr O'Connell. Of course, no one, apart from Sally, knew why she really needed a solicitor. To others, she had made up some story about an aunt leaving her something in her will.

Her appointment was for 12.30. She arrived early and was told to take a seat. She looked at the clock. 12.12. That could be a good omen or a bad omen. Even though her OCD taught her to like doubles because of her birthday, John had hijacked that, too. Her birthday was 2nd February, the second day of the second month. But John's was 22nd May, Gemini, the twins. Hence, he often referred to them as lost twins who eventually found each other. Josephine always thought that a bit odd, but gave him the benefit of the doubt. It was meant in a good sense. Not that he thought of them as brother and sister. That would be wrong. You had to know John to understand him. That's what she thought at the time. Little did she know that she would never know John, never understand John. He used to tell her she was the only one who did. Another of his convincing lies. He just wanted her to think she did. According to him, they were twins in the true sense of the word. Meant to be together forever. There was a time when one would often tell the other when one of them noticed that the time was a double, just like 12:12, 13:13: 22:22, or the number on a car number plate or a door of a building that was double numbers such as 33 or 66. Then they would kiss briefly to affirm their togetherness. Solid. Solid as a rock. That was then, when they were in love, when she was in love. When John cared, or at least pretended to care. When it was reassuring to know he was there for her, watching over her. He had told her he would be like her guardian angel, always watching.

She was now feeling paranoid. Was he outside, watching, waiting? Nothing would surprise her. She took her phone out of her bag and turned it off. Mainly so that her discussion with Mr O'Connell wouldn't be interrupted, but in the back of her mind she thought John could be listening in without her knowing. But then he wouldn't need a phone or other device. He seemed to be able to read her thoughts. They had had so many telepathic experiences during their time together. Just like twins. One knew what the other was thinking or feeling. Or was it just that she was always thinking what he was thinking. After all, mind control is nothing new.

She was glad when her thoughts were interrupted by a male voice.

"Mrs Clarke?"

She momentarily glanced to her left, then right, before realising it was her he was addressing.

No one had referred to her as "Mrs Clarke" before. Kind of ironic that it was only now, only after she decided she didn't want to be.

She looked up to see a middle-aged, dark-haired man dressed in a white shirt, red tie and navy pin-striped suit. He was good looking, handsome, well groomed. She was expecting someone older. Why? In her youth, all solicitors seemed old. Not that she knew that many. On occasion, one would come to her grandmother's house or her father's house. And everyone knew who the local solicitor was. But she was young, and everyone over twenty seemed old.

She was hesitating, looking at him longer than necessary. If he noticed, he didn't comment or change his welcoming smile. He gestured for her to go into his office ahead of him. She rose and walked past him, standing in front of his desk until he invited her to take a seat.

He sat behind his smoked-glass desk.

"Now, I believe you need some help."

She didn't know how to begin. He realised her predicament and spoke again.

"My secretary tells me it's about your marriage. Don't worry, most people find it difficult to discuss personal relationships, especially marital ones. I can assure you that everything you tell me is strictly confidential. You can tell me anything. In fact, if you want me to help you, I need to know everything, no matter how embarrassing you think it is, no matter how insignificant you think it is. I need to know the full story. Take your time. My secretary will get you tea or coffee. Which do you prefer?"

She felt better now that he had led the discussion. Taken charge of the situation. Just like John used to do in the early days. When their conversations were always so easy and so fun. Not that this conversation was going to be fun.

"Coffee, please. Milk, no sugar." He called his secretary on the intercom and asked her to bring two coffees, both milk, no sugar. She didn't know if that was what he normally took, or if he was simply trying to make her feel at ease. It didn't matter. It was time for her to talk. When she got going, she couldn't seem to stop. He was being so attentive, while at the same time taking notes without looking away. He did speak, but only when she stopped for breath. She had no doubt he was taking it all in.

She recounted all the things that were wrong in her marriage, all the incidents where John had abused her both mentally and physically, from the spaghetti on the wall to the Jack Daniels glasses whizzing past her head; and, of course, his holding her under water in the bath.

"He even wanted to have sex while I had the painters in."

He stopped writing. He was looking at her as if she had two heads.

"Sorry," she apologised. "While I had my period," she added quickly, somewhat embarrassingly, "not in front of the decorators."

She could see he was trying not to smile or laugh, trying to be serious, sombre.

"That would be too weird even for John," she added.

That did it. They both started laughing.

It created a welcome lull in proceedings. For Josephine at least. He seemed relaxed also. Her coffee was empty. She really wanted another, but didn't want to seem forward. She wasn't forward, never had been. She was proud of her manners, her consideration for other people and their feelings and sensibilities.

"Would you like another coffee?" How did he know? Don't be stupid, Josephine. He's watching you as well as listening to you. When someone lifts a cup and looks into it rather than put it to their mouth, it really doesn't take a genius to realise they could do with a refill.

"Yes, please, I'd love one."

After having called his secretary and having her bring two fresh coffees, he continued.

"Go on," he said, after she had taken a drink from her mug. Sensible having mugs. Otherwise his secretary would be in and out like... well, like a solicitor's secretary, really. She had to stifle the giggle in case he thought she wasn't taking this seriously. But she was. She really was. His words brought her to that night, probably the worst night of her life. Worse than the Dr White episode? Would you rather be raped by your husband or raped by a stranger? You would think that would be a no-brainer. It's not. She had got over the Dr White episode, or so she thought. She didn't know if she would ever get over the rape by John.

She had trusted John. With her life. He betrayed that trust. He belittled her that night. By his actions and his words. Isn't that why she was here now? She had to tell Mr O'Connell.

She couldn't look at him, so she lifted her coffee cup, took a sip, held it in front of her with both hands and gazed into it.

"I think he raped me." It was an odd thing for her to say. She knew it as soon as it came out. She felt so stupid. Who says a thing like that? To a solicitor?

She felt like burying her head in her hands or picking up her handbag and leaving.

She could feel the tears rolling down her cheeks. She couldn't stop them.

"Josephine."

She looked up again. He was holding out a box of tissues. She obviously wasn't the first woman, or maybe even man, to shed a few tears in his office. That was reassuring.

"It seems like you need to get this off your chest," he said sympathetically.

She was relieved. Maybe it wasn't as stupid as it sounded.

If she wanted his help, he needed to know. It was just so difficult. John was the only person she had confided in her entire life. Now here she was confiding about her life with John with someone who was effectively a stranger. She thought back to what her father had said about strangers being friends we just haven't met yet. She really needed a friend. Especially now. The last stranger she had let into her life was still a stranger, more of a stranger now than ever.

"You said you need to know everything. How long have you got? You probably have other appointments."

"You might not believe me, but I haven't. I had a feeling that this would take some time. It generally does. Breaking up is hard to do."

Had he just said what she thought he said? Was she dreaming? Had she told him about the game she and John used to play. Was he being facetious? Her head was spinning now.

"Josephine." This time it wasn't sympathy. It was like "snap out of it". She did.

"Sorry." It sounded so lame. "I'm sorry," she added, "I feel overwhelmed."

"We can stop, if you want. Take this up another day."

At first, she didn't know how to respond. Then he added, "I meant what I said. I have the time, but I'm not going to put pressure on you to continue if you're not ready."

For some reason, she recovered her resolve. Maybe it was because she didn't want to seem like she was here for sympathy; maybe it was because she felt like he was winning again, that he was still in control.

"No," she almost shouted. "Let's continue."

"He raped me. John raped me."

Would he believe her? Did he believe her? He did. It showed on his face. He had heard this before. It was beginning to dawn on her. I'm not the only one. I'm not alone. She began to recount the events of that night. She expected him to say, "Why didn't you go to the authorities?" But then why would he? He knew how the system worked. He knew how futile that would be.

"I believe you, Josephine. I won't say thousands wouldn't. But that's the reality. Some men believe that a husband can't rape his wife. He can have sex with her whenever he wishes. That it's his entitlement. That's what you signed up for. Somewhere in the past, a husband could sue for restoration of conjugal rights, demand that his wife give him his dues, and a judge would order her to. Can you believe it? But then the judge, the person making the order, was inevitably a man. Those were the days when a man was a man and a woman did what was demanded of her."

"Nothing's changed there, then," thought Josephine. At the same time, she was stunned. She didn't expect such understanding. From a man. But then she had chosen to go to a man. She could have chosen a woman solicitor. It never even crossed her mind. Why should it? To Josephine, people are people. And here she was, in front of someone she was sure was a good person. She told him all about the rape, all the intimate details. She surprised herself. But she felt comfortable with him. He was there for her. He wasn't Paul. There was no danger. All this stuff was going through her head. But at the end, she felt a sense of freedom. She had got it all off her chest. She wished it was so easy with John. Get him off her chest. Not in the physical sense, although some of the last times they had sex he was so heavy she felt as if her chest would explode. He had continued piling on the pounds. God knows what he was eating. He rarely ate at home any more. She thanked God he came so quickly.

She used to count the seconds, like counting sheep, but thank God she never got so far as to make her fall asleep. He still needed to hear how good it was for her when it was all over. Then he would go to sleep happy. If she had told the truth, he would certainly be grumpy. But it didn't matter as long as he was sleepy.

Being here, talking to someone, was the most liberating experience she had had since she answered that advertisement. Why, she wondered, did she answer it? Stop. She had learned long ago not to ask why. It happened, shit happened. Now it was time to live again. She needed to ask how.

"How am I going to get him out of my life?"

The mood changed.

"Even though I know what you're here for, what you came here for, and I really want to help you, I'm worried by what you have told me."

Now she was worried, too. He leaned forward, his elbows on the desk, hands clasped.

"I'm afraid for you, Josephine."

They stared at each other, during which time Josephine collected her thoughts.

"I'm afraid for myself. That's why I'm here."

"There's no easy way out. It's not just a case of asking for a separation or divorce. I don't think, from what you tell me, that he's going to say yes, Josephine, whatever you want, no problem."

"I didn't think that it would be that easy. That's why I haven't tried that."

He sat back in his seat.

"Touché."

His response reminded her of that first night with John and how they had connected. Was she going to connect with Mr O'Connell? Not in the same way, in a professional way. Would he be her saviour?

"So tell me."

"It's so easy to get married, to enter into the contract of marriage, to bind yourself to another person, supposedly for life. But as we all know, the failure rate in marriages is catching up with the success rate, if it hasn't already overtaken it. The difference between getting married and getting divorced is that when you get married, both parties want the same thing, they want to get married."

"But they don't always both want to get divorced," she interrupted.

"You got it."

"Even though neither is happy."

"The problem is that one usually doesn't want the other to be happy."

"So can I just not get him barred from the house?"

"You can, of course, apply to the court for a barring order. And you may get it. If the court believes he is abusive and controlling."

Now she wondered if he had been listening to her at all.

"I know what you've told me," he went on, "and I believe you. A judge might even believe you. But your husband's entitled to have his say in court, and I'd be surprised if he would agree with your version of events. He'll have his own version. He works away from home because that's what he has to do to accumulate enough money for him to open his own business, your own business, your own restaurant. He's told you that. You're at home alone a lot of nights. You brought another man, a colleague, into your home in his absence and tried to seduce him with alcohol."

"But he doesn't know that," she interjected. "And I didn't," she added quickly, "try to seduce him."

"I know that, you know that, but John doesn't. He will say you have tired of your marriage. You want rid of him so you have made up stories making him seem controlling and abusive, whereas the truth is, you're the one controlling the situation. Trying to take his home from him and leave him out in the cold."

Her mouth was agape.

"Josephine, I'm on your side, but I have to play devil's advocate."

"You mean you're on his side?"

He looked at her.

"Oh, I get it, he's the devil. Well, from what you tell me, he has put you through hell. I get the feeling you're not as vulnerable as I first thought."

"I'm afraid that I am. When it comes to John, I am. I mean, how do I protect myself against him if I can't get a barring order?"

"Josephine, there's something you need to understand."

"I'm listening." It was said weakly. She was deflated. It showed.

"Despite what I said, you are probably strong enough and literate enough to convince a judge that he is what you say he is. Especially if you tell him what you told me about the rape, in the way you told me. And he will probably grant you a barring order. The problem is, that won't be the end of it. At one time, as a young, naive and idealistic solicitor, I thought, like you, like a lot of people, that a barring order did what it was supposed to do. Protect someone vulnerable — at that time that was generally a woman, who was being abused by her husband. I had a client. Let's call her Mary. She was married with two young children, a boy and a girl. He was a bully, just like John. That's why she decided to leave him, get him out of her life. She applied for a barring order and got it."

"So what went wrong?" She knew there was something else coming.

"He killed her. Despite the barring order. He came to the house to collect the children. That was allowed under the terms of the barring order. To the house, but not into the house. Mary took the children out and he put them in the car. But before she could close the door, he asked her to get his son's baby blanket, the one he couldn't go to sleep without. She had washed it, and it was still in the dryer. She had forgotten to give it to him. She went to the kitchen to get it, leaving the front door open. I guess she felt less vulnerable because of the barring order. That he would be afraid to do anything stupid. He wasn't. He followed her quietly into the kitchen. Took her by surprise. Grabbed her and tried to kiss her. She resisted, threatened to call the police. He took a knife from the knife block and stabbed her, over and over. And when that broke, he took another. He stabbed her over thirty times. He called the police and admitted to it. The children remained in the car, thank God."

She was sure he could see blood draining from her face.

"It's a piece of paper, Josephine, you have to understand that. You can't hide behind it. It's not an invisible shield; it doesn't create an impenetrable barrier between you and him. He can choose to ignore it. If he does and you survive, he can be arrested, jailed even. That's the best-case scenario."

She didn't want to hear any more.

"So what is? The way to go? Run? Hide? Change my name?" Now

she knew she was being stupid.

"That would be one way out, if a bit extreme. But most people don't want to or can't do that. The most dangerous time in abusive relationships is when the victim decides to leave, or rather when she or he threatens to leave. You don't want to let him know what you're thinking, that you have been here. There's no standard solution, no one solution that fits all.

"I know some things about John from what you have told me, but is there any possibility that given time he may be the one to end the marriage?"

This is not what Josephine wanted to hear, expected to hear. Is this guy off his head? I'm not Mary. John is not her husband. He's not going to kill me. Just get me a separation or divorce. It was all too much. She needed to leave. Go somewhere where she could think for herself.

"I need time to think. But thank you so much for your time."

There she goes again. Always polite. She would never be otherwise. She stood up to leave.

"Think about what I've said. But most of all, don't let him know what you're doing. What you're thinking."

"Thanks," she said with a forced smile, picking up her handbag.

"Do you still love him?" he asked.

That stopped her in her tracks. Surely, he's not like the others. She's only just met him. That sounds like someone who's jealous of someone. No. Not in this situation. He's trying to make a point. Make me think.

"No," she said assertively. "There's no love left. He's not the person I married."

"That's a start. Just remember that. That thought might just save your life."

"Do you really want to hurt me, John?" she thought, as she made her way back to work.

CHAPTER TWENTY-NINE
IF YOU LEAVE ME NOW

When Josephine got home later that day, she needed a drink. And time alone to think. She would have both. John had texted her.

"Sorry, hon, have to work late again; don't know what time I'll be home; don't wait up."

At least "hon" is better than "babe". That meant he wasn't angry or annoyed with her. Calling her "babe" used to really make her blood boil. In a negative sense. And it would still, if she gave a damn. Frankly, she didn't. Not any longer. Not any more. He wasn't worth it. Was he ever, she wondered? He must have been one time. Otherwise, she had to admit, she was a chronically bad judge of character. Maybe she was.

"No," she corrected herself. No one is. There are two types of people. Those who trust their judgement and those who don't. The first sometimes find happiness. The second never do. She had found happiness, but it was all over now. It was fun while it lasted. No, not fun, funtastic. Get her, funtastic. She really was moving into the twenty-first century.

Next day, she got up early. Early as in 4am. Truth is, she couldn't sleep. She really didn't know what she was going to do. In bed, she mulled it over. The thought of the word mulled made her laugh. Mulled wine? It meant it had been left for a while, absorbing things. And she was. Absorbing things, especially what she had been told by Mr O'Connell.

"Shit!" She sat bolt upright as she blurted it out. "I didn't pay the bill!"

She suddenly realised how anal she was. Was that why John had grown tired of her? Had he really grown tired of her, or was he just pretending he was in love from the start? Now her head was really reeling, reeling in the events that had brought her to where she was now.

She got out of bed. Although John said he was working late, she didn't expect it to be this late. Maybe he has trouble getting away from his girlfriend. Or boyfriend. John might not be happy if he were to hear what she was thinking. He always presented as such a ladies' man. Should that have raised some red flags? Perhaps. But when you're the lady getting his attention, it just seems that he only has eyes for you.

"Can't take my eyes off you," he used to sing to her, while gazing directly into hers.

"Who's he singing it to tonight?" she wondered. She was becoming ever more sure that there was someone, at least one. Something or someone was keeping him away from home, away from her.

It was now 4.30am. Surely, he would be home any minute, any second. She held her breath. And listened. Nothing. No car. No slamming of the door. No "honey, I'm home" in a slurred, jolly tone. Recently, those words never made her feel anything but dread. Now she could relax. For another while at least. She could have relaxed for the next six hours, but she didn't have the luxury of knowing that. John eventually made it home at 10.30am. He didn't look good. In fact, he looked like shit. She thought that appropriate, given how big an asshole he had become, or more likely had always been but had hidden it from her. He wanted to go to bed. By himself, thank her lucky stars. He was knackered, in his own words. Perhaps she should put him out of his misery. They shoot horses, don't they? Except change the word horses for arses. That would be good. But who would shoot them? Not their wives. They would be the first suspects. And rightly so. But who could blame them?

Walking past the bedroom door on the way to the bathroom, she heard the snoring. The door was ajar. She peeped in. He was fast asleep. He must have fallen asleep as soon as his ugly head hit the pillow. He looked vulnerable. He was. She could set the bed on fire, with John in it. That would solve all her problems. It could just be a terrible accident. Except, he didn't smoke and neither did she. But they could have been having sex with candles on the bedside cabinet. She awoke and went to make herself some coffee. He must have knocked the candles over. He had had a little too much to drink.

She wouldn't do it. She couldn't. She knew that, as did he. That's why he could sleep so soundly. She carried on to the bathroom. She

221

needed to freshen up. It made her feel more alive, that she actually wanted to carry on. She had long since stopped trying to lock the door. It had never been repaired since John removed the little spring from the locking mechanism. There would have been no point. He would just have done the same again once he found out. Either that or he would punish her in some other way. And she had never found it necessary to hide away from him since that incident, mainly because they were never or almost never home at the same time. Today was an exception. Any other day, she would have had the excuse that she had to go to work. Any other day, she would have been at work by the time he arrived home.

But it was Saturday. She would have to wait around at his majesty's pleasure. Until he awoke from his slumber. In case he desired something to eat or wanted her to take his shirts or suits to the laundry or cleaners. She just was never up to the task. His shirts needed to be pristine and pressed perfectly. This was just one more thing she fell down on, after her weight and her appearance. He used to tell her how beautiful she was, how attractive, be jealous of other men talking to her, or even looking at her. As she looked at herself in the bathroom mirror, she couldn't see the changes that he did. She was still the same: her skin was still clear, her eyes still blue and her hair, she thought, was in really good shape. Why, then, was she not as beautiful as when they first met?

"Beauty is in the eye of the beholder, isn't it? And now the beholder has altered his view. Maybe he needs to go to Specsavers. Hopefully, it isn't that he's been to Specsavers. But then if he only has eyes for someone else now, it wouldn't matter how good she looked or made herself look. And it probably isn't only eyes that he has for someone else. After all, he had discovered those injections for his penis. He could be a stud any day of the week without even trying. And even though she waited for him to disclose his secret of sexual success, he never mentioned them, the injections. So either it was a one-off experiment, which she doubted, or he's found another guinea pig. Well, here's the thing, Miss Doe, or Mr Doe, you'll discover soon enough that the pig is the one putting his pre-injected penis into you.

Josephine still wondered if he could be cheating with a man. After all, not to put too fine a point on it, hotels and restaurants are popular career choices for homosexual men. No offence intended, that's just the way it is. John had joked with her once upon a time that he was gay. Looking at himself in the mirror, he had said: "How could anyone not fancy this gorgeous hunk, man or woman," and then laughed hysterically to himself.

"Many a true word is said in jest," her mother used to say.

Having washed, she dressed downstairs so as not to disturb his rest. Not for his sake. The longer he slept, the less time she had to look at him, or listen to him. She could still hear his snoring as she passed the bedroom door. Maybe it was best he didn't come home last night. Best he didn't come home most nights. She was getting used to having the house to herself. Maybe with a bit of luck she would have it to herself permanently. Although she knew Mr O'Connell was right. John wouldn't give up without a fight. He wouldn't give her up, whether he had someone else or not. He certainly wouldn't give up his home, his base, even if it was only rented. It was still his. She made herself a cup of coffee and some toast and retired to the living room. As soon as she had finished eating, she felt tired, so tired.

She awoke with a start. The living room clock said 4.30pm. She had slept for hours. She heard footsteps on the stairs. John. He was carrying a suitcase and a suit bag. He put them down in the hallway, walked nonchalantly into the living room and sat on his favourite reclining chair. He didn't speak immediately, but pushed himself back in the chair and began to swivel from side to side. He was humming to himself. She couldn't make out the song. They used to play the humming game, where one would hum a tune and the other had to guess what it was. Apart from the more obvious, she was never able to guess correctly. His fault. He was useless at humming. On the other hand, she was brilliant at it, but he was also useless at guessing.

Once she had hummed "Baby I Love You". Very well, or so she thought. He guessed everything from "Bohemian Rhapsody" to "Total Eclipse Of The Heart". Useless.

"Josephine," he said eventually, "you awake?"

She felt like saying, "No, I'm asleep."

He wouldn't appreciate that answer, wouldn't find it funny. He would just ignore it.

"Yes, I'm awake," she said as non-sarcastically as she could.

"Good. We need to talk."

What had she done, she wondered, that would prompt a dressing down on a Saturday afternoon? He wasn't drunk. He couldn't be tired. So why would he be grumpy or angry. He didn't sound like he was either. He sounded like he was about to deliver a lecture, like a strict parent. But why today? She wanted to relax today. Her appointment with Mr O'Connell had stressed her. She needed a day or two to wind down. She didn't say anything, but kept eye contact. He knew by that, that she was listening.

"I think we should take a break from each other." Her jaw dropped.

"I don't know about you, but it seems to me that things aren't what they used to be."

He had a way with words, a way of making such a huge understatement sound as if it was a revelation. He couldn't seriously be that detached that he hadn't noticed how unhappy she was. No, not unhappy. Despondent. She didn't know what to say, so she stayed quiet.

"I'll stay in Belfast for a while. I can stay full-time in the hotel until I find an apartment. It'll give us both time to think."

"Think? You have obviously already done your thinking, you bastard!" she thought. It was as if he was trying to make her feel guilty. It's her fault again. Her fault he wanted to stay in Belfast, her fault he didn't want to be here with her. But wait. Isn't this what she wanted? For him to leave? And he was. But on his terms.

"We can stay in touch, maybe write to each other like we used to do," he said with a wry smile, as he got up from the chair. It was clear he didn't expect her to protest, beg him to reconsider. There was no uncertainty in his tone. She would do as he had decided. She would have no choice. She didn't get up. He stood in front of her, bent down to kiss her. She turned her cheek to him, as she had done on the morning of the honeymoon. He re-enacted the scene by putting his hand on the back of her head, pulling her gently towards him so that they were eye to eye, before kissing her passionately on the lips.

"Let's just kiss and say goodbye. Is that it, John," she thought, as he took his things, opened the door and left. She didn't bother to follow. Despite her resolve, she could feel the tears begin to roll down her cheeks. Was it sadness, fear or just the absolute relief of having her freedom back after all this time? Then she realised.

He's done it again. He's pre-empted me. Did he actually know that I was planning to look for a divorce, a barring order? That I wanted him out of the house? Now he looks like the good guy, the reasonable one. Mr O'Connell was right. He would have charmed the judge.

"He could charm the birds out of the trees," she could hear her mother say of someone she thought was less than honest or trustworthy.

"I didn't even get the chance to ask him to leave. He's always one step ahead of me." Now she was afraid. What was he planning? She felt like calling Mr O'Connell and telling him, asking him for his opinion. After all, he had experience of this sort of thing. What, did he think, was John up to? She had her mobile phone in her hand and was scrolling through it for his number. She stopped.

"It's Saturday. Of course it is. John knows it is. More and more it seemed to Josephine that he knew her every move. She would have to wait until Monday at least before she could speak with Mr O'Connell. She hoped he would be in the office. Until then, she would go through every possibility in her own mind, and that wasn't something she relished.

But she was nothing if not optimistic.

"Always look on the bright side," she thought. "He's gone. Isn't that what I wanted? Now I can do what I want. Or can I? What if John is filming me? What if he just wants to get something on me so that he can blackmail me? Wait. That supposes I'm going to do something wrong or something naughty. I wish. Chance would be a fine thing."

But if John was stalking, filming, he would catch something. A look, a laugh, a touch. A picture paints a thousand words, as they say. John would use the picture to paint as many as he could. "Dirty, rotten, cheating slut. She couldn't wait a day, a week, a month after I was gone. We were only on a trial separation. I told her that. I thought she understood."

Well, John, we'll play your little game. But you won't catch me doing anything. I'll be as good as gold.

"Like a virgin," she sang. She burst out laughing. Nothing's gonna change there, then. He hadn't even tried to have sex with her for weeks. Not since the rape. "He must be saving all his love for you, whoever you are. Has he told you about me, about us? If he has, it's probably all lies and jest."

"Yes, I'm married. But not for long. We all make mistakes. She was mine, god bless her."

Well, whatever he's told you, don't fall for it, don't believe him, don't believe a word.

CHAPTER THIRTY
DON'T YOU FORGET ABOUT ME

Josephine went into the bedroom, kicked off her shoes and walked towards the built-in wardrobes. She felt a sharp pain in her right foot that made her stop in her tracks. She bent down and picked a piece of glass out of her foot. Where did that come from? She couldn't remember the last time John had thrown a glass in the bedroom. It was a long time ago. She was sure it wasn't there yesterday. She had vacuumed the room to within an inch of its life. She needed to know it was clean, clean of John. Maybe she missed it. Poetic justice. "Walking on broken glass." A reflection of their broken relationship. The fact she was still thinking in song titles told her there was a long way to go. But she had done that before she met him. Why should she stop now? Wasn't that giving in to him again? She realised that she had never changed, despite him telling her she had.

"You've changed, Josephine. You're not the person I fell in love with."

That hurt her more than she had realised at the time. Only after he was gone did it become clear to her that she hadn't. Except that she had lost belief in herself.

"Don't Stop Believing." Her favourite song. She had. Stopped believing. That was her biggest mistake. She had lost herself, given herself to him, totally, so much so that she no longer knew who or what she was. He had been controlling her, her every move. Her every thought had to involve John: what he would want her to do, how he would want her to dress, to look, to act.

"I'm your puppet," she sang in her head. These weren't the kind of songs that used to come into her head when she was alone, before she met him, after she met him.

"There must be an angel playing with my heart" — that's what she used to sing in those early love-filled days.

227

Over the next few days, she felt more uneasy as she moved through the house. In the morning she tidied the living room, only to find the CD player starting up on its own.

"Don't You Forget About Me" it played the first morning without warning. She had loved that song, as did John. But now it was creepy.

"Please stop!" she thought, as she searched for the remote control. "I want to forget."

It wasn't there, the remote, readily to hand, so she walked over to the player and pressed "stop".

That night, she took her food to the living room and made herself comfortable. She relaxed in front of the television. "Real Housewives of Beverly Hills". She needed some mindless entertainment: women who spent their lives falling out and criticising each other and their relationships. Pretending they had problems in their lives. Pretending they were housewives. They want to have lived in Ireland in the 1950s or 1960s. Then they would know what a housewife was, a housewife like her grandmother. Hell, even like her mother. Although her mother didn't grow up in those times, she had embraced the lifestyle, or rather the lack of it.

Just as she was getting into the latest bitch-fest, the music drowned out the sound of the television.

"Every breath you take…"

The loudness and suddenness made her jump. The words made her shiver. She still hadn't managed to find the remote, hadn't really looked for it; so she leapt up and pressed "stop", turning the power off this time. She stood staring at it for a moment, remembered this morning. It wasn't the same song. She pressed the ON button, then ejected the CD.

"The Best Of The 80s". She knew both songs were on there. Could it be a coincidence that those songs would play for no reason? Okay, John would play CDs on shuffle most of the time, so who knows which song would play next? Was she being paranoid? "Paranoid", the song. That would be so appropriate now, she thought, considering the lyrics of the first few lines. Except that one belonged to the 70s, not the 80s. Still, it was sort of timeless. Not like her marriage, which now appeared to be over. Or was it? Were those songs playing a coincidence, or could John have programmed the CD player just to let her know he wasn't far away?

Maybe he wasn't. He could be standing outside, with the missing remote in his hand. He would know which buttons to push. After all, he had pushed her buttons, the right buttons. That's John. He always knew which buttons to push.

"Stop it, Josephine!" shouted her inner strength. "Get a grip."

It was time to turn off the lights and relax, with her glass of wine and something escapist.

Despite, or maybe because, the CD player having played "Don't You Forget About Me", she chose "The Breakfast Club". It always lifted her spirits when she was feeling down.

She settled back on the sofa, took a long drink from her glass and refilled it from the bottle. She looked at the label. "Vacqueras". John had explained to her that it came from the same region of France as "Chateauneuf De Pape". It was just as good, if not better. She didn't know if he was wrong or right, didn't particularly care. She liked it, had acquired a taste for it, and that's all that mattered.

She became engrossed in the movie. It was one of her favourites. She had actually copied Molly Ringwald's character in putting her lipstick between her breasts and applying it to her lips. She could do it. She impressed herself so much that she would repeat it at parties after a few drinks. John, at first, was supportive.

"Wait until you see this," he would say encouragingly. "Impressive or what?" he would say afterwards.

But his attitude to it, to her, to everything, had changed.

"You're not Molly Ringwald," he would say. Everyone else would laugh, but she knew he wasn't joking. It was his way of saying, "You're drunk, Josephine, sober up."

She would defy him and find as many people as she could to demonstrate her lipstick skills to. Until he would grab her by the arm and tell her it was time to go home. Most of the time she would acquiesce, just to please him. God knows why. All that would happen at home was that he would tell her how ridiculous she was making herself look and not to do it again, before going off to the living room again to drink himself silly and do his silly ridiculous routine. I suppose he thought it okay to look ridiculous in your own home.

But sometimes she was feeling defiant and would move on to

someone else to impress. She would look for what she thought was the best-looking man, or boy, in the room and ask him if he had seen "The Breakfast Club". Even if he hadn't, she would continue to demonstrate her dexterity. "Is that the right word?" she wondered. They weren't hands, after all. But they would certainly get people's attention, at least the male of the species. And possibly lesbians.

"Is that PC?" Josephine wondered. After all she wasn't insulting lesbians. She just assumed that they would find breasts attractive or pleasant to look at. And anyway, what does it mean to be PC, politically correct? Does that mean that politicians always do the right thing, the correct thing? Or more likely that they say the right thing, at the right time. Even if they don't mean it. John could have been a politician, a top politician. After all he had done the right thing, said the right things. In the beginning. And she believed it all, fell for it hook, line and sinker. She had thought of herself as an intelligent, independent woman. Like everyone, she had made mistakes, but she had learned from them. Or thought she had. But was it all a mistake, her marriage to John? They had been happy, hadn't they? Maybe they just weren't compatible. Some people aren't.

She was watching the final scene from the movie when Molly Ringwald gives one of her earrings to Judd Nelson. Proving there was something between them but that didn't mean that there would be a happy ever after. But she had shared much more with John. Here in this house. The good times, the bad times, the ups and the downs. It was just that the downs won in the end. So what now? Should she move, leave it all behind? Did it hold too many bad memories?

"No," she decided, "the memories aren't within these four walls, they're in my head. They will remain with me, if I let them, no matter where I am. This is not a bad place. There are no bad places. Places don't harm us or hurt us. People do.

"So," she decided, "moving wouldn't change things. It's up to me to change things. To leave the bad things in the past and hang on to the good times. To look back fondly on my time with John. And see it for what it was. Someone taking a chance on love. Me. And I would take that chance again. But not with John, obviously."

The movie was over and Josephine had almost finished her bottle of wine. She was feeling tired, really tired, mostly due to the fact that she couldn't turn her mind off, couldn't stop thinking. Mostly about John. What was he doing? Why did he leave? What was he planning? The uncertainty was draining. She had to move on, wished she could move on. It wasn't over, she knew it wasn't over. She had heard absolutely nothing from John since he left despite him having said he would be in touch. But then he had no reason to be in touch. They had their own separate lives. She had always paid the rent and utilities while he sometimes brought home the food. And drink of course. So his silence was by choice but not unexpected. For Josephine, it sort of confirmed her suspicions that he already had someone else. But she would really feel better, less apprehensive, if he would make contact in some way. She could call him of course. What would she say?

"I miss you." Not if hell freezes over. And at any rate she was brought up not to tell lies.

She could ask him how he was getting on, even though she didn't really care. What about "Who are you shagging nowadays? And is the Caverject still working?" She would have to hang up quickly.

His silence was not reassuring in any way. It was worrying, frightening. She was sure that he was watching, stalking her. He had said that they were meant to be together forever. And he meant it. It showed in his eyes, those eyes that used to go black, lose their natural blue colour, when the mask slipped and his true self appeared. But when would either self make another appearance? That's the question.

She had to go to bed, and so she did. She took off all her clothes and threw herself on top of it, spread out her arms, spread out her legs. She imagined herself like a naked snow angel on her clean white duvet cover, the one she had laundered and pressed perfectly following John's departure. It was warm in the room, warm enough for her to lie there all night. She had left the central heating running. Another nod to John. He would be horrified. One night he arrived home, drunk as usual, and burst into the bedroom, grabbed her by the arms and shook her awake.

"You left the fucking heating on" he screamed. She had. She was cold. It was one of the coldest nights of the year. That didn't matter to John. He would rather she froze to death than pay for more heating oil.

That might actually suit him as when he was making love to her at that time, which wasn't often, he might as well be doing it with a corpse. No feeling, no tenderness.

Having realised what was happening all she could muster was a weak "I'm sorry, I didn't realise."

"How the fuck could you not realise? It's like Kew Gardens in here." He let her go. She fell back on the bed. She had been that pliable.

"For fuck's sake" he blurted out as slammed the bedroom door and went back downstairs. To drink and play music presumably.

As she waited, she thought, "I pay for the utilities, including the heating oil." Not that it mattered to John.

As soon as the sound of music began, she turned over and went back to sleep in the safe knowledge that John wouldn't be coming to bed before morning, by which time she would, hopefully, be dressed and out the door on her way to work.

Back to tonight. She glanced at herself in the mirrored wardrobe doors. John had told her she had changed. She hadn't changed. She was still an attractive woman. Just then she noticed something under the bed. Something red. She thought she had cleaned everywhere. Obviously, she had been a little lax. That piece of glass and now this. She got out of bed, knelt down, reached in and grabbed hold of it, the red thing. As she pulled it out and sat on the edge of the bed, she instinctively discarded it. It was a suspender belt with a black stocking still attached to it. Not hers. She would have recognised it.

"The bastard, the absolute bastard" she muttered to herself. "What kind of game is he playing?"

Did he bring his mistress in here? And when? Has he been back? Is this his idea of a joke? Well it's not funny. One saving grace, she took her knickers with her. That's if she was wearing any. Now she had to get a torch and have a good look under the bed. And under the mattress. Nothing. Nothing else that is. Thank god she had thoroughly washed all of the bed clothes, including the sheets and pillow cases. But what if they were here today, while she was at work? He knew she didn't come home for lunch. They would have had hours. But the bed didn't look slept in. It was still perfect, just as she had left it in the morning. No lingering smell of perfume, no lipstick, no stray hairs. Would she do a forensic examination for stains or body odour? "Yuck" the thought of it. But she would either have to do that or launder everything again, thoroughly, very thoroughly. She could imagine him, or them, laughing at her now, the thought of her stripping the bed and feeling what she would obviously be feeling. But it could just be John winding her up, daring her to call him, to rant and rave, to scream and shout. He would let her, without saying a word. And when she'd finished, he would simply ask her what she was talking about. Deny any knowledge. He would have been in Belfast all day. So the only thing to do was to ignore him, let him wait. Until hell freezes over. As to the bed clothes? They were clean of odours, clean of stains. She wasn't going to be fooled. He can laugh all he wants to himself. If that's what make him happy.

"No, John, I won't take the bait. You'll have to do better than that. I won't break down. I'll harden my heart.

CHAPTER THIRTY-ONE
THERE'S A GHOST IN MY HOUSE

Although it was a relief that John had decided they needed a break from each other, Josephine had an uneasy feeling. The decision had been taken out of her hands. Once again, John was in control. He had always been in control of the relationship. In control of her. From the very moment she had set eyes on his advertisement. He had been fishing for a wife and she had taken the bait. Her uneasiness was intensified when she arrived home one day and on opening the door heard the unmistakeable strains of the beginning of "Stairway To Heaven". She stopped in her tracks, still holding the key in the door. Was this the ghost of John causing the CD player to come to life again? No. This song was certainly not on the "Best Of The 80s". Someone had to change the CD, and that's not possible to do from outside, with or without the remote. Someone is in the house, and if she had to put money on it, she would bet it was John. Damn, she hadn't even changed the locks. Was that because she knew he would be back some time and would take offence that he had been locked out of his own house, or because she thought he wouldn't be back and it didn't matter? Or just complacency?

She held her breath. She didn't know what to do. She exhaled deeply as John appeared from the living room.

"Did I frighten you?" he said casually.

"What the...?"

She caught herself before she could finish. She had promised herself after John left that she would stop swearing. She didn't want the negative atmosphere that had dwelled in the house over the previous months. The swearing, the threats, the demeaning comments.

"Sorry, dear."

She was unsure whether he was genuine or if he was being his usual sarcastic self.

"I just needed to get some more of my stuff. I didn't think you would mind. I meant to be gone before you got home, but got to playing some of my CDs. I guess old habits die hard. I'm not taking any of them at the moment. I have most of them on my hard drive anyway. It just felt good to sit in my own space and listen to one or two."

Josephine didn't want to engage in conversation, especially small talk. What was she going to say? How have you been? She didn't care.

"How have you been?" he continued. The git.

"Good, I'm good."

How was she going to make him go? All the while she was thinking of an excuse; let's be honest, a lie. But it would sound like a lie. He would know. Most people do. It's acceptable to say, "I'm so sorry, I have to meet a friend for dinner"; but it's not acceptable to say, "I know I have nowhere to go and nothing to do, but I'd rather go deaf than listen to you."

"I was just going," he said, turning back to the living room. She didn't follow him. She didn't want him to think she wanted him there. But he already knew that. He was testing her. She waited by the door and kept it open. In the back of her mind was the story of poor Mary. She contemplated standing on the doorstep and taking her shoes off. Even though they weren't that high, they weren't exactly running shoes. Too late. She had hesitated once again. He was there beside her, holdall in hand. He kissed her gently on the cheek. She hadn't realised until then that she had stayed glued to the spot all the time, the only thing moving being the myriad of thoughts going through her head.

"See you around," he said cheerfully, as he walked down the path and along the footpath.

He must have parked the car round the corner, the bastard. She hadn't noticed it. She wasn't being vigilant. What was wrong with her? Her appointment with the solicitor was wasted. He had warned her. It was all forgotten once John had left. Fuck. There she goes, using the F word again. She was losing control. She laughed at that. She never had control. He had left, but that didn't mean he had relinquished control. He didn't even leave his key, on purpose. But even if he had, he could have another one, and another one, and another one. She knew now she had to change the locks. Something she should have done the day after he left. But that was a Sunday. Well, on the Monday, then. And even though his leaving had prompted her to call Mr O'Connell, until she realised it was Saturday, she didn't even bother to consult with him or speak to him on the Monday. All she did was call his secretary and ask for a bill so that she could settle up. Even though she had gone to his office to pay it, she still hadn't asked to speak with him that day or made an appointment to do so. But why hadn't he contacted her since? Now she was being silly. He had told her to think it over and make another appointment. It was up to her. He couldn't chase down every single person who came to him for advice. He wasn't her keeper. He wasn't to know what was happening. But she had decided that she should go back to him now, now that she had been woken from the slumber of stupidity. She called his office the very next day after John's visit to schedule an appointment. Better late than never. He had a court case starting in Dublin that week and it might be a week or more before he was back in the office. But she could have an appointment for two weeks' time. She took it.

In the meantime, she would have to make her own decision as regards the lock situation. If she didn't change them, John could come back any time, lie in wait for her and… And what? Kill her? He would be the prime suspect. Or would he? After all, he left of his own accord, had come back for some more of his stuff and left again. Where were the threats, the intimidation? Where was the motive? There was none. He hadn't even asked to come back. As far as anyone knew, he didn't want to come back. And if there was going to be a divorce, why would it be acrimonious? There was nothing to fight over. No assets, no children. So why would he want to harm her, want to kill her? So why change the locks? Why not let him come and go as he pleases? But no. She didn't want that. How could she live like that?

She had to do something. But changing the locks might anger him. He might see it as an act of aggression. To him it would be an insult.

"You fucking locked me out. Of my own house. And why, dear Josephine, why? Is there something you don't want me to see? My replacement, maybe? Have you struck it lucky? A nice doctor at last?"

"Fuck you, Mr Hobson. I'm going to have to decide. But how?" It might seem a bit unconventional in these circumstances, but she decided to toss a coin. She would change the locks.

"If you're going to do something, do it properly." That was one of her mottoes. So she did. New locks on the front and back door, as well as locks on all the windows, and a new lock on the bedroom door. That would do it. Until the fitter kindly informed her that the internal walls were merely plasterboard. Anyone could punch their way through them.

"So this lock on the bedroom door serves no purpose?"

"Well, it takes time to punch your way through plasterboard; maybe enough time to call for help or escape out the window."

"And break my legs?"

"There is that," he replied. "Want me to remove it?"

"No. Leave it. Let him break through the wall if he has the balls."

She was joking, but when she had time to think about it, she felt as if she had wasted her time and her money. Not because of the futility of it, but also the ridiculousness of it. She was fortifying herself, her home, against a situation that was not going to happen. And what if John came calling again and found himself locked out? He would wait until she arrived home and challenge her. Outside. What good, then, would her fortress be to her? No good, that's how good it would be. Should she undo it all, put the original locks back? That would be ludicrous. She could just make an excuse, tell John she had heard someone try to break in; she was frightened. She was a woman on her own. She needed security now he was no longer here. Would she give him a key just to prove she was telling the truth? She would be back at square one. But somewhat poorer. Time to stop thinking. What's done is done. If John does appear again, and, like Jesus, no one knows the day or the hour, she'll play it by ear.

"Que Sera, Sera."

CHAPTER THIRTY-TWO
THE LETTER

Josephine was glad that John was gone, but he could come back any minute. Sometimes they come back, just as in the Stephen King movie. John would be back. She was never more sure of anything. But when? And why? What would he want? Would he want to make it work? He should never have left, he wasn't himself. He was having a crisis, an early mid-life crisis or something. But then he might be older than he let on, older than she realised. He did look like a middle-aged man now. And she was still young. And looked young. If he did come back, would she tell him to sling his hook or, in the words of Michael Jackson, to "beat it"?

She stopped her thoughts in their tracks and rewound. Mr O'Connell had told her it wouldn't just be a case of asking for a separation or divorce. Maybe he's wrong. Maybe it would be that simple. John had left of his own volition, his own free will. Maybe he wanted a legal separation or divorce, but was afraid she wouldn't want it just because he did. That she would oppose him for the sake of it. That she would think he had found someone else and refuse him out of spite or jealousy. After all, she had on occasion, especially since things went south, shown defiance, had gotten stronger, more challenging, been more sarcastic than compliant. Maybe he wasn't as sure of himself as he made out. Often times, people need to put up a front, seem stronger than they actually are. Surely, like most people, he has an Achilles heel. If he was sorry he married her, as he had told her more than once, wouldn't the simple solution now be to tell him he can take it back, forget it ever happened, go his own way? Start again with someone else. Chances were that he already had a someone else, that he already belonged to another. Another who might not even know she existed. After all, John was good at leaving out details when it suited him. He didn't consider it lying.

"If someone doesn't ask the question, how can I answer it?" was his logic. A logic that suited him and what he wanted.

And so, decided Josephine, I'll ask the question. I'll write a Dear John letter.

"Dear John," she began.

"I'm writing to you," she continued, "because when you left you said we might write to each other as we used to. You haven't. You haven't even contacted me in any way, shape or form. So I have to draw my own conclusions. After much thought and soul-searching, I have concluded that it's over, we're over. All that remains is for us to make it official. Someone told me that it's easy to get married, because both parties are of the same mind, want the same thing, to get married to each other; but that when it comes to ending the marriage, it's not the same. One party might not want it, the separation or divorce. I just want to let you know that whatever you want, you can have it. I won't stand in your way. I'm grateful for the times we had and I'll never forget the happiness and pleasure you have brought me. As for our troubles, I don't blame you for any of them. Trouble finds us no matter who we are, no matter what we do, no matter how happy or how unhappy we are. Let's just say it found us. Resulting in us being where we are now. You in Belfast and me here in Letterkenny. And if that's the way it has to stay, then so be it. Good thing is, we don't have many assets to fight over. I don't want anything and I don't think I have anything to give you. So just write me off. It's time to say goodbye."

She read it over, again and again. There was nothing she wanted to add or change. She did initially include "nor any children" in that line "Good thing is we don't have many assets to fight over", but thought better of it and deleted those words. She didn't want to inspire any response or conversation that included children. Even though it was clear that John was never going to have any, he knew that subject was her weakness and, although she didn't know how, he might use it against her. How was she going to sign off? "Love, Josephine" or "Your ever-loving wife"? Hardly. When in doubt, she decided, do nothing. So she did. Nothing.

Who else would he think it was from? Unless, of course, like some of the stories she had read, he was leading a double life, had another wife. But would he also have left her in Letterkenny, alone? Anything's possible as far as John's concerned. She had learned that much. But she was just being ridiculous again. She would send it. But where?

John had said he would stay in the hotel until he found an apartment. Whether he had or not, she wasn't to know. So her only option was to send it to the hotel. Would he be angry that she did that? After all, it would be clearly marked "Private and confidential", but that in itself could set him off.

"When someone receives a letter marked 'Private and confidential', it makes people wonder what it's all about. Does he or she have a secret lover? Do they owe money to someone? Are they in trouble with the police? What have they done?" That was John's thinking.

She could just send it as a normal letter addressed to John Clarke, Assistant Manager, Europa Hotel, Belfast. But then would someone else open it? His secretary? She could be the one. If so, it would probably make her happy, the contents. But it might not make John happy that she had read it, especially if she didn't know about Josephine; or even if she did, John could be using the oldest excuse in the book: that his wife won't give him a divorce.

Hobson's choice it is again, then.

She decided she would mark it "Personal" as a compromise, so that no one else would dare open it. Protocol and all that.

Just as she dropped it in the post box, she wondered if he still had his "Box 22". Was he still there in the personal ads in her local newspaper or some other newspaper? She picked up the local newspaper on her way home from work. There it was. "John Box 22". Except the wording had changed.

"Vibrant professional man with a lust for life seeking young vibrant woman who would like to dance with me, day or night. I can mambo, salsa, twist or tango. Anything as long as it takes two. Could you be the one? Write me back or write me off."

God, he was arrogant. Not what she had thought when she read his first ad. But it wasn't his first ad, was it? He was growing in confidence. Not sure about mambo, salsa or tango, but he could certainly twist anything.

She wondered if it might be fun to respond. Would he realise? Would it perhaps reignite his love for her, make him realise that she was the best thing that ever happened to him? They could start all over again, a fresh courtship. In her head, she wrote:

"Dear John,

I am replying to your advertisement for a young vibrant woman who would like to dance with you, day or night. I can dance if you want to. You can lead and I will follow. Unless, of course, like me you have two left feet. But then it's not always about how well you can dance, but how much passion and effort you put into it. So, if you're free and need a partner, write me or write me off."

Would he get the hint or would he think it a coincidence that someone other than Josephine would play him at his own game? Would the realisation dawn that he had been found out? Did he care? Is this why he hadn't written, why he hadn't contacted her? He was too busy writing to another, or maybe several others. He had spent so many nights in Belfast or elsewhere, he could be leading not just a double life but a triple or quadruple life. Whatever or whomever he was doing no longer mattered. Now there would be one less to worry about.

She hoped beyond hope she had done the right thing and that she would get the reply she hoped for.

"Please, please, please let me get what I want this time," she sang in her head.

CHAPTER THIRTY-THREE
I WANT YOU BACK

Josephine waited for a response to her letter. And waited. And waited. It wasn't days now, it was weeks. She realised that it wasn't going to happen, what she wanted. For him to respond and say, "Thanks, Josephine, for your letter, you have set my mind at ease. Let's just get divorced, as soon as possible. Let's just be glad for the times we had together."

The frightening thing was, she didn't know what he was feeling. Surprise? Sadness? Regret? Not likely. Else why hadn't he contacted her? Relief? No. He would have replied. So, what? Nothing? That's it. Nothing. He was feeling nothing. He had never felt anything. For her. For anyone. He didn't have feelings. Only thoughts. And now he was thinking, how dare she suggest something, anything. How dare she try to take control. But could he remain silent? Not like him, not at all.

So she kept an eye on the post. Maybe he would reply in his own time, that he was keeping control. Leaving her with her thoughts. She didn't get that much post. Yet every day she would take the letters from the hall table and flick through them. Bills, catalogues, offers, vouchers, promos. Two pizzas for the price of one. That one struck a chord. She wouldn't be needing two pizzas for the foreseeable future. Unless, of course, she was going to be swept off her feet someday soon by a handsome stranger. Well, it would have to be a stranger, because there just wasn't any handsome man in her circle of acquaintances, not anyone that would excite her. That was the thing. With all she'd been through, with all that John had put her through, she had to admit she missed the excitement. John was a bastard at times, he was a bully, but when things were good, they were good. Josephine had never had so much fun, so much excitement, never laughed so much, laughed with John. The sex was good. It sounded ridiculous, but she would miss him. She didn't realise it wouldn't be for long.

Since John's unexpected visit, the story of Mary's murder played more on her mind; so much so, that she never left the house now without taking a taxi. A taxi to work, a taxi home from work. Two places that John knew she would be for certain, home and work. More often than not, she would tell the taxi driver who took her home that she had no change in her bag, she would have to get it from the house, just so he or she would wait until she was sure John wasn't lurking somewhere. He was nowhere in sight. That didn't mean he wasn't there, somewhere. She could remember all the times he just appeared from nowhere. That sounded daft, but it was true. One minute he wasn't there, and then he was. She sometimes thought that he could transport himself wherever and whenever he wanted, like Captain Kirk in "Star Trek". If only she could beam him up somewhere, and leave him there.

"I'm here," he would announce; "aren't you glad to see me?" She would have to smile and be pleasantly surprised. She used to be in the early days. Later, it came to a point where she was no longer surprised, pleasantly or unpleasantly. She came to expect to see him wherever she was. She used to love the song "Someone To Watch Over Me". It was a beautiful love song. For Josephine, it took on a more sinister meaning. Someone to watch over me every minute of every day. She had learned to live with it. She was doing nothing wrong, at least as far as she was concerned. That didn't mean John wouldn't find something in a look, a word, a smile, a laugh, even a sleight of hand. He often did. One day when he called to her work, which she had asked him not to do, she had looked up just as one of the doctors walked by her desk. She realised John was staring at him. She waited for him to turn back to her.

"Fancy him, Josephine?" He was being pathetic.

"Who?" she pretended.

"You mean you didn't see him?" he quipped sarcastically.

"Him?"

Now his frustration was beginning to show, but he knew he wasn't winning.

"Anyway," he began, "I've booked a table for us at the newest place in town. Got in there even though they said they were booked out."

"Well done you," she said, as enthusiastically as she could muster.

He stood up and puffed out his chest. She swore she could see a bunch of coloured feathers pop up out of his ass. It was only the sunlight reflecting on the window behind him.

She got up, walked around the desk and kissed him gently on the lips.

"Thank you," she whispered.

She was so happy to hear the phone ring. She picked it up.

"Hello, Letterkenny University Hospital."

She sensed that John had slipped away. If she had turned her back on him at home, there might have been consequences. Here, he wouldn't dare. Not in front of all these people. Not in public. That's how his kind operate. Not John, he's much too nice. Street angel. He knew when to be nice and when to be naughty. Even Santa Claus couldn't have known. Evil finds a way, it always finds a way. Welcome to the real world. All you girls out there looking for Prince Charming, you won't find him. No. He'll find you. And when he does? Then the fun begins, but not for you. "Don't judge a book by its cover" is such a good saying. A better one for the times we're in.

"Don't judge a Facebook page by its cover."

If something doesn't look right, feel right, it's not right. Sometimes, if it's too good to be true, if he's too good to be true, he isn't true, he'll never be true.

And speaking of Facebook, he was on there now, despite him telling her social media was for losers. There he was smiling, beguiling, with a girl by his side. But then he was a charmer. She could just be a patsy. He would persuade the devil to pose with him. Oh, wait, that would be a double exposure. Whatever. If he had moved on, things were looking up. And then...

She had dispensed with the taxis. She walked to work. Walked home from work. Even went to a restaurant after work, with the other girls, had a few drinks, a bite to eat, and walked home alone. It felt good. Threw her handbag on the living room floor, put on her own choice of music, threw off her clothes and danced naked in her own house. She had even bought an expensive bottle of wine before leaving the restaurant: Chateauneuf-du-Pape, paid for with her own debit card. "It was named for Pope John XXII, translated as 'New Castle Of The Pope'," she could hear John say. But it was delicious. It was one of John's favourites, maybe because it is connected with a Pope called John. Did he have aspirations to be Pope? Her thoughts were going through that ridiculous phase again. Stop, Josephine, just enjoy the wine. There was a time you had to listen to that rubbish, but not any more.

Now here you are, alone, naked, but no longer afraid. Her clothes lay on the living room floor: dress, bra, panties. She was dancing all over them as Lady Gaga sang "Just Dance".

It was one of her favourite songs to dance to. John didn't like it, wouldn't dance to it. One night out, they were on the dance floor when it came on. John left the floor, leaving her on her own. She refused to follow him and just danced as the song told her to. She had defied him that night, and that didn't happen often. It was happening now, but this time it would be for good.

As she twisted and twirled around the room, she was happy, so happy. She wondered how it was that she was happy to be by herself. Don't people always say that they feel so lonely, so alone. She did feel alone, but it was such a wonderful feeling, to be alone after all this time. She never realised she could be happy by herself. This was it. Happiness didn't come from outside, from someone else. It comes from within, from yourself. All she needed was the confidence to be happy. It was here, it had arrived. She had forgotten the expensive bottle of wine. She really didn't need it. But she wanted it, and that's all that mattered. She wanted to do what she wanted to do. And she would. No more waiting for someone else to decide, for someone to tell you what you can do or should do. Why had it taken her so long to wake up? Why had she let life pass her by, be a passenger rather than a driver? She laughed. She couldn't fucking drive. She never had to. Isn't that what it's all about? I don't have to. No longer. She decided there and then, after she had found a corkscrew and opened that bottle of wine, she had paid too much for, it wasn't about what you needed to do, it was about what you wanted to do. And in that moment, that night, there was a lot of things she wanted to do. She sat down on John's favourite chair, his had-to-have best-quality leather recliner. It was cold on her bare ass. But once there with her glass of wine, a large glass of wine, she made herself comfortable, even though she felt as if it was sucking in her buttocks. The music kept playing. "Family Portrait". "Family" — she wondered what it really

245

meant. She had often heard the term "dysfunctional family". In her time at work, she listened to everything the professionals had to say. She had a question she had never posed.

"Is there such a thing as a functional family?"

Then she fell asleep, alone, in her own living room, naked, happy and a little bit drunk.

Next morning, she awoke in the same place she had fallen asleep. In her right hand a glass, empty. She looked at it.

"Oh, no!" she thought. "I'm turning into him."

She wasn't really. But thoughts are intrusive; they seem to come out of nowhere, out of the ether. Or is it that they are being transmitted over the airwaves by someone who is thinking about you? That thought frightened her. Thoughts do that to a person. Sometimes, like a train, they keep on coming down the tracks. She was sober now. She had to think in a sober manner. It was morning. She was sitting in her own living room, naked, on a leather chair, empty glass in hand, looking at a half-finished bottle of wine on the table. Did she want to be here? Why not. There are worse places she could be. Well, maybe not worse places, but worse situations. Saving grace? No one else is here. No. Let's call a spade a spade — John isn't here. And if she has her way, wouldn't be ever again.

She was craving something to eat. They, she and John, used to get breakfast on his and her days off together, somewhere in town. The works: eggs, sausages, bacon, fried bread, mushrooms, tomatoes, black pudding, tea and toast. Made pigs of themselves. She never realised in those days what a pig John would turn out to be, or was at heart. Funny thing is, they weren't big meat eaters. More often than not, their home-cooked meals were meat-free. But these mornings were special. Now she was a few hundred metres away from the temptation of that big breakfast. And just like Oscar Wilde, she couldn't resist.

She went to the bedroom and threw her clothes in the laundry bin. Then she went and took a shower. She felt better. She dressed casually, gathered up her handbag and headed out the door.

He was just standing there. Outside the door. Staring straight at her. She was taken totally by surprise.

Before she could speak, he did.

"I'm sorry. I didn't mean to frighten you."

"Déjà vu," she thought. "If you don't mean to frighten me, then stop just turning up here."

"I needed to talk to someone. I have no one else."

She doubted that.

"What about that bitch on Facebook?" she thought, but not out loud.

"I'll leave if you want me to. I guess I hoped you'd still have some feelings for me. Do you?"

Josephine didn't want to answer that one.

"Is there something wrong?"

Even though some say you should never answer a question with a question, it was a great way to deflect the focus from yourself. So, in her book, this wisdom was flawed.

"I've got cancer."

Whether it was that her head was still somewhat fuzzy or that she didn't expect what she was hearing, she felt her limbs go weak. She dropped her handbag, spilling its contents all over the doorstep. They both hunkered down simultaneously. They looked at each other for what seemed like a lifetime. She could imagine them in a movie. They would seem like strangers meeting for the first time.

"Say Hello, Wave Goodbye" played in her head, appropriately.

They were eye to eye. She almost felt sorry for him. Tears welled up in her eyes, no matter how much she tried to suppress them. She still had feelings for him. But then she would have the same feelings for a stranger, a cat, a dog, even a hamster. She was a softy, would always be a softy, despite everything that had gone before. She wanted to help people, all sorts of people, especially the vulnerable. And now here in front of her, John was being vulnerable. She had never seen him like this. She felt sorry for him. She had never been a vindictive person, wished anything bad on anyone. She knew now that included John.

"Where?"

He didn't seem to understand the question.

"Where is the cancer?"

There was a pause.

"Prostate," he said eventually, lowering his gaze.

Given his current body position, it was as if he was looking at the affected area.

"Wow!" she thought.

She remembered that night, the night of the Caverject, as she thought of it in her own mind since and how she had asked him to stop, to get off.

He had to have it. Raped her. Is he being punished for his past sins? No. She really didn't believe in Karma. Whatever happens, happens. We don't get a say in our own destiny. Neither reward nor punishment. Otherwise, it wouldn't be destiny.

"I want you back."

That did stun her. Had she heard him properly.

"I'll change, I am changed. I love you. I always have. We can start all over again. Be like we were with each other in the beginning."

She couldn't believe what she was hearing. Is he serious? Is he seriously expecting me to forgive and forget? Did he not get her letter? It didn't seem the right time to bring it up, to kick him when he's down. But maybe she should, mention the letter. She couldn't think straight.

"I have to go, I'm meeting someone. We can talk later."

It was such a lame way to finish this, but she was unsure what was happening.

"Okay," he said, dropping what he had picked up for her into her handbag.

She was relieved. She expected more from him, more persistence.

"Remember, I love you," he said, as he walked away.

That remark made her shiver involuntarily. But why? She went back inside and called a taxi.

She had resolved to carry on, have her breakfast, go shopping, or window shopping, do what an independent woman does — but was afraid he would be waiting for her somewhere down the road. She walked home. He surely wouldn't be back today, wouldn't wait around that long. And she was still trying to be resilient. When she got to the door, she rummaged in her bag for her keys. She couldn't find them. Where can they be? She remembered that morning.

Had she dropped them? Did he pick them up? Does he have them? Does John have them?

She was in a panic. She danced around on her own front door step. Not a happy dance this time. More of a stomp. A noise. Something against her foot. She looked down. Keys. Her keys. They were still there.

Thank God. She let herself in and locked the door. She felt relieved but tired, so tired. She wasn't used to letting her hair down. She decided to go to bed for the afternoon. She fell into a deep sleep. She dreamed of her wedding day, John waiting for her at the altar. As he turned to face her, a smile on his face, she was horrified. There was a large, gaping hole where his manhood should be, and through it she saw herself lying in a pool of blood. She sat up in bed, her heart pounding. She was engulfed in darkness. It took her a second to realise where she was. She had slept for hours. She switched on the bedside light. It was midnight.

CHAPTER THIRTY-FOUR
KILLING ME SOFTLY

After his unexpected appearance and revelation, she had texted him. He hadn't changed his number. But then he could have more than one phone. More surprisingly, she hadn't changed her number. Another case of indecision. She needed to have some contact with him, especially as he hadn't responded to her letter. She told him in her text how she felt sorry that he had prostate cancer, that she hoped that he would get the right treatment and that everything would turn out well. However, she didn't think that it was a good idea for them to get back together, to try again. That their relationship had become toxic and that being apart had made her realise that. In her opinion, it was better that they simply remember the good times and what they had together and that they both move on. She wasn't going to be difficult. In a way, she was reiterating what she had said in her letter. The letter he had never responded to. It was now clear why. She hoped that her text would get through to him. That they could both now move on. More importantly, that she could move on. Surely there would be no complications. Thank God the house wasn't theirs. She had heard stories of people fighting over the house, the furniture, the television, even down to the kitchen appliances. She wouldn't let that happen. He could take the television and trash it if he wanted, take the toaster, take the kettle. Even the microwave. Even though he rarely used it. According to John, using a microwave wasn't cooking. She learned that very early on in their marriage.

"Seriously, Josephine. You bought a microwave. For what? I thought you knew how to cook. We're not having Uncle Ben tonight, are we? Or M&S? Microwave and Spit out."

That really tickled him. Despite it all, the microwave remained in the kitchen. John never used it. He was like that. He couldn't let himself down. Not even to reheat things. Even though he had used it the night they escaped. Not that he would remember or admit to that. He would wait for the oven to heat up rather than put anything in the microwave.

But then he might be right in that regard. Microwaves don't carry a warning that says:

"Be careful when reheating food in this appliance; leave it too long and say goodbye to your tongue and your taste buds."

So, in the long run, she might just be left with the microwave.

Josephine took a tour of the house. There were, of course, certain things she would like to keep. Their bed was so comfortable, and despite what had happened to her in that room, in that bed, she would still sleep there. Had slept there since John left. She was like her mother in one thing at least. She was pragmatic. Just like her mother had given her brother her father's new shoes, Josephine wouldn't throw out a good bed, wouldn't move to another room. She liked her bedroom. John had let her choose the colours, the fittings. At the time, it didn't seem like he was letting her. More like he was encouraging her. Told her she had great taste. Whatever she wanted to do with the bedroom would be good enough for him.

No, not good enough, better than that. Would be just fantastic. It was. Well, she thought so.

And so did he, he said. But then John would say anything, any time, just to keep her happy. Or so he thought. It had worked for a time. For too long a time. But then she had no one to blame but herself. She fell for it. Fell for him. His charm. And he did have charm. But it seemed so real to her in the beginning. She wanted it to be real, and that's what made it real. She didn't realise how real it would actually become. A real nightmare. But she had had an awakening. A rude awakening. Not the sort she used to enjoy in the early morning of those first heady days and weeks together. It seemed so long ago now. Now it was time to live in the real world again. Somehow that filled her with sadness. It had been a nightmare at times. The other times it had been a wonderful dream.

What now?

They say you can never go back. Yet here she was, back in the year BJ. Before John. What was she going to do? Go back to the personal ads? Take another punt? But how could she trust her judgement? She had got it wrong, or had she? She had never had so much fun. Had never felt so wanted, so desired, so much in love. It didn't matter now whether John felt the same, had ever felt the same. She had experienced feelings that she had never experienced before. And maybe she would never experience again. If she wanted, she could relive them, concentrate on them. Edit out the bad times. Deleted scenes from a happy marriage. That's one thing no one can take away from us. We can remember what we want to remember and how we remember it. We can make our memories happy or sad. Ignore the bad times if we want. Who can tell us not to?

But it was difficult for Josephine to do when John still hadn't gone away completely. She was still connected to him. He had replied to her text. By voice call. And at first, she was hopeful. The communication had been amicable. He just wanted her to be happy. He wasn't going to make things difficult. It made her feel at ease. Everything was going to go well. Yet he never mentioned her letter. She thought that strange. But never brought it up. Why? There was no why. She had assumed he received it, had read it. Nothing told her otherwise.

Then he started the stupid stuff again.

"Josephine, you don't know how much I miss you. I've really fucked up. I didn't know what I had, what we had. I'm lost without you. I don't blame you for wanting to move on, but just think about it. We could try again. I could try again. You tried your best. You put up with all my shit. I promise you, if you find it in your heart to forgive me, I'll make your life as wonderful as it was in the beginning. More wonderful. Just think about it. Don't say anything. Goodnight. I love you. More than ever."

He hung up. She almost threw up.

She came to dread his calls. She would love to tell him to go fuck himself. He probably would if he could. After all, that's the only person he was truly in love with. She so wanted to be free of him, but if she faced him off, he would just make it more difficult. If that were possible. So she put up with it. But where would it end?

Night after night, he would call.

"Go Away."

She had changed her ring tone in his honour. She ignored it. It rang out. Then rang again.

"Go away," Gloria Estefan kept on singing. But John couldn't hear her, and even if he could, he would ignore her. She didn't know whether to answer or not. Why would she? But he would call again. And again.

"Josephine. I'm sorry." So predictable. She mouthed the rest in time.

"We're good together, you and I. As good as it gets."

"Don't give up on a good thing." That was new.

"Oh. My. God," she thought. "He really wants me to fall for him all over again. Hence the song reference. He's trying to push my buttons again."

She could now hang up and really annoy him. She didn't. Instead, she waited, stayed silent. She so wasn't in the mood for more of this.

"Are you there?"

It brought her back to those nights when he had flown off the handle, ranted and raved at her incessantly. Took himself to the living room, drank, played his music and fell asleep. Then, just as she was nodding off in bed, he would crash into the bedroom. No, not angrily. In fact, he was reticent. Reticent but paralytic. Hence why the door flew open with such force. He didn't know his own strength. Well, if you call staggering across the hallway and falling forward with all your body weight into the bedroom door strength, you've got the idea. "Josephine? Josephine? Are you awake?" he would say, while shaking her vigorously. How the hell did he expect her to sleep through the thunderstorm and the earthquake he was creating?

"I just want you to know that I love you. And I'm sorry, really sorry if I upset you tonight."

Then he would hold her, hug her, kiss her on the forehead and go back to the living room. She couldn't figure out what he was thinking. She never could. Did he remember all those horrible things he said to her, all the horrible names he called her? He remembered something. Why else would he apologise? And what exactly was he apologising for? For John, it had just become a routine. Just in case. Sometimes he apologised when he had done nothing except take his Jack Daniels and go to the living room, leaving her to clear up the dinner dishes.

Tonight, Josephine believed he knew what he was doing. So she let him go on.

"Josephine, I know you're there."

She put her hand over her phone so as not to let him hear her breathing. She was having trouble staying silent.

"I know you're there. Call me back. Please. I've changed. Everyone makes mistakes. I did. We did."

There he goes again. It's never all his fault. I did wrong. But so did you. "Well, here's some of your own medicine, John. If you have changed, which I doubt, so have I." One thing that had changed for sure was the dynamic. He wanted a response, expected a response. She could almost hear the frustration in his breathing. She had had enough. She hung up. It wasn't "not tonight, Josephine". It was "not tonight, John".

She was happy with herself, so happy. She turned her phone off. She knew where the conversation would take her. He would talk about the good times again, ask her if she could remember how it felt, how good it was. Try to pull on her heart strings. Well, he had pulled her strings for the last time. She was no longer his puppet.

Worst of all, he would make these calls when he knew she was still awake, but close enough to her going to bed. That frightened her. Of course, he knew she was a creature of habit and could assume that she had kept the same routine; but was it that, or was he watching, stalking? He was never one to make assumptions. Was he calling her from outside in his car or, more frighteningly, standing outside her window? For a time, she used to stand in front of every window in the house; well, the downstairs ones anyway, open the blind quickly and expect to see him standing there. She had to admit that once when he called, she got out of bed and opened the blind on the bedroom window. Was it because she was half asleep and it had become a habit, or did she really think he could levitate? At the moment of realisation, she thought of "Wuthering Heights". A face at the bedroom window. Not Cathy, though. John. If that's his real name. She had never seen his birth certificate, his driving licence, his passport. He dealt with everything, looked after everything. Maybe he was a spectre, a figment of her imagination. She wished. Then he might disappear. Just like he disappeared as she opened those blinds. He was never there. But he could have anticipated her movements. He had always been good at that. It reminded her of those scary movies where the bogeyman disappears just as the victim turns around. She could imagine him standing outside the window, staring in, and just as she pulls the blind, disappearing to the side, back against the wall, laughing to himself. But then she had sensor lights outside. If he was there, the light would be on. But when it comes to logic versus imagination, imagination wins hands down, every time.

When he called the next night, something was different. He sounded more upbeat. He was talkative, too talkative. He was sober. He was still talking about the past, how they had met, how good things had been, recounted minute by minute that first night they met. He had it right, he had everything right, down to the most minute detail. While he was describing it, she was reliving it. She had to admit that she could almost have forgotten everything since and taken him back. Started again. Go back to square one. Had he really changed? Become what he was before? Was it down to her? What he had become? Could she go back and do it again, differently? Her head was reeling.

"Even The Bad Times Are Good" was playing in the background of his call.

She didn't want to hear any more. She hung up and turned her phone off quickly. Hopefully, he would think that her battery had died. This call unnerved her more than any of his other ones. She didn't want to open any of the blinds. Instead, she went and checked the doors. They were locked. All locked. And he didn't have a key. Did he? What about that morning she spilled the contents of her handbag? Her keys were still there when she got home. Still there, or someone had put them back. That someone being John. And if it was? She blessed herself.

"Oh, no, pray God I'm wrong."

But what if she wasn't? Should she stay or should she go? She had watched so many horror movies. Victims always do what they are expected to do. They always try to escape. They never stay put. She would. That was her mistake.

She needed to relax. All his phone calls, all his persistence had made her stressed, more stressed than she could ever remember, even more stressed than him coming home to her in a drunken stupor. At least she had come to expect that, had learned how to deal with it. Tonight? Well, tonight was tonight. She decided she would take a bath, a hot bath. As she ran it, she had a horrible thought.

"What if he's waiting? Waiting to drown me for real, to make it look like an accident? But then she had no drugs, no alcohol, in her system. How would that go? Was she just too tired, too stressed, committed suicide by drowning herself in the bath? Has anyone ever done that? Successfully? If that's the word for it. Surely your natural instinct would be to stay alive.

"Staying alive, staying alive," she hummed in her head. Would John have got it? Probably not.

If he was in the house, and she wasn't entirely sure he wasn't, there would be signs. She would struggle this time. He would leave marks. She would leave marks on him. Bite him with all her strength. He wouldn't get away with it. So what now? Would she do a sweep of the house or just relax in the tub? She would do both. She checked every room, every nook and cranny. Even the wardrobe, where John suspected her lover was hiding. Maybe he was now. No. He wasn't there. He was nowhere. Not in this house. Safe, then, to take that hot bath. As she lay back, her head against the blow-up pillow she had treated herself to earlier, all thoughts of John drifted away. She went to sleep.

She awoke with a start. Was there a noise? She couldn't tell. So she listened. Nothing. That's the problem with sleep. We turn off. And when we awake, we're not sure what's in dreams and what's real. All she could do was carry on. Get out of the bath, the water that had now become colder, but not so cold as to make her shiver. She dried herself in front of the very same mirror that John had made her stand in front of when he demeaned her, pretended that he was going to bugger her. She hated that word, bugger. Years ago, if someone called you a bugger, it was innocuous, innocent. Now, after she had heard that some man had been guilty of buggery, it was disgusting. She was disgusted.

She was feeling relaxed after her bath, relaxed enough to go to bed, to go to sleep and hopefully forget all of this, everything. For one night only.

She had prepared the bedroom. The mood lamp was still there. Red was still the most relaxing colour. It's not just the colour of love. Or maybe it is. She needed to learn to love herself. She did love herself. She had done everything to love someone else. John. Spread the love. Except he threw it back in her face. Met it with hate. With disdain, with mockery.

Well, to hell with him.

"I'll never fall in love again." Not true. She hoped she would. Fall in love again. Not to spite him, despite him.

And so to bed, to sleep, perchance to dream. Of another lifetime. The one after this.

It wasn't long after her head hit the pillow that she heard it, felt it. Something was wrong.

Her heart was beating like a drum, and not a distant one. Someone was there who shouldn't be there. The bogeyman. He was here. In the room. Under the bed. The one place she hadn't checked. And he was. Until he emerged. She saw him standing there, just as he stood there that day he told her he had prostate cancer. He lied. He fucking lied. Why was she surprised? Because he took her by surprise. That's why.

What was he going to do? What was she going to do, what was she going to say?

"Hi, John, what are you doing here? Nice to see you", or "Get the fuck out of here before I call the police".

Neither option would do any good. She knew that. So what now? Wait for him to say something? He didn't. He didn't need to. He had that look in his eyes that told her he wasn't here for a happy reunion.

She wished now she had left this place when her better judgement told her. But then she had nowhere else to go. Then she noticed that he had a knife in his hand. The biggest knife from their kitchen block. The bedside light she had left on glinted on the blade. He noticed.

"Oh! This. I thought it might remind you. Of the night we met. Friday the thirteenth. What date is it tonight? What day is it? Am I scaring you, dear Josephine?"

There's no good answer to that, is there? Neither acquiescence nor defiance.

He dropped it. The knife. It stuck in the wooden floor. It didn't make the situation any better. Stand-off. He's there standing with a large knife stuck in the floor beside him. I'm here sitting up in bed. But what did he want? To control her again? To get her to take him back? No. That's not it. He wants it to be over. In this room, where he had exercised total control, or so he thought, he was going to make sure no one else did.

She could get up, push past him and run for the door, the front door. He wouldn't let that happen. She knew that. Remember the bathroom incident. He had been prepared. Even if she made it to the front door, would it be open? She had ensured she locked both it and the back door, and if his point of entry was either, he wasn't going to leave it open, leave her an escape route. She was sure that she was locked in, locked in with a madman. At least if a stranger broke in, he might just want her money, her valuables, her body — but there was a chance she would be left alive. What's her chances of that with John? Could she talk her way out of this situation? All John wanted to do recently was talk, for her to talk to him. Well, here's her chance.

"John?" She hesitated, waiting for a reaction. None.

"I'm sorry," she continued, hoping that would make him feel better. "I know that I've been awful to you recently, that I've ignored your feelings, that I've hurt you, but you have me so confused that I don't really know what I want." She hoped that she was sounding genuine, contrite, honest enough that he would be appeased, that he would have second thoughts. "We can talk. Let's go downstairs. I'll make us a drink."

He laughed out loud. "Do you think that I'm that stupid? I thought you knew me better than that. But then you do."

What he didn't know was that she had had a new lock put on the bathroom door. If she could make it there, she might be safe. He was relatively strong, but not strong enough to knock down a door.

She leapt out of the bed and bolted for the door. He had anticipated it. He was quick, still quick, just as he had been on the morning of the honeymoon. He caught her by the arm and swung her round, so that they ended up face to face, eye to eye. But this was no "Strictly Come Dancing" routine, even though it was clearly rehearsed. By John, that is. Whether it was the light or real, his eyeballs now appeared completely black, without a hint of colour — she literally couldn't see the whites of his eyes. He had hold of both of her arms, vice-like. She could feel the pain, despite the mounting fear. What next? She looked down at the knife sticking out of the floor.

"Knee him in the groin and go for it," her mind was telling her. Too late. He lifted her off her feet and threw her with all his strength onto the bed. Her head ricocheted off the headboard. It stunned her. Everything went hazy. When she was able to focus again, his face was there above hers, grinning. She tried to move, but realised her arms had been zip-tied behind her back. Her legs were zip-tied together. Goddamn the man who invented those.

"He's not going to rape me, then," was the first thought that came into her head. Maybe he just wanted to teach her a lesson. After all, he could just say what he came here to say, rant and rave if he wants to, get it all out of his system, and when he's done, just untie her hands and leave. What would she do? Call the police, report the assault? There was no barring order. He was legally entitled to come into the house; it was his home. He hadn't broken in, she was sure of it. He did have a key. And at any rate, she had no serious or permanent injuries. They could just have had an argument, she could have invited him in to discuss their situation, their marriage. It would be his word against hers. Likely, they wouldn't even prosecute him. Maybe a warning at the very most. Would she suggest it to him? No, of course not. John was obstinate. He would do the opposite. So only one thing to do.

"Go on, then. Get the knife. Kill me. Isn't that what you came here for?"

That only caused him to sit back and laugh. Worst thing is, when he did, he didn't do it gently. Sit back, that is. He almost crushed her pelvis.

"That won't help if I do manage to wriggle free. Damn it."

She hadn't made a noise when it happened, or not that she had heard, and he didn't react. He was too busy laughing.

He was still the bastard he had always been. Confirmation he hadn't changed.

"You shit!" she blurted out without thinking. She regretted it as soon as it had come out of her mouth. She had lost control. Just as he wanted her to.

"Enough!"

It was so loud, it echoed in her ears. It panicked her. She had convinced herself that it was just another of John's games. No longer. John had been controlling, but he always relished the comeback, the opposition. He held her by the chin, squirted something into her mouth. Something bitter tasting. She didn't want to swallow. But what was it? She had always refused to swallow when she performed oral sex on him. Was he making a point, or was it worse? Whatever it was, was it going to harm her, kill her? He held her nose. It was gone. It burned.

He lifted a pillow.

"Oh, no!"

Josephine was all too familiar with asphyxiation from the true crime programmes. Although there's no good way to die, she really didn't want to die this way. Struggling for breath or just letting go. Is it possible to just let go? She had given him the benefit of the doubt during the rape incident. He was under the influence of a drug, led by his expanding penis. Pushing her head into the pillow might just have been a result of his overzealousness. Now she wasn't so sure. They say we repeat our bad behaviour. It's inevitable. Maybe he wanted to kill her that night. But he would have left evidence. His semen, for a start.

Tonight, no one would know he was here. He doesn't live here any more.

"Love don't live here anymore" that's for sure. No one expects him to be here. He doesn't have a key as far as anyone else knows. Why would Josephine let him in the house?

"Here's the thing, John. Who else would want to kill me?" But she had watched enough of those programmes to know that suspicion is never enough. And he would ensure that someone, most likely his new paramour, would alibi him.

Actions, not thoughts, Josephine. But what action? Her hands and feet were useless. So was her body. John ensured that. All she could move was her head. And only from side to side. That is, until he put the pillow over it. He had one hand on each side of her head, gripping the pillow so tightly that she had to face forward. She felt his face on the other side of it, pressing his forehead against hers, only the pillow separating their skin. It was one of those pillows that moulded itself to the shape of your head. She wondered if her face would be etched in it forever. What do you do when you are being smothered? Open your mouth or close it? She didn't want to look like Edvard Munch's Scream when they eventually found her. In the end, she discovered that you have no control. She tried to breathe with her mouth open, then closed. Then she just relaxed, as she had been taught in her Yoga class. That felt better.

She was surprised when she felt him remove the ties on her hands and legs. He took the pillow and put it under her head. She kept her eyes closed. As she felt him move away, she gingerly opened them. He had his back turned and was putting the zip-ties in his pocket. Surely no one would believe she died naturally. But then the doors were locked from the inside and there was no forced entry.

She would play possum, play dead until it was safe. She knew that all those nights watching true crime programmes would come in useful someday. He took the knife from the floor. Began to wipe it with a cloth he had taken from his pocket. He turned back towards her. She closed her eyes quickly. Quickly enough that he hadn't noticed. Or so she hoped. Stop breathing, hold your breath. This is the most important thing you have ever had to do in your life, Josephine. Do it well. She had, as a young girl, practised holding her breath. Had competitions with her friends to see who could hold their breath the longest. Had swum in the sea beside her home, held her breath, submerged herself and counted. Now it counted more than ever. She could do it.

"One, two, three, four, five, six, seven, eight, nine, ten." Double figures

"Eleven..."

She felt the kiss on her lips. And then his tongue prying them apart. She breathed out. He almost had a heart attack. But not quite. She wished that he did. No such luck. This was her last chance. She rolled over quickly and fell off the bed with a thud. She tried to get up, before realising that the crack to her pelvis earlier was more serious than she thought. She couldn't do it. She was at his mercy. At the mercy of a man she knew to be a maniac, a maniac with a large kitchen knife. And as she was face down, she couldn't see what he was doing, what he was going to do. She felt him straddle her from behind. And then the pain as he brought the knife down between her shoulder blades.

She expected her life to flash before her eyes. It didn't. There was nothing but darkness.

CHAPTER THIRTY-FIVE
HEAVEN

Josephine realised, before she opened her eyes, that she was somewhere else, somewhere different. She could sense the bright lights, so bright she was afraid to open her eyes. She had heard people who had near-death experiences say they found themselves in a brightly lit tunnel. She wondered if this was it. Would she have to continue to the end, or would God turn her back? Was he ready for her, or not?

"Josephine?" The voice was softly spoken. She expected God's voice to be booming, powerful, commanding.

"Josephine?" The voice was slightly louder, but still soft. She didn't know how to answer or what to say. They never taught you how to talk to God in school. She played safe.

"Yes," she mumbled weakly and with great difficulty. She couldn't feel her hands, her legs. She couldn't feel anything. Physically, that is. Maybe she had left her body as they say you do when you're dead. Now she felt good. I don't feel anything. I don't need to feel anything.

"Can you hear me?"

"Of course I can hear you, God," she thought. But then God would know that anyway. Why was he asking?

"You're in hospital."

She opened her eyes quickly and saw the blur of a man's face and head looming above her.

"I thought I was dead."

"God knows, you could well have been. But you were lucky. The stab wound wasn't fatal."

Stab wound?

It wasn't a dream after all. She had woken from a nightmare. Although that happens every day to all kinds of people, she had awoken from a real nightmare.

A real nightmare? Is there anything more frightening? To find that something bad that is happening to you is not in your imagination, not in your dreams? That this is what is really happening? Her nightmares would never be the same again.

She now understood the meaning of Post-Traumatic Stress. Even working in a hospital, where she lay now, she had reservations about the people who looked perfectly healthy but came there week after week, month after month, because they couldn't cope with life, their situation, with their husband or partner. She never used to feel sorry for them. Get on with it. She used to have more affinity with those who had no one. Widows, divorcees, bachelors, spinsters. Some of those same people might take offence at those words, those descriptions. But looking back, they were the ones who appeared to have less worries, smiled more and understood more about life, even though they were alone, some of their own volition, some because of circumstance. But they were able to be alone. Embraced it. Or so it seemed. How could they smile, be of a sunny disposition, week after week, month after month, no matter what they were going through? Some had cancer, some had heart problems, some were just getting older. They all seemed more concerned with how Josephine was doing. Asked her every time they came there. Were genuinely concerned. They say wisdom comes with experience. It's true. Josephine knew now it was true. She had had that experience. Maybe not the same or as much experience as those who showed their concern for her, but her own experience. Now she had wisdom. And she still had her life. But at what cost?

It was all coming back to her. "He tried to kill me. But where is he now?"

"He's not here, is he?" Her voice was panicked, her heart rate increased.

Someone took hold of her hand. It felt reassuring.

"Who? Josephine, who's not here?"

"John, my husband, he's not here, is he?"

"No, he's not here. Do you want us to contact him?"

She couldn't help but laugh. It hurt. She grimaced.

"No," she said eventually, "unless you want him to finish the job."

There were two faces now, a man and a woman. They looked at each other. Eventually, the man spoke.

263

"Is he the one who did this to you?"

"Yes," she heard herself mumble through the tears that were pushing their way out of her eyes, despite her resolve. She was finding it hard to come to terms with it all.

"He's not here, Josephine. We don't know where he is. Do you remember what happened?"

She could remember that he was there, in their house. He wasn't supposed to be. She felt overwhelmed. Not in the way she had felt on that first night.

"What did he do to me?"

They looked at each other, searching each other's faces for an appropriate answer.

"You can tell me. I've already had the abuse, more than enough. One more thing isn't going to surprise or shock me."

She could see that they were debating who was going to speak first. Their body language said it all.

The woman spoke.

"He stabbed you in the back. Between the shoulder blades. That was his mistake. He didn't hit any major organ and just missed your spine."

Josephine turned her head to the side.

"It was no mistake. He's not stupid," she thought silently to herself. That thought frightened her more than anything he had ever done to her before. More than anything she had ever feared in her life. But what could she say to these people? They wouldn't understand. Why would someone try to kill you and not kill you? They didn't know John.

How could they? They hadn't lived with him.

"Am I going to be all right?"

"You're going to be fine," came back the answer.

"But am I? Going to be fine? I can't feel my arms or legs. Oh, God, will I be able to walk again?"

"Josephine," the male voice said, "don't worry, you're just heavily sedated. You'll be able to walk, you'll be able to run."

"But will I be able to dance?" she retorted quickly.

"Could you dance yesterday?"

That made her laugh. It hurt again, inside.

She was more awake now, alert, aware, astutely aware.

She hadn't lost her sense of humour through it all. But then humour comes with relief.

"I'm still here. He didn't kill me. He left me alive. On purpose. And I'm laughing about it."

But then she realised that we have no control over our emotions. When we feel happy, when we feel sad, when we feel frightened, when we feel comfortable. But others do. John did. He made her feel all those feelings when he wanted her to feel them. Why? How did she allow him to take control of her, of her feelings? Because she loved him? Is that why she let him do what he wanted to do? Treat her like he wanted to treat her? Make her feel like he wanted her to feel? When she felt happy, he could make her feel sad. When she felt sad, he could make her feel happy. But it was always up to him. He could make her go up and down like a yo-yo.

It wasn't something Josephine had been used to. Her life had been reasonably even before John. There were no highs, no lows. All right, there were lows, like when her father died. But they were few and far between. Highs? None that she could remember. Until she met John. Funny how their first date took them to a height. The height of Donegal. Or one of them. And then down again. To sea level. He had planned it well. He was clever.

Most sociopaths are. That's the scary thing. Everything they do is organised, planned. That's why she didn't believe he wanted her dead. If he did, she would be. But she wasn't, and he knew it. Those who think that killing you is the final act of control, it's not. That's when he has lost control. John still had control. He knew he wasn't going to kill her. He just wanted her to think he was. That's the ultimate control. Making someone think they know what you're doing when they really have no idea. That's what John had done all through their relationship, their time together. It was no different last night.

He was like the man who sold the world: he never lost control. He's not gone, he's still here. But where? Could he be right here in this hospital? No one would think to look for him.

"You need to rest now, Josephine," she heard. "We're going to give you something." And before she could remonstrate, they did. She didn't want to lose control of her thoughts, go where her mind would take her, relive the nightmare, the nightmare that was her life with John.

CHAPTER THIRTY-SIX
THE END

When she opened her eyes again, there were different people there, above her, staring at her. She waited for them to speak.

"Josephine, I'm Detective Clark." Is he serious? He has the same surname as John. Is he related? Her head was racing, until she realised she was being ridiculous. Lots of people in Ireland have the same surname. Lots of people all over the world have the same surname. And she wasn't even sure if that was John's real surname. If anything about him was real.

Details, that is. His presence was real for sure.

She was now properly awake. She had unanswered questions.

"How did they find me?"

"Someone called the emergency services, anonymously. Said they heard screams from your house. We don't know who it was. We couldn't trace the call." Josephine knew.

"Are they looking for him? Have they found him?"

"No," came the answer, "we don't have to."

"What do you mean?"

"He left a note in your house. He rented a car and drove to the beach, where he abandoned it.

They found his clothes and shoes. No sign of him."

"What did it say? The note."

There was an uneasy silence. She kept her eyes on him. As if to say, "Go on, tell me." He realised.

"The person you have found here is Josephine, my beloved wife, who vowed till death do us part. She was my one true love. But they say we always hurt the ones we love. Sometimes it goes further. I killed her. I can't live with myself, I can't live if living is without her, so I guess it's time to say goodbye. P.S. You might want to retrieve the car I am leaving on the beach at Buncrana."

Although she hadn't realised, she had been holding her breath as he read, she now exhaled.

"Are you okay, Josephine?"

She didn't know how to explain the games they used to play with song words, song titles. And even if she wanted to, it might sound trite, given the circumstances.

"I'm fine. I just can't believe he's gone."

She meant it, but not in the sense they would take it. She couldn't believe he was gone. He wasn't. She was sure he wasn't. It was clear from his message.

"What car was it?"

They seemed confused.

"What car did he hire? Leave on the beach?"

"A Mercedes. Convertible, I think."

Confirmation that he was alive. It spoke to her more than his note. But what did he have in store for her now? Or was she giving herself more credit than she deserved? Maybe he was gone for good. Gone, but not forgotten. But she couldn't depend on that. That he was gone.

Her father once told her when she was young and having nightmares about ghosts that it wasn't the dead she needed to fear but the living. She hadn't heeded his advice. She was always afraid of those zombie movies, especially "Dawn Of The Dead". It used to scare the hell out of her, keep her from sleeping. But she knew it wasn't real, that it wasn't true life. There are no such things as zombies, the walking dead. If John were to walk back into her life, he would be very much alive. But was this a case of time to say goodbye, as in his note, or is it a case of when will I see you again, as in the final song he played that fateful first night?

"Josephine?"

Her thoughts were interrupted.

"He's gone."

What would she say, what would she do? Would she tell them that they're wrong? That they should keep looking for him. That the first place they should check is right here in this building. She wouldn't. She knew it was futile. They would think she was paranoid. She was. With good reason.

"So he's presumed dead, case closed?"

"For now. Until there is some evidence to the contrary."

She wasn't surprised. That's how it goes. It's all about the evidence, and now the evidence is pointing to a "murder suicide": John kills Josephine, John kills John. Except no one is dead. But they're right in a way. He did kill her, her spirit, her hopes and aspirations, her love for him. Then killed himself in a sense, the person he presented himself as, that he pretended to be. John Clark. But there was no doubt in her mind that he was not always John Clark. He may never have been John Clark, except to her. To others he could have been John Smith, John Wayne or John Doe.

"How many 'Dear John' letters has he received from women everywhere?" she wondered. She wished it would have been one less. And what's the betting he's still receiving them? Whether it's Dear John, Dear Joseph, Dear James or whatever.

"Well, here's some advice for all you ladies out there: don't write him back, write him off. Just as I should have."